THE OASIS PROJECT

THE OASIS PROJECT
A Novel By
DAVID STUART ARTHUR

ZEBRA BOOKS
KENSINGTON PUBLISHING CORP.

This book is a work of fiction. The events and characters described in it—with the exception of historical references and persons of note referred to by their true names—are imaginary and not intended to represent specific living persons.

ZEBRA BOOKS

are published by

KENSINGTON PUBLISHING CORP.
475 Park Avenue South
New York, N.Y. 10016

Printed in the United States of America

To Ruth, Marian, and Ken.

I wish to express my gratitude to Ken, Bert, Webb, Christi, Sanders, Craig, David, Charlie, Robert, Alex, and Stuart, who have contributed so much through their friendship and faith.

Foreword

While *The Oasis Project* is a work of fiction, the technologies presented, the world economic and political motivations portrayed are real. We live in a world of exploding technology and dwindling natural resources that is pressing us closer and closer to the final confrontation. This novel deals with the development of the ASP, the aerospace plane, a highly advanced version of the Space Shuttle, even now on NASA's drawing boards, and with laser technology as the ultimate weapon.

The Space Shuttle is at last a reality, but do not presume that laser weapons and killer satellites belong in the realm of science fiction. They are real and they are with us now, soon to be in the heavens overhead.

On February 16, 1981, in response to the scheduled test firing of the Space Shuttle's rockets, the Soviet Communist Party newspaper, Pravda, issued the following statement: "The United States is preparing to spread the arms race into space by using the shuttle for military purposes." Pravda further alleged that the Space Shuttle was being equipped with laser weapons capable of destroying Soviet launched ICBMs and spy-in-the-sky Soviet early warning satellites. A UPI report dated February 20, 1981 mentioned a Draft report to be delivered to Congress in March, recommending an additional $200 million allocation be added to the Fiscal 1981 Defense budget to step up research and development that could result in the first laser battle station by the late 1980s.

Two years after this book was published in hardback, President Reagan appeared on national television to propose to the country and the world that the technologies I forecast are not only possible, but that they should be developed as an integral part of our national defense.

The race for space is on once more, and *The Oasis Project* very well may be the scenario for the future that awaits us before the end of this century.

. . . 25 December 1988

Moscow. Another vicious winter storm gripped the sleeping city. He moved like a shadow in the driven snow, his steps even and deliberate. He was tall and trimly built, his body supple, his movements alert.

A bitter wind moaned from the rooftops and wailed along deserted streets and alleys, battering shutters on blackened windows, plastering the snow in brittle piles against bleak gray buildings. His shoes grated on the icy walk, but no one heard, no one saw his shallow footprints swept away by the arctic blasts.

His thick blond hair jutted from beneath the fur cap that he wore low on his brow; his overcoat hung loosely from broad powerful shoulders. His face was gaunt, handsome in a hard way; his eyes deep set and ice blue. A hairline seam of white scar tissue traced a jagged line from the bridge of his nose to the outer corner of his right cheekbone.

He was an American, and did not care for the hardships of the Moscow winter. He was abroad that night for a purpose.

At that moment, in a government apartment house reserved for important guests of the state, there was another man; a man who for the better part of two decades had engineered the slaughter of thousands in his savage bid for political recognition in a world of moral turmoil.

He was short, rotund, and strangely reptilian in his mannerisms. His lips were thick, and his nose protruded in the way indigenous to his race. He wore the stubble of an unsuccessful beard, his single most distinguishing characteristic.

9

He rose to the soft tapping on the outer door of his suite and padded listlessly to answer it, his mind far removed from the charred school buses and mutilated children he had left in his wake. He chose not to think of the innocents cut down in airports or even the diabolical plan he had come to Moscow to discuss with his mentors in the Kremlin.

He wished only to savor the lovely creature standing before him in the hallway. She was young, perhaps twenty-five, dark haired with huge green eyes and high Slavic cheekbones. A thoughtful gift from his Russian hosts. The Palestinian smiled, revealing cracked stained teeth, and took the girl by the hand, drawing her inside. She followed without resistance, without enthusiasm. She was an object to be used to his satisfaction and discarded.

Through the flurries, the American trudged, his breath exploding in steaming shrouds, frosting his eyelashes and sideburns. It was Christmas morning, and although to many throughout the world it was a night of peace and hope, if not sanctuary, to him it meant nothing. War loomed like a storm front over the Middle East.

Every country in that part of the world was embroiled in or else threatened by political upheavals, from without or within; despite the continued efforts by the United States to find a true and lasting peace. Iran still quaked in the bloody aftershocks of the 1979 revolution against the Shah; Afghan resistance forces continued to battle the Russian occupation troups. Saudi Arabia rumbled with religious discord, and trembled at the prospect of the Russian Bear, couched to the north, waiting to sweep in and deal the crushing blow. Egypt and Israel clung desperately to their fragile peace, in the midst of almost continuous harrassment from the radical Arab factions, spearheaded by Libya's Muammar el-Qaddafi and the PLO.

As for the superpowers? They remained aligned along their fronts of opposition, waiting and watching for the beginning of the end. It was insane but true; the world balanced on the precipice of religious hatred and prejudice.

Notwithstanding five thousand years of theological evolution, the greatest minds and the wisest leaders on Earth were at a loss to deal with the situation effectively.

The American paused in the shelter of a doorway and for the first time glanced at his watch. It was one-twenty-five A.M. He looked across the street at the stark, featureless apartment house, and at the third floor windows. They were dark.

The terrorist sat naked on his bed, watching as his plaything disrobed. She tried to avoid his probing stare and struggled to block out the image of his slug-white pudgy body, by focusing on the purpose of their encounter. She was part of something much bigger, more important than her own private emotions. But she trembled as the last shred of her clothing drifted noiselessly to the carpet.

On the corner below, the American removed his Browning 9mm automatic from its holster and deftly screwed the silencer in place. He checked the clip to be sure that it was full, then snapped back the action, feeding one of the thirteen copper-jacketed hollow-points into the chamber. Setting the safety, he slipped the weapon into his overcoat pocket.

Rising from his bed, the Palestinian caressed his victim's firm white breasts with quivering fingers. She stood stiffly, shivering as he sank to his knees, sliding his mouth over the flat plane of her belly. His beard scratched her, chafed her tender skin, and she winced, almost cried out in repulsion, as he buried his face between her thighs, grunting in his growing passion.

He crossed the street in long strides and paused at the base of the high stone wall surrounding the compound. The avenue was empty, the buildings deserted. From his overcoat lining, he pulled a lightweight metal tripod and extended its legs, locking them in place with quick precise motions. The unit stood just over three feet tall, and where the camera mount should have been, there was a spring loaded bracket, shaped to fit the toe of his shoe. Placing the tripod at the foot of the wall, he stepped into the binding which snapped shut automatically, hefted his weight on the one leg, and stretched to his full height until his gloved hands gripped the top of the wall. In one fluid move, he heaved himself up, removed the tripod from his foot, and dropped into the deep snow of the rear yard.

He poised in the darkness, listening for the attack dogs, which did not come. Quickly returning the tripod to his coat lining, he slid along the wall to the corner of the building, and from there into the shelter of the rear entrance. Again he paused to listen, and heard only the howling of the wind and the spattering of ice pellets in brittle frozen branches overhead.

From his breast pocket he took a key and a pinprick flashlight, which he used to guide the key gingerly into the lock without a sound. Extinguishing the light, he drew his pistol and twisted the key, a hair's breadth at a time, until he felt the tumblers fall and the door ease open. He hesitated an instant for the alarm, and when it did not sound, stepped inside and closed the door silently behind him.

Standing in the pitch blackness of the rear hall, he waited for his eyes to adjust, listening to the ticking of a grandfather clock, smelling the mingled musty odors of the aging structure; antique furniture, books mildewing in the library, stale smoke and the evening meal. At last, by the faint light filtering down from the upper floors, he was able to discern the dim shape of the banister, and moved to the foot of the stairs, across creaking timber planks. He was relieved to find the staircase carpeted as he had been told it would be.

He took the first two landings three steps at a time, and stopped at the foot of the third. A uniformed sentry was nodding in a Louis XIV chair under a dim ceiling fixture, an AK-47 automatic rifle across his knees. Halfway up the flight, the guard heard him and raised his head, fighting the cobwebs from his eyes, but too late to raise his weapon or even cry out. One silenced shot through his throat snuffed him, and he collapsed in the tufted chair, his blood blending with the ancient crimson velvet.

In the apartment, the Palestinian paused and looked toward the door. He had heard a muffled sound, but now there was only the sighing of the wind in the eaves outside the windows. The girl had heard something too, and she summoned her courage for what was to come.

After what seemed an eternity, he resumed his passions, the wind snorting through his flaring nostrils like the gasps of a rutting camel. She lay motionless, fighting the pain of his violent thrusts.

Noiselessly, the bedroom door eased open. The hall light no longer burned, and the American moved silently over the threshold to the very foot of the bed. He watched dispassionately as the man's heavy white buttocks rose and fell, driving toward climax, his belly slapping against the firm flat stomach of his unwilling partner. Her thin white legs trembled under the assault.

He raised his weapon and aimed at the man's behind. "Sit up you pig," he said, his voice flat. The Palestinian froze. "I said, sit up!"

Slowly, the Palestinian raised himself and turned to face the intruder. In his close-set eyes, there was a treacherous twinkle and a possum-like grin split his face as he inched his hand toward the pillows for his concealed revolver. He muttered something under his breath, perhaps an oath of surprise, perhaps a final prayer. The girl lay motionless, her body exposed. But the American's eyes never left his victim's face. It was a face he had seen in his nightmares. It had haunted him since the day he had received his orders.

"Merry Christmas, you filthy bastard," he said softly, and sent two rounds crashing into the terrorist's forehead, splattering the girl, the bed, and the wall with bits of hair, shattered bone, brains and blood as the man's head exploded.

Ali Said slammed back onto the bloodied pillows, his

eyes rolled up into his brainless skull. The girl did not move. Her eyes were fixed on the man she believed in, and for one brief instant they glowed with triumph.

He shifted his aim swiftly and fired a single fatal shot. She died instantly without pain. She had paid the ultimate price for her loyalty in a game of the highest stakes.

At the foot of the stairs, a young Russian waited nervously in the darkness, listening to the winter storm and the pounding in his chest. He waited for the man who had maneuvered him into his present circumstance. It was he who had allowed the American access to the building, who had drugged the dogs and the evening meal, who had disconnected the alarm and provided the key; all under the threat of disclosure to his government. Selling contraband was a very serious offense, but nothing in comparison to the act to which he was now party. He waited to ask for asylum.

Suddenly, there was movement on the landing above. Mikhail withdrew into the shadows. He saw the silhouette of the man he recognized only too well, moving noiselessly down toward him. His heart pounding, he stepped forward, his eyes asking the question his lips dared not form.

The American raised his pistol and put two rounds into the young traitor's brain, silencing him forever. He left by the way he had come, and disappeared into the swirling blizzard without a trace.

. . . 20 January 1989

January 20, 1989 dawned cold and clear in Washington, D.C. It was the kind of day that crisped the nose hairs and blurred the eyes; but even so, the crowds formed early, and by ten Pennsylvania Avenue was rimmed with a clamoring, shivering mass of humanity waiting to catch a glimpse of the forty-second President of the United States.

His name was Eldon Parker, a forty-nine-year-old self-made millionaire from the hills of Tennessee. Up until 1986 he had been politically unknown, but he had burst upon the scene that year with a personal campaign against big government, soaring inflation, hopeless unemployment, gross ineptitude on the part of the incumbent Administration concerning energy conservation and general mismanagement from top to bottom.

In no time, capitalizing on the public's discontent, Parker had scooped up a commanding lead in the early polls, using the kind of campaign rhetoric that the people wanted to hear; lower taxes, more jobs, equal opportunity, care for the aged, but most of all, he promised a miracle cure for the nation's flagging economy, which many had promised, and none had been able to deliver.

He stood in his suite in the Watergate, straightening his maroon tie and wondering what the impact of his Inaugural acceptance speech would have, not only on the people who had elected him, but on those who had opposed him. He was not a man to mince words and had made it clear on in the campaign that if elected, he intended to act swiftly and if need be harshly to set the country back on the right track to economic stability.

He was a man who had clawed his way out of the black dust

15

of the coal mines of Tennessee to the executive suite of his own mining conglomerate which by the recession of late 1985 included twenty-four working mines, fifteen successful joint ventures in the oil-rich offshore fields of Louisiana and Texas, two hundred coal cars on the Burlington Northern Railroad, and half ownership in a hotel in Newport Beach, California, as well as sizable investments in commodities and stocks.

But in 1985, the future that he foresaw was bleak. The Administration had not adhered to sound economic practices, inflation was double digit, the balance of payments was compounding itself quarterly, and union demands were crippling American industry much like they had in Britain in the previous decade. Parker sold out to the Burlington Northern for an undisclosed sum, rumored to have been well in excess of forty million dollars, and threw his hat into the political arena.

He had seen how the previous two elections had been won, and he had adopted their style, backing it up with a saturation media campaign of his own financing. Not that he didn't believe in the promises that he was making. He was living proof of the American system at work; and he wanted to ensure that other Americans in the future would have the same opportunities that he had had.

Where he had differed from the incumbent government was implementation. Somehow, the leviathan Congress had still not figured out that it was impossible to curb inflation, lower taxes, and decrease unemployment by expanding government spending and continuing to print more money. The only way to increase prosperity in the private sector was to increase the incentive to produce, to give the investor reason to plow his savings back into American industry, to convince big business that it would be rewarded and not punished for its ability to make a profit. Because for some obscene reason, the concept of profits had become a violation of the Ten Commandments to the press and the politicians.

This, coupled with the continuing rape of the American consumer by OPEC and the unchecked influx of foreign products on the market, were the domestic issues he came

16

down hard on. Parker painted a picture of disaster unless a drastic change in the American political posture came about immediately.

The campaign had been grueling, the debates vicious, and the election returns, harrowingly close. The American people elected him with only 275 electoral votes. Now the rhetoric was behind him and it was time to deliver.

"Ladies and gentlemen, the President of the United States!"

A military band struck up a rousing "Hail to the Chief" and Eldon Parker strode across the dais to the podium amidst a wildly enthusiastic reception from the massive crowd. He stood straight and firm as a pillar in his dark blue suit and black wool overcoat, his head held high, nostrils flaring, drinking in the exhilarating morning air. He was just under six feet tall, powerfully built with broad shoulders and a straight back. His skin was tanned, his hair brown and thick, his eyes an intense sparkling green, which had a tendency to go muddy when he was angered. With his angular face and strong jaw, he looked more like a frontier blacksmith than the nation's next Chief Executive.

He waited patiently as the ovation swelled to a deafening roar, thinking about the burden of the faith that his country had placed in him. He was soon to be the leader of the greatest political experiment in the history of mankind, and the challenge both thrilled and frightened him.

He gripped the edge of the podium to still the trembling in his upper body, as the Chief Justice of the Supreme Court advanced to join him, smiling like a backwoods preacher, a comforting, reassuring smile that filled Parker with peace and a renewed confidence. In his hand the Justice held a simple black leather-bound Bible. He stopped in front of Parker and, nodding solemnly, held the Bible out in his left hand while raising his right. Parker placed his own left hand upon the Bible and stared into the eyes of the elderly Justice. In them he saw great wisdom, shielded sorrow, and a glimmer of hope. He heard the man's words clearly, but as if

17

far away, and repeated in turn.

"I, Eldon Parker, do solemnly swear that I will faithfully execute the office of President of the United States, and will to the best of my ability, preserve, protect, and defend the Constitution of the United States." Smiling gravely, the Justice shook Parker's hand, the band played once more, and the people cheered.

The Chief Justice presented him with the Bible and withdrew. Parker turned to face the nation and the world. He stood for many minutes, looking at the faces in the crowd. Some were smiling, many were cheering, others merely stared in curiosity.

One man in particular caught his attention. He was rather tall, wearing a drab grey overcoat, which despite its shapeless condition failed to conceal the man's powerful structure. He was blond, and had the most startlingly cold blue eyes Parker had ever seen. From almost a hundred feet away, those eyes stood out, bold and impenetrable. On impulse, Parker smiled, and the man smiled back.

"My fellow Americans!" Parker began before the din had died. "My fellow Americans, I stand before you today as but one example of the American dream. From humble beginnings I have risen to become the leader of the greatest, most powerful nation on Earth. It is an honor I hardly know how to accept without the most profound humility and gratitude to you, the people of this mighty nation, and to the system which allows each of us access to this same dream.

"In me you have placed your faith, your dreams, your hopes and aspirations, your futures. And I say to you now, that I will not disappoint you." He paused for a spontaneous ovation and looked again for the man with the blue eyes. He was staring back, his face expressionless. Parker waited for the crowd to still before continuing.

"I, like many of you, have known the hardships that life can inflict, the suffering and pain, hunger and sickness, cruelty and desperation that are the realities of the world we live in; and it sickens me to know that such conditions exist, as it should every person with conscience. With your help in the coming months, it is my intention to begin to right these injustices; but I am only one man, and like any other man, I am vulnerable and perishable; subject to human limitations. I am not a messiah, come to free my people from bondage with the wave of a hand or the Almighty's Holy word. I do not wish you to be misled into thinking that I have all the answers. I don't. But be aware that our world is in trouble, and that we face the gravest test imaginable if we are to survive." The crowd had stilled and now hung on his every word. "For we live in a world of disparities, in which nations are joined by vast and expanding technologies, yet threatened by extinction at the mere press of a button. In almost every country on Earth, there is starvation, sickness, poverty, ignorance; yet we live in a country where crops lie rotting in the sun and farmers are paid not to plant, lest we destroy the value of the commodities already in existence. There is no justification for these paradoxes, only the bare reality that they exist. Why should one country abound in prosperity, while another grovels in poverty? Why should greed, distrust, and prejudice prevent the nations of the world from sharing the fruits of peaceful coexistence? I have no ready answers, although I know that there should be answers.

"In the past, America has stood for freedom, equality, a chance for a new beginning. Every generation since the first settlers has opened its arms to the downtrodden, the exiled, the homeless, and the needy. The United States has been an oasis of hope in a wasteland of human degradation. But sadly, as we stand together today in this brilliant sunshine, preparing to celebrate a great political occasion, our oasis stands in peril.

"The trees that once shaded us from the sun are withering and dying. The water that once gave those trees life has become stagnant, choked off by the roots of those very trees. And the cool wind that once soothed us has grown bitter and cold.

"The trees I speak of are, metaphorically, our government. Once created to serve a free people, it has spread its roots deep into the soil and fabric of our society, choking from us our dreams and desires. Now it no longer serves, but commands to be served. The water that gave those trees life is our system of free enterprise, the success of which gave rise to the need for shelter and protection from the trees in the first place. But somehow through the years, the spirit of free enterprise has been destroyed by the government that should have protected it.

"And the cold wind that chills us, is the apathy of the American people to the decline of our nation. My fellow Americans, the oasis is threatened and with it the hope of a free world and free people living in harmony and prosperity.

"The next four years that face me as your President are going to demand the utmost sacrifice that any man can give. I accept this responsibility and embrace it gladly. But this is not something I can do alone. The sacrifice must also come from each and every one of you, the citizens of this great land. You must reach down and find the strength to resist this slow madness that is driving us to the brink of destruction. You must stop this cycle of decline.

"Forces outside and inside our society tear at the framework of our values, fraying our moral fibers, threatening to destroy what our forefathers have shaped with over two hundred years of backbreaking toil. But Americans are proud and brave people, and in times of peril have risen to the causes of freedom and excellence; and it is up to us now to save the oasis for future generations of Americans and the betterment of mankind.

"In the weeks ahead, I will reveal my plans to reverse this dangerous trend that has overtaken our country, and I will call upon every one of you to give what you can for the national well-being. I trust and pray that you will do so willingly, and join me in a united effort for independence and prosperity. We are the last hope for peace on Earth, and with God's guidance we will prevail."

He stood motionless at the podium, his eyes searching the now silent, bewildered faces in the crowd. Cautiously, as if afraid to agree but fearful not to, they began to applaud. Parker sought the cold blue eyes and found them staring back. The blond man wore a strange wry smile on his narrow face. He nodded solemnly to the President, then turned and slipped away.

Parker left the dais, dispensing with any further formalities, and made his way through the crushing throng gathered at the East end of the Capitol Building to the awaiting motorcade. At his elbow, he found the new Vice-President, Preston Holmes, who shook his hand warmly as they entered the President's limousine in the presence of several of his close advisors.

The trip to the White House was the first of many departures from protocol to come. Instead of the traditional parade, there was only the motorcade of closed black limousines. Parker waved to the cheering masses through the heavily tinted windows of his armoured vehicle. He knew that they deserved more of him, for electing him and waiting for him all those hours in the cold. But there was no time now. He had four years to undo what the previous two hundred and twelve had done, and the people would just have to understand.

Through the reinforced White House gates, the solemn procession wound to the front portico, leaving behind the clamor of the crowd and the angry chants of the perennial protesters. Almost before they stopped, Parker had the door open and stepped out smiling curtly at the security agents whose job he had usurped. A worried-looking young man stepped forward from one of the rear limousines. He was Bruce Wilson, a Harvard graduate who had been with Parker from the beginning of the campaign, and who was now his Press Secretary. Parker knew what was on his mind.

"Mr. President," Bruce began, trying to conceal the anxiety in his voice.

"Bruce," Parker interrupted, holding up his hand to cut him short. "Issue a statement of apology. Say that the matters of state are too pressing to allow me even a token appearance this afternoon and express my regrets for the Inaugural Ball, et cetera. You know how to word it."

"But Mr. President. What'll I tell the press? They're expecting at least a brief statement."

"Tell them I'm not running in a popularity contest any longer, I'm running a country. And right now the matters of

21

freedom, including the freedom of the press, hinge upon my immediate attention to the affairs of state. Extend my sincerest apologies and say that I will meet with them at my earliest possible convenience."

With this, Parker and his entourage entered the White House, leaving Bruce to carry the ball. That was his job, and Parker knew he would do it well.

The Oval Office was the way his predecessor had left it. Parker had only asked that it be swept for electronic bugs and happily it had been found clean. He felt better for having done it, however, because what he had to say to his advisors in the next few hours was not the grist for any public mill.

The men who accompanied him were Preston Holmes, the Vice-President, Dr. Arnold Kemper, President and Chairman of the Board of SPEC Technologies, a research firm closely associated with the manned space program, and Richard Montgomery, one of Parker's oldest personal friends and business rivals.

"Gentlemen be seated," Parker gestured to the highbacked chairs in front of his desk and turned back to the door. "Shirley?"

Shirley was his secretary and had been since the early days of Parker Mining. She appeared in a dark grey suit, her hair neatly wadded into a bun on the back of her head. She was in her early sixties, not very pretty, but efficient and experienced in putting up with his quirks. "Yes, Mr. Parker?"

Preston cleared his throat in surprise at the breach in protocol and Parker shot him a reproachful glance. "Arrange for coffee and sandwiches, will you?"

"Yes, Mr. Parker." Shirley shot Holmes her own challenging glare and hustled out of the room.

Parker smiled and drew out his chair so that he was sitting in front of the desk with the rest of them. He leaned back in it and sighed.

"How does it feel, Don?" Montgomery asked.

"No different than the last two years, Montie." He looked thoughtfully at each of the other men in the room. Each had been carefully selected for this moment, and each would play a key role in the plans he was about to unveil.

Preston Holmes was the only one that Parker had not known for many years. He was a former Junior Senator from the state of Washington, the youngest son in a family timber empire, who had impressed himself on the Senate and the Party with his level-headed approach to government spending and his gift for accurate and skillful management. A medium sized man, with a pleasant boyish face, he was self-assured and self-motivated, traits that Parker knew he would have to exploit if he hoped to survive the coming four years.

Dr. Arnold Kemper on the other hand, had been an associate of Parker's for the past ten years. They had met at a hunting lodge in the Pacific Northwest, at a gathering of the most influential Party leaders, both civilian and elected. Parker had quickly found that he and the disarmingly cherubic Kemper saw eye to eye on almost all matters of political and international importance. This coupled with the fact that Kemper was the founding head of SPEC Technologies, the nation's largest independent aerospace contractor, which had worked with NASA and the Air Force in developing Top Secret weaponry and aircraft, made him a natural candidate for an advisorial position. Kemper sat passively, his hands folded across his comfortable paunch, peering at the President through the rimless thick lenses of his "Teddy Roosevelt" glasses, waiting for the new Chief Executive to speak.

And finally, there was Richard Montgomery, Chairman of the Board and founding President of Montgomery Mining and Engineering. A stocky, mountain-bred man, who had clawed his way up much the same way Parker had, Montie was an old business associate—one time rival—of Parker's, dating back to the early days of Parker Mining. Montie in fact had provided Parker with some rare moments of terror by attempting to assimilate Parker's fledgling company into his own empire. The attempt had failed, but in its

23

aftermath, Parker and Montie had become close friends. When Parker sold out, he persuaded Montie not to bid on his holdings, and instead, tendered a Cabinet position as incentive to follow him into politics. Montie was the strong arm, no-nonsense spokesman Parker needed as his Secretary of State, and they had received no opposition to his confirmation due to his unblemished record in business and public service.

"An excellent speech, Mr. President," Holmes said.

"Short and to the point," Montie agreed and chomped down on one of the fat cigars that almost always found themselves wedged in the side of his cheek. "I don't know where you come up with your ideas; I never have. Just remember, you're a Tennessee hillbilly."

Parker smiled. Montie was not one for formalities and he obviously was not intimidated by Parker's office. "Gentlemen," Parker began, "what we've anticipated for nearly three years is now a reality. We've had a long hard fight, we've won, and now we've got to deliver. If you don't mind, I'd like to outline briefly our immediate course of action and then I'll throw it open for discussion." The others nodded in agreement and shifted in their chairs, preparing for what they anticipated would be a long session.

"As you're aware, the situation is actually a lot worse than I painted it, and I think I painted it pretty bleak. My latest information is that the negative balance of payments has increased by over ten percent in each of the twelve previous quarters. Most of this deficit is going to OPEC, with West Germany and Japan running neck and neck in second place. But OPEC is clearly the sore spot. And, I might add, we haven't made it any easier on ourselves by shutting down half the nuclear power plants in the country. I'm not satisfied that the present nuclear facilities are the answer, but for the interim we have very little alternative but to use them. I know this has been said many times before, and others have failed to make it happen. But we don't have the luxury of failure, gentlemen. We must establish real energy independence. In that vein, I want to offset these windfall profits taxes by creating tax credits as incentive for increased domestic production and energy research. Exxon has the biggest shale oil project in the world on ice. It's time we thawed it out. To whet their appetites, I'm going to pressure Congress into reopening the continental shelf for bidding. We've got more oil in the ground than we've consumed in the last sixty years, and by God we're going to tap it and take this bludgeon away from OPEC. They want something we have; they pay through the nose for it. No more falling all over ourselves when they say jump. Let's not make our technology so damn accessible to them. Let them come to us for a change."

"What about the competition?" Montie interrupted. "The Soviets are more than willing to jump in any time we open the door."

"Montie, the door was open when we lost Iran to the Ayatolla Khomeini. And I don't believe the Russians are that much of a problem as far as the Arabs willingly going over to them. The continued rebellion in Afghanistan is proof of that. Of course, the Saudis made overtures as early as 1978, but I don't think they want the Russian bear in their back yards any more than we do. Frankly, as long as the Arabs can continue to keep the Kremlin at arm's length and bleed us with our blessings, why should they make any concessions? To date, we have demanded nothing from them except that they sell us oil. But if we reduce our independence on them, and cut off our supply of technology, they're going to realize that they just might be losing a very valuable ally. We lay it on the line, and if they don't like it what alternative do they have? Big Brother?"

"How are we going to put these plans into operation, Mr. President?"

Parker scowled at Preston Holmes. "Preston, will you call me Don for Christ's sake? And to answer your question, legislation, détente if you want to use an anachronism, coercion, bargaining, but most of all careful coordination with domestic industry and labor. If we can get labor to ease up, we'll have the time we need. I'm sure industry will cooperate in retooling so that they can compete. And that's where you're going to come in Preston. You're going to be my chief spokesman on that level."

"Don, if you don't mind my asking," Kemper said, running a hand through his thatch of shocking red hair. "How are we going to get labor, much less the American people to cooperate? I mean, after all, the energy crisis is not a new issue, and the American people *have* cut back consumption until it hurts. Now we're going to ask them to suffer more?"

"Not if we can increase our own energy production, Arnold," Parker said. "Reagan made a good start . . ."

"And the EPA is still screaming like hell," Montie scoffed as he rekindled the stub of his cigar.

"The way I see it," Parker continued, "we enjoyed two hundred years of unchecked growth and prosperity. It came to be assumed that that was the American way of life, that it was an irreversible certainty that times would always get better and the average family income would always increase. Only in the last fifteen years have we really begun to pay the price, because we've outstripped the world in self-indulgence. We're a nation of consumers, where once we were a nation of producers. The country that falls into that trap is in for hard times."

There was a tap at the door and Shirley appeared with a tray of coffee and sandwiches. She set them on the coffee table and withdrew; and after they had helped themselves, Parker continued with his train of thought.

"What I'd like to talk about now is something that I have not discussed with any of you before. It goes without saying that anything we say in this office is not for the record. We are the core of a new concept of government, and the success of our efforts demands absolute secrecy and total commitment."

"What the hell are you talking about, Don?" Montie mumbled as he munched on an egg salad sandwich. "You keep jumping off on tangents."

Parker rose slowly from his chair and walked over to a wall chart, which he lowered, revealing a hemispherical map of the moon, both the light and the dark sides. The others looked puzzled and Montie burned his lip on the coffee. For a moment, no one spoke as Parker studied the map intently.

Then he turned to them, a strange glow in his brilliant green eyes that startled Holmes, but alerted Kemper and Montgomery that the best was yet to come.

"As you all know, on July 20, 1969, three Americans landed on the moon, here," he pointed with his finger, "in an area known as the Mare Tranquillitatis, the Sea of Tranquility. It was an historic moment for mankind, and a triumph for American technology. It impressed the Russians so much that they crash-landed one of their satellites into the moon's surface a few hours earlier in an attempt to gain worldwide recognition." There was a round of dry laughter which soon faded.

"Since that day," Parker continued, "Americans have lived in space in Skylab, probed Mars with Viking, and ventured beyond the fringes of the known solar system with Pioneer 10. The early shuttle missions proved that man could live and work in space efficiently and that private enterprise could prosper from it. Think about it. Less than a hundred years from Kitty Hawk to man living and working in space. It's an astounding achievement.

"But what's even more astounding is that the first thing Congress wants to cut is the space program, when it actually costs so little on a per capita basis and stands to generate so much. It's a little known fact, but since its inception, despite protests of squandering billions, the space program has cost the average American about the price of one soft drink a day to support!" Kemper leaned forward, as if sensing what was to come. The other two were trying to figure out where Parker was leading.

"The latest stage of the shuttle program has been severely curtailed, just when it was beginning to pay for itself. We've hamstrung America's only hope for survival in order to support make-work projects for the uneducated and welfare programs for people who refuse to work! Enormous amounts of money that would have flowed into the private sector as productive government contracts are now being doled out to nonproductive individuals who are unwilling to lift one single finger to better themselves! It's incomprehensible!" He paused, gathering his self-control. Now was no time for personal emotions. He knew the others shared his feelings. It was time for facts and issues.

"Gentlemen, we are an oasis. But I'm talking about the Earth now, and not just this country." He pulled down another wall chart featuring a full color photograph of Earth's Western Hemisphere from outer space. "As a planet, we're running out of natural resources. What took billions of years to create, we have depleted severely in less than two hundred, almost disasterously. In 1980, the Council on Environmental Quality submitted a report known as Global 2000. In it they stated that, in addition to the problems of air pollution and the threat of contaminating the oceans, sections of earth the size of the state of Maine are being lost to desert every year. They projected that by the year 2005, the earth's forests will have declined by one-third, its water supply by one-fourth, and its oil reserves by one-half. At current rates of destruction, between half a million and two million species of living organisms will perish, while at the same time the earth's population is expected to explode to some ten billion by 2025. We're in a nose dive that has been ignored, despite the warnings of a few brave scientists and conservationists. Why? Because man is basically self-centered, greedy, and thoughtless. It has never been his nature to look into the future and foretell his needs and alternatives. It was inevitable that we should come to this.

"As long as we continue to rely on old concepts, the present situation will continue to degenerate. We've got to break away, search in new directions for new concepts, in energy, economics, and most importantly technologies and new sources of natural resources that have not been tapped, resources that are under our control."

"I'm afraid you've lost me, Don," Montie said.

"Give me a minute to explain. In 1980, we were the dominant force in space. Today, NASA is confined to launching satellites. The Russians on the other hand are still flinging those flying junk heaps they call manned vehicles into space. I have all the respect in the world for those Cosmonauts when I think about the risks they are taking; but in all seriousness, the Russian technology is improving and they are eventually going to catch up with us in space as long as we sit still and do nothing. And then what happens? They that ruled the waves in the colonial days ruled the world. In World War II, who ruled the air ruled the world. Today, whoever rules in outer space rules the world. I'm not talking about a shooting war. I'm talking about a far more insidious kind of warfare . . . economic devastation.

"You can bet your ass the Russians have got elaborate plans to move into Iran, Saudi Arabia, Libya in the event of a real shooting war, and there would be nothing we could do about it short of an all out confrontation and that means nuclear. So what do we do? Reduce our dependency on foreign oil. Of course, but how? By encouraging domestic production, solar research, and converting more to synthetic fuels. But that's a long and expensive process, and it won't help our present circumstance. Revitalizing the nuclear plants that have been shut down will help some, and expanding the oil leases on the continental shelf will also. But the energy crisis is really only part of the problem. The other part is industrial competition, and we're being hamstrung because of inflation. And inflation is caused by only one thing—Government trying to cover federal budget deficits by printing too much money. Inflation causes the value of the dollar to decrease overseas, as well as at home, and the result is that foreign products become more expensive because the dollar has become less valuable. This has been especially true with OPEC oil. Now I know this is obvious, but how do we combat it?"

"If you could answer that as simply as you stated the problem, you'd be the messiah you said you weren't," Montie interrupted.

"Oh, but I can," Parker countered. "By returning to the gold standard."

"You've got to be out of your mind!" Montie gasped. "This country doesn't own enough gold to smelt a spitoon!"

"Not now," Parker smiled. "But we will."

"And just how are we going to get it? Buy it on the open market with printed money, weakening the dollar further? It doesn't wash."

"By mining the moon!" Parker shouted, slapping the wall chart so hard everyone jumped. "What the hell do you think I've been leading up to?"

"Good God, Mr. President," Holmes choked. "You're not actually serious?"

"Ask Arnold if I'm serious."

Preston looked questioningly at Kemper, who nodded gravely.

"Explanation," Montie said.

"By all means," Parker smiled. "What most people thought were picture-taking expeditions to the moon, what the critics have called a wanton waste of tax dollars, were in fact geological expeditions, which came up with some pretty significant discoveries."

"Geological expeditions?" Holmes muttered in confusion.

"Why do you think we made so much fuss about bringing back the moon rocks? And why do you think there was so much of a stink when some were stolen?" Parker asked.

"You've got me," Montie sighed, wondering what in the hell Parker was leading up to.

"Because we found that the moon abounds in mineral deposits, lignite, uranium, copper, iron, there's a long list." Montie let out a low whistle as he began to see the implications. "But those finds in themselves were not significant, since the cost of mining the deposits for the present is prohibitive. However, NASA did make one singly important discovery, which none of those dumb bastards in Congress has every heard of . . ." He paused, watching their faces. Kemper was smiling. "A vein of gold, so pure, so massive, that it far outstrips the biggest strike the world has ever known. In fact, there are indications that there is more gold in that one vein than in circulation today. And despite the enormous costs of extracting it, the economic impact of our control of that much gold can return our currency to the gold standard, and other currencies will have to base their value on us and not on the flow of crude oil."

They stared at him in shocked silence for a full minute as the realization sunk in that he was absolutely serious. Kemper's expression bore this out.

"And just how are we going to mine this so-called extraterrestrial mother-lode?" Montie asked.

"What I have in mind, gentlemen, is a fleet of interplanetary space vehicles capable of mining the gold deposits on the moon and transporting them back to Earth for refining. I have in mind America's first global colony, and we use Space Shuttle as a cover-up for the real operation, until it's too late for the Russians or anyone else to do anything about it."

Kemper began cautiously, feeling his way; aware of the need for candor. "Don, as you may or may not know, in the early years of space exploration, NASA served as the front for the military space program."

"I know."

Kemper nodded, not at all surprised. "Then you also know that the Air Force had a space research budget six times the size of NASA's in those early years?"

Parker nodded calmly, but the others were totally thrown.

Kemper continued, gathering his thoughts as he spoke, sifting through the facts. How best to tell them? "For security reasons which are obvious, NASA was only the surface layer of the space program. We were testing advanced aircraft capable of limited penetration and reentry from outer space; as well as attack satellites armed with nuclear warheads. The fact that we got away with it is something that I personally, along with a handful of other individuals mostly in the Pentagon, am directly responsible for. And I'll tell you something else that only a very small number of people know. The first manned lunar landing was not on July 20, 1969; it was on January 12, 1967."

Montie and Holmes sat forward, Montie chomping down hard on a fresh cigar. Kemper continued. "We, that is, the Air Force arm of NASA operating through SPEC, landed a manned capsule on the moon two-and-one-half years before the public saw the Apollo 11 landing in 1969. Not that that landing wasn't live. It was. It was also carefully scripted and performed for the world with practically no chance for failure. Something that crucial can't be left to fate, you understand. We had to be sure it would work. We also wanted to let the Russians know what we were capable of without letting them know exactly when we were capable of it. The fact that we functioned in secrecy allowed us to take greater risks and advance much more quickly. Luckily, there were no accidents in the Air Force program, and the only losses were the first Apollo crew and the near disaster with Apollo 13. We were very fortunate."

"That's incredible, Dr. Kemper." Preston Holmes' face was ashen from the shock. "I had no idea."

"But you did?" Kemper asked Parker.

"Yes," Parker replied calmly. "I also know that by 1980, SPEC was on the verge of testing a new rocket thruster system utilizing nuclear power, and that you were counting on the Space Shuttle funding to launch new Skylab facilities to carry out that testing."

Kemper smiled a wry smile and shook his head. "I won't ask how you know," he said.

"Arnold, I've been preparing for the Presidency for over three years. I never go into any new project without first doing my homework."

"So you know how close we were, and that what you intend is theoretically-possible?"

"It is?" Montie asked.

"It is," Kemper replied.

"I also know about the Dyna-soar and the ASP programs that never got off the drawing board."

"What's the ASP . . . and the . . ." Holmes could hardly manage to speak in his astonishment.

"Dyna-soar, Mr. Vice-President. They are two programs that actually spawned the Space Shuttle. Basically, they are winged spacecraft that rely on the principles of rocketry and conventional flight together to launch the space vehicle into orbit. The ASP is the higher, more advanced form of the concept. It is designed to lift off like a conventional airplane, cruise to a high altitude under jet power, then blast into orbit under rocket power. In outer space, we planned to utilize the nuclear thruster for the main source of power. The vehicle would return to Earth much the same way that the Space Shuttle does, except for the fact that it would be able to use its jet engines to alter its course and enhance its ability to choose its landing site and control its touchdown in the manner of a conventional supersonic aircraft. If I'm not mistaken, Don, you're suggesting that we launch the ASP Program."

"I am," Parker replied firmly.

There was silence for several seconds; then Preston Holmes ventured cautiously, "Don. How are you going to keep an operation of this scale under wraps? I mean the sheer magnitude of what you're proposing is mind-boggling. And where is the money going to come from?"

"Our research budget is going to come from the Air Force. The Space Shuttle is going to be our cover. We're going to get Congress to resurrect it. You're going to get Congress to resurrect it."

"*I* am?" Holmes gasped.

"There's going to be a hell of a fight in the Congress about the Shuttle," Montie grumbled.

"After I'm through building it up," Parker smiled, "I'll make anyone opposed to it sound like a communist sympathizer."

Holmes looked sick and averted his eyes to the wall charts, wondering how all of this could have happened without his even suspecting it. It was a speedy lesson in Presidential politics. Parker walked over to his private liquor cabinet and broke out four glasses and a bottle of sour mash whiskey. He poured a healthy measure into each glass and raised his in salute. The others joined him.

"Gentlemen. We're going to call this venture the Oasis Project. I offer a toast to its success and to American independence." He drained his glass in one draught.

The others stared at him momentarily then did the same. Montie looked him in the eye, and said solemnly, "Don, this is the biggest gamble in the history of mankind. If it works, we'll all be heroes."

"And if it fails?" Holmes asked hesitantly.

"We can't afford to fail," Parker said, filling their glasses again.

. . . 26 February 1989

Camp David lay beneath a freshly fallen snow, the brilliant morning sunshine dancing in glistening waves over the white shroud. A single black limousine hissed up the hardpacked icy road toward the Presidential lodge, its heavily tinted windows concealing the identity of the invited guest.

In his office, Eldon Parker sat at a massive desk, mounds of blueprints and dossiers spread before him. He had been studying them for nearly four hours until his eyes had begun to cloud and his brain could absorb no more. The drapes were drawn, and he had no idea of the hour when the knock came at the door. He looked up sharply and quickly buried the plans beneath several manila folders.

"Come in," he said wearily.

The door opened and a blinding burst of sunlight spilled in, silhouetting two figures against the doorway. One was Bruce Wilson; Parker recognized his shape. The other man was several inches taller, with broad shoulders and a narrow waist.

"Is it nine o'clock already?" Parker asked, glancing at his watch and rising. He made sure that the plans on his desk were completely concealed before stepping forward to greet his visitor.

"Yes, Mr. President," Bruce replied. "Deputy Ambassador Davis is here for his appointment, sir."

"Thank you, Bruce. That will be all for now," Parker said as he advanced toward the dark form of his visitor who only then moved into the room past Wilson. "Please come in, Mr. Davis," Parker said, motioning to the fireplace where a pleasant blaze crackled.

Bruce shut the door, sealing out the sunlight, and Parker

34

stared into the cold blue eyes of his visitor. He could not help noticing the white scar beneath his right eye and wondered briefly, as he always had, just how it had come to be there.

"Please take your coat off, Mr. Davis. Sit by the fire."

"Thank you, Mr. President."

"Coffee?"

"Yes, thank you," Davis replied and removing his coat stepped to the fireplace to warm his hands. He turned to study the solid structure of the young President, and ran a hand through his tousled blond hair.

"Did you have a pleasant ride up?" Parker asked.

"Yes, sir. Very pleasant. The roads were clear most of the way and the country is beautiful this time of year, although I must say I'm pretty tired of snow."

"Yes, I understand the weather in Moscow has been lousy this year."

"The climate there is even worse of late, sir."

"I'm pleased to hear that, Davis," Parker said as he handed his visitor a cup of steaming black coffee. Davis smiled and Parker turned away to take a seat in his highbacked leather chair. "Sit down, Mr. Davis," Davis sat and there was a moment of thoughtful silence. "You're to be commended on a job well done, Davis."

"I was only happy to be of service."

"There hasn't been any word from the Soviets yet. I wonder how they're going to break it?"

"I imagine they're trying to figure out who in the hell did it; whether it was a PLO splinter group or an Israeli hit. And they're probably creating a legend for the young Russians involved, linking them to a Jewish conspiracy."

"A legend?"

"Yes, sir. That's what we in the trade call a life history; a fabricated life history."

"I see," Parker mused. "Do you think it will have the desired effect? Your mission, I mean."

"I think so, sir. At the very least, you've set the PLO back several months as far as their plans for Israel are concerned. Naturally, someone will succeed Said as the official spokesman, but I anticipate some infighting and dissension in their ranks."

"I hope you're right about that. We need all the time we can buy. What do you think the Russians will do?"

"They'll wait until they have an ironclad case against the traitors, and then they'll announce the event to the world as a Western or Zionist conspiracy and condemn the action as an act of terrorism. The simple fact is that no matter what they do, they've got egg on their faces. We've compromised the hell out of them."

Parker decided to change the subject. "From your tour in Moscow, Davis, what would you say the Russian mood really is? Do you think they are interested in pursuing the START accord or have they merely been pretending to cooperate and de-escalate?"

"As I'm sure you've been briefed, sir, the Russians are appearing to comply with the START agreement, but there are ways to comply and ways to comply. Without on-sight inspections, we still have no way of knowing exactly what they're up to. If you want my personal opinion, I don't think the Russian political philosophy has changed one iota since Khrushchev told us point blank that he was going to bury our children. He meant it then and they mean it now, although they aren't saying it while hammering their shoes on the table. Their apparent willingness to cooperate and pursue détente is a ploy, their way of lulling us into complacency. They did it in World War II and I don't sense a shift in the Soviet mentality." He paused thoughtfully, then as an afterthought said, "Their incursion into Afghanistan and the continued meddling in that part of the world speaks plainly enough. They're not going to make any real move, however, until they've scouted your weaknesses and looked for chinks in your armor."

"I see," Parker murmured, his mind clearly preoccupied with another thought.

"If you don't mind my saying it, sir, I think that, true to form, they'll find some way to test you. They've done it with every other President. I think they are dangerous and should be considered a primary threat to world security. You should show no weakness and give no ground on any of the issues that are almost surely going to arise."

"I appreciate your opinion, Mr. Davis. I'm aware of their history. But I agree with you. They're not going to push the first button. What worries me is, what if someone else does? Will they react instinctively with all out retaliation against us whether we did it or not; or will they wait for all the facts?"

"I don't quite understand what you mean, sir?" Davis lit a cigarette and looked questioningly at the President. "You don't mind?"

"No go right ahead. What I mean is, if another country were to employ nuclear weapons, say the Israelis against an all out Arab assault, would the Russians assume that we would automatically become involved and move against us?"

"I see what you mean. That is a question I can't answer. Certainly *our* actions would have to be very carefully thought out, and our position made clear to the Kremlin."

"Well, that's not something we have to dwell on for the present, is it? I've had you reassigned, Mr. Davis. From now on I want you close at hand, so you will be working out of Washington until further notice. In reality, you are to report directly to me. You will have no official duties other than that. But for the time being, why don't you take a few days off and get the kinks out? Go somewhere, but leave word where you can be reached."

"I'd like that, sir. After twelve months in Moscow, believe me, I need some sunshine and relaxation."

"I'll be in touch, Mr. Davis. Can you see your way out?"

"Yes, sir. Thank you, sir."

Davis left and Parker returned to his desk. He drew aside the layer of dossiers revealing an artist's rendering of a flying machine the likes of which few men on Earth had seen, much less conceived. In it lay the destiny of life on the planet.

. . . 27 February 1989

Kathy Karpovich sat behind her desk in the newsroom of the *Washington Post* staring at a blank piece of typing paper, not knowing what the hell she was going to put on it besides her name. She had the White House beat, but since the Inauguration, getting news out of the Administration other than the nebulous releases issued by the young Press Secretary Bruce Wilson was like pulling claws out of a tiger's paw. The President was keeping a low profile, of that there was no doubt.

She had followed Parker since the New Jersey primary, and what little she knew about him convinced her that he was not a secretive man, although he was private, reserved, even introspective at times. She had also found him to be warm and sincere, holding his views of economics and politics with complete conviction. But now he was sequestered behind the veil of the Presidency, and any further insight into the man was becoming nearly impossible to obtain.

Granted, his life had changed drastically. He had spent the better part of his first four weeks in office in briefings, naming advisors, proposing legislation and steeping himself in international politics. But that didn't help her situation. She had a beat to cover, and so far her stories had revolved around thrilling observations on the influx of tourists to his hometown in Tennessee and a longer series about the mysterious past of the new Chief Executive.

Kathy was thirty-five, very attractive with shoulder length blond hair, hazel eyes flecked dramatically with specks of gold, and smooth milk-white skin. Her cheekbones were high and pronounced, her nose narrow and slightly askew giving her an exotic imperfection that differentiated hers from the many other pretty faces on the national news scene. Her mouth was petulant, turned down a little at the corners, and she had a tendency to pucker her lips when she was annoyed.

She had come to the *Post* from the Midwest, and made herself the most sought after unmarried woman in the Washington press corps. Because of her looks, her boldness, and the fact that she wasn't above using her body to get a story if she thought it was worth it, she had gained a reputation, for better or worse, as one of the best at what she did. But Kathy had only one goal; to be the best, not just one of the best. A spot on the national evening news was her target, and until she was sitting in that chair, she was not going to let any Press Secretary or President, for that matter, stand in her way. If there was no news coming out of the White House, she was going to create some.

Throwing down her pencil, she picked up the phone and dialed, then waited impatiently as the phone rang several times. Finally someone answered, "Mr. Wilson's office."

"Bruce Wilson, please."

"I'm sorry," the woman on the other end said. "Mr. Wilson is in conference. May I help you?"

Kathy sucked in a deep breath and summoned her nerve. "Tell him that I know about the cover-up, and I want to talk to him. He can meet me at Ricky's in Georgetown at seven tonight." There was silence on the other end and she hung up with a smile.

Bruce Wilson returned to his office around six-thirty carrying an armload of notes and releases. Most of his staff had gone home, and his secretary, Rita, looked as if she were eager to be on her way. She handed him a stack of messages and pointed to the top one.

"I think you'd better read that one first, Mr. Wilson."

Bruce read it and paled at the sight of the word "cover-up." "Where did this come from?"

"A woman called this afternoon and that was what she said."

"No name?"

"No name."

"Have you said anything to anyone else about this?" Bruce tried to control the tension in his voice.

"Of course not, Mr. Wilson. I wouldn't . . ."

"OK. Don't. You can go on, Rita. I'll take care of this myself."

Rita looked somewhat relieved, and gathering up her coat and purse headed out the door. "Goodnight, Mr. Wilson."

Bruce didn't bother to reply. He was staring at the phone message. This on top of the day he had had already was almost too much. What with the President's special State of the Union message under preparation and the word about Ali Said, he needed a drink.

He sat down heavily on the corner of his desk and rubbed the back of his neck, then read the message again very carefully. Jesus Christ! What cover-up? What the hell kind of sick joke was this? He thought about calling the Oval Office to ask for advice, but decided against it. This had come through his office, it was his business, and he would take care of it. He looked at his watch. Six-forty-five. Christ, he was going to have to hump to get to Ricky's on time!

Ricky's was packed as usual when Kathy arrived, and as usual she was hustled nonstop as she searched for an empty table. She found one near the rear and sat so that she could keep an eye on the front door, while she parried the unsubtle propositions from nearly every guy in the place. It annoyed her the way the bastards thought that because she was alone, she was looking to get laid, but she had learned long ago not to let it get to her. Nevertheless, she went through her first martini in two swallows and ordered another.

At seven-ten, she looked at her watch for the umpteenth time. Her quarry was late. Maybe he hadn't gotten the message. Maybe he had gotten it and had seen through it. Maybe he had turned it over to the Secret Service. That would be the shits.

Suddenly, he was standing in the doorway, arguing with

the bouncer who was obviously insisting that the place was too full to let anyone else in. She laughed involuntarily at the way he looked; flustered, his overcoat on half-cocked, his hair windblown. He was very young and seemed out of place in the fast Washington crowd; definitely the easiest mark she had had in a long time. She wondered for a moment if she ought to let him suffer a little more, but then decided to go to his rescue; it would make him feel somewhat indebted to her and might soften the impact when he found out about her hoax.

She walked casually to the front, her eyes fixed on Bruce, who was turning bright red with anger. He saw her a few feet away and froze, his face strained and flushed. She could tell he was close to the breaking point.

"There's room at my table for this gentleman, Stu," she said.

Stu, the bouncer, turned, and seeing her smiled. "Oh, sure Miss Karpovich. I didn't know he was with you. Sorry, Buddy," he said to Bruce.

"Buddy?" Bruce snarled, but Kathy grabbed his arm and dragged him away before things got out of hand.

"I wouldn't worry about Stu, Bruce. In a few weeks everyone in D.C. is going to know who you are."

Bruce looked at her suspiciously as he allowed himself to be herded to the table and assisted out of his overcoat. Kathy knew just how to handle him to make him feel completely vulnerable. She waved for the cocktail waitress. "Two vodka martinis, Betty," she said. That was the last straw. She could see his ego collapse inwardly. "You do drink vodka martinis don't you Bruce? That is if my memory serves me . . ."

He nodded and calmed himself, trying to gather up his shattered psyche. He realized, of course, it was she who had called and he stared at her wondering why she had pulled such a stupid stunt. Kathy made every effort not to smile, knowing she was going to have to play this one straight for as long as she could.

The drinks came and Bruce gulped half of his right off and motioned for another round. "Two more."

"Bad day at the office?" Kathy quipped.

Bruce's expression dulled as he grew very serious. "I got your message."

"I've left a lot of messages for you, Bruce, but you never return my calls. Which one are you talking about?"

"Hey, don't play cute, Kathy. What's this 'cover-up' all about?"

"You tell me, Bruce."

"I don't know anything about a cover-up," he said raising his voice. "And neither do you."

"Then why are you here?" she asked, boldly confronting him.

His jaw went slack and he fumbled for control. "I'm here because . . . you know why I'm here!"

"Actually, Bruce, I thought the only way to get your attention was to hit you between the eyes with a two-by-four, but you seem to be more than just attentive. Have I stumbled on something by accident?" She was clearly taunting him.

"Listen, Kathy. I know you've got a hotshot reputation in this town, but this is a dumb stunt. You ought to know better than to pull that shit with the White House. On the campaign trail pranks are expected, but we're in office now and the games are over. Thanks for the drink." He started to rise.

"Bruce, wait!" she said, reaching for his sleeve. "Don't leave. I'm sorry." She was really stunting now.

Bruce paused and allowed her to pull him back into his seat. He was angry, and she had to think fast. "I'll level with you," she said, trying to sound repentant. "Since you guys have been in office, I haven't seen more than a glimpse of you at the press conferences. I've left messages but you never return my calls. It was the only way I knew to get to you."

"What's that supposed to mean?"

She smiled seductively, lowering her eyes and twirling the olive skewer in his drink. "Did it ever occur to you that I was after something besides a story?"

"Fat chance of that!" he scoffed, waiting a little too long to sound sincere.

"What if it were true?"

"What if it were?" he echoed, unable to meet her direct

42

stare. "What do you want, Kathy?"

"You," she smiled and plucking the olive from his drink, bit into it with a display of beautifully white teeth. Bruce squirmed and looked around uncomfortably. "Is that so unusual?" she asked. "After all Bruce, this is Washington, and in Washington we do things a little differently than they do in Boston. If I want a man, I let him know it. I don't have time to waste playing party games."

Bruce's ears turned red and he was getting fidgety. "I appreciate your interest, Kathy . . . but . . ."

"But?" she challenged.

"But right now I don't have time for this kind of thing."

"Is the White House running a stable of geldings?" she chided.

"You know as well as I do . . ." he mumbled awkwardly and rose to his feet, obviously torn between wanting to stay and his obligations, either real or imagined. "I'm just not interested," he said apologetically.

She smiled and taking one of her cards from her wallet jotted down her home phone number. "If you change your mind, call me," she said, handing it to him.

He hesitated an instant, then took it and slipped it into his coat pocket. Then he put a ten dollar bill on the table. "Here's for the drinks."

"My treat, Bruce," she said, handing it back to him, and letting her fingers linger on his long enough to set off sparks.

He nodded, turned stiffly, and walked out without looking back. She smoked several more cigarettes and finished her drink, entertained by the obligatory ass-grabbing going on at the bar. It was the same every night in Ricky's.

She did not notice the little man at the corner table with nervous hands and darting eyes. To her Sergei Zeitsev was just another sad face in the crowd, a person who preferred to be alone in great numbers rather than by himself.

She had no idea that he had watched her whenever possible for nearly a year. He knew where she lived, where she worked, what hours she kept, what hobbies she enjoyed, whom she entertained; but most important, he knew where she had come from and what she had been.

He did not move when she rose and strutted toward the door, her head held high, her walk provocative. She was a marvelous looking woman, but that was of little concern to him. He left the bar a moment after she did and stood in the shadow of the front awning as she pulled away in her little British sports car. He watched until her tail lights disappeared around the corner, then he drifted away into the obscurity and safety of the night.

. . . 28 February 1989

Aleksay Kurochkin sat listlessly in the grey-walled anteroom of a drab suite of offices in the headquarters of the Komitat Gosudarstevnnoi Bezopastnosti; the KGB Center. Between his feet he had trapped a roach, which now scurried frantically across the black linoleum tile, seeking a means of escape from its tormentor.

Kurochkin smiled and edged it gingerly with the tip of his toe, back to the middle of a tile, where it sat jittering nervously. He was happy to have found something to pass the time with while he waited. He hated coming to the Center, to Markelov's office in the dreary depths of the complex, and sitting in the cold blue fluorescent light on a hard wooden bench, staring at the grey-green walls, listening to the hard sounds of indistinguishable conversations clattering down the empty corridors.

Outside, it was a sunny winter day. The snow was fresh and the air was biting cold. This place depressed him. It reminded him of his childhood and the orphanage with its dirty floors and crowded wards where boys slept two to a cot, suffering through the pains of puberty in silent torment.

Aleksay was thirty-nine years old, six foot one, two hundred and ten pounds of hardened muscle and sinew. His hair was black, just beginning to grey at the temples; his face was flat and broad, neither handsome nor homely. He had the look of the farm stock from which he had come, a hardy people used to hardship and toil. His jaw was strong and protruded slightly giving him a defiant expression, yet his eyes were strikingly innocent, deep brown and devoid of emotion, disguising his true nature. His broad powerful shoulders strained at the fabric of his coarsely woven wool coat, and his thick gnarled figures hung limply from massive hands.

He had waited nearly an hour when the door to the inner office opened and Markelov's assistant appeared and nodded curtly for him to go in. She was a hard-looking woman with short mousey brown hair and a pig nose. She wore the green uniform of the GRU and walked with the swagger of a man.

Aleksay rose to his feet and purposefully crushed the roach beneath his sole with a crisp pop while holding her gaze. He hated her. She reminded him of the orphanage mother, a brutal woman — a lesbian he thought now — who had willfully tormented the boys in the institution. Aleksay walked past her without bothering to acknowledge her shared contempt.

Colonel Vladmir Markelov looked up from his desk and smiled his mortician's smile. But Aleksay noticed only the bright ice-coated rectangles of the windows. He saw the blue of the sky, felt the warmth of the winter sunlight. He came sharply to attention and saluted.

"Sit down, Comrade," Markelov said.

Aleksay clicked his heels and, seating himself, waited stiffly as Markelov leafed through a thin dossier. He was a pale, nervous man with thick bushy eyebrows and a receding hairline. His face was lean, his nose long and hooked, and the corners of his mouth turned down in an immutable sneer. The crows' feet at the corners of his eyes gave him an expression of perpetual anxiety, but that morning he appeared much more anxious.

"How have you been, Aleksay?" he asked without looking up. He did not appear to be reading, but rather meditating about the contents of the folder.

"Well, Colonel," Aleksay replied in his usual tranquilizing tone. "And yourself?"

Markelov looked up slowly, shaking his head as he closed the document. "Not well, Aleksay. Not well. This embarrassment at the apartment house is becoming impossible to conceal from the world press. Already there are rumors circulating in the Middle East and Habash is insisting we break the story. Do you realize the compromising position

46

we have been placed in?"

Aleksay nodded calmly, trying by his manner to soothe his superior's shredded nerves. He knew that as head of Security, Markelov was being pressured from above, and that he in turn was about to receive the full brunt of that pressure.

"Everyone who had access to the campground is either dead or in maximum security undergoing interrogation. But still we have made no progress."

"Not everyone, Colonel," Aleksay said.

"No, you are correct. Not the assassin. But he has left no clues. Only bodies."

"The same as I would have done."

"What do you think happened from the evidence we have so far?"

"Obviously, the assassin had a confederate on the inside. Probably the dead valet . . ."

"Mikhail Olenov."

"Olenov, yes. By the evidence we know that he waited for some time in the alcove by the stairs. Long enough to smoke three cigarettes."

"And the girl?"

"An unfortunate witness, or perhaps an accomplice. Do we have any records on her other than her government dossier?"

"We are checking, but nothing yet. By the way, urinalyses of the other guests and the dead guard reveal traces of a tranquilizing agent, light enough to induce drowsiness and a sound sleep without arousing suspicion."

"I see." Aleksay mused. "As the valet, Olenov would have had ample opportunity. That is all very apparent. What is not apparent is why, and for whom?"

Aleksay paused as Markelov took a tiny white pill from a plain metal pillbox and swallowed it without the benefit of water.

"Who do you suppose?" Markelov asked.

"We must consider the possibility of a Jewish faction, or even a member of the PFLP directed by Habash. Then there are the British and the Americans."

"Ha!" Markelov snorted. "Impossible! Do you think so?"

He seemed suddenly unsure.

"Perhaps."

"If it were a foreign agent, why hasn't the killing been leaked in the world press?" Markelov asked.

"Perhaps they want to release the information at a time that will compromise us the most. But I am certain that if they do, they will do it in a manner that will throw us off the track, or at least attempt to. I suggest we wait for the news to be broken abroad. That way we will at least have a lead to follow."

"Nyet! I have been instructed to issue a statement today. The PFLP is insisting the matter be made public, and we must comply if we wish to maintain our relationship with them. So we have constructed a case against Olenov as a Jewish sympathizer."

"There is nothing you can say to persuade them otherwise?" Aleksay asked.

"It comes from above my head, Comrade."

"Then why have you sent for me, Comrade Colonel?"

"You have been chosen to investigate this incident. Whoever is responsible, they must be dealt with. It does not matter how long the investigation takes. Those involved are to be eliminated." He slid the dossier across the desk to Aleksay. "You will start with the apartment house?"

"If you wish, Colonel, but I doubt seriously if I will find much more there. The key to this is in Olenov's relationships. Through them we will find the assassin."

"I leave it to you then." Markelov's tone indicated that the audience was over.

Aleksay rose and saluted formally. Markelov returned the gesture and resumed his paper work.

Aleksay felt much better standing in the fresh air outside the Center. The stuffy atmosphere inside had been almost more than he could bear. He thought of his next move as he jogged down the steps toward the street. It was good to be active again. He had spent too many weeks behind his desk. The mission was routine and should not have excited him, but for one element. It was the first time that a foreign entity had violated their security. It had the smell of something much larger, much more important than the assassination of the animal Said.

. . . 6 March 1989

A group of five men clustered in a small, dimly lit, low ceilinged laboratory in the basement of the Pentagon. It consisted of Dr. Arnold Kemper, Dr. Joseph Sevrensen, General Ralph Owens, Richard Montgomery, and Eldon Parker.

Sevrensen was what might be described as the quintessential scientist. A small molish man, he moved furtively among human companions, wearing a look of complete bewilderment in their presence. Perhaps it was because he could not understand their world; his was the realm of theory and experimentation. What time had he to contemplate the inconsistencies of mankind?

General Owens, on the other hand, was the direct opposite of Sevrensen. Large and robust, Owens had a great appetite for the good life. He was raw boned and rosey faced and somewhat more human than one would have expected for a Chairman of the Joint Chiefs of Staff. He was there at the invitation of the new President, but still did not know exactly what he was expected to contribute. So he remained steadfastly attentive, alternately contemplating Sevrensen as he spoke, and the prototype model of the Sevrensen Laser, mounted on the slate-topped workbench in front of them.

"As you may or may not know, gentlemen," Dr. Sevrensen was saying, "the laser is a device in which energy that is supplied to an atomic or molecular system is released as a narrow beam of coherent light, whose wavelength depends upon the energy transitions of the atoms or molecules." He paused, noticing the blank expression on the President's face.

"In simple English," Kemper suggested.

"In simple English, the laser is a device that emits an extremely intense beam of energy in the form of light rays. It is done by stimulating atoms that have artificially had their inherent energy increased. By stimulating them, we cause them to release this excess energy."

"What practical uses has the laser been put to to date, doctor?" Parker asked.

"Well, let me see. We use it in physics as a scientific tool for nonlinear optics, plasma diagnosis, metrology, Schleren photography, seismology, solar simulation, Raman Spectroscopy . . ."

"Hold it, hold it. You've made your point," Parker laughed and Sevrensen chuckled.

"I'm sorry, Mr. President. But you see, the laser has been used in so many practical ways, I could spend the next two weeks explaining them to you. What specifically did you have in mind?"

Parker paused thoughtfully, then asked. "Is there anything that the laser cannot do?"

"Oh, sure." The doctor waved his hands in mock despair. "For instance it cannot penetrate clouds or atmospheric dust, and it is difficult if not impossible to sweep a laser beam over a wide arc. The laser requires enormous energy to operate and in most cases is less than fifty percent efficient. But these are areas where we are on the verge of making great breakthroughs. With the proper funding, there is no telling what we could accomplish. The beauty of the laser is the wide variety of uses it can potentially be adapted to."

"Then in your estimation, doctor, you would say that the laser has enormous potential for industrial use in the future."

"Why yes! We have only scratched the surface. Even now, the laser is being used in research into nuclear fusion. It is also possible that the laser could be used to generate enough power to light our cities, through chain reactions involving highly complicated stacked laser devices. One experiment to date using an optically pumped laser has produced as much as five gigawatts in a single quantum pulse."

"Five gigawatts?"

"Five billion watts," Sevrensen explained.

"In one pulse?"

"In one pulse. Naturally, there are problems in maintaining a continuous flow of power this great. The greatest power comes from pulsing lasers as opposed to continuous wave lasers. So far the highest output of a continuous wave is only 2000 watts. But consider, if there were some way to harness the enormous energy release of a pulsating laser to a continuous wave laser, then we would have something."

"And is that possible?" Parker asked.

Sevrensen smiled slyly and patted the elaborate machine on the bench. "Mr. President. It has been done. The premise for this laser has been used before, gentlemen, in Venice, Italy, in the restoration of art objects and artifacts, even the classical architecture, all of which is threatened by the destructive agents in the layers of century-old soot and modern industrial pollution.

"The continuous wave laser here," he pointed to the first of the two laser devices stacked end to end on the table, "is aimed into the prisms of the pulsing laser, here. The beam of the first is used to excite the material of the second, which in this case is gallium arsenide, and acts to build the energy level to a point necessary to allow the emission of a single burst or quantum pulse.

"The process is quite simple, and the quantum pulses can be stimulated rapidly without elaborate cooling equipment operating at room temperature. This makes it useful in the restoration of artifacts. Briefly, the way the laser affects the artifacts is that it heats the outer layer, which is usually darker than the original material underneath. When the outer layer is heated by the repetitive bursts, it literally burns itself up, without harming the delicate material below, which actually reflects the heat to some extent due to its lighter color. Of course, if the heat were allowed to build up long enough, the lower substance would also be affected; but in our case we are not bothered by that problem.

"It is desirable, in fact, for our laser to penetrate as much area as possible with each quantum pulse, and by decreasing the interval between pulses, we can cause much deeper penetration and greater heat build-up. In this manner, it is even possible to effect penetration of reflective substances due to the intense bombardment and the much higher energy output allowed by the optically pumped laser."

There was a murmur of conjecture among the otherwise stoic audience. "And now, gentlemen," Sevrensen continued. "If you will kindly put on your protective goggles, I will demonstrate."

They each were handed a set of darkly tinted goggles by one of Sevrensen's assistants who appeared from an adjoining room to aid in the demonstration. Sevrensen carefully made a few adjustments to his device, which they then realized was aimed at a piece of metal, secured to the cement wall a few feet away.

"I will direct your attention to the far wall, gentlemen, where I have positioned an inch-thick iron plate. This ferrous material is not the most resistant of substances and should exhibit intense thermal response. Now, if we are ready?"

He glanced around to make sure that all goggles were in place. The distinguished guests trained their eyes on the piece of iron plating, and waited as Sevrensen made the last minute calibrations. Then, with a flick of a switch, he activated the first device, which after a moment emitted a beam of intense blue light. Sevrensen flipped another switch, and a beam of red light shot across the room and entered upon the iron plate. Suddenly, there was a blinding instantaneous flash of white light, and a red circle appeared on the surface of the iron. The metal was glowing hot, but it remained so only briefly before the heat dissipated and the red dot faded.

"That, gentlemen, is the result of only one quantum pulse from the pumped laser. The red beam is a guide, or sighting beam, and actually creates little or no intense heat. The bright flash was the pulse of extreme heat energy. If I were to fire several pulses in rapid succession, the effect would be more dramatic."

Sevrensen again activated the device, the red beam shot across the room and centered upon the target. Then, by pressing a firing button several times, he allowed a rapid succession of pulses to strike the plate, creating a glowing circle of white hot metal. This time there was an intense round of speculative murmuring, and encouraged by the response, Sevrensen decided to show off a little.

"Prepare yourselves, gentlemen," he warned, and fired another round of bursts, this time much longer than the previous one, and the circle grew blindingly white until all at once, the iron seemed to vaporize, and a chunk of cement was blown away from the wall. Sevrensen ceased the barrage. The men impulsively gave a little cheer of excitement, and General Owens' eyes seemed to glow in the dark with his enthusiasm.

"That's very impressive, doctor," Parker remarked. "Is it possible to create the same results on other surfaces, say more resistant to heat?" There was little doubt what was on his mind.

Sevrensen was effervescent with excitement. "Absolutely, Mr. President!" He motioned to an assistant to remove the metal plate, which he did; then he installed a sheet of material which looked like tile on one side, but which was coated with a silver reflective substance on the other. The silver substance was the side exposed to the laser.

"This, gentlemen," Sevrensen said, pointing to the reflective material, "is the same substance used in the flight suits of our own astronauts. It is capable of reflecting the unfiltered rays of the sun and thus maintaining an environment that will support human life. The backing of the target is the same ceramic material used in the heat shield bricks on the undersurface of the Space Shuttle. It is designed to resist intense heat by radiating more heat than it absorbs."

The assistant stepped back behind Sevrensen, and all eyes were trained on the target. Sevrensen made an adjustment to the trigger mechanism, then pressed the button. Almost at once, a succession of one hundred white hot pulses slammed their cumulative quantum energy into the space-age materials in a span of less than fifteen seconds. By the fiftieth pulse, the material had turned red hot; by the seventieth white hot; and by the hundredth, the plate literally exploded in a fine mist and evaporated.

"Remarkable," Parker said. He turned to Montie, who was standing nearest to him. "What do you think?"

"Impressive. Very impressive."

Parker turned to Sevrensen, who was fairly gloating with success. "Doctor, would it be possible to design your device so that it could be employed from a space vehicle?"

"Mr. President. If this laser were employed from a space vehicle, its utility would be increased almost beyond comprehension."

"How so?"

"Quite simply, because heating would no longer be of any consequence. Although the smaller devices do not build great heat, this device does, and it is necesssary to provide an elaborate cooling system." He pointed out the various coils of the system. "But utilize this device in the near absolute zero conditions of outer space, and our problems are solved. The device could be operated at peak capacity almost indefinitely."

"I'm impressed, doctor. I'm very impressed. I will expect your research and development budget within the next two weeks. Dr. Kemper will coordinate with you on all the details, and he will, I trust, keep me informed."

Kemper nodded his assent.

"I'll say good day, then, gentlemen," Parker said, and with Montie on his heels left the room, followed shortly by General Owens and Dr. Kemper, in heated discussion.

Sevrensen smiled proudly at his device. At last he was to see his dream of scientific recognition realized. His name would go down in history along with Einstein's and Von Braun's. Little did he know how closely linked his contribution would be to theirs.

Bruce Wilson had had it. It was seven-thirty and he had been working the President's speech since eleven that morning, in between juggling the numerous inquiries from the usual local and national news agencies. The words on the pages no longer made sense; they were merely patterns of

54

black and white, without coherence or meaning. It was time to quit.

His day had started at five-thirty when he had gotten a call from the President, wanting an immediate statement concerning the Mexican oil-pricing conference being held in Mexico City. The Mexicans, it seemed, were considering raising their oil export prices to the astronomical OPEC level of seventy-five dollars a barrel. The President had been hot as a fire cracker, and before eight o'clock Bruce had issued a blistering press release from Parker, blasting the Mexican President, Enrique de Gonzales-Perez, and warning about the effect such an increase would have on the American economy and the status of relations between the two countries.

From that, Bruce had dived right into the State of the Union address, which he was reworking at the President's request. It was going to be a hard-hitting, albeit relatively short speech, by comparison with most of its predecessors, but its impact promised to be profound.

At any rate, it was going to have to wait until tomorrow. He rose wearily and locked the speech in the vault, put on his jacket and overcoat, turned out the lights and left his office.

On his way out, he decided to stop by the President's office, just to check in in case there were anything urgent. He found the outer door open and Shirley still at her desk, busily typing out memos. She looked up and squinted at Bruce who stopped in the doorway.

"Hi, Shirley. Is he still working?"

"He never quits, Bruce. I've been here since seven, and I'll probably be here at seven tomorrow, shackled to my desk."

"That bad, huh?"

"Not really. I think he's about through with me for the day, although I know he's got Mr. Holmes coming in later."

"Do you think he's going to need me any more tonight?"

"No. I think the country can get by if you go home and get some sleep."

"That's where I'm headed, but if he's expecting the speech . . ."

"He knows you're working on it. Just have something for

55

him to look at by ten in the morning and he'll be happy."

Bruce nodded and smiled apologetically. "I hate to leave' you, but I've got a steak and a bottle of red wine on my mind."

"Don't rub it in."

"See you in the morning, Shirley."

"Goodnight, Mr. Press Secretary."

Bruce blushed a little and stuffing his hands into his overcoat pockets shuffled out.

He stopped off and got a bottle of inexpensive burgandy and finally pulled into the parking garage of his modest Georgetown brownstone complex just after eight-fifteen. It was a cold night, and he looked forward to the prospect of a rare steak and a belly full of red wine. After that, a good night's sleep would be all he needed to tackle the rest of the speech in the morning.

He didn't notice the red MG parked on the street as he pulled in. He climbed the outside stairs wearily, and came to a sharp stop at the sight of the silhouetted figure in the inner landing near his door.

"What are you doing here?" he gasped.

Kathy Karpovich smiled, and held out a brown paper bag that looked like it contained a bottle. "I just come by to drink a toast to peace and pass an otherwise lonely and fruitless evening with someone interesting."

Bruce stared at her for a moment in shock, panting slightly from the climb up the stairs. He did not know what to do. He had been looking forward to an early evening, but seeing Kathy standing there in her tight jeans and thin wool sweater, which revealed beyond a shadow of a doubt the exact shape and size of her more than generous breasts, convinced him that a quiet evening alone was completely out of the question.

"Well, aren't you going to ask me in?"

"Sure," he grinned sheepishly. "Why not?"

Fumbling with his keys he stepped past her to unlock the door. Kathy inched closer, until she was almost touching him. She could feel him tense up and he struggled for a minute with the lock before opening the door and stepping aside to let her in. She slipped by, brushing against him enticingly, and couldn't help chuckling to herself at the immediate reaction she saw in his eyes. This was going to be easier than she had thought.

Eldon Parker and Preston Holmes sat facing each other in front of a crackling fire in the Oval Office. They were both tired from a long day, but there were still things to discuss before calling it a night.

Since the Inauguration, Holmes had been recruiting support for the President's policies, which were to be revealed in the upcoming State of the Union message. Specifics had not been dealt with in those early meetings, but general ideas had been tossed around in an effort to ascertain where the resistance was likely to come from.

"I've consulted over two hundred of the nation's leading industrialists, Don, and I've spoken with all of the representatives and senators personally. I believe we can safely say you have a majority of their support for your economic policies. That isn't to say that we aren't going to have a fight on the Hill over tariffs if it really comes to that. But for the most part, you're in the driver's seat. They're apparently willing to listen to any reasonable suggestions at this point."

"What's the position concerning Mexico? Am I going to get static from the farm machinery exporters?"

"Well, you're not going to be a hero, but I don't think it's really going to come to that, do you?"

"Yes, if they refuse to lower their petroleum prices. If they're reasonable, then maybe we can avoid a blowup. It's time we taught our southern neighbors a lesson in power politics. If they think they're going to keep bilking us at the wellhead and receiving our foreign aid and loans on purchases of our equipment, they're out of their minds. The free ride is over."

"But what about the Russians, Don? Don't you think they're just waiting for an opportunity to jump into Mexico, pick up the slack if we freeze them out?"

"Let them. The Russians can't deliver. Oh, sure, they will at first, and they'll make promises just to get their feet in the door; but their industrial output isn't high enough to meet their domestic demand which in any case will take precedent over exports, so pretty soon Mexico will find itself waiting for equipment that will never appear. Militarily, the Russians can't hold Mexico any better than we could hold Saudi Arabia. If we want Mexico, we can have it as a fifty-first state inside of a week, excepting of course Mexico City which will no longer exist."

"You're kidding of course?"

Parker smiled wryly and hesitated before answering. "It isn't an improbability if it came to that."

Holmes just managed to conceal his uneasiness with a forced grimace and consulted his notes before continuing. "What if Perez responds antagonistically to your press release? How are you going to recover?"

"I'm sticking to my guns, Preston. The time for pampering those bastards is over. The rest of the world had better get it straight right from the start that there's a new man in the White House, and he doesn't take guff from anyone. Nevertheless, I'll extend an invitation to Perez to come to Washington for some private talks. In fact, I've got young Wilson working up a list of other heads of state that I need to have private talks with. One by one, I'm going to appeal to their better judgment, if you know what I mean. They've got to understand that if America collapses, the world economic system collapses. It's as simple as that, and that's exactly what I'm going to tell them." He paused as something suddenly occurred to him. "By the way, have you set up that meeting with George Benest of the COL?"

"I've made repeated overtures to him, but so far I haven't gotten a firm commitment on the date. Obviously, since he didn't support you in the campaign, he's going to try to make you sweat a little."

"That could be fatal," Parker said offhandedly. Then suddenly his face grew red and he slammed his fist down on the arm of his chair. "God damnit!" Who the hell does he think he is? I'm the God damn President, and he'll come when I send for him! Set the date and tell him to be here. I'm tired of these petty thugs thinking they're running the country. These bastards are going to come into line!"

Holmes stared at him for a moment in shocked silence, then nodded his agreement. "I'll call him first thing in the morning."

Parker eased back into his chair, letting his head of steam escape. "I'm sorry, Preston. I shouldn't fly off like that. It's counterproductive."

"I understand, Don."

"What's next?"

"You got an appeal here from the mayors of New York, Chicago, Cleveland, and Detroit requesting a meeting with you at the earliest possible convenience. Their federal loans are coming due, and it looks like they're going to default unless they get an extension."

Parker nodded solemnly, gripping his upper lip with his lower in a sign of exasperation. "Set up a meeting for all four of them, after I've spoken to Benest. In the meantime, I want that son of a bitch Benest here in my office no later than Friday morning! It's the unions that are killing those cities, and he and his cronies are going to answer for it!"

"Like I said, I'll call him in the morning, Don."

Parker nodded and gazed into the hissing fireplace. "What's going to be the reaction to the Space Shuttle proposal?"

Holmes hesitated momentarily then proceeded with caution. "I think there's going to be some stiff opposition on the Hill." He stopped as Parker turned his glare toward him. "It's a sales job that's going to take some time, Don."

"We ran out of time when the last Administration sacrificed the program in favor of welfare and unemployment benefits!"

"I know that, and you know that; but after all, Don, when people are standing in unemployment lines, or waiting on the welfare check, it's kind of difficult to explain to them why we're pouring billions into outer space."

"For the same reason the oil companies are pouring billions into research, for the same reason we're continuing to develop new weapons systems; it's all geared to survival!"

"That's a hard concept to get across to your constituents, when survival means wondering where the next meal is coming from."

"Preston, I don't care how you do it, but you have got to impress on the leaders of both parties that I am not going to stand for any footdragging on this issue. That program is going to gear back up inside of six months, it's going to provide thousands of jobs for highly skilled individuals, and my other programs are going to ease the pressure on the unskilled people. This is an across-the-board thrust and you'd better make that clear because I'm announcing my plans tomorrow night and I don't want any dissension within the Party ranks. I'm expecting it from the liberals, but by God not from my own camp, is that clear?"

"Perfectly clear, Mr. President . . . I mean Don . . ." Preston paused, embarrassed by the President's outburst.

Parker smiled, his whole countenance suddenly changing from hostile to congenial. He chuckled and slapped Preston on the knee with his palm. "I'm sorry, Preston. I'm not jumping on you, you know that."

"You could've fooled me," Preston laughed uneasily.

"I'm just so damned tired of this American ostrich policy. The public has no idea of what could happen; and unless we act immediately to impress order on this economic chaos, we're going to have rioting, starvation, maybe even total collapse! Then where are they going to hide? We've got a potential for a depression that will make 1929 look tame!"

Holmes nodded solemnly. He was tired and his mind had begun to dull. Parker noticed. "Let me say one more thing, Preston. I appreciate what you're up against. That's why I chose you over all the other possible candidates for the Vice-Presidency. I know you can get the job done. This Oasis Project is going to be taking more and more of my time, that and foreign affairs, and you are my right arm on the Hill. I'm counting on you and I know you won't let me down."

"I won't Don. I promise you."

Parker nodded. "Let's cash it in for tonight. Tomorrow's going to be a big day."

"I'll go for that, and I'll make that call to Benest in the morning."

"Let me know."

"I will. Goodnight, Don."

Parker sat for a long time after Holmes had gone, staring into the embers and thinking. Finally he rose and walked wearily to his desk. He sat down heavily and opened a thin manila folder marked Top Secret. In it there was a handwritten list which began from the top:

Montreal
Peking
Havana
London
Paris

He began to add to the list, Bonn, Rome, Athens, Moscow . . .

"Are you sure you don't want any?" Bruce asked, finally cutting into his rare steak. It was almost eleven.

"I'm not hungry," Kathy said. "For food that is."

Bruce let the comment pass and sank his teeth into the meat, but he couldn't help feeling self-conscious with her staring at him, smiling seductively as he chewed. He smiled sheepishly and she giggled, clearly feeling the effects of the brandy she was sipping out of a water glass.

He laughed, choking slightly on the wine. She was blatantly coming on to him; but at this stage of the game he didn't care. If he hadn't been so damned hungry, he probably would have thrown her on the table and had her right there. She was definitely ready. But he was hungry, and he figured that she would stick around for dessert, which was going to be him.

"So how're things behind the Pearly Gates?" she asked.

"Hectic. I've been working on the President's speech for the last three days."

"Anything juicy in it?"

"You'll find out along with the rest of the country tomorrow night."

"Oh come on, how is the state of the union?" she teased.

"Not good." He stopped himself short. She smiled at him and ran her tongue across the edge of her glass, before taking a deep sip.

"Don't worry, I won't try to pry anything out of you. Finish your steak."

He smiled, somewhat reassured, and continued his meal.

"You don't mind if I ask you a few personal questions about Parker do you?"

"How personal?"

"I'll let you be the judge. If you don't like them, you don't have to answer them."

"What's it for?"

"An in-depth piece I'm doing about Parker's background."

"I don't know any more than has already been published."

"Can I just ask you anyway?"

"Go ahead, then. Get it over with."

"All right. Does he ever talk about his childhood?"

"Not much. Oh maybe sometimes he mentions the poverty and the bad working conditions in the mines. But nothing specific. The whole region was impoverished."

"His family settled that territory, didn't they?"

"Yes, around 1800 I think."

"Does he ever talk about his marriage?"

"Never. And no one has ever brought it up."

"How old was he when she died?"

"They were both in their teens. She died in childbirth."

"God, how unbelievable. In 1957?"

"I don't know the exact date. It was around then."

"What about the rest of his family?"

"It's pretty unclear, like I said. I know he had a younger brother who died at an early age of some fever. And his father was killed in a mining accident in 1961. His mother lived until the mid-seventies. Say, this isn't anything new. Why are you asking me . . ."

"What did she die of?"

"Old age," Bruce was losing his appetite. "They had a hell of a life."

"Until they found coal under Parker Mountain."

"Yeah. Once he got a foot in the door, he took advantage of it. That led to Parker Mining."

"He's an amazing man. You know I'm always fascinated by a man who comes out of nowhere, rags to riches. The elements of timing and skill are so critical. So subject to change."

"That's the American dream," he said in true admiration.

"Yes," she said. "It is. Do you mind if I ask you a personal opinion?"

"What?"

"Do you really believe that Parker is any different than any other President? I mean, is he the one man in the present place and time who can pull this country out of its tailspin?"

"Off the record?"

"Off the record," she conceded.

"I really don't know, to tell you the truth. He's smart as hell, his business record shows that. And after all, running the country is pretty much like running a big business. I think the most important aspect of his personality is that he thinks ahead. He's not a reactionary, he's a trend setter. He sees the future and interprets what has to be done in the present to make the future what he hopes it will be. And he's realistic. He doesn't give a flying goddamn for politics, just for politics' sake. He's in that office because he sincerely believes that the country needs him to survive; and for my money, that's the kind of man I can believe in."

"Do you think he'll run again in 1992?"

"Come on, Kathy. His Administration is less than two months old. What kind of a question is that?"

"A typical journalist bullshit question."

"I doubt that you ask those kind of questions, Kathy."

She smiled but did not respond. Partially because of the brandy, she was losing interest in the word game. She had another game in mind.

Bruce finished his steak and poured the rest of the wine into his glass. He felt a hundred percent better, and Kathy

63

was looking even more tempting. But it wasn't just the wine that made him feel that way. He liked her the more they talked, and he sensed that she was a cut above what her reputation indicated. He knew already how vicious the Washington gossip could be, and how wrong. Nevertheless, the rumors about her being a journalistic Mata Hari added to the glamour of the woman; there was nothing wrong with that.

"How about sitting by the fire?" he asked, rising from the table.

She raised her eyebrows melodramatically and followed suit, swishing her fanny provocatively as she led the way to the couch. Bruce put on another log and sat down beside her, keeping a respectable distance.

She looked at him with mock disgust and slid over cheek to cheek. "Prude," she sniffed.

Bruce smiled letting his eyes run over her shapely body. "So is the interview over?"

"Over," she whispered, staring at his mouth, wetting her lips. "I like fires," she said. "They turn me on."

"Fires?" he laughed. "The booze doesn't hurt."

"Try some of this." She extended her glass.

He took it, enclosing her hand in his, drawing the glass toward his lips. She did not resist, and allowed him to raise it. He took a sip, staring into her eyes, their faces only inches apart. The brandy seemed to fill his head and lit a fire down his insides. Her perfume was enveloping him, and her eyes were glistening invitingly in the firelight. He released her hand expecting her to withdraw, but instead she set her glass on the coffee table and ran her fingers up the inside of his leg, letting them drift to a stop inches from the knot he felt hardening in his slacks. He wondered if she were aware of it. She leaned closer until her lips were barely touching his, and gently grasped him.

He felt like an explosion had gone off in his head. She parted her lips and flicked her tongue across his mouth searching for a response. He pulled her close, kissing her passionately, their tongues entwining. She urged him on, moving against him, her breath coming in short gasps.

Cautiously, he slid his hand beneath her sweater, his fingers gliding liquid-like over her silky skin to cup one of her breasts. It was firm and hot, the nipple hard. Groaning, she pulled him with her, grinding against him in response to his own boiling passions. She wanted him not for his stories, not for his connections. She needed him and she was going to have him.

. . . 7 March 1989

General Owens arrived at the White House at seven-forty-five A.M. He had been up since five, run his usual two miles, had his customary breakfast of two eggs, one slice of bacon, and black coffee, read his morning briefings from the Joint Chiefs, and sent out a barrage of communiques to various personnel in all parts of the world.

It was a cold grey morning, but the Oval Office was warm and cheerful, the atmosphere relaxed. It was the temperament of the man who occupied it that made it so.

Owens knew little of the new President other than what he had read and observed in their few short meetings prior to that morning. But he sensed that Parker was a strong motivator of people, a leader who would be hard to manipulate in any way. Nevertheless, he was prepared to put up a stiff argument for what he considered to be a breach of protocol. He was concerned that the President and Arnold Kemper had not consulted him on the Sevrensen laser prior to its demonstration the previous morning since its military applications seemed to be obvious. But his anger was cooled by Parker's opening remarks.

"Ralph, right off, let me apologize for not consulting with you earlier on the Sevrensen laser. It was something we had to get a better grip on before we could discuss it with you. But we wanted you at the demonstration. Now that we've seen how well it works, I want to fill you in on my thinking."

Owens found himself without protest. "Thank you, Mr. President."

"Don," Parker corrected him. "I like to keep things relaxed."

"All right, Don," Owens said, although it was awkward to

address his commander in chief with such familiarity. At any rate, his previous resentments had faded completely. He studied the shimmering green eyes of the young President and felt his contagious energy. It was impossible to resist being drawn into his influence. He was someone to be trusted, believed in; and that was something Owens had felt about few people in his long service to his country.

"What I have in mind, Ralph," Parker continued, "concerns a joint effort between NASA and the Air Force working with the SPEC research teams."

"We've always worked closely in the past, Mr. President . . . Don."

"I know. Your briefings were excellent and gave me a good overview of all our military systems."

Owens inwardly swelled, although realizing how skillfully Parker could maneuver people onto his side with the proper placement of praise. "I tried to make them as concise as possible, while still covering all the main points."

"You did it very well. Now what I have in mind, Ralph, is far more important than anything we have yet accomplished in this direction. It's going to require the same arrangement that existed between NASA and the Air Force during the early Manned Space Flight programs; and that means a certain degree of subterfuge."

"If it's for the good of the country, you know I'm willing to consider anything you'd like to recommend."

"Then I'll get right to the point. In my State of the Union address tonight, I'm going to announce my intentions to rein-state the Space Shuttle Program. My reasons are going to be that the program is vital to the development of new technology that can benefit us in the areas of energy conservation and development, and that it will provide thousands of jobs for currently unemployed and highly skilled personnel; which in turn will give a much needed boost to our sagging economy."

The General chose his words carefully. "Naturally, Don, I'm pleased to hear this. I've always believed in the benefits of the space program. But I don't see the connection between the shuttle and the Sevrensen laser."

"That's because there is no connection. Not directly at any rate. The Shuttle Program is going to serve as a cover-up activity for the development of an entirely new program." He paused as a glimmer of interest appeared in the General's eyes. "And that's where the military comes in, specifically, the Air Force aerospace research budget. The Space Shuttle appropriations will be barely enough to cover the cost of the legitimate research we will be conducting in that area, some of which will benefit the new program. We're going to need the Air Force budget to carry out our primary objectives."

"All of it?" Owens asked, his tone revealing more of his emotions than he had intended.

"I think so, although I don't have the combined figures from Dr. Kemper yet." He rose and walked over to the series of wall charts near his desk. He pulled one down, revealing a large artist's rendering of a huge, manta ray-shaped vehicle.

"Is that it?"

"Yes. A preliminary rendering of what Kemper is calling the ASP. That stands for Aerospace Plane." He saw the many questions written on the General's face. "Before you ask any questions, let me explain. You will recall that in my acceptance speech, I referred to America as an oasis. Well, my analogy actually goes much farther than that. The world is an oasis. We're a living planet alone in a universe of seemingly dead worlds. At least that was the general consensus until the lunar landings. From them, we've learned that the moon abounds with raw ores, lignite deposits, uranium deposits, that are there just waiting for the taking. But our target is a vein of extraordinarily pure gold."

He pulled down a new wall chart of the moon, on which the rich gold fields were marked in bright highlights. "Our targets are here." He pointed to the highlighted areas. "And this craft, produced in number, will mine those fields and transport our cargo back to Earth for refining." Owens gasped. "It is our intention to return this country's currency to the gold standard and by so doing break the inflation-crude oil cycle. What I'm talking about is our first global colony. In my estimation, the country that controls the moon in the next one hundred years, will also control the fate of the

Earth and perhaps even the solar system. It would be a monumental feat, and if we succeed we're talking about economic independence and most probably world domination. If we fail . . ." He let his voice trail off.

"Mother of God, Don! What you're suggesting is something out of Buck Rogers."

"You might say that; but I'm afraid if we don't capitalize on our technological superiority in the area of space flight, the Russians are eventually going to surpass us and then they might be the ones mining the moon although I'm certain they are unaware of our find. I don't think we can afford to wait, however."

"Is what you're describing technically possible?"

"According to Dr. Kemper, yes. Naturally, there is a great deal of new ground to break, and that's why we need the Air Force budget. Only after the program is successful will we make it public knowledge. By that time, it will be too late for the Russians to do anything about it."

"Incredible."

"Do I have your cooperation?"

"Definitely, Mr. President. Consider my influence at your disposal."

Parker approached him and extended his hand. They shook; a reverent handshake, a bond of secrecy. "This is war, General, and we must allow nothing to stand in the way of this project succeeding. Nothing."

Bruce awoke with a violent start and stared disbelievingly at his watch. It was eight o'clock. He glanced at Kathy, who was curled up beside him under a comforter she had dragged out of a closet in the middle of the night. She was still sound asleep.

He slipped off the couch and hustled into the bathroom. It was going to be his ass if he didn't have the President's speech ready by ten o'clock. He took a fast steaming shower, shaved, and brushed his teeth. Glancing out of the bathroom window, he saw that the sky was clearing and he decided to put on his new gray suit. He wanted to look sharp.

When he returned to the living room, Kathy was dressed and rummaging through the cupboards in the kitchen. "Where's the coffee? Jesus, my head!"

"In the cabinet by the stove. It's instant. Listen, I'm late. Make yourself some breakfast if you want and lock up on the way out."

She came out of the kitchen with the jar of coffee in her hand, a make-believe pout on her lips. "Just like that, huh? Fuck 'em and leave 'em?"

He stopped at the sight of her. She looked very sexy with her face flushed and hair mussed. He took her in his arms and kissed her feeling his body respond to her nearness.

She felt it too and cooed. "Want some breakfast?"

"I don't have time for that either. I'm late as hell."

"Too bad. I hate to send you out hungry."

He patted her on the rear and kissed her again, then he picked up his overcoat which he had draped over the chair the night before. "If I don't finish that speech by ten, my ass is grass and Parker's going to be the lawnmower. Don't forget to lock up."

"Aren't you afraid I'll rifle through your drawers?"

"You already have, my dear. And very thoroughly. I'm surprised I can still walk. Goodbye."

He arrived at the office at just after eight-forty, to find the place a madhouse. One glance at the headlines in the morning *Post* told him why. "Ali Said Assassinated in Moscow"; "Officials Blame Jewish Dissidents."

"Holy shit!"

His secretary, came hurrying out of his office, a pile of manuscripts in her arms. "Thank God!" she exclaimed. "Where have you been? The President's been calling every five minutes for that release on Said. He's scheduled a press conference at ten."

"Is that it?"

"The release? Yes." She handed it to him, and straightened his tie.

"Thanks. Have you called all the news agencies?"

"We're doing it now."

"Good, I'll run this up to him." He stopped, wondering if he should call Kathy, but realized that he didn't have the time.

Kathy reached her apartment at nine-fifteen to find the phone ringing. She hurried inside and answered it. "Hello? He what? He what! When! Shit!"

She hung up and tore off her clothes on the way to the bathroom. She had exactly forty-five minutes to make herself presentable and get to the White House.

The press room at the White House was absolute bedlam, what with the camera crews jostling for position and the reporters squabbling over their seats. Naturally, everyone wanted to be front row center, and since this was to be the President's first official appearance since taking office, they were all eager to gain the spotlight for their agencies.

Kathy arrived at one minute after ten to find the place packed. She slid along the rear wall and up the side aisle, looking for a spot. None were available. She caught a dirty look from her bureau chief, but ignored it as she whipped out her pad and pen. Her hair was still damp and she hadn't had time to put on much makeup, so there was little doubt how she had spent the previous night.

At three minutes after ten, Bruce appeared through the side door and took the podium. He looked harassed but in control, and announced without any delay. "Ladies and gentlemen of the press. The President of the United States."

The crowd rose to its feet and applauded enthusiastically as Parker entered and mounted the dais, smiling reservedly to the full house through the blinding wall of movie lights. He was wearing a trim charcoal grey suit with his favorite maroon tie and a white shirt, and looked eager to get down to business. The crowd quieted quickly, and the cameras began to whir as Parker gathered his notes in front of him. He put on a grim countenance.

"Good morning, ladies and gentlemen. Thank you for coming. I feel that before we begin, I should extend to you my deepest personal regrets for being unable to meet with you before now. As Mr. Wilson has explained, pressing matters of state have demanded my undivided attention; and as you all know by now I am a man of few words. I had planned on breaking my silence tonight with my State of the Union Message, but because of the world-shattering headlines in most of this morning's papers, I felt that I had to make an immediate statement on the issue."

Kathy tried to catch Bruce's eye during this introduction, and when she finally did, she gave him a dirty look. He averted his gaze back to the President without any indication of remorse.

"Concerning the news story released this morning from Eastern Europe, I want to say that our intelligence sources have confirmed the assassination of Ali Said at the hands of an unknown entity, during a visit to Moscow in late December. The allegation that a Jewish dissident faction was responsible for this atrocity has neither been confirmed nor disproven; but I feel compelled to speak out on the issue of terrorism and the peril it presents to world peace.

"It is no secret that Mr. Said was a member of the community whose very premise dictated terrorism as a way of life. He was a leader of a troubled people, a people who have been victimized by international politics and religious intolerance. And while the horror of this man's death is overshadowed by the unconscionable suffering and slaughter that he condoned and perpetuated, I want to make it perfectly clear that this administration in no way condones this act of violence against him.

"Admittedly, he died by the sword he fashioned from the blood of many innocent people; but on a larger scale, man must live by a system of laws; and adherence to those laws is essential to the survival of our species on Earth. The world has reached a point in its history at which all peoples must work together to put an end to this type of vigilante justice and retaliation.

"The world is an oasis, floating alone in the vastness of the solar system, unique in its ability to spawn and preserve life, and in that sense, the peoples of the world are a brotherhood, undivided by race, color, or religious beliefs. Even man's politics must fall subject to these facts, and it is long past due that we learn to live together in harmony and mutual respect and cooperation. I call upon the leaders of all the nations of the world to condemn this form of political expression and gross violation of human rights.

"And while I do not feel any sense of grief at the death of this man, I feel a sense of remorse for all of mankind, and an overpowering outrage at the perpetrators of this violent act. I call upon the leaders in the Kremlin to act swiftly to bring the guilty parties to a righteous justice in the interest of humanity and world peace."

Parker paused and folded his notes away. The fusilade of questions came at once. He pointed calmly to an elderly man near the front.

"Mr. President, Miles Simpson of *The New York Times*. could you elaborate on the effects that this event might have on the already dangerous climate in the Middle East?"

"Let me say only that this act should be taken as an indication to those currently embroiled in the hostilities in the Middle East of the severity of the international repercussions that might result from their continued conflict. It is my sincerest hope that this brutal crime will not widen the gulf of misunderstanding between the factions there, but will serve instead to stimulate a greater realization of the dangers to world peace that their continued aggressions present."

"Mr. President. Williams of the *Morning Sun*. Whom do you see emerging from this as the new leader of the PLO?"

Parker measured his words carefully. "As you well know, the PLO has long been divided between the moderate and radical factions. In the aftermath of Said's death, I hope that their organization will unite constructively under a common bond for peace and not increased hostility."

"Mr. President. Kathryn Karpovich of the *Post.*" Kathy stepped forward and the President's eyes riveted upon her. It was impossible not to single her out of the crowd as the most attractive woman present. He had met her early in his campaign, and had admired her beauty and incisive intelligence from the first. She stood with an easy air of confidence and returned his gaze with unequalled assurance.

"Miss Karpovich?"

"Mr. President, on the domestic scene, there have been rumors that you intend to delegate far more authority and responsibility to Vice-President Holmes than any of your predecessors have ever delegated to their Vice-Presidents in the past. Would you care to comment on this?"

Parker smiled wryly. "I see that the grapevine not only exists, but works very effectively." There was a round of chuckles from the assemblage which quickly faded. "To answer your question, yes, I intend to delegate a great deal of authority to Mr. Holmes, but in all cases, I will remain the final authority and the responsibility for his actions will be mine alone. I do this because I feel that the Vice-President should carry a share of the responsibility of the Administration owing to the increased demands placed on this office and the limited resources of one man alone at the top. I selected Mr. Holmes as my running mate because of his unique abilities, and I intend to utilize his talents to their fullest during our term in office. I have great confidence in him as a man of wisdom, courage, and devotion to duty." He paused only long enough to take a breath and continued before any more questions could be fired. "And now ladies and gentlemen, I know that each one of you has a very important question to put to me, but my schedule does not allow me to answer them all, even though I would like to. I thank you for your valuable time. Good day."

He turned and exited without hesitation; the assemblage rose and applauded although murmuring somewhat disgruntedly. The press room began to empty, but Kathy worked her way forward in an attempt to intercept Bruce before he got out the door. He saw her coming and tried to duck out, but she cut him off.

"Mr. Wilson? Do you have a moment?"

He paused, looking trapped and compromised. "What is it, Miss Karpovich?"

She waited until the others had drifted away. "Why didn't you tell me about the press conference? I nearly missed it!"

"I didn't know until I got here."

"Did you know about Said before this morning?"

"I'm not at liberty to discuss those kinds of questions, Miss Karpovich."

"You son of a bitch, you did," she hissed.

"Is that all, Miss Karpovich?"

"Just because you fucked me, doesn't mean you have to cut me off from doing my job. That could have been a hell of a scoop!"

"I think you've misinterpreted the situation. Good day, Miss Karpovich."

He left her smoldering and vanished behind the security guards into the recesses of the White House.

Roger Davis lay on his back in the cool white limestone sand, his eyes closed to the blue sky overhead, the singing heat of the Caribbean sunshine beating down on his browning skin. At his feet, the incessant surge of aquamarine surf pounded the shore. Behind him, he felt the solitude of the Yucatan jungle.

He had gone to Cancun directly from his meeting at Camp David. After wintering in Moscow, his body, mind, and spirit were in need of the pleasures the Mexican resort had to offer; exercise, good food, and heavy drinking. In a week or two he would be refreshed and ready to return to duty.

He had rented a Porche that morning and driven down the only coastal road on the mainland to the ruins near Uxmal. There the beach was deserted and the sound of the surf was his only companion. The ruins drew a fair stream of tourists the year round, but few knew about the tranquil lagoon and the strip of sand the Mayans had called the *birthplace of the Sun*.

Removed from the troubles of his world in this tranquil retreat, he did not have to think of the morning headlines. Over two months after the fact, the Russians had finally broken the Said story, blaming a Zionist zealot for the slaying, and calling for an immediate end to the terrorist imperialism of Israel and her allies. A predictable statement, totally without imagination, as he had known it would be.

He did not hear the soft pad of approaching feet in the sand, but he smelled her perfume on the wind. Its scent was South American, distinctive and expensive. He lay motionless, his eyes leveled at his toes waiting for her to come into view. At last she appeared and stopped to look at him. He saw her only in silhouette against the glare and could tell little about her.

He waited without moving as she diverted her path down toward the water, and passed quickly, heading toward the sheltered lagoon a few hundred feet south of him.

At length he chanced a better look and was pleasantly rewarded. She was tall, almost six feet in fact, browned to a rich coffee color. Her sun-bleached brown hair hung freely to her hips which swung rhythmically as she walked. He saw legs that were slender and well shaped, a narrow waist, and attractively wide shoulders, indicating that she was probably athletic. He tried to imagine her face, assuring himself that it would measure up to the rest of her.

Suddenly, as if aware that he was watching her, she stopped and looked back. He was propped on one elbow, staring boldly. She was wearing huge dark glasses, the kind worn by women who do not wish to be recognized; but from the thin line of her nose and the soft angular wedge of her cheekbones and full sensual lips, he could tell that she was stunning. He smiled instinctively. Beauty in any form pleased him, and he felt no need to hide his pleasure.

She turned away haughtily and continued toward the lagoon, her bottom twitching a bit more than before, perhaps from annoyance, perhaps as an invitation. He watched her climb the gentle slope of the rocky rim surrounding the lagoon and disappear down the other side. He wanted to follow, but wasn't one to rush things. He waited several minutes, then he gathered up his canvas bag and towel and jogged across the cool sand, up the slope where he paused on the rim to look down into the sheltered bowl.

The lagoon was some four hundred yards long and at least

two hundred wide, separated from the ocean by a narrow sand spit. There was a shallow channel that fed its crystalline waters, which at low tide was completely dry, and rocky outcroppings protected this fragile cut from the pounding surf so that the lagoon was always calm and vividly clear.

From his vantage, he could see the coral configurations beneath the shimmering surface, blue, purple, violet, and red. The fish flashed in multicolored schools, seemingly oblivious of the rare beauty who had just entered their domain. She swam on the surface for a hundred yards or so, peering into the shallow waters through her face plate, breathing through the black tube of her snorkel. On her feet she wore large jet fins which propelled her with easy sweeps of her muscled legs.

For twenty minutes he watched as she swam and dived among the coral heads, surfacing to expel the water from her snokel in a whooshing geyser; then diving once more to glide effortlessly under water sometimes for as long as a minute at a time. She was an excellent swimmer, completely at home in the water, and easily covered the entire lagoon from one end to the other before finally working her way back to the promontory where she had left her bag and towel.

He waited for her on the edge of the rocks, and smiled as she raised her head and stared up at him. She looked frightened at first, but he smiled again reassuringly. "You're a beautiful swimmer," he said, hoping that she understood English. She apparently did by her reaction; but she said nothing as she emerged from the water, shedding her fins and mask. Her body sparkled in the sunlight, shimmering with a million diamond water droplets. She was more beautiful than he had imagined, and he found himself staring, searching for something to say. It was then that he noticed the black Nikonos underwater camera around her neck.

"I hope you don't think I'm intruding, but I saw that you had this equipment and I didn't think you'd mind my watching. Is that an underwater camera?"

She looked at him cautiously, then said bluntly, "You're a terrible liar, and yes, it is an underwater camera."

He laughed out loud and she glared at him defiantly. She

was most assuredly of the aristocracy and believed in her rank and ability to command.

"Let me buy you a drink," he said, taking a thermos out of his duffle bag. He held it up. "Margarita?"

She relaxed a little and allowed herself a forced smile. "All right. It's not often I meet a man as insistent as you. You may buy me a drink." Leaving her gear on the rocks, she climbed up to join him. He had spread his towel out and moved over to make room for her. She chose to sit on the bare rock, knees up with her arms wrapped around them, and waited patiently for him to pour the drinks.

The sun beat down. There was scarcely a breath of wind. He could smell the salt on her body mingling with her perfume. It was a wild untamed blend; and sitting there in her microscopic string bikini, she presented a picture of irresistible loveliness.

He handed her one of the plastic thermos cups and she took it with a proper smile, careful not to touch his hand. He smiled back and raised his glass. "To mermaids," he said. She looked slightly amused.

"To mermaids," she echoed and took a tentative sip. By her expression she approved.

"Well?" he asked.

"Do you always fish for compliments?" she chided him, then cooly continued. "It is fine."

"Thank you. I never serve anything I can't drink myself, and I have a very discriminating palate. And no. I don't always fish for compliments. I don't often need to."

"You're very sure of yourself, aren't you?"

"Is that a sin?"

She thought for a moment before answering. "No. Perhaps it is a virtue. I'll have some more." As he filled her cup, she studied him. He was very handsome, she thought, and his blond hair attracted her. His eyes were the bluest she could remember seeing, and she found it hard to resist staring into them, searching for hidden secrets. Only the faint scar beneath his right eye troubled her, but in some strange way it was also exciting. It gave him an air of mystery. At any rate, he was interesting to talk to and look at;

not like the men who had wooed her from early adolescence, all obsequiously polite, groveling for her attentions and a share of her position in life.

"Who are you?" she asked boldly.

"Roger Davis," he said, returning her brazen stare. She was spoiled, he had decided, and domineering, but devastatingly beautiful. He could barely keep his eyes off her. "I'm an American."

"That is obvious, Mr. Davis."

"Roger," he insisted. "And who are you?" he asked, as if addressing a small naughty child.

She hesitated and he knew that she was fabricating a name. "Maria Vega. I'm from Mexico City."

"Well, Maria. Do you come to Cancun often, or is this your first time?"

"No. We come when father wants to get away. I would not come but he insists. It's so boring here. All he wants to do is relax, but I do not want to relax."

"It seems to me there's plenty to do here; swimming, sailing, tennis, and the night life . . . the discotheque at the Camino Real is a lively place."

"I don't go out at night, here?"

"Why not?" he asked suddenly disappointed.

"I'm not allowed to."

"You're not allowed to? You mean your father won't let you?"

She rose suddenly, collecting her things. "Thank you for the drink, Mr. Davis. It was very enjoyable, but I really should be going."

"Did I say something wrong?"

"No." She paused briefly. "I did."

She turned to leave, but he got to his feet and caught her elbow. "Wait a minute. What's got you so upset?"

"I'm not upset. I just have to go." She pulled away and he made no effort to stop her.

"Can I see you again?" he asked.

She looked at him, clearly wanting to say yes. "No. It would be impossible." She turned away and hurried down the slope to the beach.

He sat back down and watched her until she disappeared into the dense strip of jungle bordering the road. He finished the rest of the margaritas staring dazedly at the shimmering lagoon. For the first time in many years he boiled with an emotion unfamiliar to him; anger.

The House Chambers were packed, the air electric with speculation on the President's State of the Union address. No one knew quite what to expect from Parker, but they were optimistic that his plans would be well conceived, his goals courageous.

Preston Holmes rose and gaveled repeatedly for order. It took several minutes, but the capacity crowd quieted and he spoke solemnly into the microphone. "Ladies and gentlemen, the President of the United States!"

They arose applauding and all eyes turned up the center aisle, where the chamber doors swung open and Eldon Parker appeared shaking hands and waving. He was smiling, but maintained a serious decorum looking solid and fit in his dark suit, white shirt, and favorite maroon tie.

In his hotel room overlooking the blue Carribbean, Roger Davis rose from in front of the television to answer the knock at his door, while on screen, Parker made his way down the aisle toward the dais. Davis slipped his pistol into his waistband and, leaving the night chain on, opened the door.

A Mayan bellboy stared back cheerfully and spoke in Mayan Spanish, handing Davis a sealed white envelope. Davis took it, tipped the boy generously, then returned to the television.

Parker was on the dais in front of the President's bench, his hands raised in salute to the enthusiastic reception. Davis glanced at the envelope and only then saw the gold embossed seal of the President of Mexico on the back flap.

Parker turned to Holmes who began to politely gavel for order, but the crowd continued to applaud. Parker looked slightly stiff, perhaps uneasy about the ovation in light of the message he intended to deliver.

Davis tore open the envelope and read the brief handwritten note: "Have only just learned of your visit to Cancun. Would be pleased to receive you at a cocktail party this evening at my hacienda. Cordially Enrique de Gonzales Perez." Davis was stunned. A handwritten invitation from the President himself. He rose and began to shave as Parker received a respectful silence.

"Mr. President. Mr. Speaker. Members of the Congress of the United States, honored guests, my fellow Americans. Tonight it is my duty to put before you my candid view of the State of the Union, and the future as we in this Administration see it. In the forty-seven days since taking the oath of office, I have yet to address you on a matter of national concern, for the express reason that the enormous problems facing this nation and the necessity of a smooth transition from one administration to the next have demanded my undivided attention. During this brief period, I have begun to assimilate the massive quantities of information that I must possess in order to serve as your President. And now, with a much clearer picture of current world conditions, I am prepared to express my views and expectations for the months ahead.

"On January 20 last, I spoke to you from the steps of the Capitol Building on a day that was bright and full of promise; but I warned even then that there was a shadow in our future, a spectre threatening to destroy the foundation of our society. Tonight, I come before you to say that the State of the Union as I see it today is far worse than the picture I painted only a few short weeks ago."

David changed his socks and underwear, listening to the President's speech. The sun was setting into the jungle and the ocean had turned a luminous purple under a pastel sky. The President's words of impending doom seemed inconceivable in this tranquil setting.

"Our country faces its greatest challenge in its entire history. Its standards and beliefs are riddled with doubt and dissension. We as a people have lost sight of the values that made our nation strong and free; and we are drifting farther and farther down a river that has no end but the cataracts of economic disaster.

81

"America has lived too long at the expense of the future. We have become a civilization of consumers rather than producers. Where once the world clamored for our goods and services, now we devour in unchecked abundance incomprehensible quantities of foreign products. We are no longer independent of the rest of the world nor have we been for many years. The world economic system is interwoven, a patchwork quilt of mutual dependence. But in recent times, the pendulum of dependence has swung drastically against us, as foreign competition increases unchecked by domestic production. If we hope to provide for the future generations of Americans, and the other people of the world, we must begin now to sacrifice, to give of ourselves, to demand more of ourselves than we have become accustomed to giving, to rise to the levels of excellence that were once the standard of American craftsmanship.

"There was a time in America's past when a worker was his employer's most valuable asset and resource. Each individual gave to his job, in the spirit of total commitment, total cooperation. These attitudes were reflected in the quality of the goods produced. Today, sadly, I don't feel that we can say this is the case. Too many of us work for only the paycheck, only the new car or the new television set. Personal achievement is a thing of the past, and personal indulgence has taken its place. Therefore we are content to let others do what we have done before, confident that we will always be able to afford the luxuries that our way of life has to offer. I'm afraid we have been sorely misguided. We are a nation of haves in a world of have nots; but the trend is changing, as more and more nations demand what we enjoy. This is the primary conflict that man will face in the coming decade before the end of this century. It will be a struggle of economics, a war of balance of payments and inflationary cycles, of inflating and deflating currencies and monetary systems.

"Therefore, if we are to continue to exist as a free nation, we must return our priorities to basics. We must strive to achieve our former greatness and focus our efforts not on self-indulgence but on personal performance and produc-

82

tivity. We must each ask ourselves in our own line of work if we are truly deserving of the salary we presently enjoy. Have we earned this remuneration by greater productivity, greater value to the companies that enjoy us, or merely by greater longevity? Are we worth the dollars it takes to clothe and feed us? I seriously challenge each and every one of you to answer yes, because statistics show that you will not be admitting the truth. We have become a country of gluttons, content to take what we can for as long as we can, with as little effort as possible in return. And, my fellow Americans, that is a sure course to ruin!"

There was a tremor of disturbed discussion in the heretofore mesmerized assemblage, and Davis let out a low whistle as he rose and poured himself another stiff slug of Bourbon. Parker was really laying it on the line.

"Tonight, I intend to outline my plans for the coming months, and prepare you for the shapes of things to come. It is not my intention to frighten or panic you needlessly, but to inform you, because the issues I have just raised are very real. It's not my intention to spare your feelings or mislead you into thinking that our problems will work themselves out for the better somehow or another. Without everyone's cooperation, they won't. They will only grow worse.

"To begin with, in the spirit of my austerity program, I am hereby forfeiting all of my Presidential salary for the next four years. Since I am a man of some wealth, I see no point in burdening the taxpayers with an expense that unnecessary."

There was an excited rumbling in the crowd, but he continued without hesitation. "Now, simply, my goals are to reduce unemployment by increasing the amount of available jobs in the private sector, with some temporary employment in public works projects; to encourage greater research into the realm of new sources and uses of energy for the future, again with the emphasis on the private sector. It is also my desire to restructure the current welfare programs in such a manner as to eliminate the circumstances that encourage people not to work, and to create where possible interim jobs by combining welfare payments with certain public works projects without increasing and in fact actually decreasing current budgets.

"In order to create more jobs in the private sector, it is going to be necessary to encourage businesses both large and small to reinvest their earnings in the economy, which will serve to expand the system and create new business, more jobs, and more prosperity. This will be done by lowering the corporate and individual tax levels, and granting substantial tax credits for reinvestment of profits and establishment of new businesses.

"Naturally, this will lower the revenue the federal government will bring in annually, and therefore will necessitate a streamlining of government agencies. Government is still far too big, despite the promises of past administrations, with nearly forty percent of any agency's budget going to cover staff and overhead, rather than into the area it is needed. This will mean that many jobs in government will disappear, but with the proper incentives, new jobs in the private sector will take up this slack. Of course this will not happen all at once. There will not be massive lay-offs, and there will not be immediate reinvestment in the economy. Our nation's problems did not arise overnight and they will not be cured overnight. But we must begin, now, this very slow process of regeneration.

"As an integral part of this process, I am going to order that all persons currently registered for unemployment compensation and welfare benefits be required to relocate at the government's expense, in order to secure employment, or have their names permanently dropped from the roles. In this manner, we will be able to combine benefits with public works projects in certain areas where labor is scarce and expensive, thus satisfying the requirements of both programs with the expenditure of one smaller budget. In short, we eliminate duplication and waste.

"In relation to this, I will call upon labor to curb the tide of inflation by severely limiting their wage demands. In the past this has been tried with little success, but I sincerely believe that if we are to reverse the present trend, temporary wage plateaus are inevitable. This is going to mean some hardship for those involved, but I call upon all employers to curb wages and curtail price increases, and I submit that it is far more palatable than the consequences of total economic collapse.

"As we all know, one single element does not create the precarious circumstances that threaten our country, but one of the chief problems is the uncontrolled consumption of petroleum products and the resulting dependence on foreign oil. I call upon Congress to draft legislation that will promote greater research into alternative forms of energy and transportation in the private sector. But in tandem with this legislation, I will also ask Congress to scrap the Department of Energy and reinstate the National Aeronautics and Space Administration as the primary source of research, and specifically I want the Space Shuttle program revived and put into service."

There was a gasp from the crowd.

"By doing this," Parker continued, raising his voice above the din, "by doing this, we revitalize this nation's only peacetime impetus to technological advancement. You may ask, why, with so many people unemployed on Earth, should we pour billions into outer space? My answer is not as simple as the question. On one level, NASA provides thousands of jobs for highly skilled and productive citizens, who have been out of work since the previous Administration's cutbacks. Therefore, in that sense it will ease unemployment through government contracts to the private sector.

"But on a deeper level, what NASA has to offer is the possible solution to the problems plaguing us. Only through continued technological innovation can we hope to cope with the problems that our modern technologies have created. If man had not been willing to experiment in the past, we would still be living in caves or grass huts, shivering in the cold and trembling in the darkness like wild animals. We would still be hunting for game and foraging in the forests, subject to disease and predatory animals. Only by continuing to expand our knowledge, do we have a chance to improve our way of life.

"True, with advanced technologies have come advanced problems, but, my friends, there is no going back. We can only go forward, and if we do so aggressively we may yet save ourselves from what otherwise seems certain destruction. Old beliefs, old concepts and values, must all change. We must look ahead and prepare ourselves for the future, and technology is the key to the future.

"In the name of economic solvency, I call upon all the peoples of the world to join with us. For we have reached the state of a global village. Each country depends on the others in some miniscule way, each is an integral part of a complex jigsaw puzzle. Together we must unite in a fight for existence, not as countries or races, but as the human species. We must put aside our greed and prejudices, our jealousy and hatred, and work for the common good of all mankind.

"In the coming weeks, I will be extending invitations to the heads of state of all nations to come and share with me in the planning of how best to proceed toward these goals. It is my hope that they will join in willingly, in the spirit of cooperation and good faith, without skepticism or distrust.

"Only by coordinating our economic goals can we hope to control the runaway inflation that now affects us all. I call upon OPEC and Mexico as well to stop raising the price of their petroleum exports. By failing to do so, they will only hurt themselves, weakening and inflating the international currencies which in turn will distort and inflame their own runaway economics. By making their countries responsive to the needs of all nations on Earth, and by our reciprocating in turn, we can achieve controlled economic expansion and world prosperity without endangering the precious balance of the world money market.

"In summation, let me say that the role of the American people in the days to come will be that of the catalyst. We must set the example. We must be willing to sacrifice the present for the long run. It is up to us, the responsibility rests on our shoulders. I thank you for your attention, and I bid you a good night."

Davis cut off the set as the Mexican news commentator began to recap the speech. He could just imagine what Mexico's official reaction to Parker's allegations was going to be, and in that light, the evening with President Perez promised to be extremely interesting to say the least. He glanced out the sliding glass door. The sun had set, and stars spattered the darkening sky. He could hear the waves washing on the beach below, and a soft breeze rustled the curtains. He thought momentarily of the beautiful girl by the lagoon, but put her out of his mind. There was no sense getting himself worked up all over again. He put on his white dinner jacket and left.

In the little village of Bronnitsky, seventy kilometers southeast of Moscow on the Moscva River, Aleksay Kurochkin trudged up the snow-packed walk of a modest farm cottage belonging to the parents of Mikhail Olenov.

The day was grey and dreary, and something in the setting reminded Aleksay of the early years of his life, the dismal years in the orphanage before Colonel Markelov had come to take him away to the academy, where each boy had had his own bunk and the food was hot and plentiful. He experienced a momentary vision of warm sunny days and fields of green grass and yellow flowers, wishful thoughts of better, happier times.

The unrelenting winter wind pierced him as he came to a shivering halt on the stoop and rapped with frost-nipped knuckles on the heavy door. From within, he heard the sound of a wooden chair scraping the floor, then the slow clicking of heels approaching the door. The door opened ever so slightly and an aged round face stared out at him.

"Mrs. Olenov?" Aleksay asked, nodding politely.

"Yes? What is it?"

"I am from the Army. It concerns your son, Mikhail. May I come in?"

The woman's face brightened, then darkened in the blink of an eye. She opened the door wider. "Mikhail? Is he well? Have you spoken to him? He is not in trouble, is he? He is such a good boy."

Aleksay shook his head, smiling warmly. "No. Nothing is wrong. May I come in?"

The old woman stepped back. "Of course. Come in, Comrade . . ."

"Kurochkin."

Aleksay entered the house, stamping the snow from his boots on the well-worn mat. The house was small but neat; a roaring fire warmed the main room. An old man, presumably Mikhail's father, rose from a wooden rocker near the fire and slid his spectacles up onto his nose so that he could see. Both of the old people were short and heavy set, stooped by years of hard work, their faces etched with worry and heartache.

"This gentleman is from the Army, Rudolph," the old lady explained. "He has come to see us about Mikhail."

The old man looked worried and fumbled nervously for his tobacco pouch. "What has he done? Is he in trouble?"

Aleksay smiled cordially, motioning for them to be seated. "Please, he is fine. May I?"

"Oh, yes. Have a seat near the fire. Would you care for tea Conrade?"

"Yes, thank you. I have come to ask a few questions."

"What kind of questions? Is he all right? We haven't heard from him in so long." The old woman seemed troubled as she poured his tea.

"He is fine. I saw him only yesterday. He sends his affections."

"Why does he not write us?" the old woman complained. "He used to write every week."

"Because Mikhail has been chosen for a very special assignment, requiring intensive training and isolation for the time being."

"Is it dangerous?" his mother asked.

"Be quiet, Olga," the old man said. "Let him speak. What is it that you want?"

"Only some background information for our records."

"Why not ask him yourself?" the old man asked.

"That is not the way it is done," Aleksay replied in a tone that did not leave room for debate. The old people looked at him expectantly as he unfolded a piece of paper he had taken from his coat pocket.

"Your son was born Mikhail Stephan Olenov?"

"Yes."

"He was raised in Bronnitsky?"

"In this house."

"He was schooled at the Institute in Moscow?"

"After he turned thirteen," his father explained.

"He was a brilliant child," his mother said proudly.

"Did he have any close friends as a child?"

"Oh yes. Many of them. He was a popular boy."

"Did he maintain any of those friendships after he moved away?"

"Only a few," his father said cautiously, sensing that this was far from the routine inquiry.

"Who were they?"

"There was a girl, but she moved away when she was seventeen."

"Where did she move to?"

"I presume Moscow. Mikhail has mentioned her in his letters, so they must still see one another."

"I see. What is her name?"

"What has this got to do with Mikhail?" the old man asked. His wife frowned and he caught her expression.

"Emilia Malinin," the old woman said.

"You said there were others?"

"Yes, there was one more than I can remember."

"Who?"

"A young man named Petr Romanshin. He too moved to Moscow. I believe he works in the Library."

"Which Library?"

"I'm not sure . . . something about Foreign Literature . . ."

"The All-Union Library for Foreign Literature?"

"That is it!"

"Did Mikhail ever mention what he and his friends did?"

"Did you say 'did'?" his father asked suspiciously.

"I meant in his letters to you over the past several years, has he mentioned his hobbies, his other interests besides his work?"

"What does that have to do with Mikhail's assignment?" The old man was on guard.

"Oh, nothing. We are merely doing a personality survey on

him. It is strictly routine, I assure you. It gives us a clearer, more objective picture of the candidates."

"Mikhail seldom mentioned his activities," the old man said. He scrutinized Aleksay carefully.

The old man was no fool, Aleksay thought to himself. "Does Mikhail ever mention what kind of work he does?"

"Never," the old man snapped. The old woman threw him a glance but kept her tongue.

"And he has never mentioned his outside interests or sympathies?"

"What do you mean by sympathies?"

"A slip of the tongue, Comrade."

"He likes to read," his mother volunteered. "And he loves the country. He used to write to us about trips into the country with his friend, Petr. Only he does not write so often anymore, and when he does, he seldom mentions much more than his health and his desire to return to Bronnitsky."

Her husband glared at her, but it was too late. Whatever trouble Mikhail was in, it was probably beyond their powers to protect him. He lit his pipe as he studied the impassive face of their visitor, and wondered why the man did not wear the army green. Was he GRU? Military intelligence?

"Well, I think that that is all I need to know," Aleksay said, rising. "Mikhail asked me to give you his warm greetings. He is well and advancing very quickly in his training."

"When will he be able to write to us?" his mother asked.

"I cannot say," Aleksay replied. "And now, I must be going. Thank you for the tea."

The old couple escorted him to the door, the old man fiddling with his pipe to keep his snarled hands from trembling. Their visitor had the smell of death about him. He had smelled it on the Western front in the long winter of 1941-42 during the seige of Lenningrad, and he smelled it now. His heart was heavy in his chest as they saw the man down the icy front walk and into his car. He drove off in the swirling flurries and was gone. Perhaps later Rudolph could find a way to tell Olga that their son was dead.

* * *

Roger guided his Porsche out of the circular esplanade of the Camino Real Hotel and down the narrow two-lane artery running south along the eastern edge of the island. On his left was the sea, with numerous lavish hotels perched on its sparkling beaches, lights shimmering in the tropical night; the Cancun Carribe, the Garza Blanca. A fair breeze rustled the palms and blew cottonpuff clouds across the moon. The bay to his right rippled in the moonlight and the lights of moored boats rocked back and forth on the gentle swells.

Soon he passed the last hotel and the road darkened. Only his headlights cut the night as he sped along past scattered palatial private residences, nestled on the edge of the sea. He had been told by the hotel manager to look for a large white archway with high metal gates and an adobe guardhouse; it was not hard to spot. He swung off the road onto the cracked shell drive and stopped short of the guardhouse as two armed soldiers approached the car, automatic rifles slung over their shoulders.

"Is this His Excellency's estate?" Davis asked in rusty Spanish.

One of the guards nodded gruffly and asked if he had an invitation. Davis showed him the handwritten note from the President, and although the man could not read, he recognized the President's seal and signature at once; he came sharply to attention.

"Si señor," he said and ordered his companion to open the gates. He then told Davis to follow the road directly up to the hacienda.

Waving to the two guards, he slipped the Porsche into gear and followed the short winding road to a sprawling white adobe hacienda built in the traditional style of old Mexico. Multicolored spots painted gay splashes on the outer walls, and uniformed car attendants waited under the portico to receive him. Already, the drive was lined with many expensive automobiles, and he could hear the lively strains of a mariachi band. Beyond the house, the surf pounded the shore. He felt the damp salt spray in the heavy air.

He followed a graceful staircase up through an arched entrance onto a partially covered terrace which opened onto the water. The moon painted the sea dramatically with a wide swatch of pale yellow across the darkened firmament. Gas torches flickered in the sea breeze and blue spotlights bathed free-form flying buttresses which supported a crown of superstructure surrounding the terrace and a lush garden situated in its center, where brightly colored tropical birds cawed irreverently from the limbs of banana and palmetto trees.

He paused in the foyer to survey the interior, looking for any familiar faces in the crowd, but he soon found that he was a stranger. Suddenly, from his right, a uniformed doorman appeared and bowed smartly. "Señor? May I announce you?"

"Yes," Davis replied. "Roger Davis of the United States Foreign Service."

The man perked at the sound of his name and smiled broadly. "Ah, Mr. Davis. I have been instructed to show you in the moment you arrived. Will you please follow me?"

Without waiting for a response, he led the way across the terrace, circumnavigating the garden where a great number of people were clustered over cocktails. A few ventured glances his way, and some of the more attractive women allowed their eyes to linger a little longer than idle curiosity required. He fixed a pleasant smile on his face and stuck close to his guide, eager to reach his host without creating a stir, specifically with any jealous husbands. For the most part, the men were very thin, their clothes chic, their skin perfectly tanned. The women were strikingly groomed, expensively dressed and bejeweled, and practiced at looking somewhat bored.

He found himself presently approaching a group of more casually dressed men, who were clustered around a low glass table at the end of the terrace, drinking and listening intently to the short, chubby man who held their undivided attention. He was, of course, His Excellency, Enrique de Gonzales-Perez, President of Mexico; a good-natured looking little man, dark skinned with a broad grin, a receding hairline, and thick greying sideburns which he had allowed to grow well below his ear lobes. His eyes sparkled as he spoke, and his manner was easy as he expounded on his topic in predictable latin style.

The servant stopped and waited respectfully for Perez to notice, which he did at last. "Excuse me, Excellency. Mr. Roger Davis of the United States Foreign Service." Bowing, he slipped away, leaving Davis to face the hushed gathering which had turned all eyes toward him. Perez rose showing a generous display of glistening white teeth, and stepped forward extending his pudgy little hand.

"Mr. Davis. How nice that you could come."

"Mr. President," Davis said, shaking the man's hand firmly, staring directly into his bright eyes. "I am honored by your invitation."

"Not at all, Mr. Davis. Please, won't you join us?"

"Thank you."

The President turned and introduced him to the others in English. "My friends, please meet Roger Davis of the United States Foreign Service. I hope you don't mind my giving you away," he teased Davis.

"Not at all, Mr. President, although I think I should point out that I'm here on vacation."

Perez laughed. "We are having Scotch."

"Scotch would be fine, Mr. President."

The little man waved his arm to no one in particular, and before Davis could look around for a seat, a servant brought him a glass brimming with Scotch and a little water.

"You will sit by me, Mr. Davis," Perez said. One of his cronies jumped up to make room for him.

"Thank you," Davis said, and sat down rather self-consciously, aware that he was the center of attention.

"We were just discussing your new President's State of the Union address. Did you see it?"

"Yes, I did," Davis said, without venturing to say more. He was acutely aware of the probably effects of Parker's speech on these men. They were all obviously members of the inner circle, and probably all involved in the development of the Mexican oil reserves, which in only a few short years had raised the standard of living for the average Mexican citizen from rampant squalor to mere poverty, while no doubt making millionaires of every one of the men sitting around him at the table.

"We found his position to be somewhat different than we had anticipated," Perez continued, probing for some point of contention upon which to launch into a debate. Davis knew full well why he had been invited and chose his words carefully.

"What little I know of him, President Parker seems to be fairly consistent in his views, which haven't changed appreciably since he campaigned for office."

"That is true, indeed," Perez conceded as did all the others in hasty unison. "Now tell me, Mr. Davis. How do you like Cancun?"

Davis smiled with relief, having expected the third degree to continue. "It's beautiful. Especially after having served in Moscow for a year."

"Ah, Moscow! Wasn't that startling news from Moscow today? Quite a delicate situation for the Soviets."

"Yes, isn't it," Davis agreed and said no more.

"You know, Mr. Davis, Cancun has been many years in the development. And only now have we reached a level of completion that will allow us to compete with almost any resort area in the world. There is nothing that Cancun cannot offer — sun, sand, water sports, golf, tennis, nightlife, and soon casino gambling. What more could one ask of a vacation spot?"

"Frankly, Mr. President, I hope you don't mind my saying so, but I find the underdeveloped areas of Cancun far more enchanting. But that is only my personal opinion."

"I myself feel the same way," Perez said. "But for the average tourist, we must provide all the amenities. And that has taken a great deal of money."

"I'm sure it has, sir."

"In the beginning, we were incapable of the capital expenditures necessary to develop such a resort area. So we were compelled to take on American partners who could provide the needed funds. Unfortunately, for a variety of reasons, those original investors have withdrawn one by one, leaving us with the burden of our partially realized plans. It has worked great hardship on the people of Mexico, but we have finally succeeded in reaching financial stability, thanks to our petroleum exports, without which we would have been severely injured by the American withdrawal."

Davis bit his tongue and resisted the urge to say what he was thinking. The truth was that one by one, the American investors who had poured millions of dollars into the partnerships controlled by their Mexican associates had been driven out by exorbitant government demands and dwindling profits, when there were any at all. Unchecked labor demands had bled the investments dry, leaving little if any incentive for a sane financier to remain.

Davis personally knew of one individual from Texas, who had literally walked away from the substantial resort investment in Acapulco after squatters had moved onto the grounds and the government had refused to act. Once the American financier was out, the government swept the area clean of the vermin and reopened the resort which was now running at a lucrative ninety-five percent occupancy with absolutely no remuneration to the original American partners.

But his role was not to criticize. After all, under the Mexican political system, it was expected that the man in charge would take all he could in his single six-year term, leaving the despoiled country to his successor. Therefore he gritted his teeth and determined to remain silent, no matter what lies the strutting little Latin Napoleon might concoct.

"But tell me, Mr. Davis. What do you think your country's position will be with respect to our petroleum price increase? Surely your people realize that with our heavy burden and the decline in the dollar, we must raise our prices to keep pace with our plans for economic development?"

The question was loaded with double-ought buckshot and Davis was reluctant to make any form of response. Nevertheless, he had been asked a direct question. "Naturally, Mr. President, I am not in a position privy to the policy making of our country. I only serve as its representative in isolated instances, and fortunately I am not acting in an official capacity during my stay here. I will only say that I think that

95

your country and mine should follow the course suggested by President Parker in his speech tonight, and work very closely in our mutual best interests. In that manner, we both profit from our relationship."

Perez smiled a broad cheeky smile, and his eyes twinkled brightly. He looked lika a fat mouse gloating over a piece of cheese. "Spoken like a true diplomat. Mr. Davis. I commend you." He raised his glass and the others laughed in accord.

Davis sighed inwardly, relieved to be out of the pinch. There was nothing he would have liked more than to tell the fat little fart what he really thought of Mexico's oil-gouging policies, but he knew that in the very near future, Parker himself would do exactly that and with a lot more clout.

He had scarcely had time to recover, however, when Perez again led into a delicate topic. "Tell me, Mr. Davis. What do you think about our agricultural agreements with your country? Don't you feel . . ."

"Oh father! Must you always discuss business with your guests? How can I meet this handsome American if you refuse to allow him to enjoy the party?" Her voice came from behind them, light and amused, but it cut the conversation as if it had been a shot.

All heads turned. She stood in semidarkness, wearing a flowing white chiffon pants suit that clung to her graceful figure, enhancing the rich coffee brown of her skin.

Davis nearly dropped his drink when he saw her. His beautiful mermaid from the lagoon; the President's daughter? Perez rose chuckling and embraced her bestowing an affectionate peck on her cheek.

"Gentlemen, you all know my daughter Mercedes?" The other guests grinned and bobbed respectfully, expressing their admiration in glowing terms. Davis rose slowly, his eyes riveted on her, and she returned his look with an expression of triumph. She was even more beautiful in the soft light of the torches. He tingled as he again caught the distinct, earthy smell of her fragrance.

"Mr. Davis. May I pesent my daughter, Mercedes?" the President said.

Davis extended his hand to grasp her delicate outstretched

fingers. She smiled at his touch and spoke softly. "How do you do, Mr. Davis?"

"Mercedes. What a beautiful name. It suits you."

Their eyes said the rest, and Perez cleared his throat nervously, aware of an attraction between them. "Mercedes, my dear. Perhaps you would like to entertain Mr. Davis while I finish discussing my business here. I will join you later."

The mariachis were playing a sensuous Latin melody and she smiled. "Do you like to dance, Mr. Davis?"

"I'm a bit rusty, but I'll give it a whirl." He offered his arm, and she took it with more enthusiasm than he had expected, digging her nails into his forearm in a teasing pinch.

"By all means," Perez proclaimed, patting Davis on the back in a fatherly fashion. "Dance. Enjoy yourselves." He had covered his discomfort well.

"Thank you, Mr. President," Davis said, and led her onto the dance floor. He pulled her close and felt the firm pressure of her young breasts against his chest. The sheer material of her outfit left little to the imagination, and the sensation was maddening. She did not resist, following his lead as if she had been made to dance with him, her thighs rubbing tenderly against his. The drinks had made him bold. He held her tighter until she whispered, "My father asked you to dance with me, not make love to me."

He laughed sheepishly and drew back to look at her. Her lips were barely inches from his and the temptation was almost too much to resist. "You dance very well for never going to discotheques," he said.

"I wasn't raised in a convent, Mr. Davis."

"You didn't tell me you were the President's daughter."

"You didn't tell me you were a diplomat."

"It seems there's a lot we didn't say."

"What more was there to say?"

"You could have agreed to see me again."

"How could I have? Father does not let me go out with just anyone. How could I let you think that there was even a chance of seeing you again?"

"You admit that you wanted to?"

She did not answer at first, but leaning closer she rested

her cheek against his for the briefest of moments. "Yes," she whispered as the dance ended.

"Would you like a drink?" he asked, his heart pounding from the excitement of holding her.

She smiled and took his arm as they threaded their way through the very observant guests to the bar. Everyone, it seemed, had nothing better to do than discuss who it was that had attracted her eye.

"I seem to have made a great hit with your father's friends. They're all staring."

"They're only wondering who you are that I would allow you to hold me that way."

"And who am I?"

"I don't know," she said.

With drinks in hand, they strolled to the north end of the veranda, away from the crowd and the strains of the band, and stood in the gentle moonlight, looking out over the sparkling Caribbean. The wind was sweet with the smell of wild orchids and Mercedes' exotic fragrance.

"Why did you come?" she asked.

"Your father invited me."

"Is that the only reason?"

"It's a great honor to receive a personal invitation from a head of state."

"You didn't suspect that he intended to use you for some purpose?"

"Naturally. Why else would he invite me? But my job is to manage delicate situations, and considering the precarious circumstances alluded to by President Parker, I felt I owed it to myself to stick up for our side, to express our point of view in a manner that would not offend your father."

"Are you sure you didn't come out of curiosity? To see if he had two heads or horns on his nose?"

"You don't need to take the defensive with me. I told you . . ."

"I'm not being defensive, Mr. Davis. This is my house. I have no reason to be defensive."

"If you'll allow me to explain, I merely suspect that your father wanted to explain his position to someone, and I happened to be handy."

"But you don't see his point of view?"

"What is this, the third degree?" His tone was harsher than he had intended and her expression darkened.

"If you are asking me if I'm spying for my father, the answer is certainly not!" she hissed, starting to turn away. He grabbed her elbow and turned her back around.

"Wait a minute! You've got a habit of running out on me. I didn't mean it to sound that way, but I'm also not in the mood to be interrogated by a beautiful woman whom I would rather be making love to."

She glared at him, her hackles up, but he could tell she was also flattered by his impertinence. "You're very rude," she said, sipping her drink with a little pout on her face.

He wanted to kiss her but that was out of the question. "I didn't mean to be. I was only being honest."

"Sometimes it is best not to be too honest with certain people."

"I quite agree, but I don't feel that way with you."

"You know nothing about me."

"But I intend to by the time you get through showing me Cancun."

She jerked her head up like a yearling and stared defiantly into his cold blue eyes. "I what?"

"Well, you aren't going to let me sit in my hotel room all by myself for the rest of the week, when you could be showing me the island."

"You're very sure of yourself, Mr. Davis."

"You said that before." He smiled at the spark of anger in her eyes.

"What makes you think I ever want to see you again?"

"The way you deny it," he laughed.

"Oh! You Americans are all the same!"

"No we're not."

"You are!"

"I'm not like anyone you've ever met."

"How would you know?" she snapped testily.

"Because I know, that's all. But I don't want to talk about me. Let's talk about you."

"I don't want to talk about me!"

"Are you going to pout?" he teased.

"No!"

"Good. You're too seductive when you pout, and I don't want to get thrown out of here for trying to kiss you."

"You wouldn't dare!"

"No, you're right. Not unless you wanted me to."

She looked at him in shock, as if seeing him clearly for the first time. "I've never met a man like you," she said.

"That's what I just got through telling you." He could see that he had gotten to her. She was confused, out of stride, and the confidence she had shown a few moments earlier was fading quickly.

"I think I should slap your face," she said, her voice searching for the anger she had lost.

"That would be too predictable," he said.

Suddenly, she took his hand and led him down a narrow stone staircase that descended to the beach below the hacienda. Out of sight from the terrace, in the moon-cast shadows against the rocky cliff, she turned and kissed him passionately, burying herself in his arms.

She broke away and stared up at him defiantly.

"What was that for?" he asked.

"Nothing. I just felt like kissing you."

"And do you always do what you feel like doing?"

"Yes."

"So do I," he said, crushing her to him and kissing her fiercely. She did not pretend to struggle. She had gotten what she wanted.

. . . 8 March 1989

Bruce knew immediately that it was going to be a lousy day
when he stepped through his office door and saw the bags of
telegrams already piling up in the corners. Several staffers
were ripping through them, tabulating the public's reaction
to Parker's speech. That was at six-thirty.

He found a note on his desk from Parker requesting him to
prepare a statement as soon as a trend could be predicted.
That did not happen until eleven o'clock, after nearly three
thousand opinions had been sampled. The trend was forty-
six percent in favor of Parker's policies, forty-three percent
opposed, and the remaining eleven percent were lumped
somewhere between noncommittals and reactionaries
predicting the apocalypse.

At eleven-fifteen, Bruce picked up the phone and dialed
the Oval Office. "Shirley? Is he busy? Can I have a few
minutes before lunch? I'll be right down."

He grabbed his notes and bolted through the outer office,
which was still frantic with staffers. "Clean this crap up, will
you? We've got other things to do today," he said, and was
out the door. He found the President in conference and
Shirley looked flustered.

"Have a seat, Bruce," she said. "He's still in there."

Bruce sat on the edge of a chair near the door, and
skimmed his notes and the brief statement he had worked up.
Through the door he could hear voices, sometimes raised in
heated debate. Parker's voice was easily distinguished and
sounded angry. Bruce pretended to be preoccupied, but he
fidgeted on his chair.

At last, the door opened, and Parker appeared, his face
stone sober, his eyes muddy hazel. He stepped aside and

allowed the House majority leader to slip out, looking thoroughly pissed off. Parker stared at Bruce, trying to cover his anger. "You have something for me?"

"Yes, sir. The tabulations you requested and . . ."

"Come in, then. Shirley, get me Holmes on the telephone. I want to know when that bastard Benest is coming in."

"Yes, Mr. President," Shirley said and rolled her eyes at Bruce as he followed Parker into the Oval Office.

Parker returned to his cluttered desk and flopped into his chair. Bruce entered cautiously. He approached the President's desk and poised by a chair as Parker rummaged through a pile of file folders.

"Sit down, Bruce. Don't stand there like a moron. I'm not going to jump on you." He was having difficulty finding what he was looking for.

Bruce sat down stiffly, pretending to study his notes.

"That liberal son of a bitch had the nerve to say he was going to urge his colleagues to oppose me. Seems like he thinks that having to relocate to take a job is unconstitutional! I wonder how he explains the fact that I have to live in Washington, D.C. in order to be President? Is that unconstitutional too? Liberal jackass!"

"Yes, sir."

"Well?"

"Well, I've tabulated the results."

"And?"

"They're pretty much what we expected. Forty-six percent for you, forty-three percent against you, eleven percent just making noise. Labor is in stiff opposition as we expected . . ."

"That cocksucker Benest hasn't set a meeting yet, I'll bet you any amount of money! If he thinks he can keep avoiding me! I'm going to have his nuts, I'll tell you that!" He slammed his fist on top of a stack of folders, and then sat back in his chair rubbing his eyes. He looked tired. "Have you got a statement ready?"

"Yes, sir." Bruce cleared his throat and read, "Reaction to President Parker's State of the Union address has been mixed, but preliminary results indicate that a majority of public opinion is in his favor. Congress has not officially expressed itself concerning the issues raised by the President, but it is expected to split along party lines in most cases, with labor taking a strong stance against many of the programs proposed last night in Mr. Parker's first major speech since taking office. As promised, the President is extending invitations to foreign dignitaries as well as domestic officials to meet with him in an attempt to work out the complex details necessary to facilitate Mr. Parker's proposals." He stopped and looked up as Parker began to ransack his desk again.

"That's it?" Parker asked.

"Yes, sir."

Parker thought for a moment then smiled cunningly. "Put this in. Parker intends to hold fast to his position and come down hard on any elected official or government employee who fails to cooperate with the spirit of his program for economic independence. You can also include union officials in that, and make it sound like any bastard who isn't with us is a Communist sympathizer intent on the collapse of the free enterprise system. You know how to work it. I want the fire under their fannies when the lobbyists start in on them."

"Yes, sir. Shall I release this right away?"

"Yes. We've got to keep one step ahead of the opposition. And by the way. Will you draw up a personal note from me to everyone on the Hill? Invite them to a cocktail function here tomorrow night. Shirley will give you a list. I want them all here, so they can express their views. It'll look good in the press. And make sure every news agency has at least one representative here. I want as much positive momentum on this as possible. The head of NASA is going to be here and so will some of the Joint Chiefs. Let's play this thing up real patriotically and get the media on the bandwagon."

"Yes, sir. But isn't this kind of short notice?"

"I think you'll see that everyone will be here. They won't pass up a chance to get to me personally." Just then the intercom buzzed, and Parker answered it. "Yes?"

"Mr. Holmes on the line for you, Mr. President," Shirley said.

"All right, put him through," Parker said and waved Bruce on his way. "Let me know of any developments, Bruce."

"Yes, sir," Bruce said and quietly slipped out.

"Preston? Where the hell is Benest? What's he doing there? Have you talked to him? What did he say? What the hell do you mean he can't meet with me until next week? What's his room number? No, I'll take care of it!"

Parker slammed the phone down and jumped up, bellowing through the closed door. "Shirley, get my car around front and tell the shadows we're going out!"

Bruce rechecked the statistics when he returned to his office. They had not changed. He quickly reworked the press release and gave it to his secretary for retyping. As she was leaving his office, a security agent appeared in the doorway with a potted plant of geraniums. Rita beamed with surprise.

"For me?" she asked.

"No ma'am. For Mr. Wilson," the agent explained.

Bruce said incredulously, "For me?"

"Yes, sir," the agent said and handed the plant to Rita. Bruce flushed as she set the flowers down on his desk and found a card tucked in them. She handed it to him.

He read. "No funeral would be complete without flowers. K.K." He couldn't believe his eyes. The stupid bitch! Nevertheless, he did his best to cover his embarrassment.

"They're from my brother," he explained to Rita. "He's a practical joker. Here, why don't you take them? They'll look nice on your desk."

Rita broke into a broad grin and removed the plant at once, leaving Bruce simmering in his own juice. He looked at the phone for a minute, then a flash outside caught his eye. He saw Parker getting into his limousine with the Secret Service men, and watched as the motorcade pulled out. He glanced at his calendar but saw nothing about a Presidential appointment at noon. He puzzled about it for a moment, then picked up the phone and dialed the *Post*.

"Kathy Karpovich," he said, trying to keep his voice down.

He waited for what seemed a very long time as the phone buzzed on the other end. At last she answered out of breath.

"Karpovich!"

"What the hell is the meaning of this!"

"You got my flowers!" she exclaimed excitedly.

"Kathy," he snapped, then lowered his voice. "Kathy, this is not play school around here. Don't you realize those had to come through security? Everyone knows about them! What the hell are they going to think?"

"Oh come on, Bruce. I thought that they were very appropriate after Parker's speech last night."

"What do you mean by that?"

"Haven't you seen the public opinion poles?"

"Yes. I've just made one of my own, and the majority supports the President."

"Not according to ours."

"I'd hardly call yours unbiased; besides yours doesn't mean a damn. Listen, Kathy, I don't have time to shit around with this sort of thing. Don't ever do anything like this again or else I'll . . ."

"Or else you'll what?" she challenged him.

"Or else I'll jerk your White House pass!" he snarled and slammed the phone down before he really got hostile.

Parker's motorcade pulled to a stop in front of The Madison hotel at precisely twelve o'clock. Secret Service men swarmed into the lobby, securing it before they hurried him out of the car and into an elevator — almost before anyone knew that he was in their midst.

At the penthouse level, where George Benest kept a year-round residence, they again scoured the hall and stairwells, then escorted the President to the end suite.

Parker knocked on the door firmly, hard enough to make his knuckles tingle. His blood was boiling. After a moment, the door opened and one of Benest's aides stood in the doorway. It took him a moment to realize who he was facing, but when he did, he paled and stepped back in astonishment. The Secret Service agents pushed past him into the suite and

Parker followed, regarding the young man sternly.

"Tell Mr. Benest I'm here."

"Yes, sir. Right away," the man stammered and hurried out of the room.

Parker paced back and forth in front of the broad picture window overlooking the parkway which was jammed with room traffic. The day was dull and it made his mood even blacker.

In a few moments, the door to the bedroom opened and Benest himself appeared, straightening his tie and running a hand through his thin white hair. He was a big man, around sixty, whose belly hung generously over his belt, giving him a slovenly appearance despite his expensively tailored suit.

"Mr. President," he said. "This is indeed an honor."

"Cut the bullshit, Benest. You know damn well you've been avoiding me!"

Benest looked ashen and glanced around at his retainer and the agents. "Would you mind if we conducted this in private, Mr. President?"

"Fine with me," Parker replied, sweeping his hand to motion his men from the room. Benest's aide went with them, eager to be out of the line of fire, leaving Benest and Parker glaring at one another across the low coffee table by the windows.

"Mr. President, I spoke with Mr. Holmes only this morning, and I assured him that I would be very happy to meet with you at the earliest possible convenience." He fumbled for a cigarette from the eighteen-karat gold case on the coffee table.

"Not until next week, as I heard it." Parker was tight-lipped. "Sit down, Mr. Benest. You and I have some things we need to discuss."

Benest puffed nervously on his cigarette as he sat on one of the low expensive couches that flanked the coffee table. Parker remained standing, his back to Benest, facing out onto the gray setting below. Benest had met the President several times before the election, but always in situations that demanded absolute diplomacy. He was therefore unprepared for this encounter.

106

Parker seemed much larger than he had remembered him, perhaps because of the sheer force of his personality and ability to seize command of a situation just displayed so convincingly. At any rate, Benest gripped the arm of the sofa with one puffy white hand, trying to calm his nerves and collect his ego which had just received a smashing blow.

"Mr. Benest, it's obvious the impact that my proposed policies are going to have on your union, so there's no sense beating around the bush." Parker's tone was more controlled, but there was an edge of warning in it. He turned to face the older man. "I want your cooperation, plain and simple. If we're going to stop this inflationary cycle, it has to begin with organized labor, and your endorsement will go a long way toward that end."

"Mr. President. I represent hard-working people who expect to earn a decent living for what they do. I don't think it's unreasonable to ask for cost-of-living increases and increased benefits so that they can maintain the standard of living to which they have become accustomed."

"Under normal circumstances, I would tend to agree with you. But these are not normal circumstances. I'm asking everyone from the top to the bottom to share in the sacrifice, and that means labor putting a ceiling on its demands."

"It's our legal right to bargain for higher wages! My people keep this country running. If it weren't for them, the wheels of industry would grind to a halt. I'd hate to see that happen, but I'm afraid if you try to force mandatory wage controls on us, it just might."

"Are you telling me that you would call a general strike?"

"If that's what it takes to maintain the status quo."

"Even if that meant crippling our economy?"

"It's our legal right."

Parker turned and faced the windows, his hands folded so tightly behind his back that the knuckles turned white. He fought to control the anger in his voice. Now was the time for logical debate, not emotionalism.

"All right, Mr. Benest. I've listened to your philosophy, now you'll listen to mine. As you probably know, I started off working in a coal mine at the age of seventeen. I was a member of the United Mine Workers. I enjoyed the benefits and wages that all other members shared. From my point of view, I was entitled to them, as long as I continued to enjoy a fair profit.

"That was at a time of economic expansion when nearly all businesses were prospering, so we felt justified in increasing our demands with every new contract—higher wages, more benefits. There were bright days ahead and we wanted to share in the fruits of our labors.

"But then something happened none of us expected. Cost increases began to outweigh the pricing structure. By the time I moved into management, I saw firsthand that, despite higher wages, better benefits, and more efficient operating techniques, we were losing money by remaining in business. There was only one thing to do, and that was to raise our prices. But that price increase caused our customers to raise their prices, and the resulting domino effect reached all the way down the ladder: to the grocer and the barber, even to our own laborers. One price increase touched every facet of the local economy. And so when the next round of negotiations failed, the workers struck again for higher wages and better benefits because something called inflation was devouring their paychecks. And the same thing was happening in almost every other industry throughout the country. The pie that everyone was so eager to get a bigger and better piece of was shrinking, rather than expanding. But no one was willing to give in. Are you getting my drift, Mr. Benest? Where once a raise was based on merit and productivity, it had come to be based on tenure and labor's needs whether they had earned it or not. It has become an endless and vicious cycle.

"I'll grant you; unions were based on noble objectives and principles. I've never disputed that. But in the American tradition of pendulum overreaction, those principles have faded and new values have replaced them. Unions are unresponsive to the needs of business and the realities of economics. Somewhere, this cycle has got to stop. We can't go on raising prices and wages, prices and wages, thinking that the cycle will never end. Someone has to pay for it! The American worker is not worth the price he is being paid right now, but he is demanding more and more every day. Why? Because otherwise he would have to tighten his belt a little!

"And there's another thing, Mr. Benest. The justification for raising their demands is because the company's profits are increasing, and labor feels like it is due its fair share. But let me ask you, on the other hand, if labor would be willing to share in company losses on an equal basis. When times are hard and sales are down, when the company opens its doors every day knowing that it is going to lose a hundred thousand dollars by remaining open, are the workers willing to take a reduction in pay to help the company through the crisis? I've only seen one situation like it in history and that cost the taxpayers as well, through federal subsidies.

"So you see, what I'm talking about is a philosophy and a spirit of capitalism that is missing from today's industry. Labor only wants to get, get, get, and they are increasingly unwilling to give, even a little."

"Mr. President, it sounds to me like you are not in favor of collective bargaining or the free enterprise system. Don't you believe that a man has every right to make as much money as he possibly can?"

Parker's eyes turned a muddy green, as he glared at Benest. To suggest that he was against free enterprise was to imply that he had worked his whole life for nothing. He had lived and breathed free enterprise and was a direct product of it. And now he was willing to risk everything for it, even his life. "Mr. Benest. I believe you're distorting the facts to suit your own perspective. First of all, I'm going to ignore your statement about my not believing in free enterprise. I don't feel it deserves the dignity of a response. But I will address myself to the issue of a man making as much as he can, with the sky being the limit. I believe wholeheartedly that a man should be able to amass as much money as he can. That is the American way, that is the incentive that in the past made this country great. Remove that incentive and you have communism, where no man is worth more than any other, where all men are created and treated equally. And I don't believe in that.

"No man is created equal to any other man. No woman is created equal to any other woman. That is a fantasy promulgated by the glorious euphoric wording in the Preamble to the Constitution and it is a lie. If it were not a lie, then no man would be able to run faster than the next, no man would be able to earn more than the next, no man would be more talented in playing music or painting greater masterpieces than the next. If that were so, man would be a machine. But he is not. He is mortal flesh and blood, subject to the demands of nature, the forces of time and destiny. The concept that all men are created equal is a vicious falsehood and should be stricken from the minds of modern man.

"The concept that we should all have equal opportunity, however, is valid. Each man and woman should; it is their right under our system of government; and because of this they have the right to rise as high as their worth can take them. The key to that is the word 'worth' because man is valued and rewarded in relation to his worth, his ability to produce and contribute. That is, he used to be. Now workers expect to be advanced because they have survived another year on the job, whether they contribute to greater prosperity or not!"

"What you're saying, Mr. President, is that my people are not entitled to a pay increase to offset the cost-of-living increase. You're asking me to sacrifice my people's security in the interest of your own political ambitions!"

"Benest, I have no political ambitions any longer. I've realized those. My goals are in the interest of the national welfare; that means that I'm asking everyone to sacrifice as much as the next guy across the board, man for man, woman for woman."

"I don't care what you say, my people aren't going to stand by and become the scapegoats for the national government's inability to provide the services they should provide. If you insist on this wage freeze, we'll fight you in the factories, we'll fight you in the courts, we'll fight you in the streets. Without my people, this country will collapse and you'd better remember that. The people are the power of America. The workers who break their backs and sweat away their lives to make the industry bosses rich deserve a share of the profits and we intend to get them!"

"Even to the point of destroying the firms that employ you? Even to the brink of national economic disaster? Are you willing to push your power that far to satisfy yourself and your own private interests? Don't you realize the people you call industry bosses are men and women who sweat day and night to make ends meet so that they can continue to operate their companies, so that they and the people they employ by the millions can continue to earn a living?"

"What about the profits? What about the fatcats who pocket all the corporate wealth?" Benest was fuming, his face blazing red. "They're not out there on the line day after day, sweating blood to earn a living! Not the fatcats!"

"Wrong Benest! Wrong on two counts! First of all the corporate executives are on the line not only every day, but every night. When the workers go home from their shifts, the day is over for them. But the day never ends for the corporate executive. He lives with the pressures day and night. He never escapes the responsibility of providing thousands of jobs and still managing to make a profit. Second, the people you call fatcats, the average American stockholder, is an aging grandmother with three grandchildren, living on Social Security and her life's savings and what meager dividends she gets off a couple of hundred shares of corporate stock. I wouldn't call her a fatcat! But you would deny her her profits from her investments!"

"You're twisting the issues!" Benest snarled. "What about the corporate executives drawing down six figure salaries, smoking cigars, and pushing paper around their desk? They're getting rich on the labors of hard-working people! That's obscene!"

"You're obscene, Benest. How much do you make a year? Two hundred thousand plus expenses, according to my figures. And what do you do to earn that? Smoke cigarettes, fly around in your Lear jet making speeches, push paper around your desk, wear expensive suits. You're getting rich from the efforts of your own people, Benest. Would you be

111

willing to take a cut in salary to lower their dues, to make their paychecks stretch a little further?"

"I've earned my position, Parker. I've worked hard for nearly forty years!"

"And so have the corporate executives. They've earned their money by using their brains and risking millions to provide new jobs and products for the American consumer. Are they no less deserving than you?"

"I represent the people, and I say we deserve a share of the pie!"

"Not when your share keeps getting bigger and corporate profits keep dwindling to mere percentage points."

"That represents billions of dollars. How much do they want?"

"It's not a question of how much they want, but how much they deserve and how much they need to have to stay in business. Because without them, Benest, there would be no more jobs to strike."

"We're entitled to our share and if it means striking to get it, that's what we're going to do. It's our constitutional right to maintain our standard of living!"

"Wrong. The Constitution guarantees you the opportunity to make a living. It does not guarantee that you will be successful."

"That's easy for you to say. You're a millionaire. You don't have to worry about where the next meal is going to come from or new clothes for the kids. You don't have to sweat when your TV set goes on the blink and you don't have the money to fix it."

"Mr. Benest, life is not a spectator sport. There are no guarantees of happy endings. The fact that I'm a millionaire is due to my own efforts, and my ability to make myself more valuable, more productive. I didn't get rich by demanding the same salary for less work, or more salary for the same amount of work. I got rich by working harder, longer, and better than everyone else; by risking everything I had to move up so that I was worth more and I earned more. The hard facts are, there is only so much money a man can expect to earn by being a coal miner or a truck driver. If he wants to make more, he'd better get a job that pays more. That's the American way, Benest. Every man has the right to try to do what I have done, if he has the brains and the guts. But there's no guarantee that he will succeed!"

"I say that's wrong!"

"Then, Benest, it's you who does not believe in the system of free enterprise. Let me tell you, there's going to come a time when your workers will cost more than machines, and then the jobs are going to disappear. Then the workers will be forced to reevaluate their ambitions and their goals and come to grips with their priorities or see their children starve.

"I came here today hoping to reason with you, to convince you to voluntarily help me win this battle against inflation so that this country can return to prosperity. I'm asking everyone to sacrifice, from the front office to the back door; but that's something you can't understand from your perch here in this expensive hotel suite, wearing your thousand dollar suit. If you really had your people's best interests at heart, you'd stop blowing their dues and pension money living like a king, and you'd get down to the task of helping me save this country from total collapse!"

"You can't frighten me, and you can't push me around! You'll feel the power of the American labor force if you keep this up!"

"Mr. Benest. If you take me on, you're going to lose. I promise you that!" Parker said no more. He walked quickly out the door, leaving it wide open. The stage was set.

Aleksay followed the uniformed guard down a long grey corridor, past innumerable iron doors with no windows; their footsteps echoed harshly into the concrete silence. He tried to think of something other than the misery that existed behind those closed doors. The Ministry of Intelligence was not a pleasant place to visit, especially for those who had no choice.

At long last, the guard stopped and opened one of the locked cells. The door swung open with a cold grating sound, and Aleksay squinted into the blackness. Someone inside

113

moaned. The guard stepped in and cut on an overhead floodlamp, filling the sterile chamber with harsh white light. On a solitary iron bed frame, covered with a dirty thin mattress, lay a man of about thirty-five. His skin was pale, his beard thickened to a black stubble, his hair tousled and matted with dried blood. He was gaunt and almost too weak to turn his head and stare with frightened sunken eyes at their entry.

"Petr Romanshin," the guard said gruffly.

"How long has he been here?"

"Since his arrest just over three weeks ago."

"His official crime?"

"Selling contraband."

Aleksay approached the bed and leaned over to stare into the man's semiglazed eyes. Romanshin's face was lacerated and bruised in many places, and his lips were swollen and clotted with blood.

"Has he made a statement of confession?"

"No, Comrade Kurochkin."

Aleksay sat on the edge of the bed and cradled the man's face in both hands. The man did not have the strength or the will to keep his eyes open. "Petr?" Aleksay said. "Can you hear me?"

Petr opened his eyes, but did not respond.

"Can you hear me?"

At length he mustered the energy to blink and nod his head slightly.

"I am here to help you Petr. But in order for me to help you, you must help me. Do you understand?"

Again Petr managed to nod his head, but then he averted his eyes and looked anxiously at the guard's harsh face.

"Don't worry. No one is going to harm you. Not if you cooperate," Aleksay said in a soothing voice. "They tell me that you were arrested for selling contraband. Is that true?"

Petr stared at him for a long time, then finally nodded.

"Then you admit that you sold contraband?"

Petr hesitated and looked anxiously toward the guard.

"You must trust me, Petr, if I am to help you. You are in very serious trouble. No one will hurt you if you tell the truth, but you must tell the truth. Do you admit to the crime of selling contraband?"

There was no response.

"It will go easier for you, believe me, Petr. Why should you resist? We have evidence of your guilt. It is senseless to persist."

At last Petr nodded.

"Then you admit your crime?"

He nodded feebly.

"Good, good. Thank you Petr. Now I can help you. You see, I am not a bad man. I do not like to see you suffer. Why should you suffer for your crime when the others go free?" He paused to let this sink into Petr's dulled brain. "There were others, weren't there. Petr?"

Petr resisted and tried to roll his face away with a pained groan. Aleksay gripped his head firmly and turned it back.

"There were others, weren't there?"

Petr nodded.

"And where did you get the items you sold?"

Silence.

"Tell me who helped you. Tell me where you got the items you sold. Why should you suffer for their crimes?"

Petr stared hopelessly into Aleksay's eyes. He had the desperate confused look of a dying animal. Aleksay smiled reassuringly, like a priest at confession.

"Tell me Petr and your suffering will be over. It is not right that you should go on suffering."

Petr's look of desperation faded into a glimmer of hope and he struggled to form a word.

"Give me some water, quickly," Aleksay snapped at the guard.

The guard responded and Aleksay gently lifted Petr's head and helped him manage a few sips from the battered metal cup. The water ran from the corners of his swollen lips, but he seemed relieved by what little he swallowed.

"O . . . Ol . . . Oleno . . . fffl"

"Olenov? Did you say Olenov?" Aleksay asked intensely.

Petr nodded and closed his eyes in remorse.

"Would that be Mikhail Olenov?"

Again a nod.

"And where did he get the contraband?"

Petr immediately shook his head that he did not know. His eyes were wild and pleading. Aleksay could tell that he was telling the truth. The man had already broken. There would be no sense in withholding that information. Nevertheless, he pulled Petr's face up toward his and hissed. "You are lying! This is making me very unhappy! You do not trust me! How am I to help you if you do not trust me?"

Petr shook his head helplessly and struggled violently to speak. "I . . . do not know!" he gasped; then his body was wracked by a spasm of coughing. Quite obviously, he had sustained multiple internal injuries during his interrogation.

Aleksay lowered Petr's head to the mattress and stood up. The guard locked the door behind them, as Aleksay stood in the corridor, staring at the bare lightbulbs placed at intervals down the low-ceilinged passage.

"Do you believe him, Comrade?" the guard asked as they retraced their steps.

Aleksay shrugged. "He has at least told me more than he did you. That is something. He is not to be interrogated further. He is of no use to us dead. Inform me when his condition has improved. I may wish to speak to him again."

Mikhail's single room apartment had been sealed shortly after the assassination and lay in the same disarray in which the agents had left it. Aleksay sifted through the broken pottery and scattered papers on the floor with the toe of his shoe, mulling over in his brain what he knew to be the facts. Romanshin had been selling contraband, and Mikhail had been supplying it. Mikhail had also been involved in the murder at the apartment. Was Petr also implicated in the murder? Where had Mikhail gotten the contraband for Petr? The goods were of varied origin, obtainable only through a source that had access to the West. What was the connection?

He spent a futile hour scouring the disheveled apartment, looking for a clue, something, anything that the agents had missed. The way the KGB had ransacked the place disgusted him. It was thoroughly unprofessional. How could anyone make sense out of the chaos they had created? Only through methodical study of each detail would the case unfold. Perhaps a valuable clue had been destroyed in the mindless violence of the initial search. The pigs! He would see that they were reprimanded. They had smashed every piece of furniture, every glass, ripped open every pillow. He decided to have the apartment swept clean and each and every scrap of rubbish examined at the Center.

As he walked briskly back toward his office in the dark along deserted sidewalks, a piece of the puzzle kept trying to fit itself into place. What was the connection with the young girl? Did she belong in the scheme of things? Something told him that she did.

It was after eight P.M. and Ricky's was packed with the regular crowd. Kathy sipped deeply from her first martini and scanned the bar for familiar faces. There were a lot of them, but she did not know their names.

She wondered if Bruce would show. She had called him back and managed to smooth things over, but he was still pretty hot when he agreed to meet and talk things out. Now he was ten minutes late, and she began to doubt that he would come.

She jumped at the light touch on her shoulder and turned smiling only to stare into the darting eyes of a nervous little man she had never seen before. He wore a crumpled grey overcoat and held a shapeless hat in one hand. His other hand hovered furtively on the back of the adjacent chair. "May I join you?" he asked.

He was a pathetic looking little man, she thought, and not wanting to be rude she smiled politely. "I'm expecting someone."

"It will not take long, Miss Karpovich."

She was startled that he knew her name. "Do I know you?" she asked, wondering about the thick accent she had caught in his few words. What was it?

117

"No, but that is not important," he replied softly. "What I have to say will not take long . . ."

"I said I was waiting for someone," she said, letting her irritation filter into her voice. *Russian*. His accent was Russian!

He glanced around anxiously, as if about to take flight. "Perhaps Mr. Wilson is not coming."

Kathy jumped like she had been hit and her face darkened. "Who are you?"

"If you will allow me to sit down, I will explain. It is very important that I speak to you."

"Listen, I don't know you, and what's more I don't care to know you."

"Oh, but I know you," he said. "I know all about you."

It was more the way he said it than what he said that gave her the clue, and she did not resist as he drew out the chair and sat down close beside her. "I will be brief. I know that you call yourself Kathryn Karpovich, that you work for the *Washington Post* on the White House beat. That you are a woman of ambition. I also know that there are certain unfortunate circumstances in your past that might, shall we say, hinder your climb to the top of your profession should they become public knowledge."

Kathy's face paled and her hands trembled as she gripped the martini glass. She said nothing, waiting for him to speak.

"I am glad that you choose to remain calm. It would be unwise to create a scene."

"What do you want?"

"Your cooperation."

"With what?"

"I want you to apply for a job."

"I already have a job."

"There is currently a position open at SPEC Technologies that is ideally suited to your qualifications. My government would be very interested in having you occupy that position."

"Your government? Say, what the hell is this?"

"Please, Miss Karpovich. I would hate to think that you were uncooperative. Then I would have to inform your publisher of your unsavory relationships from the past . . .

the SDS, the Weather Underground?"

Her expression told him that he had struck a nerve. She tried to speak but was incapable of finding the words.

Suddenly, the little man noticed something over her shoulder and rose. "Apply for that job, Miss Karpovich, if you do not wish to have your past spread in the headlines of your own newspaper. I will contact you again!"

With this he slipped toward the exit near the bathrooms and disappeared. Kathy downed the rest of her drink and gripped the edge of the table to still her shaking hands.

Scarcely a moment later, Bruce sat down looking solemn and tired. "Sorry I'm late," he said, looking around for the cocktail waitress. He did not notice Kathy's near catatonic stare focused on the door where the little Russian had disappeared.

"I hope you haven't been waiting too long. Things at the office got out of hand." He spotted the waitress and waved her over. "Another martini?"

"Make that a double," Kathy said, coming out of her state.

"That goes for me, too," Bruce said. He glanced at Kathy for the first time and noticed that she looked strained. "Do you feel all right? You look a little pale."

"No. I'm fine, really. I was just thinking about a story I'm working on."

"God what a day it's been! The phones haven't stopped ringing."

The girl brought their drinks and he took his eagerly, relishing the first biting swallow. He sighed and seemed to relax until he remembered the reason for their meeting.

Kathy gulped most of her drink and avoided looking at him.

"Kathy. You've got to promise me you won't pull any more shit like you did this morning. It could really be embarrassing."

She looked genuinely sorry. "I didn't think you'd get that upset, Bruce. I'm sorry. I should've realized the position it would put you in."

"Well, let's forget it."

"I'll drink to that," she said, and did.

He noticed that she was still distracted; it bothered him. He had felt angry and self-righteous, but her immediate apology had thrown him. Now her distant manner annoyed him. The least she could do would be to pay attention to him after he'd rushed over to meet her leaving a desk full of work still unfinished.

"Are you sure you're OK?"

She nodded, perhaps a little too quickly, and forced a smile. "Sure. I told you, I'm working on this big article and I can't seem to keep it out of my mind."

"Well don't let me interrupt," he said, sounding irritated. "After all, I realize you're the only person in town with a hectic schedule. I only came over here because you insisted . . ."

"It's not you, Bruce. Believe me. So drop the martyr shit! I'm not in the mood!"

"This is great. I leave a fucking desk full of paper work to listen to this crap!"

"Oh for Christ's sake, Bruce! Will you stop it? You're the biggest baby I've ever met. So you had a bad day. You're not the only one! Other people have troubles too, you know!"

"What the hell is wrong with you, Kathy? All I said was . . ."

"All you've said since you sat down was that you've had a rough day and you're really pissed off at my practical joke. OK. For the last time, I'm sorry. It was a dumb stunt. Now can we drop it and enjoy our drinks?"

She drained the rest of hers and sat sullenly staring at the ice. He was stunned by her outburst and confused at its intensity. Something more than his remarks had set her off, and she was obviously not in the mood to discuss it. As far as he was concerned, the evening was a total loss.

He started to rise and she looked at him with a mixture of surprise and fury. Her expression told him at once that he had made a mistake.

"Is that your answer to everything, Bruce? Running away?"

"I'm not running away. I just figured you weren't in the mood to be sociable tonight, and there's no sense wasting my time or yours."

"You know what? You're right. You're absolutely fucking right!" She got up and sent her chair clattering to the floor. Several people turned to stare and Bruce sank lower in his seat. "Go back to your goddamn office, asshole!" she snarled, and turning on her heel, stamped out, leaving him to pick up the bill.

He sat for an embarrassing moment, looking for the cocktail waitress and when she didn't appear, dropped a twenty-dollar bill on the table and pushed through the crowd toward the front door.

On the street, he stopped and looked around only to see her flash by in her red MG and disappear up the street. He wanted to punch something, but there was nothing available, so he kicked the curb and bruised his toe instead. Then he limped to his car and drove back to the office, in a slow boil.

. . . 9 March 1989

There is a ferry that runs from the mainland of the Yucatan Peninsula to Isla Mujeres, the Island of Women, some twenty miles north of Cancun. It is a journey of less than an hour by car to the landing, and a similar period of time for the crossing in good weather. In foul weather, the ferry doesn't run at all.

March 9 was a brilliantly clear day, warm with a refreshing breeze from the northeast. The sea was a tableau of aquamarine, turquoise, and violet under a sky filled with faint puffy clouds that by evening would blossom into thunderheads, perhaps to bring a cooling shower to the steaming jungles.

But, for the moment, the day was perfect, the road was relatively free of the regular slow-moving traffic, and Roger Davis was in tune with his rented Porsche as he maneuvered it over the narrow two-line roadway along the coast. Mercedes lounged in the passenger seat, enjoying the sunshine and the fresh sea air. Her hair blew free in the wind, swirling around her head and shoulders like a golden brown halo. She looked truly happy for the first time since Davis had met her, and he was mesmerized by her innocent beauty, her almost angelic demeanor—almost angelic save for the hint of seductive petulance in her expression.

"You look happy," he said.

She turned to him, and smiled. "I am."

"I'm glad," he said. "I'm glad you came with me."

"I had a hard time convincing Father. He wanted to send along some bodyguards. But I told him you could take care of me."

"I'm sure he didn't buy that."

"No, you're right. But I threatened to have a tantrum if he didn't trust me this once."

"It sounds as if he treats you like a teenager!"

"Worse. Like an infant, incapable of using common sense."

He laughed out loud and she suddenly frowned. "I'm sorry," he chuckled. "But if he really knew you, he wouldn't worry about you. I've got a feeling you can take care of yourself."

"You're making fun of me."

"No I'm not. I'm making fun of him."

"That's disrespectful. Remember he is . . ."

"All right. No lectures. I just don't like to see you treated like a child."

She smiled to herself and let her gaze return to the sea as they emerged from a jungled stretch of road onto a broad sweeping bay. In the distance, she saw the blue and white ferryboat churning through the shimmering waters toward the landing, which was little more than a concrete bulkhead and several cement block buildings clustered at the edge of the shoreline. "There it is," she said, excitedly pointing. "It looks like there's a line. Hurry or we'll have to wait for the next one."

Roger downshifted into third and accelerated through a sharp curve as the road bent back into the jungle. They followed it for about half a mile, before it again veered and brought them unexpectedly into a shabby little community of wooden houses with thatched roofs, open sewers, and dirt footpaths.

Several scrawny chickens flushed from the roadway as he braked hard and slowed to a crawl past the filthy little homes. Thin children, with distended bellies and hollow pleading eyes stopped to watch them pass. Mercedes tried not to notice their dirty faces and the pools of stagnant fouled water in which they were playing. Pigs and goats milled in fetid pens and the stench of animal and human excrement was almost unbearable.

It was a heart-rending contrast to the opulence of Cancun, but Davis understandingly tried to ignore the conditions and accelerated quickly once they had passed through. He knew that she was painfully aware of the gulf between her way of life and that of her people.

Not long after, they approached a wooden guard post, and several uniformed soldiers moved lazily out of the shading trees. He glanced at her, questioningly.

"The ferry is operated by the army. It is a military outpost. You'll have to pay toll at the gate."

He slowed to a stop just short of the soldiers, and waited as one of them approached, eyeing Mercedes with unconcealed appetite. Inwardly, Davis smiled, thinking how the man might grovel at her feet if he were to learn who she really was. But he kept quiet and paid the toll, then jamming the car into gear, roared past the soldiers toward the line of cars and trucks that had already formed at the landing.

He stopped the Porsche at a safe distance behind a truck-load of pigs and cut the engine. The ferry was only just docking and would have to be unloaded before they could board. They sat without speaking as other cars filled in behind them. Casually, Davis checked out the occupants of a black Volkswagen close to his rear bumper. They were Mexican, both males, both wearing tropical print shirts and dark glasses. His instinct told him to be aware of their movements during the crossing.

The wait for the ferry was short, and in no time they were on board and steaming out into the gentle swells of the straits separating Isla Mujeres from the mainland. Shortly after leaving the dock, Davis and Mercedes climbed to the upper deck and stood at the guard rail, staring into the ever-changing waterscape slipping by below. Sandy shallows of cobalt glistened like pearls between massive ranging purple coral jungles. Deep trenches of indigo cut meandering paths across the bottom, the light filtering like fracturing diamonds into the fathomless depths of every imaginable shade of blue. They stood close together, their shoulders touching. Her skin was warm and soft; her hair wisped across his face and the smell of her distinct fragrance filled his head. Had it not been for the two men in the Volkswagen he would have been at peace. They did not leave their car, but he could tell they were watching.

During the crossing they hardly spoke. There was pleasure enough in their closeness and the breathtaking beauty of the sea. Isla Mujeres rose from the horizon, a thin strip of green jungle, but soon they saw the white limestone beaches and white-washed adobe buildings, glistening in the midday sun.

They returned to the car and waited patiently as the ferry docked and the forward vehicles began to unload, one by one, onto the narrow access road. Davis followed the pig truck, the Volkswagen followed him. His eyes darted back and forth between the mirror and the snarled traffic ahead. The market was jammed and they inched forward, hopelessly committed to a snail's pace.

Davis watched for his first opportunity, which finally came when a vegetable truck scraped the front right fender of the pig truck. Both vehicles screeched to a halt and the drivers leaped out and began shouting at each other. Horns began to blare. Just beyond the two trucks was a narrow alley running down to their right, toward the ocean. The instant Davis spotted it, he turned the wheel hard, whipped around the stalled trucks, cut in front of them, and zipped into the alley before the traffic became inextricably tangled.

The men in the Volkswagen cursed and tried to duplicate the maneuver, only to run into an oncoming battered old Ford. The market erupted in a cacophony of car horns and angry words.

Mercedes let out a whoop of excitement as they careened down the narrow artery past startled old men snoozing in the sun. Sure enough, at the bottom of the alley, there was another narrow road running parallel to the main one. Davis downshifted into second and slid the Porsch onto it in a spray of dust and gravel. An old woman washing her clothes in a bucket by the road cursed them.

Mercedes was laughing gleefully, unaware of his real intentions, which had been to lose the tail. Davis glanced in the mirror, but saw no sign of the other car. Another three-quarters of a mile brought them to an intersection with the main road again. There was no traffic coming from town, so they scooted out onto the blacktop without slowing down, and roared away toward the north end of the island.

Isla Mujeres is not a large island and the drive took them less than twenty minutes. At the northeasternmost point they came to a cantina at the very end of the highway. A narrow dirt path led down toward the blue-green swells past the cantina's white adobe walls and open rear veranda.

Mercedes jumped from the car the moment he stopped, laughing gaily and shaking her hair free. "Oh, that was fun!" she said. "I love to drive fast!"

"I'm sure the local police would not approve. Watch yourself, I'm going to pull in behind that wall." He slipped the car into reverse and backed up behind a crumbling wall of some former residence, out of sight from the road. "The car should be all right here," he said and climbed out dragging the canvas equipment bag and the picnic basket with him. "Let's see if we can get some beer to take down with us," he said and led the way to the cantina.

The place was surprisingly dark and cool inside, with a low-beamed ceiling and heavy whitewashed walls. The bartender, a heavy-set fellow with a round face and a thick black mustache, immediately sized Mercedes up and swaggered to their corner of the bar.

"Buenos dias, Señor. Señorita?"

Davis' Spanish was rusty and he decided not to give it a try. "We'd like to buy some beer to take down to the cove with us."

Happily, the bartender's English was better than his Spanish.

"You are going swimming in the lagoon?"

"Yes, I understand the diving is good."

"Si. That will be twenty pesos . . . apiece."

Davis glanced questioningly at Mercedes, who nodded that he should pay the man. Davis gave him an extra twenty. "I'm parked outside. Keep an eye on my car, will you?"

The man nodded reservedly. "Si. Si. What kind of beer you want?"

They left by the rear entrance and crossed the open veranda to a stone staircase that led down through a natural garden to the dirt path they had seen from the road. On either side, the path was bordered by lush vegetation and bright flowering vines. Mercedes stuck close to him, clearly uneasy about the bartender.

"Nice fellow," Davis remarked wryly.

"He gave me the creeps!"

"I don't think you have anything to worry about, as long as he doesn't steal our car. Then we might have to walk home."

"You're not funny."

"Relax, dear. These are your people, remember?"

She frowned.

"Oh cheer up," he said. "You're in for a great experience. A friend of mine told me about this place a couple of years ago. He said the diving out by that point is tremendous."

From their vantage, they could see the placid cove below, sheltered by a jutting finger of limestone rock. A glistening strip of white sand bordered the gentle surf and disappeared into thick jungle only a few yards up from the shore. Beneath the waters of the cove, the coral heads could be clearly seen, vividly colored in purples and blues.

They followed the ragged path down a rock cliff and emerged on the beach in absolute isolation. They could see nothing of the cantina overhead, and as far as the eye could see to the east, there was only the blue sky and shimmering sea.

"It's beautiful," she sighed.

"You're beautiful," he said, watching her eyes turn to him.

She smiled shyly and chose to let his comment pass as she slipped out of her cutoffs and T-shirt top, revealing the tiny string bikini she wore underneath. He stared in awe.

"What's wrong?" she asked.

"Nothing. Absolutely nothing."

"It's not polite to stare."

"I wasn't staring. I was lusting," he teased.

With an indignant sniff she picked up her diving gear and camera and headed for the water. Chuckling, he followed suit.

The water was surprisingly cool and invigorating, and soon they were fanning their way over sprawling coral heads and brilliantly colored schools of tropical fish. The sun beat down on their backs, warming them as they dived time and again into the crystalline depths, Mercedes snapping pictures for nearly an hour. Roger was a strong swimmer, but she apparently was a stronger one, or at least had the advantage of age, because he was the first to call it quits. Motioning to her, he began to swim back to the beach. She hesitated, took a few pictures of him retreating, then followed.

He sprawled on the hot white sand when she emerged from the water and sat down beside him. He took her hand and kissed her fingertips, and they listened to the gentle wash of the swells, letting the sun drive the chill from their bodies. He closed his eyes and drifted.

After a time, he felt her close, her breath on his face; he opened his eyes to find her lips only inches from his. He folded her gently in his arms and pulled her down, their lips lingering in a tender kiss, not like the kiss of desperation the night before. She was restrained, inquisitive, but he sensed her concealed desire.

He released her when she drew away, and studied her large questioning eyes, the alluring line of her mouth, the velvet texture of her golden skin. She was clearly fascinated by him and, something told him, a little afraid. That excited him. He tried to pull her back, but she resisted. "Not now. Later."

They ate a leisurely lunch of bread and soft Mexican cheese, complemented by the stout Mexican beer. For dessert, there was fruit and coffee liqueur. He smoked a cigarette and she watched him, like a child, hypnotized by something she did not understand.

They lay on the sand, content to be alone with only each other, far from the pressures of their worlds, which were so far apart.

Kathy's phone rang at around four o'clock. She stopped typing in midsentence to answer.

"Kathy? It's Bruce."

For a moment, she did not reply. "Hi," she said at last, sounding cold.

"I'm sorry about last night, Kathy. I want to apologize."

Again there was a very long silence.

"No need, Bruce. We were both on edge."

Bruce sighed to himself and continued hopefully. "The real reason I'm calling is that the President is giving a cocktail party for some VIPs on the Hill tonight, and I wanted to know if you'd like to come."

"Well of course I would!" she blurted out without bothering to hide her excitement.

"Great!" He tried to control his own enthusiasm, remembering his official position. "It starts at seven-thirty. Should I send a car for you?"

"No, I'll get a cab."

"Are you sure?"

"Positive. No sense wasting the taxpayers' money on me."

"Maybe after it's over we can have a quiet drink somewhere."

"Your place or mine?" she teased.

"Whichever," he chuckled. "Well, listen, I've got to get back to work here. I just wanted to call and invite you . . ."

"I wouldn't miss it for the world. See you around seven-thirty!"

"Right. Bye." Bruce hung up feeling smug. He was beginning to enjoy the powers and privileges of his rank.

Kathy hung up also feeling smug. She was surprised that he had called back, but pleased that he had, because she'd been feeling like an idiot all day for blowing her inside contact with him.

She glanced at her watch, then suddenly remembered the little man in the bar. She had been repressing the incident all day, but now it came back to haunt her. Was he for real? She shuddered to think that he was serious about her applying for the job at SPEC in order to spy for the Russians. It had to be a cruel hoax put on by some of her more jealous colleagues. But if that were so, where had they gotten their information about her past? And would they really be willing to use it? She told herself that the man was bluffing, but what if he weren't? Would he really expose her past?

The outcome was unthinkable, so she put it out of her mind and picked up the phone to dial the State Department.

She had a story working on the Soviet buildup of the dictatorship in Surinam that they were holding for the late edition, and if she didn't get it finished, she was going to have to apply for that job at SPEC in earnest.

"Gentlemen, quite frankly your situation is bleak."

Parker faced his four visitors across his cluttered desk in the Oval Office. They were the mayors of New York, Cleveland, Chicago, and Detroit, and each had come to request an extension of the federal subsidies which were the only buffers standing between their municipalities and bankruptcy.

"What assurance can you give me that if you were granted an extension of your loans, your municipalities will ever be able to pay them off?"

The four men squirmed like schoolchildren before their principal and cleared their throats.

"Your silence tells me that you can give me no assurance."

"Mr. President," said Wilson Bernstein, the mayor of New York City. "Our cities have fallen on hard times. Labor is driving the costs through the ceiling. Right now we're operating with only two-thirds of our police and fire department services; the garbage workers are threatening another strike if negotiations on their contracts don't resume immediately, and there's no way we can afford to meet their demands without postponing our debt commitments. What else can we do?"

"Default," Parker said passively.

The four men flinched in unison. "Mr. President," said Mayor Krensky of Cleveland. "The last time something like this happened, we nearly had a riot on our hands. You know that only a last minute federal guarantee saved us. Do you realize . . ."

"Have you got any other suggestion?" Parker asked, his tone chillingly calm.

"Give us an extension. Until we have time to get things under control!" Chicago's Mayor Jordan pleaded.

"I don't see why the federal government should pick up the tab for your municipalities' deficits. Hundreds of other cities are able to survive without special assistance. Granted, your governments are faced with grave problems, but what justification can possibly be given for burdening the American people with your support?"

"Surely you realize that a default will leave our cities without public services!" Detroit's Mayor Works exclaimed.

"It's time to pay the piper, Mr. Works. I can't sanction what amounts to public blackmail. If labor thinks they can push for more money, without any limitations whatsoever, they'll continue to do so. It's time to show them what fiscal responsibility really means. Government has to be run like a business. Revenues have to meet expenses or you go belly up. Your present resources are going to have to meet your current needs. If you default, the major lending institutions are going to be severely injured, and the responsibility is going to be yours and yours alone. That's the long and short of it. Now I suggest you find some way to convince your local unions of this fact, because if you default, there won't be any jobs for any of their people. Frankly speaking, even if you are able to avoid higher wages, I doubt if you're going to be able to survive. But in any event, I'm not going to be able to do anything for you."

"But I represent the greatest city in America!" Mayor Bernstein exclaimed. "You can't turn your back on me. It's unconscionable!"

"Who says you represent the greatest city in America, Mr. Bernstein? You are the mayor of the most inefficiently run municipality in the United States. Your government is the most corrupt, your welfare system the most abused, your citizens the least productive. I don't consider that a mark of greatness."

"What about our cultural contributions, our heritage? The theater, the arts, our museums?"

"Meaningless in terms of your present dilemma and current values. After all, in times of extreme crisis, luxuries such as the arts and museums have no place in the realities of day to day survival. Times are changing, gentlemen. You're going to have to reevaluate your priorities. When garbage workers make more than nuclear physicists and college

131

professors, I think it's time to take a second look at the system. And since it's difficult to eat great masterpieces, I suggest you consider selling them to offset your outstanding debts."

"Surely you're not serious?" Krensky gasped. "You can't expect us to liquidate our cultural institutions in order to subsidize our public services?"

"You're talking about priceless treasures!" Bernstein stammered.

"I'm sure private investors would be willing to put a fair price on what you call priceless treasures, Mr. Bernstein. In fact, they'd be more than willing to snap up what you've got if you gave them the chance. I'd look at it as a logical source of badly needed funds if I were you. After all, in hard times, businesses sometimes have to divest themselves of nonliquid, burdensome assets in order to meet current expenses. Why should your municipalities be any exception?"

"Do you realize that you're challenging the basic fiber of western civilization?" Bernstein asked angrily. "How do you expect the public to react? Those masterpieces belong to them. How do you think it will look if we tell them what you've said?"

"I'm not running a popularity contest, Mr. Bernstein. I'm running a government, and I'm trying to plug some leaks. Your cities are sieves when it comes to the federal budget, and in the overall scheme of things, you are expendable."

"I've never been so humiliated in all my life," Jordan hissed, leaning forward on the edge of his chair. "If you think we're going to sit by and let you get away with this you're out of your mind. The people will never stand for it."

"They will when they realize it's the only way to keep food on their tables. As for you being humiliated, I suppose that's a good lesson for you. After all, why should you be rewarded for running an inefficient government? Your failure is a betrayal of the public trust. Just like my granting you a reprieve would be a violation of the public trust. I'm sorry gentlemen, but you're going to have to stand your own ground. The battle against inflation has to start with local government. Labor is your enemy, not me. And if it's allowed to have its way, it'll ruin this country just like it's almost ruined Great Britain. I won't let that happen. If you can't handle your own problems, then the natural sequence of events will just have to follow."

"But our cities will be wastelands. There will be riots in the streets, mass exoduses, maybe even mass suicides. Do you want that on your conscience?"

"I think you're placing too great an importance on the value of your cities, gentlemen. The fact that they're some of the oldest communities in the country is no excuse for granting them immunity from the basic laws of economics. The country isn't going to collapse if your cities do. Your citizens will move on to find work in more productive areas of the country. They'll learn to work for wages that the market will support, and they'll adjust their standards of living accordingly. We're facing a national crisis, gentlemen, and I can't allow you special dispensation at the expense of the entire country. If you can't settle your own affairs, then the results will be on your heads. My conscience is clear. I wish I could be more sympathetic, but you see, I'm more concerned for what this country used to stand for — freedom! Freedom connotes risk, and risk connotes the possibility of failure. What you're asking me to do is remove from your lives the threat of failure. That's something that the unions have been demanding for the last forty years, and that's something I am definitely not going to do. The role of the federal government is to protect and to serve the people of this country. But that doesn't mean provide for them, clothe them, feed them. We are a free people, and we must learn to fend for ourselves if we want to remain free. If not, then we ought to convert to communism, let the government run our lives, tell us what to think, what to do, what to say, what to wear, where to sleep, when to live, and when to die. That's an alternative that is anathema to me, and as long as there is a breath in my body, I will resist it."

"Then you're going to sit by and let our governments collapse?"

"I told you before, if your governments collapse, it will be because your administration failed, not mine. And if violence erupts, let me assure you, I will send in the National Guard to restore order."

"Do you realize you would be creating a state of martial law?" Krensky squealed. He was white and trembling. "It's unconstitutional!"

"I don't think the Constitution makes any mention of that, Mr. Krensky. If it becomes necessary to establish a state of martial law to keep order, then I'll do so until your governments can restore control. I'm not going to fail in my responsibilities to this country, gentlemen, and I suggest you act very quickly and purposefully so that you won't either. Don't try to lay your failures on me. I won't let you."

"You haven't heard the end of this" Works whispered, as if afraid to speak but too afraid not to. "The press is going to get the whole story and when they're through with you, you won't have enough support in Congress to get a street sign approved. You can't spit on our cities and get away with it!"

"Gentlemen. Your degenerate cities have succeeded in soiling themselves. And you've either got to clean up the mess or sit in it. It's up to you. Now if you'll excuse me, I have other appointments this afternoon."

The four men stared at each other in horror and disbelief. Parker buzzed for Shirley, who appeared and held the door open, waiting for them to rise. Silently, they filed out. Parker opened one of the many files on his desk, and glanced up when the last of them had left.

"Bring me some coffee, will you, Shirley, then I want to place a call to Mr. Roger Davis at the Camino Real Hotel in Cancun, Mexico."

"Are you asleep?" Mercedes whispered. It was getting late, and the sun was slipping away behind them, dipping toward the palm-studded cliff top.

Davis awoke with a start and reached instinctively to his left breast before he realized where he was. He saw Mercedes smiling curiously at him and gave her a sleepy grin.

"I must have been asleep."

"You were. I was watching you."

"I hope I didn't talk in my sleep."

"Afraid of revealing state secrets?"

"Something like that."

"Did I frighten you?"

"No," he said and sat up stretching. The ocean had roughened, and a stout breeze whipped white caps on the once calm lagoon.

"You jumped as if I did," she laughed.

"I don't frighten easily," he said and tossed sand at her.

She dodged and tackled him, driving him back into the sand. "But you do frighten," she insisted.

He smiled but did not respond. In his eyes, she saw something that told her he did not know the meaning of fear, and it troubled her for a moment. But she pushed the feeling aside. "Come on," she urged. "What frightens you?"

"Pushy girls," he teased, and pulled her close, kissing her playfully. She nestled in his arms and moaned softly with sudden desire. Their bodies entwined briefly, then she broke away and rested her head against his chest.

"Who are you?" she sighed.

"I told you. My name is Roger Davis, and I work . . ."

"Who are you really?"

"I'm a spy," he said, mocking her.

"I think I believe you."

"No you don't."

"I don't know. If you were a spy, I could understand you better."

"What's there to understand!" he laughed. "I'm a man who happens to find you very attractive and would give anything to spend all my time with you while I'm here."

She was silent for a moment.

"Does that upset you?"

She turned to him, a soft glow in her eyes. "No." She kissed him.

"Come on," he said. "It's getting late. If we want to make the late ferry, we'd better get going."

She groaned in mock protest as he dragged her to her feet. She raised her lips and he kissed her tenderly.

"Come on," he insisted, breaking away. "I don't want to

135

spend the night on this little island. Not when I've got an expensive suite and a bottle of champagne waiting."

"Champagne?" she laughed and hugged him affectionately.

By the time they had climbed the cliff, the breeze had freshened and from the top, they saw a slate-colored line of clouds on the horizon. A storm was brewing over the mainland. Neither spoke as they walked up past the cantina, which was now crowded with thirsty locals, wetting down their throats after a long hot day. They found the Porsche where they had left it, apparently untouched.

There was no sign of the Volkswagen as they drove back toward town along the lonely highway. The sky was growing more and more threatening with every passing minute. He sensed her anxiety. When they arrived at the landing, they found the traffic snarled all the way back to the market, and by the looks of the line, they were not going to make the boat, the last one of the day.

"Damn it!" he said. "I don't think we're going to make it on."

"That would be terrible," she teased and blew in his ear, trying to ease her own tension.

"Come on, cut it out. Your father will have my head if I don't get you back. Get in the driver's seat. I'll go see what I can do."

He climbed out and she slid over behind the wheel. Casually, he walked up the long line of cars toward the ferry. One in particular caught his eye immediately—the black Volkswagen. As he passed, he took care to conceal his face from the two hombres inside, and they were too concerned with the long line and dwindling space on the ferry to notice him.

At the landing, Davis found several guards supervising the traffic. He approached them and in his broken Spanish tried to find out how he could get on the ferry. He was told gruffly to wait his turn, and if he missed it, there would be another one in the morning, if the storm was not too bad.

He whipped out his wallet and peeled several hundred-peso notes from the pocket. The guards eyed them calmly but made no suggestions in his behalf. He peeled out several more and their interest increased, but not to the point of cooperation. He tired of the game and spoke bluntly.

"I don't know how to tell you this, men, but if I don't get the President's daughter back tonight, he's going to want to know your names and just why you weren't more helpful."

"El Presidente?" one of them asked, sounding skeptical.

"That's right. His daughter is waiting in line back there behind a stinking chicken truck, and she is not happy about the possibility of missing this ferry."

The two guards conferred quickly and turned to him all grins. One of them took the notes he still offered and gestured politely. "Please, señor, bring your car right up to the front. I will hold a spot for you."

"Thank you, gentlemen. You've been very understanding." Davis turned and walked swiftly back along the line of cars.

The two men in the black VW saw him coming and watched suspiciously as he sauntered past with a wry grin on his face, noticing their stove-in front end. They craned their necks to watch him pass, and broke into a heated argument a moment later.

Back at the car, Davis opened the driver's door. "Scoot over. I'll drive." She moved over and he slipped the car in gear and roared out of line up the empty lane to the landing where the guards were holding the other vehicles back to allow him to fill the last available spot on board. Both guards bobbed and saluted as they pulled past, and Davis gave them a friendly wave.

"What's that all about?" Mercedes asked, as if she didn't already know.

"They were very glad to help out El Presidente's daughter, with the help of a few hundred pesos' subsidy."

"You mean they actually accepted a bribe?" she asked with mock despair.

He laughed and climbed out of the car to look back at the cowering soldiers who were raising the gangplank under the heated harangue of the two fellows from the VW.

Davis smiled and slipped his arm around Mercedes as they

137

walked casually to the observation deck. The sky over the mainland had grown very black, and the water appeared to glow phosphorescently in contrast. The swells pounded the hull with the thunder of kettle drums, and the wind blew the spray from the bow wave high in the air, as the ferry churned across the straits.

By the time they crossed the narrow bridge onto Cancun and roared up the divided esplanade toward the Camino Real, the rain had begun to fall lightly, but the pitch black of the sky was a portent of more to come.

"I don't want to go home yet," Mercedes said.

"Who said anything about going home? I had my place and a bottle of champagne in mind."

She grinned and squeezed his hand. "Lovely."

The rain began to fall in torrents about the time they pulled under the huge front portico of the hotel where Mayans dressed in khaki uniforms greeted them and helped them inside with their belongings.

The sheltered poolside bar was jammed to the hilt with afternoon merrymakers and the rain hissed on the surface of the lighted pool. Davis and Mercedes passed quickly by lest she be recognized and went directly to the bank of elevators near the front desk. A clerk behind the desk looked up and spotted Davis. He turned and withdrew a note from the mail slip, then hurried forward with it.

"Mr. Davis. This came for you a short while ago."

"Thank you," Davis said and slipped the folded note into his pocket as the elevator came.

He opened the door of his tenth floor suite and cut on the hall light. "Make yourself at home. I'll call room service."

The curtains were open. Through the driving rain, a bright line of sky could be seen to the east. The clouds were black as slate, the sea the color of the sky, the lightning flashed brilliantly in jagged forks, highlighting the scene in stark relief.

"We just made it," she said, slipping her sandals off and wandering to the sliding glass door. "I love storms. Don't you? Violent storms."

He called room service and ordered champagne and caviar

sent up, then went into the bathroom and turned on the shower. When he returned, he found the room in darkness, and by the light of a lightning flash he saw her standing near the window, her naked back to him. She turned at his approach and he saw desire in her eyes. She was beautiful, too perfect to be real.

But when he touched her, felt her warmth and excitement, he knew that she was much more than any fantasy could hope for. Her breasts were firm, the nipples small and pointed. She shivered slightly and moved to him, seeking his caress. He took her in his arms and kissed her. She trembled and nuzzled against him, her fingers gripping his broad muscular back.

Suddenly, she slipped away into the steaming mist of the bathroom. He let his clothes fall to the carpet and followed. She stood in the shower, her body glistening, her hand outstretched to him. He took it and she drew him in, pressing her body to his.

All at once there was a shattering knock at the door and he broke away. "Damn it!" he hissed. Stepping out of the shower, he grabbed a towel and went to answer the door, slipping his Browning out of his coat pocket as he passed the closet. It was the bellboy with roomservice. "Leave it, will you?" he asked. "And charge it to my room?" The boy smiled knowingly and vanished down the hall. Davis pulled the cart inside and turning back into the room, he found the shower off and all the lights out.

He caught her movement in the darkness and saw her slipping into bed. She lay on her back, waiting for him. He went to her and softly caressed her, eliciting sighs of pleasure from her parted lips. She ran her fingers through his hair, then pulled his head down to her, driving up to meet him insistently. He pulled away the dampened sheets and kissed her tracing delicate circles with his tongue on the inside of her thighs.

She groaned and arched her back, beckoning him to explore further. He responded, drawing from her sobs of pleasure. At last she could take no more.

"Roger please!" she gasped.

He pretended not to hear.

"Roger!" she begged.

He poised above her. She drove up to meet him. Their bodies moved in unison, clinging desperately in their passion to the only true sensation they could trust.

They lay coupled in exhausted rapture, aware of their hearts beating as one, their breath flowing in rhythm. The storm raged in the night, the surf pounded the shore. He withdrew and lay by her side and she snuggled close seeking his warmth and tenderness. Burying her face against his neck she sighed contentedly, "I think I love you."

The Grand Ballroom of the White House was filled with candlelight and the genteel flow of conversation, released by the soothing effect of a river of alcohol.

As Parker had predicted, everyone who had been invited was present, all eager to put in his or her two bits about whatever pet project they happened to be pushing through committee. He was pleased with the turnout and moved through the throng, shaking hands, exchanging meaningless pleasantries with men he scarcely knew beyond their images in the press or the Senate and House chambers. Bruce Wilson was his shadow, parrying questions that dealt with tender issues. The State of the Union address had sent seismic waves shuddering through every branch of the government, and many were eager to learn firsthand just what effect the Administration's policies were going to have on their particular special interests.

It was nearly nine when Kathy finally arrived, looking harried. Bruce spotted her from a distance and excusing himself from the President's company, hurried to intercept her.

"Kathy, where the hell have you been? This thing's nearly over. I told you seven-thirty."

"I know, Bruce, and I'm sorry. But at the last minute I got this insane phone call from Wilson Bernstein."

"The Mayor of New York City?"

"The same. He insisted on meeting with me, said he had a

story he wanted to give me. An exclusive."

"And?"

"Well, it was some story. It's running tomorrow morning, but they're holding the presses until I get a comment from the White House."

"What's it about?"

"It seems Parker was pretty rough on the Mayor, and the mayors of Cleveland, Detroit, and Chicago. They met this afternoon."

"Yes, I know. What did Bernstein say?"

"Basically that Parker was abandoning the four cities in question to their own fate. He apparently isn't going to lend his support to the extension of their federal loans. The way Bernstein put it, he's going to fight against the extensions and veto any measure passed through Congress."

"And you're going to run that?"

"Of course I am. It's the hottest item I've had since you tight-lips took office."

"Easy, Kathy . . ."

"Just kidding, dear. Any chance of getting an interview with him?"

"Parker?"

"Who else have we been talking about?"

"Absolutely none. This is a social affair, a chance for the press and policy makers to mingle, get to know each other."

"You mean a show of solidarity for the President, don't you?"

"Precisely, Miss Karpovich." Parker's voice came from behind them and they both wheeled in surprise.

"Mr. President," Bruce gasped. "I was just explaining . . ."

"It's all right, Bruce. I know what she wants." He regarded Kathy quizzically, with just the hint of admiration. "You have some questions you want to ask me, Miss Karpovich?"

"Well, yes, Mr. President. But I don't want to intrude."

"You look like you could use a drink. Why don't you come sit at my table for a while. Maybe I can shed some light on the issues."

Kathy looked questioningly at Bruce who stood with his mouth agape. "I'd be delighted, Mr. President. Bruce . . . ?"

Bruce tried to muster a smile. Parker sized up the situation.

"Come on, Bruce. You can mediate this thing. If you think Miss Karpovich can be unbiased, I think it might be helpful to have her air my side as well as the opposition's." Parker's request had the hint of a direct order.

"Anything you say, sir. I'll get the drinks."

"Bourbon for me, Bruce," Parker said.

"Scotch," Kathy said, and followed the President to his table.

Bruce walked to the bar puzzling over the President's apparent sudden shift in policy, making himself available on a one-on-one basis to a reporter.

"I couldn't help overhear you mention Wilson Bernstein's name, Miss Karpovich. I assume he's been in communication with you?" They had seated themselves at the President's table, and as the other members of the press corps looked on with varying degrees of indignation and jealousy, Kathy tried to make herself comfortable in the presence of the security agents and the Secretary of State, Montie Montgomery, who was in a heated conversation with Dr. Arnold Kemper of SPEC Technologies.

"Yes, Mr. President. Mr. Bernstein called me this afternoon and told me he had a story he wanted me to print. I met with him and heard his side of your meeting this afternoon. Bruce invited me tonight, and I came hoping I might be able to get a comment for the story I'm going to run tomorrow morning."

"Oh, you're seeing Bruce are you?"

"Only professionally, I assure you. We've had dinner together a couple of times."

"No need to explain. I suppose Mr. Bernstein was pretty hot under the collar?"

"To put it mildly. He accused you of every political sin under the sun."

"Any chance you can put off this story a day or two, to give Bruce a chance to draft a statement?"

"I'm afraid we have to run it tomorrow or lose the exclusive."

"Then Bruce is going to have to burn the midnight oil . . ."

Bruce arrived just in time to hear the good news and tried not to look put out. Parker laughed out loud.

"I'm sorry, Bruce, but your friend is going to run the story. You'll have to give her a statement tonight."

"By all means, Mr. President . . ." He served their drinks and sat down at Kathy's right elbow, facing Parker past her shoulder.

"Are there any specific questions you want to direct to me?" Parker asked.

"Yes, a few."

"Shoot."

"Well, Bernstein implied that you are abandoning the cities at a critical time, jeopardizing thousands of jobs and the security of millions of people. Is that true?"

"I'm not abandoning them. I'm letting them solve their own problems. The role of the federal government is not to play nursemaid to local government. If they can't do the jobs they're elected to do, then their constituents should elect someone else who can."

"But don't you feel a certain obligation to the general welfare of the American public, and if so, aren't you bound to lend your support to critical situations on the local level?"

"When circumstances permit it. But, unfortunately, these problems have been growing unchecked. If I were to sanction any form of extension or subsidy at this point, it would mean calling on the lending institutions to further jeopardize their security as well as fanning the flames of inflation. I'm afraid those cities are on their own."

"But past Administrations . . ."

"This is not the past. This is the present, and this Administration intends to make everyone financially responsible for their actions. The free rides are over."

"That's a pretty hard line, isn't it?"

"I think it's about time someone took a pretty hard line, don't you?"

"No comment," Kathy smiled despite herself. She admired the man, even if she did not agree with his

143

philosophy. She also saw a stream of articles coming out of this situation that could put her right in the limelight.

Just then, one of the Secret Service agents leaned over Parker's shoulder and whispered in his ear. Parker looked intent and turned back to them gravely.

"You'll have to excuse me, Miss Karpovich. I have a very important phone call. Bruce, see me after this is over and we'll work up something for this. It's been nice chatting with you, Miss Karpovich," he said smiling, and left the table.

Bruce sat sulking, sipping his drink. Kathy on the other hand was overjoyed. "This is incredible. Two months of silence and suddenly an exclusive!"

"And I've got to help you write it. Not exactly what I had in mind for later on."

"Oh, come on Brucey. We'll eat a late supper at my place."

Bruce smiled at the inflection in her voice that indicated what the menu might include.

"Parker here."

"Mr. President? I received your message," Davis said over the phone. "How may I be of service?"

"When can you get back to Washington, Mr. Davis?"

"First thing in the morning, if I can get an early flight out. I'll have to call the airlines . . ."

"Don't bother. I'll send a charter jet down from Houston to pick you up."

"As you wish, sir. What time should I be at the airport?"

"It's nine our time," Parker said. "Say midnight your time?"

"Done, sir. Until tomorrow morning then?"

"Goodnight, Mr. Davis."

Davis replaced the phone on the hook and looked at Mercedes. She lay naked beside him, the sheets draped gracefully over her body. The look in her eyes told him she did not understand why he was going. He wanted to stay, more than anything else, to preserve what they had for as long as they could. But there was no choice. He took her in his arms. There were only a few hours left for them.

Aleksay thumbed through the dossier he had compiled so far. The facts were sketchy, disjointed, but something gnawed at him, telling him there was a pattern.

The room he occupied was a dim cement block enclosure on the first floor of the Center. A single shaded lamp hung over the wooden table. There were three hard-backed wooden chairs set around it. In the leaden silence of this bunker, his thoughts could be focused entirely on the clues.

What were they? Mikhail Olenov, age twenty-nine, implicated in the murder at the apartment house, also implicated in trafficking contraband. Petr Romanshin, old friend of Olenov's from the village of Bronnitsky, an admitted accomplice of Olenov's in the trafficking of contraband. Was he also involved in the murder? And what of the girl, who was also killed by the assassin?

He opened the folder and read her brief dossier. Name: Claudia Mashkanstev; age twenty-eight, recruited into the service twelve months before her death. Born and educated in Leningrad. No previous associations with either Olenov or Romanshin. An innocent victim?

Suddenly, the heavy wooden door opened and Colonel Markelov entered. Aleksay rose and saluted. Markelov's response seemed lethargic. "Come with me, Aleksay. I have something that will interest you." Without waiting, he turned and marched out of the room.

Aleksay gathered his papers and his leather overcoat and followed Markelov down the long subterranean passage leading to the Ministry of Medicine. Through a series of staircases and dim corridors, they worked their way into the bowels of the structure, until they came to an unmarked door at the end of a short hall. Markelov knocked, and in a moment the door opened and a balding man in a white lab coat looked out at them past the rim of his wire glasses. "Come in Comrade Colonel."

They entered to find a complete medical laboratory, equipped for chemical analysis and post mortem operations;

a morgue. On the single operating table, there was a body covered with a pale green sheet.

The technician walked to his desk and picked up a file from which he extracted a scrap of paper. This he handed to Markelov who examined it and in turn passed it to Aleksay. It was a portion of a black and white photograph that had apparently been burned; only this section had remained untouched. It showed the lower part of a woman's face, from just below the eyes to the base of the neck.

"What is this?" Aleksay asked.

"A clue," Markelov said, sounding annoyed. "It was discovered in the waste basket in Mikhail Olenov's apartment, during the search that you deemed counter-productive."

"Why was I not informed of this?"

"Because I thought it wiser to refer it to the department of records for possible identification."

"And?"

Markelov looked at the technician, who took the cue. "Colonel Markelov brought this to me because I specialize in reconstruction drawing as a part of the identification process of badly maimed subjects. A search of the records revealed a number of possible young women to whom the photograph could be matched. I very quickly eliminated all but two file photos." These he handed to Aleksay. Both were women in their late twenties, both very beautiful with high cheekbones, full sensuous mouths, and narrow chins. They could have been sisters.

"Who are they?" Aleksay asked, aware of the familiarity of the faces.

"One is a woman named Emilia Malinin, killed in an automobile accident in early 1988. The other is Claudia Mashkanstev."

The sound of their names rang in Aleksay's brain. "What?"

"The woman found in the apartment building with Said. She was in the government service," the technician said.

"Since early 1988," Aleksay said.

Markelov nodded.

The technician took both photographs, the one of Emilia in his right hand, the one of Claudia in his left. He walked to the operating table and drew back the sheet, revealing the body of the young woman found in the apartment house.

Aleksay gasped in astonishment as the truth became apparent. The technician held the two photographs next to her face, and the likeness was clear despite the slackening of the facial muscles and the single dark hole that yawned in her forehead just above the eyes.

"This woman was not Claudia Mashkanstev. She was Emilia Malinin!" Markelov snapped. "But she was posing as Claudia Mashkanstev, using her own photograph and medical records."

"Except for the dental records," the technician interjected. "Those she did not need for her purposes. But I have cross-checked them both against this cadaver, and there is no doubt that this person was Emilia Malinin."

"And according to your early report, Emilia Malinin was from the town of Bronnitsky, a childhood friend of Mikhail Olenov's," Markelov stated.

Aleksay nodded numbly. Emilia Malinin, posing as Claudia Mashkanstev had entered the government service in early 1988, at about the same time that she was supposed to have been killed in an automobile accident. It was obvious that the real Mashkanstev had been killed in that accident, and that she had been buried in Emilia's place.

"They are very thorough," Aleksay grumbled.

"Apparently," the technician agreed.

"Another piece of a growing puzzle," Markelov fretted.

"But it fits," Aleksay said. "They were the inside contacts. Of that there is now no doubt. But what of Petr Romanshin?"

"The assassin?" Markelov speculated hopefully.

"*Nyet!* Never. He is a weakling. No, he was on the periphery. Someone else arranged this. Someone who had access to the West, to foreign contraband. This same person maneuvered these two into compromising themselves so that they would have to cooperate. That would would not be easy. He . . . or she . . . is obviously very adept."

"But who would have such access to the West besides . . . ?" Markelov cut himself short as the truth hit him.

"A foreign diplomat," Aleksay completed his thought. "And I think that Romanshin knows who it is."

Markelov turned to the technician. "Tell no one of this. I will keep the record in my files. Destroy the body!"

Aleksay looked once more at the beautiful young woman on the table. He felt sorry for one so young, so attractive, sacrificed in such a way. It angered him and he burned to find her killer and take revenge.

"Come with me, Aleksay," Markelov said and stamped out.

They did not speak until they had almost reached the main lobby of the Center. It was clear that Markelov was bothered by the extent of the conspiracy; it reflected poorly on his ability to maintain security. "Aleksay. I'm counting on you to get to the heart of this before anyone else becomes involved," he said at last.

Aleksay stopped and looked at his superior. They had known each other for many years, and he knew the man seldom revealed his inner self to anyone. But he saw the fear in his eyes, a fear that Markelov either could not or did not want to hide. "I understand, Comrade Colonel."

"The level of penetration is the highest ever achieved by a foreign source. It means that there are others still in government service."

"I will investigate everyone in the records department thoroughly."

"No. Leave that to me. Your duty is to find the assassin. He may be German, he may be English, he may be American, Israeli, evern Arab. But he must be found and eliminated, is that clear?"

"Yes, Comrade Colonel. It will be done."

One of El Presidente's huge Cadillac limousines swept through the steaming jungle toward the airport. Inside, Davis and Mercedes were silent. The storm had passed, but the sky was filled with lightning and the road was awash with

148

the run-off.

"I wish there was some way to delay this," he said at last. "But the President has just reassigned me to service."

"I understand," she said, unable to look at him.

"Thank your father again for lending me his limousine."

"He was very impressed with you. He asked me to have you extend his best wishes to President Parker."

"I will."

They rode on in silence for the better part of half an hour, until the driver turned off the main road onto the airport cutoff. The two-lane blacktop wound through the jungle for another two miles and finally emerged in the clearing cut from the Yucatan wilderness. The lights of a few buildings burned intrusively in the sullen stillness of the night. The field was deserted. Only when they approached the terminal did they see the armed sentries languishing at their posts.

The soliders jumped to attention at the sight of El Presidente's car, and hurried out to greet it, snapping to a sharp attention by the curbside. One of them opened the rear door and saluted as Mercedes emerged. They all looked surprised to see Davis follow her.

Together, he and Mercedes walked past the chain link fence into the terminal proper, while the guards brought his luggage. There was still no sign of the plane. He turned to her and smiled resolutely.

"I'll wait until your plane comes," she said.

"You don't have to."

"I know." Again they were silent as the soldiers deposited his bags on the concourse and took up positions at a respectful distance.

"When will I see you again?" she asked, her voice almost breaking.

He hesitated, wanting to tell her the truth but unable to. He wanted more than anything else to see her again, but knew that the probability of it was slim. "I don't know."

Suddenly she embraced him, holding onto him desperately. "I wish you didn't have to go!" she sobbed under her breath.

"I do too, but I have no choice. I promise you, it won't be long."

149

She accepted this even though she sensed he was lying. Suddenly, the roar of jet engines split the jungle silence and the landing lights of the charter jet appeared out of the threatening sky. It passed overhead, and the field lights were switched on by the guards in the control tower.

"Roger," she said, her voice quavering. "I told you tonight that I loved you. I've never told anyone else that in my life. I meant it. Whether you love me or not, I can't change the way I feel. You are the only happy thing in my life, the only thing I have to live for. No matter what happens, I will always feel that way about you."

He started to speak, but she put a finger to his lips to silence him, then kissed him lightly. "Don't. You don't have to explain anything to me. I gave my love to you freely, and you returned it. I want to remember it just that way. If we never see each other again, we will always have tonight."

He held her tight, memorizing how she felt in his arms, the smell of her hair, the taste of her lips, the glistening desire in her eyes.

The harsh blue landing lights of the jet swept through the open side of the terminal, and they watched in silence as it swept down over the blackened tree tops at the far end of the field and glided onto the wet tarmac. With a roar, the plane slowed quickly to taxi speed and approached the terminal. The night creatures cried out in protest from the forest.

He looked into her eyes, searching for the right words. "Mercedes, what I feel for you is something I've never felt for any other woman in my life. I don't know if the word love describes it, but you're the only person in my life that I truly care for." He kissed her and she began to weep softly as their lips parted. But by the expression on her face, they were tears of happiness. "Take care of yourself," he said. "I don't know where I'm going to be, but if I can I'll let you know soon."

"Oh, Roger. Promise me you won't forget me . . . promise me I'll see you again."

"I promise," he said.

He held her tightly as the soldiers carried his bags to the waiting plane, then reluctantly released her. It was time. He left her with a gentle kiss and walked across the wet pavement to the open hatch of the Sabre jet. The second officer saluted him, and the soldiers snapped to attention as he boarded the plane. He turned once and waved to her. Still standing at the edge of the terminal, she returned his parting gesture.

Within minutes they were streaking down the short runway toward the black wall of jungle. The pilot lifted the nose and the jet thrust sharply into the night sky toward low hanging clouds. From his seat, he watched as the lights of the terminal fell away. Just before they slipped into the clouds he spotted the twin beams of the limousine's headlights winding along the narrow road to the main highway.

Then there was only the impenetrable shroud of gray around the plane. He closed his eyes and thought of what the future held. He knew the President's plans were bold and dangerous. The chances of his ever seeing Mercedes again were remote, and he silently prayed to whatever universal force might be watching over them that if they never were together again, she would find happiness in her lonely world.

The plane tossed violently, but he was asleep within minutes.

. . . 10 March 1989

Bruce hurried down the corridor to the Oval Office, in his hand the statement he had given to Kathy at two that morning. Tucked under his arm was a copy of the morning *Post*, and the banner headlines were alarming: "City Mayors Rebuffed by Parker."

He paused in the outer office, and Shirley looked up. It was clear from the scowl on her face, that the President had already been on the warpath.

"I take it he's in?"

"He's expecting you."

Bruce drew a deep breath and opened the inner office door. He found the President pouring over the front page, but he was not prepared for the expression on his face. It was a look of amusement, even victory.

"Excuse me, Mr. President. You sent for me?"

Parker looked up, trying with some effort to conceal a smirk. "Good morning, Bruce. Sit down. How about some coffee?"

"Uh, no thank you, sir. I've already had mine. I see you've seen the headlines."

"Yes. He's hung himself this time, hasn't he?"

"Excuse me, sir?"

"Benest. He's thrown the first punch."

"But . . ." Bruce opened his copy of the paper and looked at the smaller headlines of a feature article: "Benest Draws Bead on White House Policy."

"Oh. I haven't read that article, sir. I was talking about Kathy's . . . I mean Miss Karpovich's piece."

"Yes, I read that. Thanks for drafting that statement. I hope she didn't keep you up half the night?" Parker's tone implied more than his statement, and Bruce flushed.

"No, sir. It was no trouble. But I didn't expect her to come down quite so hard on your position."

"Freedom of the press, Bruce. I'm glad it's out in the open. The sooner the public sees my position, the sooner they are likely to agree with me."

"Not the citizens of those cities."

"They didn't vote for me anyway."

"True. That's very true."

"No, this Benest article is what I'm pleased with. The press is going to have a field day, making me look like a bastard, and at the right moment, I'm going to drop a bombshell."

"Sir?"

"Just between you and me, Bruce, I've got a dossier on that son of a bitch an inch thick, linking him with every major underworld figure in the country, going back to 1956. Let them make him out to be a patron saint, then I'll release this to a federal grand jury and see if labor doesn't come into line with their kingpin under indictment." Parker chuckled to himself.

Bruce's jaw dropped. "You'd actually do it? Take on organized crime and labor?"

"You're damn right! Some of my predecessors might have let labor and organized crime run free, but not *this* boy. I want this to come out after the labor lobbyists have sunk their claws in and after Congress has bogged down in debates over my policies. This is my hole card."

Parker was silent a moment and Bruce fidgeted as he returned the President's gaze. At last Parker asked, "What's your relationship with Karpovich?"

"Sir?"

"She's quite a looker isn't she? Got a reputation, I hear."

"I wouldn't know anything about that, sir. I only know her professionally."

Parker again laughed out loud. "I don't care if you know her like Adam knew Eve. That's your business. Frankly, it wouldn't hurt us for you to get to know her better if you don't already. We can leak the kind of information that can help us through her. Discreetly of course."

153

Bruce was flustered and couldn't find anything to say. Parker continued to amaze him.

"Relax, Bruce. It's in the family. Now, I want you to work up a statement responding to Benest's charges. Base it on my previously stated policies, nothing new. Just make the points clear and reiterate my determination to stop inflation and put this country back on the road to financial independence." Just then, Shirley buzzed on the intercom.

"Mr. Roger Davis to see you, sir."

"Oh, yes, Shirley. Show him in, will you?" He returned his attention to Bruce. "Work that up and let me go over it before you release it. And don't show any favoritism to your friend. We don't want to appear too well connected."

"Yes sir. I'll get right on it."

Bruce rose at the sound of the opening door and turned to see the tall blond man stepping past Shirley into the Oval Office. As before, at Camp David, Bruce was struck immediately by the coldness of the man's vivid blue eyes. He stared for an instant, mesmerized.

"Thank you, Bruce."

"Oh, yes sir. Excuse me," he said and slipped past Davis. As he did, he noticed again the thin white scar under the man's right eye and felt suddenly chilled. Shirley closed the door behind him.

"Come in, Mr. Davis. Have a seat."

"Thank you, sir."

"Did you have a good flight?"

"A little bumpy, but pleasant enough. I slept most of the way."

"Sorry to drag you away from your vacation, but something's come up." He buzzed Shirley. "Shirley, hold all calls," he said and regarded Davis thoughtfully. "I'll get right to the point, Mr. Davis. How do you feel about carrying out certain covert operations on a domestic level?"

Davis studied Parker for a long time before answering. He was aware of the implications and painfully conscious of the legislation under past Administrations severely limiting such activities. "That depends on the nature of the operation, Mr. President."

154

"I thought you'd answer something like that. Let me explain. You've seen the morning headlines?"

"Yes, sir. About the mayors?"

"No Benest of the COL."

"Oh, yes sir. Typical response. You apparently really put the screws to him."

"I asked for his cooperation and this is his response. Very unfortunate for him. You see, my domestic policies are going to call for voluntary cooperation among labor, business, and government. Now I know I'm going to have a hard time with the liberal faction on the Hill convincing them they can't go on spending like there was no tomorrow. And I'm going to have a tough time convincing the welfare leeches that they're going to go off the sugar tit and start earning a living. Business is going to go along with me all the way because they want the tax credits and reinvestment incentives. But if labor opposes me, that's going to make the whole thing damn near impossible to pull off."

"How do I fit in?"

"I've got a dossier on Benest that will hang him in any federal court in the land. But I'd much rather not use it. That could get messy and the whole thing could be drawn out for years; and time is something we don't have enough of. We've got to convince labor to go along with us, make the average worker responsive to the general welfare and the idea of prosperity in the long run. That's a hard concept to sell to people who have been used to regular raises. How do you persuade them to suddenly limit their own upward mobility, especially when the leading union boss is not in the frame of mind to lend his endorsement. I'm afraid it's going to take another type of persuasion, if you get my drift."

"I think I do sir."

"Of course, I'm not talking about anything immediate. But I want to convince labor that there is a higher authority in the land than Benest and organized crime. That might necessitate a show of power, maybe even force."

"I understand."

"Would you be willing to be involved in such activities?"

"If it will benefit the country, sir."

"Good. For now I'd like for you to familiarize yourself with Mr. Benest's history, his life style, his associations, and so on. This dossier will help you. It's the latest FBI file on him. As I've said, I could use this, but it would take too long. We can't afford that."

"I agree. May I suggest a surveillance?"

"It's already established. You'll find all the information you need in that file."

"Then I'll get on it right away, sir."

"Thank you, Mr. Davis. I knew I could count on you."

Kathy had returned to the office in time to get the story in the late edition. Then she had gone home for a few hours sleep. She awoke late, and took a hurried shower, eager to get to the paper and follow up on her exclusive. She was totally pleased with herself; the situation with Bruce promised to become more and more productive.

He was waiting for her in the dim recess of the stairwell, his glasses misted from having just come in out of the cold. His thin body trembled slightly in the icy stillness. He heard the door open, the sound of footsteps on the stairs. When she paused at the mailbox he spoke, his voice soft but challenging.

"Have you forgotten my instructions, Miss Karpovich?"

She wheeled to face him, dropping her mail at her feet, and froze. He stepped out of the shadows, looking carefully up the stairs. They were alone.

"Perhaps you thought that I was joking? I assure you I was not. I am prepared to go to your publishers this very morning with enough evidence to cost you your job and possibly send you to jail."

She gasped but could make no response.

"But all of this is unnecessary if you simply agree to cooperate. My government is eager to work with you. You see, because of your association with the SDS and the anti-Vietnam war movement, we suspect that your sympathies are not dissimilar to ours."

"That was twenty years ago!"

"Come, come, Miss Karpovich. Are you so changed from the days of your involvement with the Weather Underground and the disturbances at the 1968 Democratic convention in Chicago?"

"I was a kid! I didn't know any better! I wasn't responsible for . . ."

"You weren't responsible for planting the plastic explosives in the mail box in front of the Marine recruitment station in 1972? You weren't responsible for the maiming of the young postman in the subsequent explosion?"

"Stop it!" she screamed. "I didn't know anyone was going to get hurt! We only wanted to frighten them!"

"Oh, but someone was hurt. That young postman was the father of three small children. He now must be constantly nursed by his wife when she is not working at menial tasks for the neighbors. You see, a postman's pension is very small, Miss Karpovich. It is another criminal example of the evils of capitalistic society."

Kathy's mind reeled as the memories came swirling back. For years, she had lived a life free from her past. But, suddenly, the spectre of her mistakes loomed up from the ashes and threatened to destroy the career she had struggled so hard to create.

"It would be a shame," the Russian continued, "for such information to become public. I do not think that the *Washington Post* would like a former student radical, who is still wanted on a John Doe by the FBI, on their payroll. It would hardly be good for business, as you Americans say it."

"This is blackmail!" she cried in desperation.

"Worse than that, I'm afraid. If you do not cooperate, we will turn over our information to the FBI and the Secret Service. You will be arrested and charged with crimes against the state. Your association with Bruce Wilson will become public knowledge, and the Administration will be humiliated. You will most likely go to prison for a very long time."

"And if I do cooperate?"

"You will be able to enjoy a prosperous career in public relations with SPEC Technologies. You will live well, make many new friends, make a lot of money, which somehow has become important to you, and be free of criminal prosecution. All it requires is your cooperation. The choice is yours. Happiness and prosperity or . . ." he let his voice trail off, and shrugged his shoulders.

Pulling his collar around his face, he brushed past her into the swirling eddies of snow that had begun to fall in the early morning hours.

Kathy felt her knees give way; her bladder released fouling her clothes, and she fell trembling and sobbing to the floor. It took her several minutes to regain control. Feebly she climbed the stairs and managed to let herself into her apartment. Once inside, she bolted the door and staggered to the bathroom. She stripped off her soiled clothing and rinsed it out in the tub, then took a long shower.

Afterwards, she made coffee and laced it with Scotch, then sat for a long time trying to sort out her next move. She couldn't bring herself to believe what was actually happening. Since leaving the radical movement in 1972, she had divorced herself of all former associations, changed her name, and moved from New York City, covering her tracks. Everyone involved in planting the bomb in the mailbox had done the same, because of the tragic results. Since then it had been their own horrible secret—they thought. But somehow, the Russians knew.

Were they bluffing? What would happen if she were to go to the FBI with the whole story? Would they believe her? Would they grant her immunity from prosecution in order to turn state's evidence against the Russians? She had seen enough plea bargaining in her journalism career to know that she might possibly get off with a suspended sentence. But her career would be over; in fact her whole way of life would be over. She had grown accustomed to her privileged position at the *Post*. She craved the power of rubbing shoulders with the most important people in the country. Gone would be the White House visits, the trips to foreign countries, the excitement of her semicelebrity life style. And what about her future? There would be no anchor spot on the national news. How could she give it all up?

And then there was the possibility that the FBI wouldn't play ball, or if they did, she would be the ball. What if they took her information and used it against her? She had a history of being an outspoken student leader from an era fraught with bad feelings on both sides of the law. Could she ever hope to find justice in the courts? Would she end up in prison?

She realized that she had no other choice but to cooperate with the Russians. It would mean leaving her position at the *Post*, lowering herself to a public relations job. But maybe if she went along with the game, they would eventually release her from her obligations. Then she could return to journalism. A little older maybe, but still her reputation would be intact and she would be free to pursue her career.

It was a possibility, she told herself. She had to tell herself that. It was the only way she could make her feet carry her down the stairs and out to her car. She found herself driving aimlessly in the direction of the Potomac. Suddenly she realized that the SPEC labs were located on the Potomac, not far from the Pentagon. What was she doing? This was insane. She wasn't going to apply for that job! Her fear melted into anger as she flushed with embarrassment at the way she had been acting. Who the hell did they think they were?

She first noticed the dirty blue Dodge sedan as she turned east toward the river. It did not particularly stand out in the relatively heavy trafic on the snowy street, but she was suddenly aware that she had been conscious of it in her rear view mirror for some time. Inside were the dark figures of two men. Both wore hats. She strained to see their faces but it was impossible. Where they following her? Were they the Russians? Or perhaps the FBI or CIA?"

She told herself to get a grip on her nerves. She was beginning to imagine things. She didn't know if the car were following her or not, and if it were might it not be simply a coincidence? Of course. You're overreacting, she thought. Your mind is playing tricks. But she felt that she had to know for sure.

She made a hard right at the next intersection, but instead of punching it as her emotions urged, she eased the accelerator down aware that she could easily skid on the slushy road. Then she gradually increased her speed, and when she checked, she saw that the sedan had been stopped at the light. She could not see its blinker flashing and her heart jumped. Better not to take chances, she thought, and continued to accelerate.

The street she was on led to a light industrial district near the river. She had never been in that part of town, and soon became confused by the numerous cross streets and alleys. She reasoned, however, that if the car were following her, it would be better to turn onto a side road in hopes of losing it rather than to continue on this one. She chose the next street and turned left. The street wound around a gradual curve of dreary deserted-looking warehouses, and dead ended near the river. Her heart sank.

Doing her best not to panic, she put the car into reverse and with tires spinning backed around and headed up the street in the direction from which she had come. If they had not seen her turn, wouldn't it be best to stop and wait there and hope they would give up the search? But if they had seen her turn, what would they do if they caught her? She glanced around at the lifeless buildings slipping by. There was no one around to help her if they did.

Breathlessly, she approached the intersection with the main road and stopped at the light. There was a steady stream of traffic coming from the right, but none from the left, and there was no sign of the blue sedan. She turned right and eased her foot to the floor, speeding toward the bridge leading over the Potomac, her heart pounding in her throat.

As she reached the bridge, it was suddenly there again in her rear view mirror. She had not seen it pull out. But the blue sedan was directly behind her. She desperately fought the urge to try to outrun them, knowing it would be hopeless on the icy streets. She began to tremble as a wave of nausea overwhelmed her.

On the other side of the bridge was an exit for SPEC Technologies. She took it at the last minute, sliding dangerously through the banking curve. To her horror, the blue sedan did the same. Tears blinded her, increasing her panic. The SPEC parking lot came into view. Visitor's Parking, the sign read. She whipped off the street and skidded to a stop just short of the gate. The startled guard stepped out looking annoyed.

Kathy glanced over her shoulder and watched the blue sedan drift by. She couldn't get a clear look at the men inside. But at the last minute she caught sight of the license tag. A diplomatic plate! For the second time that morning, she felt as if her bladder were going to release. Her mind was made up. She was going to apply for the job.

Aleksay sat passively on a wooden stool, staring at the pale face of Petr Romanshin. Although his cuts were healing and his lips had returned to their normal size, his face was sallow and yellowed by the severe bruises inflicted during his interrogations. Enormous black circles ringed his sunken eyes, and when he spoke the jagged remnants of broken teeth glinted in the cold light. He stood near the center of the room in a small circle painted on the floor.

The room they occupied was bare cement twelve feet on a side. The floor sloped to a three-inch drain in the center. There was no furniture save for a stool. A faucet and hose jutted from the wall near the only door, which was solid steel with a tiny grating that opened from the outside. Once inside this tomb, time ceased to exist; day and night became irrelevant; life and death were figments of the imagination.

Aleksay spoke with the same regular cadence and cajoling tone he had managed to maintain for the past forty minutes. "Petr. We know that you and Mikhail Olenov and Emilia Malinin were friends. We know that you kept close ties with each other. You have admitted that you and Mikhail were involved in the sale of contraband. Yet you refuse to acknowledge any connection with Emilia Malinin concerning this activity."

"She was not involved in the sale of contraband. I have told you that repeatedly. Why won't you believe me?"

"When was the last time you saw her?"

"I don't remember. I don't even know what day this is."

"This is March 10."

"I can't remember the exact date."

"Approximately, then."

"Three months ago, perhaps."

"I see. And who was she with?"

"Mikhail."

"Where were they?"

"We were having dinner at Mikhail's apartment."

"The three of you?"

"Yes."

"There was no one else?"

"No."

"What did you speak of at this dinner?"

"I don't remember."

"Try."

"I can't."

"You must!" It was the first time Aleksay had raised his voice, and Petr flinched.

"It was just talk between friends."

"They are very old friends of yours, aren't they?"

"Yes."

"They are perhaps the closest friends you have?"

"Yes."

"They are both dead!" Aleksay snarled, his face contorting brutally.

Petr reeled as if he had been struck and stared in horror at his inquisitor. "I don't believe you!"

Aleksay picked up a file folder from the floor and took out two black and white photographs. He held them out to Petr. "See for yourself."

Petr hesitated, afraid to look.

"Take them. See for yourself." Aleksay's tone was once again blasé.

Petr took the photographs which had been taken by the KGB at the scene of the murder. Mikhail's body lay crumpled against an ancient china cabinet, his brains spilling out of a gaping hole in his skull. Emilia's body lay completely exposed on the bed next to Said's hulk. Her face and the hole in her forehead were clearly visible. Petr cried out and began to vomit, staggering back against the wall for support.

Aleksay sat motionless as he retched, and only spoke when his spasms had passed. "Do you have any idea who might have killed them?"

"No," Petr sobbed.

"Do you know that Emilia Malinin was a whore?"

"No! You're lying!"

"What do you think she was doing in bed with that fat pig you see in the picture there?"

"I don't know. I don't know. Let me alone!"

"Was she your lover?"

"No!"

"Was she Mikhail's lover?"

"No! Yes. Once. A long time ago in Bronnitsky."

"Did you know that Emilia Malinin supposedly died on January 13 of last year?"

Petr stared at him in bewilderment. "If I had known that, do you think I would have told you that I saw her three months ago?"

"No, and because of that, I think that you are not involved in their murders."

"How could I be . . ."

"Silence! Return to your spot!"

Petr moved on trembling legs to the circle in the middle of the floor.

"Since you were not involved with their murders, surely you are willing to help us find the guilty party?"

"Yes, of course!"

"Tell me where you got the contraband you sold."

"I've told you. Mikhail got it. He would not tell me where. He said it was better that I did not know."

"Did Emilia Malinin have any other friends? A lover perhaps?"

Petr remained silent.

"I asked you a question. Did Emilia Malinin have a lover?"

"I'm not sure."

"That is not an answer."

"I'm not sure. I think she was seeing someone, but she was very secretive about her private affairs."

"Why do you think she had another lover?"

"Mikhail said something about . . . I think he was still in love with her."

"Did Emilia ever discuss her work?"

"Never."

"Not even to say what she did?"

"No."

"Did that not strike you as suspicious?"

"I never told her what I did."

"What did Mikhail say about Emilia's lover?"

"I can't remember."

"He must have said something."

"Let me think. I can't think. Give me time!" Petr's nerves were reaching the breaking point under Aleksay's continued harangue. "He said that she was seeing someone. That he was worried because it was dangerous for her to be seeing that person. That if she were caught, she would be in a great deal of trouble."

Aleksay's eyes sparkled with excitement; at last they were making progress. "Why was that?"

"I don't know."

"Did Mikhail know the man?"

"Yes."

"Was he a friend?"

"Once."

"What do you mean?"

"I mean that the man was once his friend, but that Mikhail resented him for seeing Emilia."

"How do you know he was Mikhail's friend?"

"He used to give him things."

"Like what?"

"Luxuries. Liquor, cigarettes . . ."

"What kind of cigarettes?"

A look of realization came over Petr's face. "American cigarettes . . ."

Aleksay stiffened.

"Did it ever occur to you that Mikhail's friend could have been the person supplying him with the contraband?"

"I never thought of it."

"Think of it now!"

"I suppose it could be true."

"And if Emilia were caught with that man, most likely an American, most likely a diplomat, naturally she would be in grave trouble, since she was working for the government," Aleksay stated.

"Yes. Yes, it could be. It could be." Petr looked hopeful. He was aware that the interview was concluded, and he prayed against all possibility that he would soon be released from this manmade hell.

"Thank you, Petr. You have been a great help to me." He rose to leave.

"You will help me, won't you?" Petr asked. "I've tried to cooperate. You will speak well of me at my trial!"

Aleksay turned to Petr with a blank look on his face. "I assure you Petr that your troubles will soon be over."

He left the wretch pondering the meaning of this statement. Outside, after the steel door had been closed, Aleksay turned to the guard. "Kill him," he said.

It was late when Aleksay returned to his single-room apartment in the projects near the Center. It was a plain room, with simple furniture, a well-worn rug, an old stove, and a noisy refrigerator. But it had a window that faced south, and on clear days sunshine flooded the room. It was all that he required, for he was seldom home.

Already, the sun had set, and a cold wind shook the glass in the window frame. He pressed a ragged towel tightly against the sill to keep out the draft, but it could not block out the lonesome howling of the wind. It brought back memories of the orphanage, the cold tile floors, the dark crowded dormitories. It was there that Colonel Markelov had first found him.

He remembered the day clearly as if it were yesterday. It had been grey and bitterly cold. The night before, Aleksay had beaten an older boy brutally with a chair for suggesting a homosexual act. He had been placed in isolation, and Markelov had come to observe him, to evaluate him. They had spent that dreary day in conversation about his likes and dislikes, his hobbies, his dreams for the future.

Shortly after that he had been transferred to a special school for boys near the Baltic Sea. Those had been the happiest days of his childhood. There was farming, athletics, sailing in the summers, and plenty of good food. He had not even minded the long hours in the classroom or the military regimen of their daily life. He found that he thrived in the face of challenges, that he learned quickly, and Markelov gave him hours of special attention, grooming him for the years to come when they would work together.

There was great affection between the two, and he wanted more than anything else to solve the riddle that now threatened his mentor's career. He also sensed an adversary of extreme ability against whom he was eager to match his skills.

He made himself a steaming bowl of potato soup and sipped it contentedly by the heat of the stove as he thumbed through the new file which he had obtained on his way home. It was an exact accounting of all international travel of foreign diplomats stationed in Moscow over the past two years. Any passage in or out of the Soviet Union was logged by date, destination, flight number, time of day, return date and time, and intervals between trips for each individual. The section he had brought with him dealt only with the American Embassy corps.

He skimmed the pages looking for the most frequently repeated names, and soon one stood out above all others. Roger Davis, Deputy Ambassador, assigned to the Embassy in 1987; November 4 to be precise. During the man's first three months in Moscow, he had traveled to the West nine times, most of the time staying less than a week. His destinations were varied: London, Paris, Rome, and once to the United States.

During the following months, the man had made fourteen more sojourns at irregular intervals. That information in itself was not damning. Many attachés traveled regularly throughout Europe during the course of their tenure at the Embassy.

But he stared with intense interest at the date of the man's last departure. December 25, 1988. He had left Moscow at six A.M. less than four hours after the assassination of Ali Said. He checked for a return flight entry. There was none. Quickly, he cross-referenced the man with the present Embassy staff. Davis was no longer assigned; he had been transferred to duty in the United States!

Coincidence? Possibly, but highly unlikely. The pieces fell too neatly into place. His numerous trips would have given him ample opportunity to secure contraband for Mikhail's operation. Coupled with the other critical dates involved in the case—the supposed death of Emilia Malinin on January 13, 1988, her enlistment under an assumed name a week later, and Davis' final departure from Moscow on December 25—the chance for coincidence diminished considerably.

There was one more reference for him to check before he was sure. The domestic surveillance of all Embassy officials' movements in or around Moscow. That file would hold the proof he would need to make his move.

He arrived at the Center just after ten o'clock. The night was thoroughly disagreeable, and snow clouds hung low over the city. He went directly to the Section for Domestic Surveillance and requested the file on the American Embassy for the period begining November 4, 1987, and ending December 25, 1988.

Within fifteen minutes, he was seated in another dim cubicle, scouring the pages of the binders, searching for the one item he needed to close the investigation. There was page after page of detailed surveillance. He checked the index for Davis' name and found there was a substantial amount of information on him.

By eleven, he found the evidence. On the night of September 5, 1988, Roger Davis had been seen entering an apartment house on Peski Street; 497 Peski Street! His stomach felt hollow, his mouth dry. His palms were wet and he felt the beads of perspiration forming on his brow.

The fools! The incompetent imbeciles! There was the

proof! Had they not thought to investigate who lived at that address? If they had they would have known that Claudia Mashkanstev, whose real name was Emilia Malinin, had lived at 497 Peski Street, and that she was in the employ of the state. How could they have been so blind? Malinin had gone over to the Americans. She had entered the service and survived for nearly a year. That meant there were still others involved, as Markelov had suspected. Their entire system had failed to detect the most blatant violation of security, and the result had been disastrous.

He closed the file wondering how he would break the news to Markelov. He knew what a blow it would be, but he had no other choice. At least now he would be able to close the case and avenge this act of aggression. From that moment on, Davis was a marked man.

. . . 24 March 1989

For the better part of two weeks, Davis had spent every waking hour studying his quarry. George Benest was a creature of habit, he had learned, who rose precisely at five-thirty each morning, took ten minutes of mild calisthenics, then showered and dressed for breakfast, which was served in his suite at six A.M.

He ate a meal of two poached eggs, a stack of toast with butter, half a grapefruit, and several cups of black coffee. Davis watched him through a telescope from a nearby apartment building, and often thought how easy a target the man made himself.

By seven, Benest was invariably on the phone to his colleagues in other parts of the country. He spent most of the morning running his empire in this manner. Whom he spoke to was a matter of record on lengthy tapes currently on file at the FBI. The President had commissioned a microwave monitoring system similar to the one used by the Russians against the American Embassy in Moscow during the sixties and seventies. Of course, this had been done without a federal warrant, because Benest had more than one federal judge on his payroll who would promptly advise him of any request for a wiretap or listening device directed his way.

Usually by noon Benest had concluded his routine business, and prepared for either a luncheon speech or business conference that took him out of The Madison. These activities were always planned months in advance and so were easy to allow for in scheduling surveillance. Davis never bothered to attend any of these functions, not caring to listen to overblown rhetoric.

As far as his afternoons were concerned, Benest sometimes

traveled by private jet to New York, Boston, Chicago, or Cleveland — any of the relatively nearby cities — to confer with locals and lend his support to whatever labor action happened to be in progress at the time. On these occasions, he was almost always back at The Madison by seven in the evening, at which time he would take an hour to recuperate over drinks and small talk with his advisors or close personal associates. The man didn't have any close friends; friendship would make him vulnerable. In his long career he had been noted as a loner, a ruthless negotiator, and a conscienceless motivator of underlings who carried out the dirty business he masterminded.

Often, at dinner, he entertained well-known politicians, both national and local, and some of the most infamous of underworld figures. They were his power base, and their cooperation enabled him to hamstring big business in more ways than through labor manipulation. These were facts well known to the FBI, and all were carefully detailed in the thick briefing that Parker had given to Davis in their meeting on the tenth.

Benest's connection to organized crime naturally gained him access to the world of big gambling, and he was personally involved in various operations from Las Vegas, to Reno, to Atlantic City, as well as the recent meccas established in Miami Beach, Galveston, New Orleans, and Mexico. In point of fact, many of the new operations opened in these areas were funded in part by the massive pension funds of the major unions.

Gambling had become the biggest business in the country after the opening of Atlantic City. Crippling inflation, dwindling gasoline supplies, and soaring prices at the pump had throttled the resorts, and it had been necessary to open more areas to legal gambling in order to revitalize the tourist trade. The alternative was to close down, leaving billions of dollars in hotel investments moldering under lock and key.

Miami Beach had been the first to convert, despite fierce local opposition and several special elections in which the repeated attempts to legitimize gambling had failed. Galveston had followed quickly, sensing the opportunity for rebirth after the years of gradual decay that had set in after World War II; and soon after came New Orleans, whose French Quarter and deteriorating inner city had reduced that city to a thin shell, crumbling within from a collapsing tax base and eroding tourist trade.

What was interesting to note, and frightening as well, was the fact that somewhere in the rank and file of nearly every new entertainment corporation that had sprung up in response to the gambling boom, there was at least one of Benest's hand-picked lieutenants looking out for the union's investments, which meant that Benest had enormous influence in an expanding and rich power base.

It was not hard to see for anyone who cared to look that, with the exception of the President, the military hierarchy, and a few of the legitimate industrial magnates, Benest was probably the most powerful man in the United States. Because of this, when George Benest spoke, Washington and every major industry in the country listened.

Everywhere that Benest went, he was accompanied by four of the biggest, most dangerous-looking henchmen conceivable. Each was reputed to be a combat-tested killer who had risen through the ranks of the underworld to their esteemed, albeit infamous, positions of trust and responsibility by ruthless and mindless adherence to their employers' directives. Yet despite all of these well-known facts, the legal system had failed to act against this self-proclaimed modern Caesar. After all, what was good for George Benest was good for the U.S.A., and if someone dared to think otherwise, he was prone to end up in cement waders.

Davis found Benest to be a most uninteresting prospect. Where Said had been cunning and politically astute, if somewhat misguided, Benest was brash, and brazenly open about his throttlehold on the country. Privately, Davis wondered just how far Parker would be willing to go with Benest. Intuition told him all the way, and he looked forward to the day when he would stand over the union boss and dictate the terms of an even high authority. It would take time, he knew, just as Said had; but he consoled himself with the knowledge that someone had once called patience a virtue. It was perhaps the only virtue he, Davis, had.

During this period, he thought often of Mercedes, of the brief tenderness they had shared and the abruptness of his departure which he knew he could never explain to her. It had been impossible to contact her and would be until his operation was concluded. This caused him some anxiety. Unlike most women he had known, she was untouched by the troubles of the world, partly because of the sheltered existence she had been forced to endure. To her, a serious complication was a cloudy day in Acapulco, which prevented her from basking in the sun. He marveled at her simplicity, and the fact that someone like her could exist in this world. The women he had known were from his world; calloused, hardcore products of treachery. Through necessity, or sometimes boredom, he had slept with many of them, but with never the hint of compassion.

There had been one exception besides Mercedes. That had been a long time ago, shortly after he had joined the CIA in Europe. She had been his first contact in Berlin, which at that time was crawling with double agents on both sides. Berlin was, to put it figuratively, a simmering cauldron of intrigue and betrayal, laced with sex and strychnine. One false move could have been deadly, and in his case almost was. The woman he had thought he could trust had gone over to the other side, sacrificing him as proof of her allegiance.

He had survived the ordeal thanks to his wits and superior skill, but it had destroyed the last remnant of trust he had in humanity. It was decided officially that he should die, and legally he did. That was a strange experience; death always is, especially when one must witness his own demise from the sidelines. Ties with the past were forever broken, friends and relatives were committed grief. With the passage of time, all traces of his existence were erased. He had taken the name Roger Davis, and since then . . . he had lived as a man no one knew or could ever know. He was isolated in a world full of people, but it was his way of life, the only way he could hope to survive

For the present, he was committed to a relatively mundane existence, free of practically all danger. And, it was sadly devoid of the one thing on Earth he would have given up everything for—the woman he found himself missing night and day.

Two weeks to the day after her interview with SPEC Technologies, Kathy received a phone call at her desk in the newsroom. She was hard at work on a piece about the upcoming renewed START negotiations, and picked up the phone expecting to hear her editor ranting about the deadline.

"Miss Karpovich?" a man's voice said.

"Yes."

"I'm calling about your application for the public relations job at SPEC Technologies."

"Yes?" Kathy felt her heart beating rapidly. She had prayed that she would be rejected. She had done her best to blow the interview.

"I thought that you would like to know that you've got the job if you still want it." The man's voice was strangely impersonal and chilling.

She paused. She wanted to hang up. Since the interview her terror had waned into the feeling left by a bad nightmare. The man's voice on the line rekindled that nightmare and reminded her of the serious and possibly dangerous nature of the work she would be doing for the Russians. But try as she might, she could not lower the receiver to its cradle. She was too afraid of what might happen if she failed to follow through.

"Yes. That's fine," she replied, trying to sound enthusiastic.

The man continued without a hint of interest in her feelings. "Naturally, we have had to run a security check on you, due to the nature of the work conducted here at SPEC, and you'll be glad to know that you checked out just fine. When can you begin?"

"Well, I'm not sure. I've got to give notice here. Probably not for another week or two." There was an icy silence at the other end of the line. "Unless that's too long," she added quickly.

"No. A week will be fine. You will report to the personnel office."

"I see."

"Do you have any questions?" the man asked.

"No, I don't think so." She had thousands of them, all unspeakable, and most assuredly unanswerable for the present.

"Very well, then. We'll look for you in a week."

The man hung up with a decisive click, and Kathy stared at the phone for many minutes afterward. She wondered how it had all been arranged so easily. Certainly the implication was that SPEC was already infiltrated by the Russians. Why then did they need her? Desperately she thought of calling back and refusing the job. There was still time to go to the FBI. But she didn't. She stoically typed her resignation and sealed it in an envelope. She was committed, no matter what the future held. Only time would tell if she would ever be free from her past.

. . . 3 August 1989

Death Valley is, in geological terms, a graben or rift valley; a depression in the Earth's crust sprawled between two parallel uplifted and tilted fault-block mountain ranges. The Panamint and the Last Chance mountains jut skyward from the desert floor, forming the western border of the great basin. To the east, the Black Mountains, the Funeral Mountains, and the Grapevine Mountains make up the Amargosa Range.

Of these, the Black Mountains are the most recent orogeny, their rugged lower slopes showing little erosion from the chiseling dry winds that sweep the valley floor. The basin itself was formed some ten to thirty million years ago, at the beginning of the Miocene Epoch, and has been sinking ever since.

Through the eons, it has been filled with hundreds of feet of alluvial sediment washed down from the peaks and mountain canyons by the flash floods which follow the few winter cloudbursts that account for almost all of the region's two- to three-inch annual rainfall.

In primeval times, successive lakes were formed by the prodigious runoff from these storms, but the last great inland sea evaporated nearly a million years ago when the present dry climatic phase began. Now only faint strands and traces of ancient beaches mark the parameters of the waters that once stretched for nearly one hundred miles with depths of over six hundred feet.

Much of the basin floor is barren sand and salt deposits, and only for one brief period has man's industry touched that Godforsaken hell pit, when the white gold salt sediments offered quick profits for the bold and hardy early miners. But when word came that the choice alluvium of the Mojave provided richer bounties, the pioneers moved on, leaving Death Valley once more to the lonely desert winds and the buzz of an occasional angry rattler.

Death Valley is a place that time and man would sooner forget and leave to some distant age when perhaps the basin will again fill with life-giving waters and a valley paradise will spout from the parched soil. It is a land totally hostile to human existence, named for the toll in lives of the unwary settlers who sought a short cut to the West and found only death in the blinding glare and lethal heat of that waterless wasteland.

A few highways cut bravely across the desert floor, from tourist outpost to gas station, to National Monument markers; and a trickle of travelers speed hastily over these lonely blacktops, conscious of the highway warning signs not to travel in the heat of summer, when temperatures rise to more than 120 degrees Farenheit in the shade.

To the north of the main east-west highway, U.S. 190, the earth rises slowly into the confluence of the bordering ranges, untouched by human habitation, unnoticed by all save the curious airline passenger who happens to peer from his window thirty-five thousand feet overhead to see the monochromatic patterns of mountain ridges descending to the shimmering sunblasted salt flats. For nearly sixty miles in a north-south direction, there is complete arid wilderness, a barrier stronger than any wall that man could build. Only in that timeless cavity in the Earth's crust could President Parker bring to fruition the plans he had nurtured for so long; only there could he be assured of the security that was imperative to the success of the Oasis Project.

The B-52 banked sharply and nosed into a gentle descent toward the desert floor, settling down like a great King Condor swooping from a mountain crag. On either side, two companion fighter bombers perched in formation on her wingtips. Miles and miles of white salt flats rushed by as the three jets dropped, the roar of their engines racking the silence; then the lumbering bomber touched down with a bump, sending clouds of salt dust flying into the air. The

176

two escort fighters peeled off and up into a wide circling pattern, their jets roaring.

The bomber drifted to a halt on the open tundra and cut its engines, returning the desert to its prehistoric state of solitude. General Owens, dressed in his summer uniform, was the first to emerge from the shimmering steel thorax of the metal bird. At the first blast of heat, he removed his handkerchief and mopped his brow as he stood in the shade of one enormous wing, surveying the unbroken horizon around him.

Parker and Kemper were the next to appear, followed closely by Montgomery, who was busy peeling off his suit coat and opening his shirt collar. The heat rose in sheets from the blinding sand, and there was not a breath of wind. The escort screamed by overhead, and vanished toward the distant Black Mountains.

Parker walked slowly out to the end of the wing and stood for many minutes staring into the distance. Out of the shimmering mirages, the mountains rose wavering before his eyes, seeming to float on a mercuric sea. Nothing he had ever read or heard about the place could have prepared him for the feeling of loneliness and isolation he now felt. He was pleased.

"Gentlemen, look around you," Parker said, his voice shattering the stillness. "What do you see?" They made no response. "Nothing!" he continued. "We're more than sixty miles from the nearest living human being, and between him and us lies the most hellacious land on God's green Earth." He walked back toward them and leaning down picked up a handful of the powdery white sand. "We're standing above what will soon be Oasis Project Headquarters. Within six months there will be a labyrinth of tunnels and caverns beneath our feet, hidden from above by the desert floor, protected from the outside world by this . . ." he let his voice trail off and waved his arm to indicate their surroundings.

Montie stooped to examine the soil, letting it drift through his fingers. General Owens watched him thoughtfully then faced the President.

"How in the hell are we going to keep an operation this

177

size under wraps, Don? The manpower needed to excavate the cavity alone will need a small city to house them and produce a jigsaw puzzle of security problems."

Parker looked at Arnold Kemper, who took the cue. "You've got to remember Ralph, that we're not operating under normal circumstances here. In fact, we're going to need only one-third the personnel we would require using conventional techniques. And those selected for the program will be screened and chosen for their specific qualifications and reliability."

"When will the laser be ready, Arnold?" Montie asked, rising and brushing the white dust from his trousers.

"For all intents and purposes, it's ready now. The impulse energy is operational at ninety percent of maximum capacity, and the sectional displacement we anticipate will be about 200 cubic yards per impulse; that's an area ten yards by twenty yards by one yard deep. The only factor holding us up is the overheating that will occur in these temperatures, but Dr. Sevrensen is developing a refrigeration unit to house the instrument, using liquid hydrogen as the coolant. So far, he seems pleased with the results, and he assures me that barring any complications the functional units should be ready within six to eight weeks."

"And you really think this device is going to speed up excavation?" Owens asked, clearly skeptical.

"Absolutely, Ralph. One laser can do the work of ten bulldozers in half the time. By blasting the sediment instead of excavating, most of the debris is removed, part is completely disintegrated, and much of the rest is altered into a crystalline silicon state. That means that the walls will be much more self-supporting and require less reinforcement. You see, the intense heat actually changes the silicon in the soil to a quartzlike hardness. With less reinforcement, we need less labor."

"How many laser units are you going to use in the primary excavation?"

"I've projected five, three working at all times. As I've explained, they'll be mounted in the belly of your jet hovercraft and will be fired from a height of two hundred feet for maximum sectional displacement. We'll work three shifts around the clock, and we estimate the main cavity can be hollowed out inside of two months, with construction following immediately on the roof structure. Once the roof is in and the area is refrigerated, we'll work four six-hour shifts, with auxiliary excavation continuing on minor chambers and corridors, until the entire complex has been carved out. Additional lasers mounted on sleds will be used for corridors and shaping the lesser compartments."

"I hope you know what you're talking about," Owens muttered in bewilderment.

"We hope so, too, Ralph," Kemper smiled.

"The Congress votes today on the Shuttle appropriations bill," Montie said. "Let's hope we have the votes."

"Preston assures me that we do," Parker said. He looked around in reverent silence at the vast emptiness of the valley. "Take a good look, gentlemen. After today, nothing will ever be the same."

"Jesus, it's too fucking hot!" Montie scowled and stomped off toward the hatch.

"I've seen enough," Parker agreed. "Let's have a cool drink and get our butts back to Washington."

"I'll second that, Don," Owens smiled, and they filed back into the enormous belly of the bomber, just as the fighters made another pass overhead and fanned out in opposite directions.

Soon the bomber was thundering across the flats, throwing up a plume of dust a hundred feet high, looking like an ungainly gosling on its first solo flight. But with speed came lift, and the huge wings flexed their steel sinews, raising it from the desert floor, streaking skyward in a sharp ascent. The fighters took up their positions on its wingtips. Somewhere over eastern Nevada, the men inside toasted the future with tall drinks and settled in for the long ride and serious discussion. There was a multitude of problems yet to be sorted out as well as solved. It was only a brave beginning.

* * *

Some three thousand miles away, in his penthouse suite at The Madison, George Benest was dealing with his own problems.

"Son of a bitch! The bastards passed it!" He threw the telegram to the table and scowled at his four sour-looking associates. Each in his turn picked up the communique and read it as Benest continued. "Thirty billion dollars to put satellites into outer space when we've got people out of work right here on Earth! Where the hell did he get the votes? What the hell kind of organization are we running here? Cubbi, you told me we had that bill killed!"

Cubbi Bertone frowned and flipped the paper to the man on his right. "The senator said we did." His tone was dangerous, intimating that he wasn't in the mood to be browbeaten by Benest or anyone else present.

In fact, none of the four were men to be used as scapegoats. Cubbi Bertone, swarthy and of medium height, was the head of the International Carriers Union. To his right was Alfredo Fontana, of the American Factory Workers Alliance. Larger and bulkier than Bertone, Fontana wore thick glasses that steamed up when he got excited. He was busy wiping them with his handkerchief.

To Benest's left sat Rudi Markowitz of the United Weavers Guild. He was older than the others, but very fit and shrewd as an old wolf. He sat cooly, his hands folded on the table, only his eyes moving while the telegram passed from one man to the next.

The last man, an old adversary of Parker's from the early days of their respective careers, was Wallace Penchinski of the International Brotherhood of Coal Miners. He was thin, frenetic, and dangerously impulsive.

"This fuckhead is challenging us to open warfare on the picket lines," Benest ranted. "Not only is he ramrodding through this kind of crap legislation, but he's holding out fat government contracts to big business in return for their pressuring us for across-the-board wage controls. And I'm here to tell you he isn't going to get away with it."

"Why don't we just knock the son of a bitch off?" Fontana muttered nervously, looking around the table for

180

possible support. The others were hardened veterans of many battles with difficult administrations, and each had more than once called a man's number for one reason or another. But none was willing to agree with him at that point, although Benest looked like he was seriously considering the possibility.

"Why don't you shut your mouth, Fredo?" Cubbi snapped. "We don't need that kind of talk right now. We can whip this cocky bastard into line without that kind of stuff."

"It's going to mean sticking together," Benest emphasized. "No side deals, no early settlements, no private interest intervention. It's all or nothing with Parker. I told you what he said to me."

"We've heard it, George," Markowitz said in a soft, chilling tone.

"Parker's a dangerous man," Penchinski scowled. "I've dealt with him for almost twenty years and I tell you that once he gets an idea in his head you can't beat it out of him. I've seen him close down an operation for twelve months. He took enormous losses, but he held out and we finally had to meet his terms — our people were starving."

"The problem is, this bill is going to provide lots of jobs," Fontana offered.

"Not for our people!" Bertone said angrily. "We got five thousand garbage workers on strike in New York City, and the trash is ass-deep on the sidewalks, but Parker cuts off the federal extensions and there's no way the city's going to make good the loans. The cities are going to go belly up, and then we've got real shit!"

Bertone was more hostile than the others and with good reason. His life for the past four months had been a continuous barrage of negotiations, legal battles, and wildcat strikes, all pointed at trying to force the crumbling city governments of New York, Cleveland, Chicago, and Detroit to accept the new contracts and maintain civil service manpower at their former levels before the cutbacks.

"So what're we gonna do about this Space Shuttle bill?"

Fontana asked.

"We can't do anything about the bill now, but we can sure as hell make it tough on 'em at Cape Canaveral. That means your boys, Cubbi, are going to have to slow up their supplies. Wildcat walkouts, missing shipments, unexplainable delays. Let them feel the pressure. When that program starts going over budget, then we got ammunition to use against Parker."

"What about the other bill before Congress? The welfare reform act?" Penchinski asked. "That thing is going to change the whole picture of employment in this country. Who ever heard of making a poor sap relocate to take a job or become ineligible for unemployment benefits?"

"Not only that, but there's no provision for organized labor in the present form of the bill," Benest fumed. "That means they can pay minimum wage in the work camps. Do you know what that can do to us? That's thousands of jobs out of our control. We ought to be getting a piece of the action!"

"I don't think it's got a chance," Cubbi said. "It's so full of unconstitutional provisions, the whole thing will bog down in committee. I mean, how can they limit the family size to three kids? Legally, how can they think of doing something like that?"

"They're not limiting the family size," Benest replied. "They're saying you got more than three kids—no additional benefits. But it'll have the same effect."

"I tell you it's un-American!"

"So what do we do?" Markowitz asked.

"We make it tough for them everywhere. Walkouts, shut downs, pickets, violence if we have to. We've got Parker's word that as long as he's in office, he's going to veto any measure to extend the federal loans to the eastern cities." Benest said.

"Doesn't he know that if the cities default all hell's gonna break loose? There's going to be rioting, looting; hell, business is going to make a mass exodus for the west coast. New York and every other eastern city in trouble is going to be a no-man's land." Fontana sounded close to hysteria.

182

"I'm tellin' you we got our work cut out for us," Cubbi said. "Those congressmen that are getting the benefits of these public works jobs are the ones who are taking it out of our back pockets. They're spreading the word that Parker is the messiah, and let me tell you the fever is catching on. Christ, except for the east coast, just about every other state in the union is in favor of more state's rights and what Parker calls 'responsibility for their own solvency.' Those assholes in Texas are bitching about having to sell us their oil and natural gas. Why don't we do more drilling off New Jersey, they want to know? Don't they understand we got major resorts up here? One big oil slick and our investments could be ruined. They treat New Jersey like it was some sort of shit pot!"

"Sure Cubbi, sure," Benest said. "But that ain't the issue here. The issue is, are we gonna let Parker take the country away from us? Because if this *new* bill gets passed, and the public works are allowed to hire people at minimum wage, we ain't got a pot to piss in."

"So what the hell do we do?"

"We shut this fucking country down!" Benest snarled. "Everywhere we got people, we start problems. Make the fat cats feel the heat, let them know who holds the strings. If they crumble, the President's support is going to go to hell, and we're back in the driver's seat."

Across the street in the surveillance headquarters, Davis and the FBI agent on duty exchanged smiles.

"You want a transcript of this?" he asked Davis.

"Yes. I think the President will be very interested to hear what these clowns are planning."

"I'll have the transcript ready first thing in the morning. Do you think they were serious about an attempt on Parker's life?"

"I suggest you pass the word along upstairs, have a complete team assigned to each one of these guys. There's no telling what they'll pull if they get desperate, and something tells me things are going to get pretty desperate before this is all over."

Kathy drove north along state highway 97, her eyes riveted on the dark road, barely aware of the white lines whipping by in the fringe of her headlights. Her destination was a diner near the intersection of 97 and Interstate 70 called Molly's Place. She had never been there before, and until only a few hours earlier, she had never even heard of the place.

He had called her at work on her private line, his voice muffled, as if he were speaking through his hand. Nevertheless, she had recognized his voice immediately. Calmly, as if he were an old friend, he had invited her to meet him at the diner, limiting what he said, knowing that the line would be tapped. He had only told her the time and place and to order two martinis.

Night had shrouded the green hillsides and trees in its veil. The air smelled sweet, the temperature was mild; but despite this, she felt cold inside and yearned for that first drink.

Her heart beat faster when she caught sight of the shabby little sign set back too far from the highway to notice unless one happened to be looking for it. At one time it must have been brightly lit, but only two bulbs burned now, and the word MOLLY'S was missing an "L."

She pulled into the partially paved parking lot and rolled to a stop just out of the glow of the single street lamp. Cars droned by on the highway, and for a few minutes, she sat silently in the dark, watching the blackened lot for some sign of movement. It was seven-thirty when she glanced at her watch; she was still ten minutes early. She took a deep breath, mustered the courage to open the door, and stepped out of the car fully expecting someone to jump out of the darkness. She was surprised to find herself untouched, standing in front of the battered front screen door, her pulse pounding in her temples so hard she thought she would faint.

She paused to look back at the lot and happened to notice

a late model Chevy slow down and glide by as if the occupants were looking for something. Her, perhaps? She turned and swung open the screen, pushing in through the glass-paned inner door, where she was greeted by the smell of stale beer, cheap country cooking, and the tinny complaining of a juke box, which was turned up just to the point of discomfort.

The place was surprisingly crowded, but scarcely anyone seemed to notice her as she stood in the doorway waiting to be seated as the sign requested. After a moment, a dumpy middle-aged woman with a blond beehive hairdo and heavy eye makeup appeared with several frayed menus in the crook of her arm, her jaws pumping on a wad of gum.

"One for dinner, honey?"

"Uh, no. Two." Kathy stammered. "A table near the rear, please."

The woman looked past her for the other person.

"I'm expecting someone," Kathy explained.

"Oh. Well, I don't know if we got anything in the back, honey. Let me check." She shuffled away to have a look, and Kathy felt the eyes of several men at the bar giving her the once over. She glanced to the side, without letting her head turn. Several semitanked fellows at the bar were watching her with dazed curiosity. She pretended not to notice.

"We just got one bussed," the waitress said, returning. "This way, honey." She led the way into the back, where the lights were dimmer and the sound of the juke box was somewhat muted by distance and the endless clattering and occasional shattering of dishes in the kitchen. The table was stuck in the very back corner, and was set with plain cutlery, paper napkins, and placemats. A solitary jewell-light candle provided an incongruous touch.

"You want a drink while you wait, honey?" the woman drawled.

"Yes. Two vodka martinis, on the rocks please."

The waitress gave her a funny look, then waddled away, her backless flats slapping the floor. Kathy breathed a sigh of relief as she settled into one of the uncomfortable metal

185

and vinyl chairs, her back to the wall so that she could face the rest of the room. On impulse, she leaned over and blew out the candle, plunging the table into semidarkness.

While she waited for the drinks, she studied the other patrons. They were mostly truckers, whose rigs she had seen scattered along the roadway and in the lot out front. And there were traveling salesmen types, whose eyes kept straining in the dim light to catch hers.

Nowhere in the room was there anyone who even remotely resembled the little Russian. Nor was there anyone who looked like an FBI or CIA agent, although she had little idea what one of those was supposed to look like. Slowly she began to relax, realizing that perhaps she had not been followed as she had feared. Her mind flashed momentarily to the late-model Chevy that had slowed outside the parking lot, but she quickly put it out of her thoughts.

The waitress brought the drinks and set them down unceremoniously, spilling part of one on the placemat without bothering to wipe it up. "You wanta run a tab, honey?"

"Yes, that would be fine," Kathy mumbled, and took a deep sip from one of the drinks, trying to appear less in need of it than she really was. The waitress turned away, then noticing the extinguished candle, set her tray down and fumbled in her grimy apron for a book of matches.

"That's all right," Kathy said, forcing a smile. "I really don't care for the candlelight."

The woman looked at her for an instant then shrugged. "Have it your way, honey. Just trying to give the place a little atmosphere." She walked away with a slightly irritated twitch and Kathy drained her drink and reached for the other.

By the time she had finished that one and was thinking about ordering another round, it was eight o' five. She was beginning to have second thoughts about staying. Then suddenly she saw him weasling through the narrow path between the tables, his hands shoved into his shapeless overcoat, which he wore despite the warm evening. He wore the same hat, pulled ridiculously low on his brow, his hair splaying from under the brim.

Nevertheless, his appearance was far from amusing to her. She stiffened as he stopped in front of the table, smiled briefly, then pulled out a chair and sat down next to her. He removed his hat and placed it on the table.

"You have been waiting long?" he asked, his voice surprisingly warm.

"Not long."

"I see you have had your drink."

"I was just going to order another one for you."

"No, thank you, Miss Karpovich. I intended them for you. You see, when one is nervous, it is very difficult to concentrate, and I want your undivided attention. So relax. You may have one more, but only one."

Kathy felt like shoving the glass into his face and bolting, but she scarcely moved as he motioned for the waitress to bring one more. He looked at her, his eyes kind, almost fatherly.

"And how have you been enjoying your new job?" he asked.

Kathy breathed out sharply but declined to answer.

"No matter. I have it on good authority that you are doing well. I understand you have passed the necessary clearance investigations. Within a few months you are expected to be cleared for classified information." He broke off as the waitress set the drink on the table in front of him.

"You folks want to order now? Kitchen's running out of baked potatoes if you want a baked potato."

"Nothing for me," Kathy said.

"Oh, but you must eat, my dear," the man said. "Please, bring us two of your best T-bone steaks, baked potatoes, and whatever else comes with them. Coffee for me," he said, sliding the drink over in front of Kathy. "And bring me the bill. I am treating my daughter tonight."

"I said nothing for me," Kathy snapped.

The waitress looked questioningly at him and he

shrugged. "Nothing for her, then. You know these young people always watching their weight. When you get to be my age you can eat all you want because it no longer matters."

"One T-bone, with a baker and coffee," the waitress said in a bored tone and ambled off toward the kitchen.

Kathy sat motionless, staring at her drink, trying to steady her trembling fingers long enough to reach for it. He was aware of her fear and spoke soothingly in his heavy accent.

"We are pleased with you, Kathy. You seem to suit your job, you make friends quickly, and you mix well in the right circles. This is very important for our work."

"Listen, who are you, and just what the hell is it you want me to do?"

He smiled. "My name is Sergei Zeitsev. I work at the Soviet Embassy. For the present that is all you need to know about me. As for what you are to do, you will learn that in good time. First I want to instruct you in certain procedures we will follow in the weeks ahead. Drink your drink and listen carefully. You must remember everything I tell you, because nothing of what I say will ever be written down."

Kathy reached for her drink and downed half of it. The alcohol was beginning to have its desired effect. Her hands no longer trembled.

"In the future, Kathy, you and I will seldom meet at this diner. It is not safe to return to the same place again and again. Nor will I contact you by phone unless it is absolutely necessary. Rather, we will correspond by messages and signals, left at designated locations. I have chosen several sites to begin with and from time to time I will change these sites. For now, we will use the stop sign on the southwest corner of Henry and Duke streets. Every other Thursday, you will drive by this stop sign after work. If I desire a meeting with you, I will leave a piece of reflective tape like so on the inner edge of the 'P.' " He indicated that the tape would be placed half on the white of the letter, and half on the red. "If you see this signal, you will buy a copy of the evening paper.

188

Under the classified personal section, you will look for an item addressed to Darling. The message will be simple. For instance, tonight's message would have read: 'Darling. Molly's Place, highway 97, seven-forty.' Do you understand?''

Kathy nodded numbly, although her head was spinning. Did spies actually behave this way?

"Good," Zeitsev said. "Upon occasion, I will complicate the message in order to confuse anyone who happens to be noticing a trend. For instance, I might give you an address where you would find a phone booth. You would consult the yellow pages. I would give you the page number and you would find the meeting place circled. In such a case, you will memorize the address, tear out the page and destroy it. The meeting times will vary, and I will always give you the exact time. If I do not appear within ten minutes of the appointed time, you will leave immediately. If you do not appear within ten minutes, I will leave. I will assume you have been unable to keep the appointment, and I will contact you in the same manner the following Thursday."

The waitress brought his meal and they sat in silence for several minutes as he ate voraciously; his appetite was like that of a shrew. At last he continued in between mouthfuls.

"Once you have received my signal at the stop sign, you will take the piece of tape and place it in the center of the 'O.' This will tell me that you have seen it. Then you will proceed to buy the paper and follow my instructions."

"What's the purpose of all this?" Kathy said, unable to keep quiet any longer.

"The purpose, my dear, is to gather information— information that my government would very much like to obtain. At our meetings, I will give you specific instructions as to what sort of information to deliver, what documents my government is interested in. At first these documents will be fairly innocuous; often they will be of your own choosing. The assignments will be kept simple until you have become accustomed to the routine and the pressures of your task. As you mature, we will require more of you."

"How do you know what information you want?"

"You will help us to determine this by the information

189

you provide. SPEC is developing new systems and instruments all the time. We are interested in almost anything you can get, and if we find something of particular interest, we will want you to dig deeper into the records in that area."

"But how do I get the information out without getting caught?"

Sergei withdrew a plain white envelope from his pocket and slid it casually under her fingertips as they rested on the table. She stared at it without moving. He continued. "Use this money to buy a camera. The make and model number as well as the necessary lens requirements are written on the inside of the envelope. Memorize these and destroy the envelope. The camera will cost $875 plus tax. Once you have purchased it, read the instructions thoroughly and become familiar with the instrument until you can operate it without having to think. That will be imperative since you will be working under extreme pressure and often with little time. You will also want to purchase a compact and light-weight monopod, to steady the camera while you are shooting the documents."

"You mean I'm to photograph the documents you want?"

"Yes. The best method, we've found, is to place the documents on the floor and turn a desk lamp so that its light falls on them evenly, being careful not to create a glare on the paper. Then you photograph every sheet and return the documents to their proper place. No one will suspect that the material has been copied and your cover will remain intact."

"What do I do with the film once I've shot the documents?"

"You will take it home, and in a completely dark closet you will wind it into this." He handed her a ballpoint pen.

"What? How do I . . . ?"

He smiled. "What appears to be a ballpoint pen is in reality an ingenious film container. Inside you will find sprockets that correspond to the sprocket holes of the film. Wind the film around the inner core of the pen and screw it back together. Do not open it once you have done this. You will then place the pen inside an empty Coca Cola can, which you will deposit at a predetermined *debok* . . . excuse me . . . that is 'dead drop' in English."

She shivered at the way he spoke the words.

"Once you have dropped off the film, you will go to the post office box at the corner across the street from your office building. You will take along a letter to mail, a legitimate letter. As you are mailing it, you will place a piece of masking tape on the dot above the 'i' on the left side of the box as you are facing it. That is the side facing the street. I will check the box each day, and when I see your signal, I will remove the tape and retrieve the can from the *debok.*"

"What happens if I get caught?" she said, suddenly aggressive. She noticed how his manner changed at once.

"That would be very unfortunate."

"Unfortunate?" Kathy said, raising her voice.

He looked around quickly.

"What the hell do you mean, unfortunate?" she asked in a lower tone.

"What I mean is, you will have to leave the country. We will arrange for you to be smuggled out."

"Oh, fine. Where to?"

"Why Moscow, of course."

"No way!" Kathy's voice suddenly contained a note of command.

"I'm sorry," he said, clearly surprised at her response. "I don't understand . . ."

"I said *no way.* There's no way I'm going to spend the rest of my life in Moscow. I'd just as soon turn myself in right now and get it over with."

"But you would enjoy living in Moscow."

"Forget it. You'll have to do better than that."

"You have another suggestion?" Sergei's voice had taken on a slight tremor of uncertainty.

"South America, Brazil maybe. Or even Mexico. Somewhere I could live comfortably. And I'll need money."

"Now just a minute, my dear. You are hardly in a position to make demands. If you refuse to cooperate . . ."

"I know. You'll turn me in. You've said that before. But I don't care. If I'm going to do this thing, then I'm going to go all the way, and that means I have to have some assurances in case something goes wrong. Now you either come through with a sizable amount of cash in addition to the salary at SPEC, or I go to the FBI myself and turn you in. I'm sure they'd be very interested to know about your connections at SPEC."

Sergei was becoming more and more agitated. His eyes searched furtively around the room, and he fumbled with his empty coffee cup. "But I have no authority to make such arrangements without consulting my superiors."

"Then I suggest you consult them," she snapped. "I want a guaranteed payment with each delivery. Those are my terms. And the payment had better be generous."

"You are playing a dangerous game," he said sternly.

"You don't have to tell me that."

"I will ask . . . I will see," he said.

"And if I don't get caught," she continued. "How long does this little routine go on? How long before I buy my freedom?"

"I don't know."

"You'd better find out."

"Usually, the relationship lasts as long as your position is not in jeopardy. After all, you are of no use to us if you are being watched."

"How long can I go undetected?"

"Some have gone as long as twenty years. Others as short as a few months. It depends on how careful you are."

"Well, I'm not sticking around for twenty years. You may as well know that right off. I'll make a pact with you to stay around for a year."

"Impossible. You will hardly be able to penetrate the classified material in that short a time."

"How long then?"

"Shall we say three or four years?"

"Two."

"I will check. I must have the proper authority."

Kathy slid the envelope from the table into her open

purse without letting her eyes leave him. She wanted him to think she wasn't kidding, that she could be as tough as he could. She hoped her bluff would work.

"I'd like to go now," she said.

"We'll leave together. Act as if you are my daughter." He rose and she followed suit.

Once outside, Kathy suddenly no longer felt afraid. Her life had taken a drastic, unexpected turn; it was beyond her control. But she was determined to maintain some semblance of sanity and to shape her outlook for the future on the premise that in two years she would be free to pursue her goals.

They parted in the lot without speaking. He melted into the darkness as she pulled out onto the empty highway and gunned her engine. An instant later, Sergei's blue Dodge rolled out and headed toward the distant lights of the city.

In a dim corner of the lot, a white late-model Chevy suddenly turned over, and drove off in pursuit of the other two cars. Inside were two men in dark suits. One of them was busy writing in a small spiral notebook.

. . . 4 August 1989

The next morning, Parker met with Dr. Kemper, General Owens, Montie Montgomery, and Dr. Sevrensen in a classified section of the SPEC complex, where many of the prototypes for the NASA and Air Force aerospace vehicles had been developed. On the drawing boards at the present were the detailed plans for the next two years, including the projected Space Shuttle launchings, a new Skylab facility, and the development of the ASP. On the walls of the conference room were various charts and artist's renderings. On the conference table was a mockup of the current ASP design and a slide projector.

"Gentlemen, this morning I would like to outline our timetable for the next twenty-four months, at the end of which we hope to have the ASP operational and in service. These plans include the launching of four Space Shuttle flights per year for the purpose of testing guidance systems and rocket fuel mixtures, as well as servicing the Skylab which we hope to put into orbit in the next nine months.

"The purpose of the new Skylab will be to establish a working laboratory above the Earth's atmosphere for testing and perfecting the SPEC atomic fission thruster, and to carry out some other NASA experiments, which will take place after our purpose has been satisfied. In that vein, I would like to touch on the reactor now, and later explain how it will affect the development of the ASP.

"As you probably all know, the single most critical factor in nuclear reactors is containing the heat of the reaction. For this reason, we have so far found it impossible to test the SPEC thruster safely on Earth. The fission reactor operates on the same principle as the atomic bomb and the present fission reactors used to generate power in the conventional power plants throughout this country.

"The shields used in these plants, by the very nature of the reaction, must be enormously heavy and very large—totally unsuitable for use in a thruster that must carry a craft into outer space. It has been thought for some time, however, that the fission process could be contained in a much lighter, more functional chamber, highly suited for our purposes. Still, we have been faced with the possibility of accidents which could prove disastrous should this testing be carried out in a conventional manner.

"The new thruster utilizes a specially formed synthetic diamond bottle to contain the reaction. It is conceptually very simple. The diamond bottle would serve as the primary container for the reaction, but owing to its transparency, it would allow the heat of the reaction to pass through its walls without causing them to absorb this heat, in much the same manner that sunlight heat passes through a window on a winter day. If you sit in the sunlight, you feel its warmth, but if you press your hand against the glass, you will feel that it is still cold. The heat energy passes directly through. The problem with the transference of the nuclear heat energy of course, is that once it has passed through the walls of the bottle, it still must be contained or expended.

"Therefore, we place the diamond bottle inside of another container, whose inner walls are of a highly polished tungsten 184 alloy. This alloy is both highly resistant to heat and also tends to regulate the reaction; that is, keep it in check, under control. Now the inner walls will cause the heat energy to be reflected back and forth within the chamber, but this itself will not prevent the temperature from eventually rising so high that it will destroy the outer chamber walls. Therefore, we fill this outer chamber with our propellant, and assuming that it is opaque, even black, it is theoretically possible to expend or absorb all the heat energy released into the outer chamber, and therefore control the heat output in a relatively light and compact unit.

"The propellant we propose using is a water-ammonia

solution supersaturated with graphite particles to create the necessary opaqueness. We chose ammonia and water because of their greater efficiency as liquid propellants, lighter weight, and enormously lower costs when compared with the conventional rocket propellants liquid helium and liquid hydrogen. We also eliminate the necessity of providing liquid oxygen to support the combustion. The graphic has one other quality besides opaqueness, and that is it too tends to regulate the nuclear reaction.

"Furthermore, the entire unit is cooled by radiant coils running from the reactor to the surface areas of the space vehicle. We will circulate liquid hydrogen in this system, and therefore we will be able to maintain the heat of the reaction at a functional level.

"Naturally, the propellant when heated will be transformed into a gas, and it will escape through a conventional rocket nozzle, which will provide the thrust for the space vehicle, in this case, the ASP. Because of the risk of accident, and because of the lack of funds since the Shuttle program was cut this is, of course, all theoretical. There have been no tests. I might add, there is also a hitch in the nuclear test ban treaties of 1963 and 1972 concerning the testing of nuclear devices in outer space."

"Then what you're proposing is technically against those treaties?" Montie asked.

"Since when have you been concerned over treaty violations, Montie?" Parker asked. "Considering that just about every treaty we've ever made with another country has either been broken or seriously challenged, I don't have any compunctions against giving the go-ahead to this project."

"Actually, Don," Kemper interrupted. "If you will allow me to point out, there are really no clear-cut guidelines to what we are proposing. The nuclear test bans refer to the testing of nuclear weaponry and make no specific reference to nuclear reactors or thrusters. The only reference to this issue is the fact that all signatory countries agree to consult each other before potentially hazardous activities are undertaken. I myself would not call these projected tests potentially hazardous. Should there be an accident with the reactor, it would occur in space, and in such a case, any fallout from an explosion would be filtered by the Earth's atmosphere in the same manner that solar radiation is, allowing only minimal, indeed, negligible amounts of radiation to enter the Earth's upper atmosphere."

"There's no risk during launch?" Parker asked.

"None at all. The reactor will not be activated until it is in outer space, or at least on the fringes of the atmosphere. During the testing, in fact, we will assemble the reactor in orbit in Skylab, and the reactor test unit will be equipped with a detonator with which we can terminate the test in space should there be any danger of the reactor entering the atmosphere."

"What about when it's installed in the ASP?" General Owens asked.

"The reactor unit will be a detachable element that can and will be jettisoned and detonated in the event of over-heating or malfunction. For instance, if the ASP has to make an emergency reentry into the atmosphere, and if there is a chance of a crash landing, the reactor will be jettisoned in outer space and destroyed. This is a safety measure for the crew as well, if we decide to man the vehicle on certain flights."

"When will the testing begin?" Parker asked.

"As soon as Skylab is in orbit. We will then launch a Shuttle with the components of two reactors on board. They will be assembled in Skylab and tested. If the tests are successful, we will order a full complement of the units. Now, if there are no more questions, I'd like to get on to the ASP itself."

"By all means," Parker said.

"Generally, the ASP's basic design will be similar in concept to the Space Shuttle. Both are aerospace planes; that is, they employ the elements of winged flight combined with rocket power and a capacity for orbital injection, giving them the ability to leave the Earth's atmosphere and navigate in outer space."

Kemper switched on the slide projector, which threw an

artist's rendering of the ASP on a small screen hanging on the wall. It was shaped in a delta wing configuration with drooping wingtips, a thin nose resembling the SST, or Concorde, as the French aircraft was dubbed, with a wide fuselage like the Space Shuttle and a high rigid tail section.

"This gentlemen is the latest design, which we are presently testing in laboratory wind chambers for aerodynamic responses. In a little while we'll go down there and see the models in operation. The ASP is a fully powered winged aerospace glider, capable of jet takeoffs and landings and rocket powered outer space flight. It measures just over two hundred and eighty-eight feet from wingtip to wingtip, and one hundred and forty-four feet from nose cone to tail. Let me briefly explain the various power systems. First, we have six of the latest vector thrust J-58 turbojet engines, like the ones employed in the SR 71 reconnaissance aircraft. Each jet is capable of generating over 53,000 pounds of thrust, giving it a total takeoff thrust of some 318,000 pounds. These engines may either be utilized to effect a conventional horizontal takeoff in the manner of a modern jet, or they may be channeled into rotatable nozzles on the under surface of the fuselage to effect a vertical takeoff like the British Hawker Harrier. This system allows the craft to hover up to an altitude of some eight hundred feet, and the conversion from hover to forward thrust is computerized to allow for a smooth transfer with a minimal loss of efficiency.

"Assuming a normal takeoff, the ASP will use any conventional airfield capable of jet air traffic to become airborne. It will quickly climb to high altitudes and attain an air speed of close to Mach 3.9 or somewhere around three thousand miles per hour. Now remember, these are not normal jet engines but engines capable of lifting the SR 71 in an almost vertical, straight up and down ascent, like a rocket. Because of the massive wing structure, the ASP will achieve enormous lift, allowing it to carry a payload of much greater weight than the thrust of its engines, as opposed to the rocket, which must rely on only its engines for lift and therefore must have more thrust than weight.

"As the ASP climbs toward the stratosphere, engine

efficiency and lift will begin to decline, and at this point the on-board computer will activate the secondary system, twin solid propellant rockets similar in concept to those used in the more conventional takeoff of the Space Shuttle." Kemper pointed to the image on the screen, locating the rocket housings in the tail structure. "When these kick in, they will rapidly accelerate the craft to somewhere close to 21,000 miles per hour, which is in excess of parabolic escape velocity, the speed needed to escape the atmosphere of the Earth and put the craft into orbit. At the point where these rockets flame out, in a low altitude orbit, the nuclear thruster will be activated, driving the vehicle to a maximum escape velocity of somewhere around 26,000 miles per hour, or what we call hyperbolic escape velocity, a speed capable of propelling the craft beyond the pull of the Earth's gravity so that it will eventually be able to fall toward the moon.

"I should point out that the specific mass of nuclear fission thrust is expected to be much lower than that of conventional rocket fuel thrust, and is only efficient in a vacuum environment like outer space. Therefore, acceleration toward hyperbolic escape velocity will be slower than with conventional rockets, but will be more efficient with a specific impulse or maximum burning time well over a hundredfold that of our present rockets.

"Once in space, then, the ASP will function completely under nuclear power, and minor course adjustments will be performed in the same manner that former space craft have been maneuvered, that is, reaction thrust, or opposite push to guide the craft in one direction or the other. To go left, the rockets fire to the right, and so on. We will channel the exhaust from the reactor into a system of nozzles located throughout the vessel, much like the Shuttle.

"Touchdown and liftoff from the moon will be powered by these systems as well, by nozzles on the underside of the wing structure and fuselage. Since the moon is one-sixth the size of the Earth, liftoff thrust is also one-sixth that of the Earth; thus the ASP can easily take off with a full payload using the lower density nuclear thruster.

"Reentry into Earth's atmosphere will be guided up until

the very last minute by nuclear thrust; then once it begins its descent, the reactor will be shut down and the reaction killed. At this point, the jet system will again take over to guide the landing on the targeted airfield, almost anywhere on Earth.

"Should there be a failure of the nuclear thruster at any time, the liquid hydrogen coolant from the radiant coils will be channeled into a small backup conventional liquid propellant rocket engine, and a small reservoir of oxygen will be employed to provide the necessary burn needed to send the ship home for an emergency reentry and landing. Again, the jet system will take over once the craft is back inside the Earth's atmosphere." He changed to a new slide showing a blueprint of the ASP's design, and pointed to the reactor section.

"As I mentioned before, the nuclear thruster section will be detachable with the firing of these explosive bolts." He pointed them out. "In the event of malfunction, the on-board computer will automatically fire these and eject the entire section into space, where it will self-destruct after the craft has reached a safe distance. The separation will also serve as a backup form of thrust for the crippled craft, aiding the liquid hydrogen rocket." He cut off the projector and pulled down a wall chart showing both the ASP and the Space Shuttle in relative sizes. The ASP literally dwarfed its little "older" brother.

"Unlike the Shuttle, the ASP is designed to take off empty and return with a full payload. For this reason, we use smaller rockets to accommodate our design. The wings of the ASP provide not only guidance on reentry but the very important aspect of lift to compensate for the greatly increased weight of the full cargo bay, which for our purposes will contain raw ore. I might point out that this vehicle may also be used to effect outer space rescues of small space craft, whereas the Shuttle has only the capacity for placing and retrieving satellites.

"Now the aerodynamics are such that the ASP can land without the use of jet power if necessary, in the same manner that the Shuttle does, but the use of jets allows us to make last minute changes in landing sites and support a much greater payload. It will be landed just like any large multijet aircraft."

"Absolutely remarkable, Arnold," Parker sighed. "An incredible feat of engineering."

"If it flies," Ralph Owens remarked.

"It will fly, Ralph." Kemper replied. "We're testing the models in the wind tunnels. Already it is more aerodynamically sound than the modern jetliner. Remember, this craft is designed to land without power if necessary. What modern jet can do that? And stress-wise, it is the difference between steel and balsa wood."

Owens muttered to himself, but no one questioned Kemper further.

"Now, why don't we take a walk down to the wind tunnel and have a look at what we're doing?"

As they filed out of the conference room and walked down the brightly lit corridor, Parker continued to press for more information. "What about the mining system, Arnold?"

"For the laser, I'll defer to Dr. Sevrensen."

Sevrensen kept pace with the President, his enthusiasm running over, his eyes sparkling with the prospects of his pet project. "The laser may be programmed to excavate any given set of coordinates on the moon, or the Earth for that matter. Sonar and infrared soundings will allow the on-board computer to calculate the relative depth of ore deposits and relay the data to the laser brain. The laser will then excavate to the proper depth to expose the top layer of ore, and then the remote mining unit being designed by Mr. Montgomery's company will be employed to excavate the ore itself.

"The plan is to have the ASP hover above the lunar surface while excavating the chosen site. Once the programmed area has been cleared, the ASP will land and deploy the RMU as we have chosen to call it for short. The RMU will excavate the raw ore and transport it to the cargo bay until it has filled the bay to capacity weight, which will automatically be sensed by the bay decking. This information will be transferred to the RMU by the on-board computer and digging will cease. The RMU will return to the ASP, and the vessel will depart for Earth with a full cargo."

"What's the status of the RMU, Montie?" Parker asked as they approached the flashing red sign above the entry to the wind tunnel testing section, designating the area Top Security.

"Right now we're bogged down trying to develop the right energy cell. We're trying to adapt the nuclear cell already in use in our latest satellites. The unit itself will perform essentially in the same manner as the unit I designed for our mines in Tennessee two years ago. But the big challenge is making it compatible with the on-board computer."

"Here we are, gentlemen," Kemper announced as they passed through the security checkpoint and entered a large control center, jammed with electronic equipment and scores of white frocked technicians who all rose to their feet at the sight of the President.

"Keep your seats, ladies and gentlemen. We're only here to observe," Parker smiled, motioning for them to be seated.

Kemper took Parker's elbow and guided him toward a computer console. "If you'd care to look through this window, Don, you'll see what they're testing right now."

Parker peered into a small window, approximately one foot square. Inside, illuminated by one harsh spotlight, was a scale model of the ASP they had seen in the slide show. It was perhaps three feet in length, but accurate as far as he could see to the minutest detail, right down to the window slots on the front of the nose section.

"Remarkable," Parker mused, and stepped back so that each of the others could have a look.

"This is where we first test the aerodynamics of any aircraft we design, atmospheric and otherwise," Kemper said. "This particular tunnel is designed to test the craft's response to wind, temperature, and the effect of sound waves, which is a very real barrier that we have never conquered but have only learned to live with.

"All these factors come into play when building a supersonic aircraft or a space vehicle and affect the flight from liftoff to touchdown. The first and most obvious is wind. In the case of rockets, the needle shape and enormous thrust of the vehicle minimize the effect of wind on the structure. But in the case of a winged spacecraft, the presence of wings gives us the advantage of lift to conquer both the wind and gravity. The design we are testing today has tested out very well in terms of lift efficiency and is capable of greater response than our larger jets.

"However, just as wings give us the advantage of lift and greater control, they also expose the craft to greater drag on reentry and therefore much greater heat buildup than with conventional reentry vehicles. We are using for the skin of the craft an alloy called Rene 43, an improvement on the alloy projected for the old Dyna-Soar craft. The heat shield of the ASP will consist of the ceramic material used in the Shuttle, designed to radiate more heat than it absorbs and which has a melting point of some 4000 degrees Fahrenheit. This is very important, since reentry will take approximately twenty minutes and the heat generated by the bow wave will reach approximately 20,000 degrees Fahrenheit, although this temperature will never actually be transferred to the craft. And, finally, for the belly of the craft we will use a cobalt-based super-alloy.

"All of this is calculated to meet the requirements of the heat buildup during reentry, but there is another critical factor that will affect the craft on reentry and liftoff and that is stress. Because of the extreme temperatures and enormous speed on reentry, the craft must be designed so that it is actually more structurally sound under stress, in effect becoming harder when placed under great stress. We do this by designing the outer skin of the craft in sections, leaving gaps in critical places so that when heating occurs, the skin will expand to fill those gaps and press tightly together, giving the craft much greater strength to endure the stress of reentry."

"You mentioned earlier, Arnold, that the ASP can either be manned or unmanned. Can you elaborate?" Parker asked.

"Yes, sir. The ASP will be capable of totally programmed unmanned flight in the case of routine mining operations, or it can be adapted to accommodate a crew of six with room for six passengers."

"In the event of unmanned flight, what sort of guidance system will be used?" Parker asked.

"One developed for use in the high altitude unmanned reconnaissance aircraft, the Drone."

"How does it work?" Parker asked, pressing for understanding.

"In the most general terms, the coordinates of the target area are fed into the on-board computer through the master computer terminal on the ground. For our purpose, the master computer will guide the ASP's flight from liftoff to touchdown, including the mining operations during which it will locate the prescribed coordinates, operate the laser bombardment, land and deploy the RMU, etcetera. It will be totally remote controlled, subject to the program tapes in the master computer which will be located in the Death Valley compound."

"I see," Parker said, his thoughts momentarily far away from the present. "Well, I've seen enough," he said at last. "I suggest we let these good people get back to work."

"I hope I've been able to put this all into perspective for you," Kemper said.

"Very much so," Parker replied and the others agreed. "Dr. Sevrensen, if there is anything the military can do to hasten the development of the laser, I wish you'd contact General Owens personally. I've given him carte blanche on all matters pertaining to the Oasis Project."

"Thank you, Mr. President, but just yet we have but to test our apparatus, and since I anticipate no complications, I feel safe to say that we can deliver the prototype within the month."

"I'd be grateful, Doctor. Gentlemen, it's been a pleasure."

The presidential party left the testing section and returned down the long busy corridor to the elevators that took them up to the main lobby of the compound where the President's security men were waiting.

Parker stepped out of the elevator last, and just as he was preparing to leave, someone coming up the corridor caught his eye. He stepped past the circle of agents. "Kathy?"

Kathy Karpovich looked up from the stack of mail she was sorting as she hurried toward her office, and her face brightened, then suddenly flushed with embarrassment. "Mr. President . . ." she stammered.

"What are you doing here? I haven't seen you since the Press party. How're things at the *Post?*"

"Kathy is our new publicity director, Mr. President," Kemper interrupted. "She came on board in late spring and has been doing a marvelous job for us. She was responsible for getting that Shuttle piece in the *Post* just before the vote in Congress."

"I thought you were a die-hard newspaper woman, Kathy. What made you decide to come over here?"

"Let's just say that SPEC made me an offer I found difficult to refuse," Kathy said, trying to smile.

Kemper and Parker both laughed and Parker held out his hand to Kathy who shook it self-consciously. "Well, it's nice seeing you again, Kathy. Good luck."

"Thank you, Mr. President. The same to you."

"Mr. President, you'll be late for your appointment with the Mexican Ambassador," Montie reminded him.

"Right." He turned to Kathy and smiled once more, noticing the unhappy and almost frightened look in her eyes. "Hope to see you again. Goodbye Arnold. Thanks for the tour."

"My pleasure, Mr. President."

Parker left with his entourage and Kathy and Dr. Kemper exchanged undemonstrative stares for a brief instant, then went their separate ways.

"Mr. Ambassador? The President will see you now," Shirley said, stepping from the Oval Office with an armload of dossiers.

Eduardo Muniz, rose to his full five-feet, six-inches, stroked his thick neatly trimmed mustache, straightened his beautifully tailored three-piece suit, and marched past her through the open door into the Oval Office.

Parker stood with his back to the door, facing out the window deep in thought. He turned at the sound of the man's entrance and stepped forward to greet the diminutive Mexican Ambassador. His six-foot solid frame fairly dwarfed the man, and Parker made certain that his handshake was on the bruising side of firm as he gestured his visitor to a comfortable seat near the windows.

"Come in, Mr. Muniz. Have a seat."

"Thank you Mr. President. It is a pleasure to meet you at last." His accent was heavy, but his English was carefully cultured.

"The pleasure is all mine, Mr. Muniz. I've looked forward to having a frank discussion with you for some time now, only matters of State being what they are, I've scarcely had a free minute in the last six months. I'm sure you understand."

"But of course, Mr. President. Let me personally extend the compliments of His Excellency, Enrique de Gonzales-Perez. It is his sincere hope that our two countries can continue to live and work in harmony and share a warm and fruitful friendship."

"Thank you, Mr. Muniz. I share Mr. Perez's desires. However, if you don't mind my getting bluntly to the point, I'd like to discuss with you some of the issues that are standing in the way of our two countries' sharing 'this warm and fruitful friendship.' "

"Please Mr. President. This is why I have come, to speak to you frankly as I have been directed by my President. He too feels that only by candid discussion of the issues can we reach the true heart of the differences that plague our great nations."

"I'm glad we see eye to eye, Mr. Muniz." Parker paused, letting the Ambassador savor the sumptuous silence of the Oval Office. "Frankly, Mr. Muniz, I've been concerned with the relations between your country and mine ever since late 1978 when President Carter and your President Portillo had a falling out over the price of oil and natural gas. It was a rift that in my opinion was unnecessary and counterproductive. The asking price of fifteen dollars a barrel was a fair price in my estimation, in light of the subsequent developments in

Iran that have since driven the price on the open market to the current level. However, I don't see how the OPEC nations can continue to ask seventy-five dollars a barrel and expect to continue to sell all they have. It's a prohibitive price, and I'm concerned over your country's apparent willingness to go along with OPEC's pricing policies. I don't think we can go on paying that much for low sulfur crude oil." Again he fell silent and stared directly at the Ambassador. His tone had been totally impersonal without the hint of castigation, but the little man shifted uncomfortably in his chair.

"But surely, Mr. President, you are in favor of a free market system?" the Ambassador said.

"Yes."

"And is it not the axiom of such a system to let the market find its own level?"

"Yes."

"Then with all due respect, sir, I do not see how the market price can ever return to the level of the late seventies."

"Let me ask you a question, Mr. Muniz. How many millions, no, how many billions of dollars do you estimate the United States has poured into your country through trade, subsidies, private investments, and salaries to illegal aliens, who we allow to remain in this country despite our laws?"

Muniz remained silent for a moment, then fumbled for a reply. "I . . . I have no way of knowing, Mr. President. But I don't understand . . ."

"I would safely say somewhere in the realm of one hundred billion dollars have been siphoned out of this country into yours, much in the form of investments that have been nationalized, much in the form of federal loans that I might add are still outstanding and at interest rates several points below the prime rate based upon the figures of the seventies."

"I am not privileged to that kind of information, Mr. President," Muniz stammered, aware that the tone of the conversation was quickly shifting.

"And how much cooperation has the United States received from your country in return for our benevolence?"

"I don't know what you mean."

"I mean how many times have you voluntarily offered your

oil and gas to your largest and friendliest neighbor at prices below the OPEC level? How many times have you encouraged American investment in your country by offering reasonable incentives such as controlling your outlandish union demands and guaranteeing the investor's security in his investment, security against nationalization or premeditated bankruptcy? As I recall, not once in more than twenty years."

"Mr. President, with all deference to your office, I am the offical representative of my country and President, and I did not come here to be insulted." The little man's feathers were getting ruffled, and Parker had to fight to keep from laughing out loud.

"It's not my intention to insult you or your country Mr. Muniz. Personally, I have nothing against you, and I am informed that you are a very effective diplomat. That is the reason I have granted you this interview and have chosen to speak to you so candidly. I'm trying to point out that in any relationship, be it political or personal, there is a two-way give and take that must exist in order for that relationship to remain smooth and mutually beneficial."

"Mr. President, I assure you that my country stands ready to listen to any reasonable proposal for mutually beneficial trade arrangements and investment opportunities. But after all, we are a growing nation, a developing nation and naturally our needs are great. Our people have known much deprivation and suffering."

"I can sympathize, Mr. Muniz."

"And you must understand that though in our hearts we feel we must do one thing as government officials in order to encourage continued good relations with our neighbors, we must also think of the needs of our people and our growing economy. That is often the deciding factor, for in order for our nation to prosper, we must have capital, both to reinvest in our country and to purchase foreign technology. And for us, there are only two commodities that we produce that will bring the amount of capital we need—oil and gas. Surely, you would not condemn us for trying to rise out of three centuries of poverty to join the world community as a nation to be trusted and respected."

"No, Mr. Muniz, I don't condemn you for your noble goals. Your country is entitled to reap the benefits of its resources, just as every other country is entitled to do. But sometimes there arises a need for agreements which somewhat compromises the short run in favor of the long run."

"What exactly do you mean?"

"I mean there may be certain deals I want to make with Mr. Perez that in the short run seem to be more than reasonable, perhaps even foolishly below market level. But those deals may be made in return for goods and services that in the long run are more beneficial to your country than an extra ten or fifteen dollars a barrel for instance?"

"You're not suggesting that we sell you oil at below current world market prices?" Muniz gasped in shock.

"I'm suggesting that you sell us your oil and gas, as much as we want to buy, at well below the market price, in return for our continued good will and aid in developing the aspects of your economy that today might be considered at best rudimentary."

Muniz stared at him in horror, but Parker's expression was fixed, although there was a filmy glaze over his green eyes and a faint crease in his brow.

"What aspects of our economy are you referring to Mr. President?" Muniz asked. It was clear from his voice that he was trembling with either fear or rage or a combination of both.

"Your agricultural development, your nuclear development, your communications, your educational system, heavy and light industry . . . do I need to go on?"

"How do you propose to exchange these favors for our lower prices?"

"I don't think there is necessarily a formula, Mr. Muniz. I think rather there is a philosophy that we should exchange, one that takes into account our mutual good will, our responsibilities to each other as friendly neighbors, our economic necessities on both sides of the border — simply put, a promise to bargain in good faith out of mutual concern for our future well being. After all, Mr. Muniz, should the

United States fall on any harder times, we would be hard pressed to continue pouring millions of dollars into your country. We would be ill-advised to allow so many of your citizens to remain in our country, either under temporary visas or illegally. Think of the impact if the United States could no longer afford to import your produce or even your oil. What if it became necessary to impose tariffs or embargoes? You realize, Mr. Muniz, that in the event of a real emergency I have the authority to take drastic steps in the national interest. That might mean doing without many luxuries, restricting our imports, which might tend to work a hardship on your country as well."

Muniz's face turned red and his nostrils flared slightly. Nevertheless, he maintained control and forced an amicable smile. "But, of course, Mr. President, neither of us would wish to see something like that happen. As you have said, we are two nations joined together in a struggle for prosperity for our people and the Western Hemisphere. I am sure President Perez would agree with me when I say that we will do everything in our power to come to terms with the United States."

"Fine, Mr. Muniz. I hope that you will extend my best wishes to Mr. Perez and tell him that I look forward to meeting with him personally as soon as possible so that we may begin a sincere dialogue toward this end. I can't stress enough the urgency of our situation."

Roger Davis, dressed in a light blue summer suit with a white shirt and pale grey tie, emerged from his hotel at seven-fifteen in the evening and stepped into the limousine waiting at curbside. The night breezes brought the smell of green grass and fruit blossoms.

The drive to the White House took less than a quarter of an hour, and shortly after his arrival, he was ushered into the President's private elevator and escorted to the President's library on the third floor by two dark-suited security agents.

"Make yourself comfortable, Mr. Davis," one of them said. "The President will be right with you. There's ice in the bar if you'd like to make yourself a drink."

"Thank you," Davis said, and after they had withdrawn made himself a weak Bourbon and water. He strolled casually around the library, looking absentmindedly at the shelves of books, ranging from legal texts to current best sellers. It seemed the President was a voracious reader of all manner of literature, and he marveled at the energy of the man to assimilate this matter in addition to the mountains of highly technical and legally complicated documents that crossed his desk daily.

Davis was just finishing his drink and thinking about another when the door to Parker's chambers opened and Parker appeared wearing a pair of khaki slacks and a fresh dress shirt open at the collar. He was tanned and looked fit and refreshed. It was the first time Davis had seen him in something other than a suit and he immediately liked the image the President presented at home in the privacy of his chambers. He was suddenly approachable, vulnerable, although still undeniably compelling.

"Ah, Mr. Davis. Punctual as always, I see. I'm sorry to keep you waiting, but I took a longer workout than usual. The pool really helps me unwind, you know. And these summer nights remind me of home. We used to go skinny dipping in Parker creek at dusk, just us and the water moccasins," he laughed. "I see you've got a drink."

"Yes, sir. Some of your fine sour mash."

"I think I'll join you," Parker sighed. "I've earned one today." He poured himself a tall drink. "Can I freshen yours?"

"Yes, thank you, sir."

Parker poured him another then raised his glass in salute. "Your health," he said and drank deeply, savoring the sweet essence of the strong Kentucky whiskey. "My God! There's few things I like better than a good sour mash."

"I quite agree, Mr. President."

Parker sat down in a highbacked dark green leather chair near the open windows and leaned back closing his eyes. "Sit down, Mr. Davis." He breathed in deeply, enjoying the scent of the evening air. "It's a beautiful night, isn't it? This is the time of day I like best. Everything seems to slow down, become less urgent. I usually sit here for an hour or so and try to unwind."

Davis took a seat in a matched chair directly in front of the President.

"It's a pity you have to spoil it by telling me about that S.O.B. Benest."

Davis stifled a smile. "Believe me, sir, it's no pleasure."

"Well, let's get on with it. What's he up to?"

"Pretty much of what you anticipated. He met with Cubbi Bertone, Alfredo Fontana, Rudi Markowitz, and Wally Penchinski yesterday in his suite at The Madison. I've got a transcript of their conversation."

"Leave it with me," Parker sighed. "Can you give me a synopsis?"

"Yes, sir. Their initial response to the Shuttle was hostile as you predicted, and their stance with regard to the legislation in Congress is to fight you with everything they've got; wildcat strikes, boycotts, lobbyists, wholesale walkouts if necessary. In their words they want to shut the country down, make big business suffer, put the fear of God in the consumer, and put you in the dog house. To put it delicately, sir, one of them even suggested eliminating you from the picture."

"Fontana?" Parker asked.

"Yes, sir."

"That so and so is getting to be annoying," Parker mused. "You'd at least think he'd come up with something original."

"I wouldn't take him too lightly, sir."

"I don't, Mr. Davis. That's why I've got you working this operation."

"At any rate, sir. I instructed the agent on duty to pass the word along upstairs and put a full team on each of those guys, just in case they are seriously plotting against your life."

For a moment, Parker looked troubled, then his expression changed as his thoughts took another course. "So they're going to take it to the streets are they?"

"Yes, sir. And apparently they're willing to press their members to the limits in order to discredit you. Benest vowed it was either you or them."

"I wonder what he'd say if he knew we were listening to him? Probably scream that his civil rights had been violated, his right to privately plot my assassination with his thug friends."

"I'm sure he would, sir."

"Well, it's too bad Mr. Benest will never get his day in court." Parker paused for a very long time, his eyes shut, appearing after a while to be asleep. "Mr. Davis," he began suddenly. "It's time to give Benest and his kind a taste of their own medicine. But it's got to look like an inside job. Like the Hoffa thing. Rivalry among the bosses, big money, bad blood, and messy solutions."

Davis remained silent for a moment, considering the possibilities. "Is Benest the only one?"

"No. All the rest have to go, but not all at once. In fact, I want them all to think about Benest after he's gone and wonder who was responsible. Let them struggle with the uncertainty of not knowing who will be next."

Davis said nothing.

"You understand why they have to go, don't you Mr. Davis? We're desperate. The country can't stand a major economic setback. If the unions start trouble, it's going to send repercussions into every facet of American life, and there's only so much I can do legally under the Taft-Hartley Act. But if we remove the main source of irritation, as we did with Said, then we buy time while the hierarchies reorganize, which means in-fighting and a disruption in the normal flow of business."

"I understand, Mr. President," Davis said. His commitment to Parker was total and he had his instructions.

Parker opened his eyes and let them stray to the lights on the avenue beyond the White House compound. Davis set his empty glass on the coffee table and rose slowly.

"I'll leave it to you, Mr. Davis—the place, the method— only I ask that you do it within the next thirty days."

"Yes, sir." Davis remained for another few instants to see if there would be more, but Parker seemed lost in another dimension. "Goodnight, Mr. President."

"Goodnight, Mr. Davis," Parker said without looking at him. "And good hunting."

Parker sat for nearly an hour after Davis had left, running it all through his head one more time to make certain he had made the right decision. It was the only way he could see, the only way to achieve total independence, the only way to assure absolute freedom for mankind; something that had not existed since the end of World War II when for a few brief moments in history the world had breathed a unanimous sigh of relief. Then, of course, the doors had shut, the minds of free men were once more throttled with prejudice and nationalistic misconceptions, and the cold war had begun. In every part of the world, the Russians were disrupting the delicate balance of peace, and counting on the reluctance of the United States to take firm action, to continue their expanding influence and agitation.

Parker was certain that the message he had imparted to Muniz that afternoon was already being turned over in Perez's mind. He knew that Mexico could and would be most difficult to deal with, despite her obvious vulnerability. But more serious than that was the information Parker had received concerning clandestine conferences between Perez and special envoys from the Kremlin. There was little doubt what had been discussed. What had the Soviets offered in return for a shift of loyalties? Undoubtedly everything the Mexicans had demanded. What would they deliver? Political unrest, leading to open confrontation and violent internal conflict; perhaps ultimately the overthrow of Perez or his successor and the insurgence of a strong leftist government with the support of the Kremlin.

And how long could Saudi Arabia hold out? Her oil supply to the free world was too critical to leave untouched. Already the West had felt the impact of a stoppage from the Middle East when the Straits of Hormuz were shut down for a brief three weeks by a terrorist bombing of a supertanker. There would come a time in the Russian scheme of things, when the flow of petroleum would have to stop, when the West would be hamstrung, when OPEC's policies would be dictated by the Kremlin. Already, OPEC had taken a puni-

214

tive position toward the U.S. and an uncompromising position with respect to world economic stability. Did they not see the bear looming over them, its giant paws rushing down to crush them?

When would the Russians move on Mexico, Venezuela, even the North Sea? It was of course inevitable that they should try. Only for a short time had the alliance between China and the U.S. thrown them off their stride. But it seemed they had redoubled their resolve to continue the pattern set in the wake of the war to end all wars. Why had so few of his predecessors not seen it more clearly. Why had all but Reagan chosen to ignore the domino principle after Vietnam in the hopes that it would go away? Now the chips were falling into line.

Brazil was the latest Latin American country to suffer major disturbances. Silent for so long, the sleeping giant of the Southern Hemisphere had erupted with angry conflict between the haves and the have-nots, a tragic confrontation precipitated by the rapid growth of the country from primitive to industrial leviathan, leaving its people desperately torn between the old and new, wealth and poverty. It was a bitter situation that still existed despite continued efforts by the U.S. to reach a negotiated peace between the Cuban-backed rebels and the government.

Eventually, Russia would even turn toward China, border disputes would arise, and the United States in its own interests would find itself in a situation that would most probably end in global decimation.

Of course the tension in the Middle East made that possibility a day-to-day reality. The peace treaty negotiated by Carter, Sadat, and Begin was a noble effort of foolish and nearsighted good will, like so many treaties of the past that had been engineered by men whose hearts were true, but who in the long run would have very little to say about the course of human events. There were too many variables, too many sides to satisfy to ever allow that treaty to remain intact, and what it did was to drive a wedge into the Arab world and add fuel to the fires of religious hatred that had burned for over five thousand years and would continue to do so if something weren't done to change the entire perspective in that part of the world.

The fact that a major confrontation between Russia and the U.S. had not erupted in the Middle East was a miracle, and only served to increase the probability that such an event would soon occur, as the PLO once more geared up its macabre killing machine to grind into mincemeat hundreds of innocent people in the name of religious and national devotion. It was inevitable that armed conflict would come before the end of Parker's Administration, either in China or the Middle East; the end result would be the same.

Therefore, there was absolutely no place for internal conflict as far as Parker could see. The United States was not only going to have to shine as a beacon for the other free countries of the world, it was going to have to make certain that its own affairs were in order, that its own borders were safe, and that its own people were prepared mentally and physically to protect themselves or bow to Russian Communists at the foot of the Washington Monument.

Union disorder, financial instability, political unrest, all were conditions he could not allow to exist. The coming months would prove to be the most trying in the history of mankind, if humanity were to survive; and if freedom had any hope of surviving, the United States was going to have to survive. Parker was going to have to survive.

. . . 16 August 1989

Thirty-five miles off the southern tip of Florida, on that muggy summer evening with thunderheads threatening in a heavy sky, a forty-eight foot fishing boat plodded through sullen seas, bearing northeast toward the Keys. The vessel *Allegro* was Cuban, its dark-skinned crew a motley assortment of unfortunates who scavenged the Caribbean waters for a meager living and sometimes hired out for the right price to perform certain favors for the government, even though it meant the risk of being captured, perhaps even killed if they were unlucky. These were men to whom yesterday was best forgotten and tomorrow did not exist until they opened their eyes and saw the sun.

On board, the evening meal had been taken, and the crew had made preparations in anticipation of some rough weather before the night was through. The captain was drunk on rum in his cabin below, as he was every night, and José, the mate, once again took the helm, his eyes trained on the horizon that time and again was streaked with forks of lightning from the approaching storm. It was nothing more than a squall, a seasonal storm common in those waters, yet vicious and unforgiving of the unprepared. A bottle crashed against the bulkhead and José cursed the captain under his breath.

Aleksay Kurochkin stood at the bow, his eyes straining into the gathering darkness. They had strayed north of the Cuban fishing waters and soon they would be entering United States territory. Every man on board knew what would happen if they were caught by the Coast Guard, but no man, save for Aleksay, knew what lay in store for them that night. The storm worried him, but in the event that they were spotted, it

217

just might give him the cover he needed to slip away. He turned from the bow and walked toward the hatch across the gently rolling deck.

Two hours after sunset, the wind died and the sea grew calm. It was the lull before the storm, and nervous hands fashioned repeated knots in coiled lines or mended the tattered fishnets as the crewmen impatiently awaited the tempest. Their mood was murderous, for they would have chosen to be anywhere but in this patch of coral and shark-infested waters on such a night.

The horizon was a tapestry of sheet lightning, and across the glassy sea, the thunder rolled like cannon fire. The sputtering chug of the diesel engine was the only other sound to break the vacuum of the sweltering night air.

At nine, Aleksay rose from his filthy bunk wearing only a short pair of bathing trunks. Sweat dripped from his body and he felt limp, drained by the oppressive humidity and merciless heat of the cabin. From a battered foot locker, he laid out his wet suit, the helmet, jacket, legs, and boots, and checked them carefully for punctures. Next to these he placed a waterproof bag containing a service automatic and two hundred rounds of ammunition, a change of clothing, and a diver's knife and compass. He double checked each piece of equipment, before removing his air tank and regulator from the trunk. With a special gauge he tested the air supply; the tank was full, 2250 PSI. He took a few short tugs at the mouthpiece to make sure it was functioning properly. The air tasted cold and faintly metallic.

Shoving the trunk back under the cot, Aleksay drew out a wooden crate with a locked top which he opened, removing several layers of cardboard insulation. Inside was an oblong metal cylinder with two plastic handles on one end and a metal propeller on the other; a miniature electric-powered sea skate measuring 100 centimeters long and weighing 20.25 kilograms, about forty-five pounds.

Carefully he removed the skate from the box and placed it next to his other equipment, freeing the cardboard stops from the propeller and rotating it several times to be certain that the bearings were not bound. From the bottom of the crate, he took two compact chemical battery packs, which he installed in the watertight compartment on the underside of the skate, then checked the level and found them charged to peak capacity. He pressed the drive button and the propeller whirred softly. Everything was in order.

He unscrewed the single dim lightbulb in its fixture, plunging the cabin into darkness, then opening the door stepped out into the gangway. He could see the light under the captain's door and assumed that he was by now completely obliterated as he had been for the past two nights. Silently, he made his way forward and emerged on deck just in front of the tiny wheelhouse.

José looked at him sullenly as he approached. "What is our position?" Aleksay asked in fumbling Spanish.

"Ask the captain," José grumbled.

Aleksay understood well enough to turn red with anger, and he gave José a look that sent shivers into his bowels.

"Twenty-eight miles from the Florida Keys," José said grudgingly. "If this fucking storm does not blow us off course, we should reach them by morning."

"Maintain your heading as instructed, and notify me when we have passed the twenty-five mile limit."

The Cuban glowered but did not respond, and Aleksay disappeared back into the hatch, taking careful note of where the other men were. Two were in the stern playing dice and drinking; one was forward asleep against the bulwark. And the captain was drunk in his quarters. They were all accounted for. He returned to his cabin to wait.

At five minutes to ten, the mate stomped on the deck above and shouted, "We're entering U.S. waters!"

Aleksay stood in the blackened cabin dressed in full diving rig, his tank on his back, his knife strapped to his left forearm. The storm that had been threatening was beginning to whistle in the riggings, and the swells slapped the hull with increasing force. There was one more task to perform.

Clutching a wax paper parcel in his hand, he slipped silently into the gangway and moved aft toward the engine room, his ears straining for the sound of approaching footsteps. He made the door unobserved and entered, closing it behind him. He found a single dim light bulb burning and immediately went to work. From the parcel he took a half pound of plastic explosives and a timer-activated detonator. Deftly he molded the explosives to the boiler of the ancient engine, and attached the detonator, setting the timer for ten minutes. That would give him just enough time to get over-board and safely away.

He paused at the door long enough to unscrew the light bulb, then slipped out and hurried back to his cabin, where he hefted his equipment and turned sharply back into the passage. Suddenly, there was a second shattering of glass from the captain's cabin and the door was thrown open. The captain stood in silhouette staring at him through a blur of rum.

There was no time to think. Aleksay moved through instinct, reaching the doorway in two strides, heaving the sea skate at the man's bobbing head. It struck with a resounding smack, the skin parted to the sound of crunching bone, and the captain reeled backward and crashed to the floor striking the back of his head on the bulkhead. He lay motionless, blood oozing from his gaping wounds.

Certain that the disturbance had alerted the others, Aleksay bolted toward the forward hatch, climbed the steps, and reached the side an instant later, vaulting over the bulwark into the black seething waters with an explosive splash.

In the wheelhouse, José rose and squinted into the dark-ness. He had been thinking of Rosita, and was not sure what he had heard or seen. But Manuel, who had been playing cards with Jorgé in the stern, came running forward yelling, "He jumped overboard! The foreigner jumped overboard!"

José stepped from the wheelhouse, puzzled. It had been the plan for the foreigner to go overboard, but only when the coastline was in sight. He did not know what to think. "Go below and tell the captain!" he ordered, and cut the engine back to idle.

Manuel scampered below as José stepped to the bulwark and stared into blackness. The wind was singing in the lines, and the force of the rising swells sent spray wheezing from the bow. He did not understand.

Hidden in the sea, Aleksay activated the power packs, and using his luminous compass, pointed north toward Florida and squeezed the throttle button. The prop whirled, and the skate jumped forward, pulling him through the surging waves away from the doomed fishing boat.

Manual reached the captain's door to find it open and the captain sprawled against the bulkhead in a pool of his own blood. His eyes were wide and staring and Manuel knew at once that he was dead. Nevertheless, he instinctively felt for a pulse. There was none. Whirling, he bolted toward the companionway.

José was still at the side when Manuel burst from below screaming, "José! He's dead! The captain's dead!"

José turned in surprise to see Manuel silhouetted by a blinding flash and lifted in a tumbling somersault through the air toward him. In the same instant, he felt the hammering impact of the concussion against his chest. The breath left his body as he too was hurtled aloft, deafened by the roaring in his ears. Something burned his skin like the fire of hell itself, and he was barely aware that his clothing was ablaze as his fractured body hit the water and began to sink. He tried to move his arms, but they were useless. His lungs raged for air, but he was powerless to struggle to the surface. At last he could refrain no longer, and succumed to the irresistible impulse to breathe. His lungs filled with tepid salt water and his corpse sank into the fathomless depths.

Aleksay turned briefly at the sound of the explosion, long enough to see the flaming fragments of the shattered wooden ship rise out of the water in a blaze of fire, then plummet back into the sea and sink beneath the waves. The echoing roar that rocked the night faded swiftly in the wind, and he flattened himself once more and squeezed the throttle, knowing that his only chance was to reach the Keys before the power cells died.

. . . 31 August 1989

"Pending your approval, Don, this is the final site plan."
Ralph Owens spread a large blueprint on the conference
table of the President's private library, showing the master
plan of the Oasis Project compound, a sprawling maze of
subterranean caverns and cubicles connected by miles of
tunnels, covering an area roughly one square mile.

"Arnold's approved this?" Parker asked.

"Yes, and he's waiting for your go-ahead."

"Run me through it," Parker said, leaning forward to
study the matrix of lines and rectangles.

"All right. Here's the main chamber, roughly half a mile
long and a quarter of a mile wide, two hundred feet below
the surface. The ceiling will be retractable in sections,
hangar doors, made of corrugated reinforced steel and two
feet of external silicon insulation tinted to match the surface
of the salt flats. When they're closed, no one will have any
idea what's underneath. Around the periphery will be the
dormitories, officer's quarters, recreation facilities, medical
facilities, mess, power plants; in short, everything an
underground city could possibly need.

"The control tower will be there." He pointed to the center
of the north wall of the main cavern. "And underneath it will
be the computer and back-up computer system, which is
identical and designed as an override in the event of a failure
in the primary system. If there's no failure, the primary
system cannot be overridden without a special code, similar to
the fail-safe system."

"How many people will have access to this code?"

"Only you, me, and Arnold."

"What about security?"

"Security will be provided by a hand-picked garrison selected from various branches of the service for special assignment. They are being enlisted on a tour basis and will be committed for the duration of the project. Secrecy and loyalty oaths will be administered to all personnel and will be enforced to the full extent of military law."

"What about outside security?" Parker asked.

"A ground level perimeter has been established with an average radius of ten miles from ground center of the complex. This perimeter will be patrolled by armed details. The fences are wired with a light charge to discourage any sight-seers without serious injury, and they are clearly marked.

"One mile inside the perimeter remote control machine gun bunkers have been placed four hundred yards apart and will command a 360 degree sweep of the landscape. They will be activated by seismic sensors implanted every one hundred feet at a distance of one hundred yards outside the bunker line. No one entering this area on foot will escape alive.

"There are only two passages through this line of defense. One road to the north and one to the south, which leads to the landing strip shown here on the map. Our troops will move along this route in armored vehicles using coded transmitters.

"There is only one main gate, and this gate will be manned by a garrison of fifty men at all times. If the gate is violated, they will be the first line of defense, with orders to hold that position to the last man. If they fail, then the backup remote system comes into play and lastly the armored garrison at the compound itself. As you can see, everything has been designed to prevent surface entry, while limiting visibility and therefore avoiding any undue notoriety."

"What about an assault by air?" Parker asked.

"Should there be an airborne entry into our restricted airspace, the alien craft would be picked up one hundred miles out. That will include commercial airliners that have strayed off course, and I might add that all commercial flights have been rerouted around the compound site. Our air traffic control will demand that any aircraft violating the airspace identify immediately and vacate the area at once. If they refuse to do so, the warning will be repeated and a fighter intercept squadron will be scrambled from the Top Secret Navy base in the Black Mountains foothills. Air to ground missile sites are also projected where you see the black crosses." He pointed them out at various spots around the complex. "In addition, we will have back-up support available from Edwards Air Force base on a twenty-four hour alert basis. Frankly, Don, the only thing besides a bird that could enter this airspace is a nuclear warhead, and we both know what the result of that would be."

"Excellent, Ralph."

"Then you approve?"

"Yes."

"I'll give Arnold the word," Owens said, rolling up the blueprints.

Parker looked pensive as he walked out of the library back into the Oval Office. Owens followed in silence. From his desk, Parker took a thick manila folder and opened it, reviewing something written on a single sheet of typing paper.

"Ralph, I want to run something by you."

"About the project?"

"No. I'd like to have a feasibility study done on these items, concerning aerial reconnaissance."

Owens took the piece of paper and scanned it. The sheet contained a list of most of the major world cities, alphabetized by country:

Montreal, Canada	Yokahama, Japan
Ottawa, Canada	Amman, Jordan
Peking, China	Kuwait, Kuwait
Havana, Cuba	Pyongyang, N. Korea
London, England	Seoul, S. Korea
Paris, France	Tripoli, Libya
Berlin, Germany	Mexico City, Mexico
Bonn, West Germany	Muscat, Oman
Munich, West Germany	Lima, Peru
Athens, Greece	Warsaw, Poland

Teheran, Iran
Baghdad, Iraq
Jerusalem, Israel
Tel Aviv, Israel
Rome, Italy
Tokyo, Japan
Moscow, USSR
Leningrad, USSR
Kiev, USSR
Chicago, USA
Cleveland, USA

Doha, Qatar
Jiddah, Saudi Arabia
Mecca, Saudi Arabia
Riyadh, Saudi Arabia
Madrid, Spain
Damascus, Syria
Detroit, USA
New York, USA
Washington, D.C., USA
Caracas, Venezuela

The general looked questioningly at Parker. "What sort of reconnaissance?"

"Aerial photography using the new Drone."

Owens suddenly looked skeptical.

"Arnold tells me it's ready for a real mission, and I can't think of anything better to test it out on than what I have in mind."

"That may be, but we're already capable of this kind of surveillance by satellite."

"Not to the extent I want. Am I correct in my understanding that with the Drone, any city on Earth can be surveyed from a height of ninety thousand feet with pinpoint accuracy? Even greater than satellite surveillance?"

"That's what it was created to do."

"With your cooperation, I'd like a study prepared."

"What exactly do you have in mind."

"I've been developing a theory, and I'd like to know what you and the DIA think about it. I've always thought that if a complete systematic survey of all the major cities of the world were carried out, from the standpoint of population flow, density, activity, traffic movement, rail traffic flow, and so on, we might learn a great deal about the continuous mood of the people in those cities, the psychological response they displayed in relation to current world events."

"Such as?"

"I'll give you an example. Suppose a major conflict was shaping up in the Middle East. And suppose we determined

225

by aerial photography that certain Russian population centers were undergoing unusual activity, both military and civilian, say, a massive relocation or even evacuation. Wouldn't that tell us something about the Kremlin's outlook on the future? Wouldn't that warn us that they were preparing for something other than a debate at the UN, that perhaps they considered the possibility of open hostilities imminent?"

"Yes, it's possible."

"Wouldn't that be worth knowing? Wouldn't we have an edge, an ability to read their minds?"

"If we could correctly interpret their responses."

"That's what I think this surveillance will tell us, when coupled with our ground-based sources and our knowledge of world events."

"But why American cities? I see you've got . . ."

"Because we would know exactly what was happening in those cities, and they would give us the control data we needed to make comparisons with other population centers."

"Damned interesting concept."

"Do you think it would work?"

"I haven't the slightest idea. But it's sure worth a feasibility study."

"Commission the study. Put the best minds we have on it. If I'm right, it could give us the edge we need to keep ahead of the Russians. I don't mind telling you, I don't trust the bastards. Not with this thing in the Middle East boiling. I want to be prepared on all levels, and I don't think our conventional surveillance can react quickly enough to interpret all the factors involved."

"I'll give it to Defense Intelligence immediately. They can work up a prospectus and give us an evaluation."

"Keep me informed, Ralph. I think we've got to assume that the Russians are going to make another move in the Middle East. Maybe Saudi Arabia. Maybe the whole fucking Persian Gulf. I don't like to think what that could mean."

"I think we both realize what that would mean, Don."

Parker nodded gravely.

"I'll call Arnold this afternoon and tell him to proceed

with the excavation. I know he's eager as hell."

"I'll expect to hear from you, then, Ralph. Thanks for coming in."

He sat behind his desk for a long time after the general had left, watching the traffic flow by on the avenue. It was rush hour, and he wondered what the streets of Washington would look like from ninety thousand feet up, jammed with moving piles of metal, the sidewalks crammed with pedestrians. Would they look like so many milling ants, indiscriminately scurrying to and fro, or would the experts see something else? A chink in the psyche of an entire people, a vulnerable Achilles heel that could spell defeat for the enemy?

The enemy, however, was only a few blocks away, pacing the plush carpets of his penthouse suite in The Madison. Benest was a troubled man. That morning he had found a handwritten note on his breakfast tray, warning him that he was being watched and that his life was forfeit.

Not that Benest had not received death threats in the past. Threats and warnings were the price he paid for his tumultuous rise to the top. He himself had made a living, and a damned good one, from coercion, bluffs, and outright blackmail, and to receive the same was part of the bargain. But this note was not coercion; it was a promise.

What concerned him was the obvious penetration of his security. Naturally, it led him to consider the possibility of a traitor within his ranks, a secretary, a bodyguard, perhaps a driver, or even one of his personal acquaintances. To that end, the bellboy who had delivered the note with his breakfast had been questioned rigorously, but to no avail. He obviously knew nothing; nevertheless he lost his job.

Benest quickly rejected the idea that it came from one of his fellow labor bosses. Granted, the men with whom he conspired were completely untrustworthy, and it was not inconceivable that each and every one of them could strike out against him; but not now. They had as much at stake as he did. They were at war, but not with each other.

In fact, they needed each other to survive. Their success

would mean the establishment of absolute power over the government, big business, and the American taxpayer. Their failure would mean the degeneration of years of struggle that had brought them to the pinnacle of command over the ignorant, the fearful, and the weak. It was said that the meek should inherit the Earth, but according to Benest's gospel, only through the brutality of a few strong leaders who drew their power from many timid voices.

United, the labor leaders were a driving force, an unstoppable momentum of raw, shortsighted greed, bent upon their own self-aggrandizement, no matter the cost in human souls or ruined businesses. The American ideal of one house, two cars, a recreational vehicle, and unlimited televisions was their dogma; and Benest and his kind would see bloodshed in the streets before they would yield to the forces of reason.

Under Benest and his ruthless associates, the American worker had ceased to be the most valued asset of American business and instead had become its single most destructive liability. It was no longer profitable to continue to produce. Capital reserves, good will, lines of credit, return on investments, profits, dividends to shareholders—all were dwindling with no certainty that a change would come.

But these were none of Benest's concerns. He was interested only in the unlimited power that his constituents placed in his hands. With one proclamation he could shut down the industrial output of the most powerful economy on Earth. That was true power! With a few words, he could reduce a thriving business to a ruin of accounts payable and bad debts. That was true power! And in return for his power, what did he offer the employer who provided the jobs that paid his people, that provided the benefits and wages and dues? Nothing!

And for the unlimited authority that they bestowed upon him, what did he offer his constituents? What did he and his cohorts provide for the common man, who broke his back in the fields, in the factories, who sewed the garments and poured the steel? Assurance that food would be on the table, that TVs would burn brightly in every living room, that every three years new contracts would be wrung from the captains of industry; more benefits, higher wages, greater security, until those villains, those infidels, the representatives of big business who demanded that a man work for his living, crumbled under their attack and yielded to that last great act of selfishness—bankruptcy!

And after that, where would be the security, the benefits, the salaries, the food on the table, and the TVs shining brightly? That was not Benest's concern. His concern was the threat; that someone had finally decided to put an end to his insane rule of fear and uncertainty.

But who would have the nerve, the audacity to threaten him? A crank? Preposterous! A frustrated litigant? Most unlikely. Businessmen were little more than frightened paper pushers. Who then? Higher up? He banished the thought. The government was predictably pusillanimous. Congress was in his back pocket; they all needed to be reelected. Not even Parker with all his warnings had effectively challenged him. To do so would mean political suicide. But just the same, the simple handwritten note in its last two lines had spelled it out clearly and simply: "Benest, your time has come. Count the hours on your fingers."

There was a meeting of the executive council at one o'clock. He called his assistant and ordered two extra body-guards just in case. There was no sense in taking chances.

He drank his lunch, three double martinis, and rang for his car at twelve-thirty. Dressed in his habitual black suit, starched white shirt and dark blue tie, he stared impatiently into the mirror of his dressing room, wondering what was keeping them. He was eager to get to the meeting, to set in motion the plans they had formulated for the coming months. He could hardly wait to smell garbage rotting on the New York sidewalks and see the shelves in supermarkets barren in the wake of a nationwide Carrier's walkout. Those were the visions of his dreams, the fruit of his lifelong efforts. Because once government and business caved in to his demands, the last vestige of free enterprise would be crushed. There would be union men on every board of every major corporation in the country. Nothing, not even a death threat, could keep him from this meeting.

At twelve-thirty-five, the front desk buzzed and, accompanied by his assistant, he went out into the hall where six of his most trusted bodyguards were waiting to escort him into the elevator. They started down.

Between the penthouse and the lobby, Davis moved like a precision instrument. Having positioned himself on top of the car at exactly twelve-fifteen, he had assured that this would be the only elevator to service the penthouse by using a simple electronic cutoff switch to stall the other car at the second floor level.

Now as they slid down the narrow shaft toward the ground, he checked the AR-15 Army issue automatic rifle. The clip was full. He fed a round into the chamber at the seventh floor. At the sixth, he hooked the wire loop, secured to the trap door in the ceiling with his toe. At the fifth, he jerked his foot upward, pulling the door open, and sank to one knee. The occupants below stared up at him, their eyes questioning in that instant between confusion and horrified realization.

They saw the cold steel muzzle of the weapon, heard the metallic crack as Davis depressed the trigger, and saw the first blast of fire as the machine leapt into action, spitting death into the enclosure.

It was over by the third floor, and at the second, Davis transferred to the roof of the stalled car and reactivated the switch, causing the car to rise quickly away from the descending carnage.

Just below the penthouse, he stopped the car once more and leaving his weapon on the roof, climbed down through the hatch and exited into the peaceful corridor. Entering the stairwell, he pulled on a pair of dirty grey coveralls hidden in a trash bin and jogged down the stairs to the basement.

At the first floor, a bellboy recoiled in nausea at the mangled, bullet-ridden bodies, entwined and lying motionless in an expanding pool of their mingling blood. The acrid smoke of the rifle fire hung in the air, filtering slowly out the open hatch in the roof.

Patrons of the hotel ran screaming into the Washington

sunshine, away from the slaughter. Benest lay twisted below the heap of bodies, his carcass riddled with holes, his starched white shirt stained with his own red blood, his eyes staring upward in disbelief. He had seen, but his wordless mouth would never betray the ultimate confidence Davis had shared with him.

The police came and cordoned off the area, Ambulances arrived to carry away the dead in brown plastic bags on bloodstained sheets. Passersby stopped and wondered who might have been under those shrouds. Mothers shielded their children's eyes and hurried away, afraid to face the reality. Here and there a policeman shook his head in silent disgust.

Aleksay stood at the corner, watching the scene, trying to figure out what had happened. He had followed Davis to the hotel at a little after twelve, and had watched him go in, as he had for the four previous mornings. Knowing that there were only two means of access and egress, he had waited patiently for his quarry to come out the alley exit as he had the previous four days. He was not concerned. Davis was easy prey, his any time he chose. He was curious. Did the man have a lover in the hotel? Perhaps, but he always reappeared at about the same time, twelve-forty, and walked away down the side street to a car parked at the curb.

The first clue he had that something was different that day was the muffled but unmistakable reports of automatic rifle fire from inside the hotel. He had thought first of leaving, but realizing that no one would notice him in the gathering crowd, he had stayed. At precisely twelve-forty-three, he had seen Davis appear from the alley, dressed in his coveralls, enter a white cleaning van parked at the curb, and drive away in the swirl of lunch-hour traffic.

He had known at once that Davis was involved in the disturbance, but watched passively as the van turned the corner and disappeared. He knew where to find the man. The Americans were such fools in their own country, so sure of their own security.

It was nearly an hour later, while dining at a little outdoor cafe, that Aleksay overheard the news from a man at a nearby table. The victims of the shooting had included

231

George Benest of the COL. Was that not the most powerful labor union in the United States? What a curious victim for an American agent. It raised several perplexing questions, the first of which was, who was Roger Davis working for? The American government? The sudden realization that the United States government was conducting covert operations against its political opposition struck him as a singularly important piece of propaganda, which could be used to great advantage by the Kremlin against Parker's Administration.

If, as Aleksay suspected, Davis was a CIA operative, carrying out covert acts of violence both at home and abroad, might he not be more valuable alive than dead? Could they penetrate his apparat and perhaps discover the source of this master plan of action? Would it lead to the top of the CIA or perhaps even the White House? It was certainly worth investigating, and for the present, Aleksay elected to postpone his mission and contact the Center, even though it meant surfacing from deep cover to do so.

He would arrange a meeting with the man he had been instructed to contact in the event of complications. It would be safer to go to the Embassy in person, rather than to arrange a meeting by phone. He finished a leisurely lunch of filet of sole and white wine, hailed a cab, and gave the driver instructions to take him to the Russian Embassy. The afternoon was warm, and he felt relaxed, in control, and happy to be in the heat of the action once more.

"Shirley?" Bruce said into the phone. "Is the President in conference?"

"Yes, Mr. Wilson," she replied.

"Will you see if he can be interrupted. I've got some urgent news for him that I think he should hear."

"May I tell him what it is?"

"Tell him George Benest was assassinated at The Madison just after noon today."

"Hold the line, Bruce."

Bruce waited scarcely fifteen seconds.

"Mr. Parker says for you to come right down."

Bruce was out the door and down the hall to the Oval

Office almost before Shirley had hung up the phone. Seeing him, she pressed the intercom button and Parker buzzed back. "Go right in, Bruce," she said gravely.

Bruce entered the Oval Office to find Parker in conference with Montie Montgomery and Preston Holmes. They all looked slightly white in reaction to the news.

"I'm sorry to interrupt, Mr. President, Mr. Vice-President, Mr. Secretary. But I thought you would want to hear the news right away."

"What exactly happened, Bruce?" Parker asked.

"I don't have all the details, but at about twenty to one, Benest and seven of his assistants were shot as they were taking the elevator down from the penthouse. The police say it's obviously a professional job. They found the weapon on the roof of the other car and an electronic device that had caused the car to stall just before the attack."

"Do they have any leads, any witnesses?"

"None at the present. Of course there's already speculation that it was a mob killing."

"A what?" Preston Holmes said in shock.

"It's not surprising, considering his connections with organized crime, Preston," Montie said in slightly derisive tone.

"Is there anything else, Bruce?" Parker asked.

"Only that I think you ought to issue a statement, expressing the White House's dismay and shock at the brutal slayings and promising full FBI support in the investigations."

"I agree, Bruce. Will you get that out right away, and keep me informed of any further developments?"

"Yes, sir. Excuse me, gentlemen."

Bruce hurried back to his office and sat down to work on the press release. Then he had a sudden thought and picked up the phone. He dialed and waited for a long time. "Kathy?"

"Hi, Bruce. You just caught me on my way to a meeting."

"I just thought you'd be interested. Did you hear the news?"

"What news?"

"George Benest was shot gangland style in the elevator of The Madison at twelve-forty this afternoon."

"No shit?!" Kathy said on a rising note, then lowered her voice remembering where she was. "No shit?" she whispered.

"No shit. Looks like either mob or union in-fighting."

"God! I wish I was still at the paper!" Kathy exclaimed before she could catch herself. Her secretary looked at her coldly for an instant, and Kathy turned her back to the door. "Uh, listen, Bruce. I can't talk right now. How about doing something after work?"

"Fine with me. I think I can break free. How're things going, anyway? You've been incommunicado for the past three weeks."

"I know. It's just that with all the projects over here and the stuff I'm having to learn, I haven't had much time to do anything but eat, work, and sleep."

"Well, I don't know about the eating and working, but I could handle the sleeping part," he chuckled.

"I could go for that," she said. "Listen, call me later. OK?"

"How about just coming by my place when you get off work? I'll pick up some steaks and a bottle of wine."

"It's a date. See you then." She hung up feeling good for the first time since she had been in the new job; but as she walked past her snippy little secretary, she remembered what she was about and that there were probably spies all over the place. Her mood changed once more to grey, as she hurried to the meeting she was already five minutes late for.

Bruce turned to his typewriter with renewed enthusiasm and pounded out a powerful statement full of moral outrage and political innuendo.

Aleksay was announced to Sergei Zeitsev as a Tass correspondent, and at first Zeitsev refused to see him. After all, he was busy with more important matters than the problems of journalists. And, besides, that was not his department. He sent his assistant back downstairs with the name of the man on the ground floor for Aleksay to see.

When his assistant returned a few minutes looking cowed

and somewhat frightened, with a strong message from the man in the lobby, Sergei decided that the visitor was either an illegal seeking refuge or a very stupid and stubborn journalist.

But he was not prepared for the person he saw walking through his door a short time later. Aleksay Kurochkin's face was well known in the GRU and it was a face that men like Zeitsev did not care to see more often than necessary.

Aleksay extended his hand and Zeitsev bounded forward to shake it eagerly. "Comrade Kurochkin. Had I known it was you . . ."

"Sit down Comrade Zeitsev. Don't trouble yourself. I did not want to allow the young man to know my real identity." He glanced around at the rather dull walls of the little office by the elevator shaft. It was not much, but then neither was Zeitsev in the overall scheme of things. "We may speak without being heard?" Aleksay asked.

"Yes, Comrade. May I offer you tea?"

"No, thank you, Comrade. We haven't time. There is some very important information I must transmit to the Center. I was given your name as my contact in such an event. I have taken the liberty of encoding it for you, if you will be good enough to send it for me."

"But of course, Comrade. May I ask . . . ?"

"No, you may not. Just send the communique. I will wait."

Aleksay sat stiffly in the single chair in front of Sergei's desk, while Sergei rose with the communique and exited. In a few hours, Aleksay would know the course he would follow. Whether he were instructed to proceed with his mission at once or to continue his surveillance, he sensed in Davis an adversary of some talent, albeit limited, and looked forward to the hunt which could only end one way—with a bullet through the American's brain.

By the evening news hour, the country was abuzz with the story of Benest's untimely death. The FBI was calling it a gangland style hit, but no one was guessing that there may have been connections to other labor leaders.

Predictably, all unions in the country issued a statement more or less to the effect that they were unanimously shocked and horrified at the act of violence, and assured their memberships that their brotherhoods were strong and united in the causes for which Benest had lived his life.

The press, it appeared, was warming up to have a field day with this, the hottest news item since the Said killing. There was so much news on the tube that evening, in fact, that normal programming was set back a full hour to allow the networks to hash and rehash the startling events and sling their readymade personal profiles of the great union boss into the airwaves from coast to coast. Anyone who had been within four blocks of The Madison that afternoon was interviewed, and most had a theory or claimed to have seen a suspicious black limousine or a shady-looking character lurking near the hotel all morning. No one mentioned the nondescript panel truck leaving the alley behind the hotel, nor did anyone suggest that a particularly foreign-looking man who had lingered near the street corner since shortly after noon to just before one, had anything to do with the unseemly events.

It was carnival atmosphere, and Parker watched enough to hear Bruce read his prepared speech and see the sacked bodies rolled from the hotel lobby to the waiting ambulances.

At six-fifty, the phone rang and he answered it.

"Parker."

"Don? Arnold, here."

"Yes, Arnold."

"I just thought you'd like to know that the lasers are going to be ready to go earlier than we expected. I think we can start inside of two weeks."

"Wonderful, Arnold. By the way, did Ralph talk to you about my proposal?"

"About using the Drone to run reconnaissance . . . ?"

"Yes. What do you think?"

"Very ingenious."

"Do you think he bought it?"

"I don't see why not. I'll get on the programming tapes right away."

"Better wait until the feasibility study has been completed, for appearances' sake."

"Anything you say, Don. Have you seen the news?"

"Yes, I'm watching it right now."

"Really something, huh?"

"Live by the sword, die by the sword, they say, Arnold."

"I'll let you go, Don."

"Thanks for calling. And keep me informed on the feasibility study will you?"

"Will do."

Parker hung up and switched off the television. The news that construction could begin two weeks early made him feel very good, and coupled with the success of Davis' mission he felt good enough to treat himself to an extra Bourbon before dressing for dinner with His Excellency Enrique de Gonzales-Perez and Ambassador Muniz. The night promised to be as exciting as the day had been.

Kathy left her desk at eight-forty-five, locked the office door, and walked briskly down the semidarkened corridor into the lighted front foyer. Gus, the night security guard was at the desk and smiled his warm grandfatherly smile.

"Hi, Gus."

"Evenin', Miss Karpovich. Put in another busy day?"

"They're all busy, Gus."

Just then, the sound of a phone ringing crackled along the tiled corridor. They both stopped to listen.

"Sounds like it could be yours," Gus said.

"My private line, maybe. Switchboard's closed, isn't it?"

"Yeah."

"Well hell. Let it go. I've had enough for one day."

Gus laughed and took the pen as she handed it back to him after signing out.

"That's right, Miss Karpovich. There's only so much an employer can expect from you in one day. You go home and have a nice supper and watch some TV. That's what you need."

"Goodnight, Gus. See you tomorrow."

"Goodnight, Miss Karpovich. Drive carefully."

Kathy pushed through the front doors into the warm air of an Indian summer evening, feeling free at last and looking forward to a quiet intimate dinner, and afterwards something she both needed and wanted.

Gus listened as the phone continued to ring, but just as he stood up and began walking toward Kathy's office, thinking that it might be something important, the ringing stopped. Shrugging, he walked back to the front door.

Sergei hung up and looked at Aleksay across his desk. "I'm afraid she has already gone for the day. We can try calling her later at home."

"She is trustworthy?" Aleksay asked.

"So far, she has proven helpful and her work is relatively good. She appears to be learning. What shall I say to her when we do reach her? I've been using a sign method to contact her. She may become overly excited if I break the routine."

"Tell her nothing over the phone. Arrange a meeting. You will introduce me to her, and I will do the rest. Are you positive of her connections?"

"She has been seeing him for almost six months, on and off. I know they sleep together, although I am not certain of the extent of their relationship beyond that."

"Then what guarantee do we have that she will be able to extract the information from him?"

"I'm afraid none. We can only try. There is one thing in our favor, however. She is both greedy and eager to end her relationship with us. I told her at the outset that she might expect to work for us for two years. Perhaps we can convince her that by doing extra special favors like this, she can shorten that time period."

"Perhaps. At any rate, once this operation is over, it may

be necessary to eliminate her, especially if she refuses to cooperate."

"If it becomes necessary, I will make the arrangements myself," Sergei said. "But now, come. I have instructed the kitchen to prepare a special treat for tonight. Steaks, baked potatoes, and Chivas Regal Scotch. You will be pleased."

He escorted his important guest out of the office down to the private dining room on the ground floor, reserved for the lesser dignitaries. Tonight they would dine like czarists.

Dinner at the White House was served promptly at nine. In attendance were Eldon Parker, Montie Montgomery, Ambassador Muniz, and His Excellency El Presidente, Enrique de Gonzales-Perez.

The summit level dinner had not been publicized. Perez had arrived by private jet at eight o'clock and had been taken under military escort directly to the White House. Parker had thought it best to keep the meeting quiet, knowing the sensitive areas that needed to be discussed would quite probably touch off a minor tiff between the two until Perez had had a chance to think the issues over more carefully.

To say that the meeting was informal, however, would be far from the truth. Since Parker's meeting with Muniz, the two presidential staffs had been dickering about the format for the meeting, Perez wanting a full summit, Parker sticking to his request for a quiet personal dinner at which they could discuss the issues informally without restraint.

It was no secret that Perez's nose was officially out of joint after Muniz's rather undiplomatic treatment at the hands of the American President; and at first he had been insistent on demanding an official public apology from the United States to Mexico. Muniz, however, having experienced firsthand Parker's unique form of intimidation, sensed that an open apology would neither be forthcoming nor productive. As Ambassador, he took it upon himself to promote a more rational approach and at long last reason had prevailed.

It had been a difficult three weeks, but at last they were all assembled over veal Picatta, braised asparagus tips, new potatoes, and a fine selection of California wines. The President was a stickler for domestic products and refused to allow any foreign products to be served, purchased, or otherwise consumed by the White House.

Dinner conversation was guardedly polite and innocuous as had been the brief cocktail hour discussions, which had scarcely lasted the length of one drink per the President's instructions. But as the evening wore on toward eleven o'clock and the four men's stock of trivialities dwindled, the topic of discussion inevitably turned to the issues on everyone's mind; political and economic relations between the United States and Mexico.

It was, in fact, Perez who finally broke the truce as the dinner was removed and apéritifs were poured. "And now, Mr. President. You have served me a fine dinner. I have sipped your excellent domestic wines, I have listened patiently to conversations about professional golfers, the World Series and the upcoming professional football season. But may I respectfully suggest that we address ourselves to the purpose for which we have gathered this evening? And that is to discuss an official apology from your Administration to my country for the gross fallacious accusations and innuendoes perpetrated by yourself in the presence of my foreign Ambassador, Señor Muniz."

There followed an oppressive silence, during which Muniz stifled a smile and turned to Parker, anticipating the aftershocks. But Parker stared unflinchingly across the lengthy table at his Mexican counterpart, his lips pressed tightly together in an expression that resembled neither smile nor frown. Muniz, however, winced painfully and sank a little deeper into his seat cushion. With one glance, Montie swept the servants from the room.

"Mr. President," Parker began calmly, with an edge of annoyance in his voice. "I have no intention of even entertaining the possibility of making a public apology to your country or your government or yourself; nor will I ever make any such statement to any foreign government or diplomatic representative. It is my habit to choose my words carefully before I speak, and once spoken, I do not intend to ever retract them, for I believe them to be the truth."

Perez's jaw went slack. He glanced first at Montie, who was doing his best to keep from laughing. Then Perez glowered at Muniz who looked like he was about to lose his dinner. Perez was in such shock that it took him fully fifteen seconds before he burst from his chair and pointed an accusing albeit trembling finger at Parker, who still had not moved more than his lips and eyes. "How dare you!" Perez shouted. "Do you think you are addressing a servant? Do you think that you can speak to me in this manner and not be prepared to support your words with action?"

"I have every intention of supporting my words with action, Mr. President," Parker said solemnly, a muddly film veiling his green eyes.

"And just what do you mean by that?"

"Anything you wish to interpret it to mean."

Perez froze. He suddenly saw something in Parker's face that he had not seen in any stateman's face ever before. There was a layer of hardness beneath the skin, a wall of steel, a sinew of iron will, and the glint of danger. Parker looked like a prize fighter or a Roman gladiator, prepared to stand his ground to the death but confident of his ability to survive.

"Sit down, Mr. President," Parker said patiently. "And let's conduct this discussion realistically and sensibly."

At first Perez did not move. He was trapped. To sit would cause him to lose face. To leave would almost certainly sever ties with both a very powerful neighbor and a potentially dangerous enemy.

Muniz, the diplomat, did the thing he was paid to do. He stood slowly, stepped to his President's side, and positioned the chair so that Perez could sit back down. In this way, it was his suggestion that they stay and all the shame was placed on his head.

Perez looked at him, trying to conceal the gratitude in his eyes, then sat down stiffly, his hands placed flat on the table. Muniz took his seat and they waited, all eyes focused on Parker.

"It is not my intention to insult you, Mr. President,"

Parker said at last. "I have the utmost respect for your office, for your government, for your aspirations for your people, and for your belief in your own good intentions."

Montie privately took his hat off to Parker's marvelously worded statement. In one breath, he had not only saved Perez's face and opened the doors for a frank and meaningful discussion, but he had totally alleviated the necessity for a formal state apology, which he knew would never be forthcoming in any case. Even though he had known Parker for years, the man's mind and courage never ceased to amaze him.

Muniz almost audibly sighed with relief but made no outward sign save to raise his chin an inch or so and sit a little straighter in his chair. Parker continued to stare directly into Perez's dark brown eyes.

"What I wish to accomplish with you, Mr. President, is to arrive at an understanding man to man—not country to country, not ego to ego—by which both of our peoples can prosper. It is imperative that we ascertain exactly what each of us must do to meet the requirements of such a relationship."

Perez reached for his glass of champagne and sipped it in silence, indicating that he was willing to listen. Parker continued.

"The essence of what I have to say is that both of our countries have something that the other not only wants but desperately needs. Both of us have something valuable to exchange, and should we fail to reach a compromise, both of us face the same perils. In the case of the United States, we require your oil at well below market price, in return for which we are prepared to offer a great deal. We are willing to provide sizable investments in your country's developing industry, creating thousands of jobs for your unemployed. We are prepared to offer consultants to train your people in the skills they badly need and have no other means of acquiring. We are prepared to encourage greater trade with your country in the areas you are the most deficient in. In short, we are willing to offer your economy a chance to develop in close association with ours, each sharing in the

242

benefits of the other, each prospering from the growth and solidarity of the other, achieving a political and economic symbiosis unprecedented in modern society.

"That is the essence of the situation. Work with us, share with us, grow with us, and the return to you will be tenfold what you give." Perez started to speak, but Parker raised a hand to stop him. "Let me say, before you speak, that in this relationship we will expect honesty, fairness, and no surprises. We will not sit passively by as we have in the past while you nationalize our investments or run them to ruin by graft and laziness. We won't let you bastardize the spirit of good will that we have offered in this relationship. If there is a breach of faith, my administration will act quickly and decisively to correct the situation on terms far harsher than I have outlined to you here."

Perez's eyes widened. He was aware that he had just been handed an ultimatum, the likes of which had never been made except in times of war, when the victor dictated terms to the vanquished. Though he had not said it in so many words, Eldon Parker had just sworn that in the event of national emergency, the United States would move against Mexico to conquer, indeed subjugate her. It was tantamount to a declaration of war before the fact.

"Now I've spoken my mind, Mr. President. I don't want you to respond to me now, because you haven't had time to carefully consider my words, whereas I've had plenty of time to give this situation a great deal of thought, and believe me, sir, I have. I know you came here expecting to debate the issues, but frankly there are no debatable points. Should you determine to accept my offer, we will meet in your capital where we will refine the exact terms of our agreement. It's my fondest wish to create a bond of brotherhood between our peoples, so that together we can establish our independence before the entire world reaches a point of no return."

Parker rose swiftly and stepped around the corner of the table extending his hand to Perez. The Mexican President stared up at him in disbelief, his head reeling. Slowly he stood and took the President's hand, shaking it firmly but without enthusiasm. He noticed that once more the President's eyes were sparkling green and clear as gems.

After the two Mexicans had gone, Montie, who had remained silent save for terse farewells, sat down and poured a stiff shot of California brandy for them both. Parker paced to the window and stared at the lighted landscape of the White House lawn.

"I hope you know what you're doing, Don," he said at last.

"So do I, Montie. So do I."

Bruce and Kathy lay entwined, their bodies drained, soothed by the tenderness of their passion. Somewhere in the distance, the hum of cars on the freeway came to them like the crashing of waves on an unseen shore. In their minds, there was no Washington, no Middle East, or spies, or tomorrow, or even yesterdays. There was only the present, the gentle warmth of their closeness and the fresh clean smell of autumn in the air.

"Football," she said softly.

"Football?"

"Football."

"The air smells like football, and pompoms, and overcoats, and hot dogs and beer."

"More like exhaust fumes, if you ask me."

"Spoilsport. Where's your spirit of romance."

"Between your legs," he chuckled.

She punched him playfully and pretended to be angry until he kissed her. In the cool glow of the moonlight splashing across the bed through the open balcony door they looked into each others eyes, both searching for something they were afraid of not finding, yet not really expecting to find. Nor did they, but it was all right just the same. They had what they needed—each other and the darkness to hide their disappointment.

"Are you unhappy?" he asked.

"Do I look unhappy?"

"Not particularly."

"Then why do you ask?"

"I don't know. It just seems since you left the *Post* you

haven't been yourself."

She did not reply, but averted her eyes to stare out into the night.

"Did I say something wrong?"

"Not really."

"You are unhappy, aren't you?"

"Let's just say the job is not what I expected."

"Why did you take it?"

"Maybe I copped out for money."

"A woman with your ambition, with her sights set at the top where the big money is?"

"Do we have to talk about this?"

"Not if you really don't want to, but I think you do. I think that's what's been bothering you."

"Who said anything was bothering me?"

"The way you walk, the way you smile, the way you hesitate before speaking."

"Ridiculous."

"Why did you take that job, Kathy?"

"I told you."

"No, you gave me an answer, but it wasn't the right one."

"Bruce, can we talk about something else? All day long all I do is talk about work. When I finally get some time off, I don't want to talk about work. OK?"

He shrugged and looked at the ceiling.

"Well, do you always want to talk about work?" she asked defensively.

"Sometimes I'd like to, but I can't. There are things I know that keep me awake at night, and I'd like to tell somebody."

"Let's just say we're in the same boat but for different reasons. There are things associated with my job that I can't talk about."

"But you can quit."

"So can you," she said.

"Not as easily as you might think."

"That goes for me too."

"I wouldn't say they were exactly the same."

"I didn't say they were."

245

"You mean if you really wanted to, you couldn't leave?" he asked.

"Probably not."

"Why not?"

"Let's just say I made a bargain and I intend to stick to it."

"Well, I can't fault you for that."

"You Harvard lawyers are all the same, you know?"

"No, we aren't."

"Yes, you are. Your commitment to duty is all consuming, and the minute anyone mentions it, you buy whatever they say in the belief that duty is everything."

"Isn't it?"

"I'm not sure."

"Well if your word isn't the most valuable thing you have to offer, what the hell good is anything else?"

"I don't know."

"Is there something better?" he asked.

"Freedom."

"There's a conflict?"

"Sometimes."

"What do you mean?"

"I mean that sometimes we're compelled to do things we don't want to do because of forces beyond our control."

"What would you rather be doing?"

"Sailing to Tahiti, I think. Or working at the *Post* again."

"Why don't you go back?"

"I will eventually. I've got a contract to fulfill."

He looked at her earnestly. "With all your liberal ideas, you're just as old fashioned as I am."

She did not respond.

"You don't have to apologize for that," he said. "It's a rarity today." He smiled but she did not. "But I still don't understand why you left in the first place."

"Bruce, please! *Please! Please! Please!*"

"Please what?"

"Please . . . just shut up and kiss me. Hold me!" She sobbed and clung to him, as if by doing so she could forget the nightmare of her double life.

He found her lips and pressed his to them. His embrace tightened and they came together in forgetful pleasure.

246

. . . 1 September 1989

The morning papers hailed him as a giant among men, the patron saint of the working class, an American success story, a martyr to the cause of freedom and equality. George Benest was eulogized in articles and editorials; his picture was on every front page, the grisly details of his death spattered from front to back of every major publication and tiny gazette in the country.

Moralists proclaimed ruination and foresaw the coming of the apocalypse. When so horrid a crime could be perpetrated in the nation's capital, was the judgment day far away? Why was it the good should always perish for their acts of charity? Men such as George Benest were a dying breed, the country's last hope for salvation. What was the world coming to?

Somewhere in a tiny column on the back page of the editorial section of the *Post,* a relatively unknown reporter dared to suggest that Benest might have suffered his fate at the hands of the unsavory company he chose to keep; that his associations for the past four decades were suspect at best and there were strong ties between George Benest and organized crime figures currently under investigation by the FBI. That writer and the editor who had allowed him to run the story nearly lost their jobs.

Davis read it all with moderate distaste while taking coffee on the balcony of his apartment in the bright morning sunshine. The day was refreshingly cool, and despite the glowing heroic terms used to exalt the fallen demigod of national labor, he managed to enjoy the brief solitude, content with his own small taste of personal achievement.

But he was troubled that the American public should be so misled. Could they actually be that blind, that naive? No doubt the union lobbyists had been up all night feeding the newspapers reams of propaganda, pressuring them with all their cumulative might to ignore the rumors and print the gospel according to the brotherhood. Freedom of the press! A much abused phrase, used to distort the true purpose of the publishers, which was to print their own thoughts, their own conception of reality. And if their views did not coincide with the truth, not to mention the facts, who was there to challenge them? After all, they were the press, they were the media, their word was law. Theirs was the voice of the people, the words and thoughts that the average man and woman formed in echoing choruses across the nation at cocktail parties, in the corner taverns, over the dinner table. It was in the paper; it must be true. And if it came out later that the paper had been wrong, if it turned out that the national anchorman had read copy prepared contrary to the facts, would they believe it? First impressions meant a lot to the average American.

The truth would come out. It had to. The FBI investigation would turn up Benest's associations. There would be congressional hearings, union backlash, accusations and denials. But it would all take time; and with time came apathy, and with apathy forgetfulness. Who would really care? The whole thing would blow over and die in the headlines of tomorrow. And what would have been accomplished? One disgustingly corrupt individual would have been eliminated, quite probably to be replaced by someone just as bad. But if it bought the President precious time, if in some way it took the pressure off the faltering economy, it would have been worth it.

The phone rang and he stepped inside to answer it, drawing it back onto the balcony with him. "Davis, here."

"Your call to Mexico City, Mr. Davis. Please hold," the operator said.

"Hello?" said a delicate slightly accented voice.

"Mercedes?"

"Roger? Is that you?" Mercedes nearly shrieked into the phone. "Where are you?"

"I'm in Washington! How have you been?"

"Lonely!" she replied. "You bastard! You haven't even so much as written!"

He could not help laughing. "Careful, darling. The wires might be tapped. Mercedes, when can I see you?"

"Why should I want to see you? It's been six months!"

"Darling, please. Don't ask me to explain. I told you I might be involved for some time." Up until this point, Davis had not realized how desperately he had missed her. But hearing her voice, having her this close but still so far away caused him to fear not ever seeing her again. He wanted to feel her warmth, touch her silken hair.

"Just the same, you could have written."

"Believe me, Mercedes, if I could have I would have."

"Liar!" she said.

"Are you going to pout?" he teased. "I can just see your lower lip sticking out."

"Go to hell," she said, not sounding like she meant it. She could hardly conceal the excitement in her voice.

"Now is that any way to talk to the man who . . ."

"Not another word, Roger Davis!"

"When can you get away?"

"To where?"

"Lake Tahoe."

"Lake Tahoe?"

"Yes. I've got some time off. I thought we could meet there at least for a week."

"Another whirlwind affair?"

"Mercedes, you know it wasn't like that. If it was, why would I call? You don't know how much I've missed you. I've got to see you."

There was a long silence.

"Mercedes?"

"I'm still here."

"Well?"

"I'll have to check," she said cautiously.

"Check what?"

"Father has just returned from Washington and he is in an awful mood. I don't know what about, but it has something to do with your President Parker."

"Parker? What has he got to do with it?"

"They had dinner last night in Washington."

"Oh really?"

"Yes, and Father came home early this morning and called a cabinet meeting. They've been behind closed doors all day. I think it must be something very important."

"Well, what does all that have to do with us?"

"Nothing, but I have to get Father's permission to go. What shall I tell him?"

"Tell him the truth."

"Are you out of your mind? He would never allow me to meet a man at a foreign resort."

"For Christ's sake, Mercedes, you're over twenty-one whether you like to admit it or not."

"I'm also the President's daughter."

"Yes, I know," he said sullenly. "Have you got any suggestions?"

"I might be able to come with a girlfriend."

"Oh, great," he said not bothering to conceal his annoyance.

"Have you got a better idea?" She sounded hot.

"No. If that's the best you can do, it's the best you can do. I suppose we can find someone for your friend."

"Oh, I don't think she's that kind of a girl."

"Good God, Mercedes! Is everyone in Mexico a virgin princess? I thought that was a bordertown come-on."

"Very amusing, Mr. Diplomat!"

"All right, look. See if you can swing it with your father, and then call me back."

"At this number?"

"Yes. If I'm not in, the switchboard will take a message."

"All right."

There was a long pause.

"I miss you," she said at last.

"I miss you, too. Call me."

"I will. Goodbye."

She hung up and Davis held the receiver to his ear an instant longer, long enough to hear the second click on the line. He froze in amazement, then lowered it to its cradle.

Someone else had been on the line. But who?

"It's confirmed," Ralph Owens said solemnly.

"I can't believe it," Arnold Kemper stammered. "Why wasn't I informed at the beginning?"

"We didn't have any indication at the beginning. Only her record, which was no real grounds for refusal. After all, there were lots of bright kids her age involved in those things in the sixties and early seventies. Being a member of the SDS and burning your draft card or your bra was part of being in."

"That's a very liberal attitude coming from you, Ralph."

"I've got kids her age. Believe me, I know what I'm talking about. I'd be mad as hell if someone refused them a job on the grounds of the childish things they did in high school and college."

"But how did you find out?"

"Well, her background was enough to make us do some extra digging. After all, we thought it kind of strange that an ambitious journalist would suddenly drop a very successful career to become a P.R. type."

"Didn't you check that out before she got the job?" Arnold asked.

"Of course. And she checked out fine. Seems she'd been after SPEC for some time. We've got four separate applications from her for that job. But still, we had some questions, and so after she was hired we put a tail on her to see who she was associating with on her own time."

"How did she meet him?"

"Apparently he contacted her. That's the way they usually operate. They pick a likely subject, study them for a long time, and finally make contact. The first time we got wind of him was at the diner. They came in separate cars and had dinner together. Then they left separately. Our men couldn't get very close, so there's no way to know what was discussed. But we ran a make on the diplomatic plate and found out it was assigned to the Russian Embassy. That was our first surprise. We have to assume that she was in league with him before she got the job and that she was cooperating

251

freely. It's not unlikely, however, that he's got something he's holding over her head."

"Such as?"

"Some form of blackmail. They operate like that. Threats, blackmail, promises of large sums of money; any way they can subvert their quarry's natural tendency to resist. We're checking into her case to see what might exist in her past that would give him some leverage; but we do have some indication that she is receiving sizable payments for each delivery."

"How many have there been?"

"Five. The method is predictable. Dead drops, soda pop cans, coded messages in the newspaper. They think they're being tricky, but all their roaming around just makes them stick out like sore thumbs. Naturally, the DIA was brought in once the FBI got wind of what was going on."

"Do you think she's violated the Project's security?"

"No. She hasn't got access does she?"

"Definitely not. She's only qualified for midrange clearance. It'll . . . or it would have taken her another year to qualify for high level clearance."

"So far we've got a record of everything she's taken. It's all in this file I'll leave with you. You'll see it's mostly preliminary stuff, studies on guidance systems, proposals for new rocket fuel mixtures."

"But why on Earth did you continue to let her operate when you knew she was spying for the Russians?"

"She may do us more good than she does them."

"What do you mean?"

"I mean, if we know that she is stealing military secrets and selling them to the Russians, we can determine what she will have access to and provide her with exactly the information we want the Russians to have."

"You mean enlist her as a double agent?"

"No. She's not good enough to pull that off. She won't know we're onto her."

"You mean you're going to let her continue . . ."

"Let me explain, Arnold, before you get excited. We let her continue on as if nothing is wrong. We advance her in security clearance, although what she's going to be seeing will be no more classified than what she sees now. She won't know that and neither will the Russians. They're so paranoid they classify a new brand of toilet paper. We let her think that she's unobserved, and we provide her with information that will mislead the Russians or information that will do them absolutely no good. That way, we neutralize an entire apparat while we build a case against the Embassy officials. Once we get what we need, we drop the boom and haul everyone in. Then we rub the Russians' noses in it in the world press."

Kemper stared nervously at the Karpovich file. "I don't know if I can do it. I mean, how can I face her knowing what she is, what she's doing?"

"Because you know she isn't doing you any harm; that she's really screwing the Russians, keeping their attention away from the touchy stuff." He paused for a moment. "There's just one one more thing, Arnold. We've got some indication that there's another agent inside SPEC, but we're certain he's in deep cover."

"Another?"

"I'm afraid so."

"But how?"

"It explains a lot of leaks in the past programs, leaks that we couldn't ever plug. Like the Stealth bomber. The DIA has assigned a full team to finding this person. We're replacing certain personnel at the main facility with our people, mostly security guards and secretaries. And that brings me to the other point. We're going to shift the Oasis Project team to the Pentagon. That way we'll know precisely who has access to the material, and we'll make it impossible for peripheral people to even get close to any sensitive information. All your records, data, research equipment, everything will go over to the Pentagon. We've already got a facility prepared. With the exception of your wind tunnels. We'll be supplying extra guards in that area."

"You don't think this will alert her?"

"I don't think so, as long as we continue to provide her access to some kind of information."

"This is totally demoralizing," Kemper sighed.

"Don't let it get to you. By the very nature of our legal system, we enable spies to operate with enormous freedom. We've got to build up an ironclad case before we move, because if we're wrong, we're in deep shit. So it isn't your fault. The important thing is that we know what she's doing."

"What kind of information are we going to provide her?"

"Let her continue rummaging around where she is for now. Those records are mostly outdated and should have been reclassified long ago. If she decides to dig deeper, we'll create bogus information to feed her."

Kemper shook his head reluctantly. "All right, Ralph. If you insist. But I want it clearly noted that you gave clearance for that information to fall into the Russians' hands."

"I'll take full responsibility."

"Who's he?" Kathy asked, sounding frightened. She did not like the looks of the other man with Sergei Zeitsev. He had a cruel face.

"This is Comrade Grechanin," Sergei said, using the fabricated name they had chosen. "He has come to speak to you."

"What's this all about?" she asked, looking around at the deserted park benches. It was not yet lunch time and the park was empty. But soon it would be crowded. It was as risky as hell meeting in broad daylight, and Kathy could tell by Sergei's expression that he too was afraid, but she could not tell what of—the meeting or the man he was with. "I haven't got much time," she said.

"This will not take long," Aleksay said in his most pleasant voice.

Kathy was surprised by his courteous manner, but she was genuinely uneasy. "Well, it had better not. You've got to be crazy meeting me here like this."

"Believe me, Miss Karpovich. We are perfectly safe," Aleksay said. "And if it were not of great importance we would have waited until the normal time. Let us walk as we speak. We will look less conspicuous."

They began to walk, Sergei hanging back watching the surrounding trees and sidewalks.

"Well?" Kathy said.

"It has come to my attention that you are intimate with a Mr. Bruce Wilson of the White House staff, the Press Secretary, is he?"

Kathy turned bright red with anger. "What the hell is this?" she snapped, surprising herself by the strength of her response.

"We do not wish to pry, Miss Karpovich, but in the course of our routine surveillance of you, we have determined you are very close to a source we would like to pursue."

"Forget it! You've got the wrong girl."

"I beg your pardon?"

"You're barking up the wrong tree, Comrade. If you think I'm going to try to pump Bruce for State secrets, not that he has access to any, but if you think I'm going that far with this goddamn business you're out of your fucking minds. As a matter of fact, I'm getting sick and goddamned tired of this crap!"

Aleksay looked questioningly at Sergei, who immediately interrupted.

"Forgive me, Comrade, allow me to explain. Naturally, Kathy, if you feel that you have no influence over Mr. Wilson, it would be pointless to pursue the matter. But hear us out before you make your final decision." The way he used the word "final" sent a chill up Kathy's spine. "What we are asking you to provide is some simple information about a certain individual's visits to the White House. We do not wish to know what he said, only the dates of his visits, in return for which we are willing to offer a large sum of money."

Kathy scrutinized them but remained silent. She wanted to crush Zeitsev, and was certain that she could if she ever had to. The other man was a different matter. He stood relaxed, his hands shoved into the pockets of his overcoat. Why did these Russians always wear overcoats? She wondered briefly if he had a gun in one of his pockets, if it were pointed at her that very moment. What if she refused to cooperate? Would they kill her? Suddenly she was afraid, despite her anger. She had spoken hastily, before she had realized the true nature of her predicament. With sickening awareness she understood at last that it was impossible to refuse these men anything they asked. There was nothing keeping them from killing her except her value to them. She fought the sudden impulse to run screaming for her life.

"How do you know this person visited the White House?" she asked.

"We don't. That is part of what you are to find out. That and the exact time and dates of any meetings he *might* have had with the President."

"This is really out of my line, you know. I mean, how am I supposed to get this kind of information?"

"You were a reporter, Miss Karpovich. I'm sure you have gotten information in the past that was denied to you." Aleksay sounded less persuasive than demanding.

"I can't make any promises other than that I will try."

"Trying is not good enough," Aleksay said.

Kathy wanted to cry. She felt her knees growing weak.

"You've got to give me time," she stammered, trying to maintain control. "What's the man's name?"

"Roger Davis."

"I've never heard of him before. Who is he?"

"That is none of your . . ."

"A member of the American diplomatic corps," Sergei interrupted, receiving a wicked glare from Aleksay. He was taking a great risk.

"I'll work on it," she said, looking around at the groups of people filtering into the park from the office towers nearby. "I've go to get back. I'm going to be late as it is."

"We will contact you in the prescribed manner next Thursday," Sergei said.

Kathy nodded, then shot one more look at Aleksay. He stared at her coldly, almost hatefully. She turned and hurried away.

When she was gone, Sergei smiled obsequiously. "I apologize for interrupting you, Comrade, but you see, I know her. I know how to influence her. It is senseless to challenge or command her. She is strong willed and stubborn."

"A poor choice for an operative," Aleksay said chastisingly.

Sergei winced. "Perhaps, but we shall see. She is very effective once she puts her mind to a project."

"I hope so, Comrade. For your sake."

"Are you certain, Ralph?" Parker said in surprise.

"Positive, Don. The only reason I bring it to your attention, though, is because she's seeing young Wilson."

"Good God, Ralph, you're not suggesting he's involved?"

"No. We've checked him out thoroughly. But if this should break and it's revealed there was an association, it could be very embarrassing for your Administration."

"What the hell do you suggest we do?"

"I suggest we level with Wilson, tell him what's going on, and let him break it off."

"What if he can't handle it?"

"Leave it to me, Don. I've had a lot of experience with this kind of thing."

"Gladly. I don't want any part of it."

"Good. Now I've thoroughly briefed Arnold. We've arranged for the Oasis Project team to relocate to the Pentagon. We're going to let Karpovich play her game for another couple of months and feed the Russians some bad information. That way we keep them occupied and out of our hair."

"Do you think that's wise? I mean, there's a lot more vital research going on at SPEC."

"We'll contain her activities, believe me. And we're after another deep cover operative at SPEC anyway. If we bust up this operation, he or she might submerge and that would be the end of it."

"Will you handle all this then, Ralph?"

"Yes. Leave everything to me. I just wanted to let you know about young Wilson."

"I appreciate it, Ralph. This can't go any farther or it could be damaging."

"Of course."

Shortly after Owens left, the phone rang.

"Parker."

"Don, Arnold here."

"Yes, Arnold?"

"Has Ralph spoken to you?"

"Yes, he just left. I can't believe it about Kathy Karpovich."

"You know that Ralph wants her to stay on?"

"Yes."

"And did he tell you he wanted to feed her bogus information?"

"Yes, and I don't like it."

"Believe me, Don. It'll be all right. I'll make sure I edit everything she sees."

"If you say so, Arnold. But keep me informed."

"I will."

Parker hung up, his complexion considerably paled.

Down the hall, Ralph Owens faced Bruce Wilson, who sat rigid in his chair, his eyes staring, his jaw set. He dropped two photos of Kathy and the Russian agents on his desk.

"I can't believe it. It's impossible. You've got to be mistaken."

"I'm afraid not, Bruce. I know it's a shock. We feel they must be blackmailing her, forcing her to cooperate."

"What do you want me to do?"

"Break it off," Owens said.

Bruce sat motionless, his stomach knotted, wanting to throw up. "I suppose it's the only way."

"You've got to think of the President." Owens rose.

"Does he know?" Bruce asked.

"Don't worry. He understands the situation. You weren't to blame."

"I appreciate your speaking to me in person, General. If I'd known . . ."

"There was no way you could have."

Owens left Bruce staring at his typewriter. It all fit. Their conversation of the night before, Kathy's leaving the *Post* so unexpectedly, her obvious unhappiness. He was sure that she was being forced to cooperate with the Russians, but he was powerless to help her. To save his job, to prevent any embarrassment to the President, he had to break it off.

It was eight o'clock when Davis returned to his apartment to find that no call had been left at the desk. He thought nothing of it until ten; then he began to wait for the sound of the phone with increasing impatience. Nevertheless, he fought the urge to call her until five minutes after eleven.

It seemed as though he waited a very long time for the call to go through, and when the phone on the other end began to ring, it was an equally long time until someone answered.

"Hello?" It was a voice he did not recognize, an older woman's voice.

"May I speak to Mercedes, please?" he said, trying to sound polite despite his irritation.

"She's not in. Who is calling please?"

He waited an instant. "When is she expected?"

"She has gone on vacation. I will relay a message. Who is calling, please?"

Davis was stunned. He did not want to leave his name; but he was angry now. What the hell kind of game was she playing? "Where can she be reached?" he asked.

"I am sorry, but I am not at liberty to give that information. I will take your name?"

"No. Thanks." He slammed the receiver down and thought about hurling it against the wall. He didn't. Instead, he made himself a strong drink and stood on the balcony watching the city lights, letting his temper subside. It was not like him to fly off. He reminded himself that only once before had he let a woman get to him that way, and it had nearly cost him his life. He wasn't going to let that happen again. He calmed himself and thought it out. She was probably out and the servant who answered the phone was mistaken about her being on vacation. But how could that be? Was she deliberately taunting him? What if her father had been the other person on the line? That would explain it.

He poured another drink, got into bed with a good spy novel, and tried to put the whole thing out of his mind. He was sure she would call the next day with an explanation.

At that moment in the Presidential palace in Mexico City, Mercedes was locked in her room, her phone ripped from the wall.

An expanding patch of blue marked her cheek below her left eye where her father had struck her in his rage. Never before had he laid a hand on her. She had wept for hours, until there were no more tears, until her feelings were numbed by exhaustion and the rum she had swallowed.

What had President Parker said to her father that had so turned him against the Americans? Why was he even now meeting with his cabinet and military advisors? It was beyond her understanding.

There was a knock at the door and Carmela, her aging nurse, came in with a dinner tray. "Look what I have brought you, my dear," the kindly old woman said. She looked sadly at the bruise on Mercedes' face.

"I'm not hungry," Mercedes said, turning her back to the woman. She did not mean to hurt Carmela's feelings. It was not her fault.

"But you must eat."

"Did he call?"

Carmela was silent.

"Did he?"

"A man called, but he would not leave his name."

"What did you tell him?"

Carmela did not want to respond.

"What did you tell him, Carmela?"

"What your father instructed me to tell him. That you could not be reached."

Mercedes began to weep.

"There, there, little lamb. Don't cry so." Carmela set the tray down and cradled Mercedes in her arms. Since her mother's death, Carmela had raised Mercedes like her own daughter. It grieved her to see such suffering in one so young.

"You will forget him, child."

"No. You're wrong. I won't. Why should I have to forget him? I love him."

"It is your father's will."

"I hate him. He has no right!"

"Sssh. Hush now. Perhaps he will change his mind. He is very troubled now. In time he will regret his actions and perhaps he will give his blessings to this young man."

Mercedes could not speak. She buried herself in the comforting folds of her nurse's arms, as she had when she was a lonely child. It was the only comfort she had ever known.

"Gentlemen, we must be prepared to defend what is ours. President Parker has as much as threatened to invade us if we refuse his offer!" Enrique de Gonzales-Perez was drunk and angry. He ranted in front of his horrified generals and advisors like a madman. "This pompous American inperialist. He will know the sting of defeat if he tries to move against us!"

They had all heard the story in its entirety several times over, but sat patiently letting His Excellency's temper rage.

"Beginning tomorrow morning we will fortify our oil fields. I want all available troops deployed. And I want the Marines along the border. We will show the American's the power of our military. We are not poor peasants to be spat upon and dragged through the streets like scum! Do you understand? If it is war he wants, it is war he will have!" They all knew, including Perez, that his threats were hollow. But no one dared to state it. They would follow their orders and pray that somehow His Excellency would come to his senses.

. . . 6 September 1989

They were to meet at Ricky's, the place they had first met for drinks what seemed like a very long time ago. The night air held a faint chill, a promise of the changing seasons, and everyone in the place seemed close and friendly at the prospect of the descending autumn. He thought it curious how people always seemed to need an excuse to get close, let down their inhibitions. Unfortunately, Bruce felt very alone — an outcast out of time and in a strange place.

He had arrived early and had a double martini to bolster himself, knowing that he would otherwise not have the courage to say what he had to say. Glancing around, he saw plenty of attractive girls, all apparently single and very available. Why couldn't he have gotten involved with one of them? No complications, no serious hang-ups, no diplomatic embarrassments.

The drink didn't seem to loosen the knot in his stomach, so he ordered another and tried to remember the speech the way he had rehearsed it. It was no good. If it sounded phony to him, it sure as hell would to her. No, he had to do it quickly and simply.

He still couldn't believe it was true. Kathy a Soviet spy? It gave him a peculiar feeling of isolation and estrangement from her, as if he had never really known her at all.

He had known from the first, of course, that she wanted him because of his position. But after he had confronted her, after they had been through the awkwardness of their beginnings, after all the pretenses and defenses were dropped, there had been something there; if not love, then a bond, a mutual need, a desire to please and comfort and share each other's company. That surely amounted to something and he was reluctant to see it end.

"Bruce? Hi."

He turned and saw her standing close by, looking as good as she had ever looked. Her blond hair was freshly done and hung full over her shoulders. Her lips were moist, her smile warm, inviting. But he realized at once there could be nothing more between them. His insides were cold, his hands trembled involuntarily.

"Hi. I was early so I ordered a drink."

"I'll have what you're having," she said, sitting on the stool next to him.

He could tell by the way she looked at him that she sensed a change. He tried to act as before, but only succeeded in being awkward, telecasting his indifference.

"Had a busy day?" she asked.

"Yeah. Pretty much so. How about you?" He suddenly wondered if she had spent the day stealing military secrets. Jesus, how could his feelings change so radically in such a short time?

"Hectic," she said. "There's some sort of move going on. I think one of the divisions is getting relocated, but no one's saying much about it so it must be top security."

He tried not to reflect his suspicions. Everything she said reminded him of her other life.

"Here's your drink," he said, being overly helpful. She looked at him oddly as he paid the bartender and tipped him too much.

They sat in silence for an unbearable few minutes, while Bruce mustered his courage and Kathy braced herself for something she sensed was coming.

"So, how are you?" she said finally, not wishing to appear put off by his coldness.

"Fine. Fine. Kathy?" he said, then stopped. She looked at him and in her eyes he saw that she already knew what he was going to say. "I've got something to tell you."

She smiled grimly, controlling her voice. "You don't think we ought to go on seeing each other?"

He lowered his eyes and nodded. "It's not that I don't still like you."

"You don't have to explain, Bruce. There are no strings." Her mind was racing, struggling with the mixture of relief and disappointment she felt. After all, if she were no longer involved with him, she would not have access to the information the Russians wanted. But she was not sure she wanted out of the relationship either, no matter what the cost of keeping it together.

"It's just that . . . well, I've met someone else." Bruce could feel his ears turning red and wondered if she knew he was lying. He glanced up and saw a look in her eyes he had never expected to see. She was hurt.

"I see," she said coldly. Suddenly she was angry. He had never meant that much to her, but knowing she had been replaced by someone else wasn't pleasant. "Anyone I know?" she asked, trying to pretend she wasn't injured.

"No. No one. She's just someone I met by accident. I haven't been seeing her very long."

"Is it serious?"

"I don't know. I mean, yes, I guess it is."

"Well, the least I can do is say good luck." She extended her glass in a toast. "Good luck. No sense in being a bad loser."

He took her free hand and held it. "You're not a loser, Kathy. No way. You're a winner. No matter what happens, remember that. I know if you put your mind to it, you can do anything you want to." He stopped before he said too much and released her hand.

"You don't have to say that, Bruce."

"But I want to. I mean it. This is hard for me to say. I know we were never really close, but we had our moments, and they meant a lot to me. They always will. I don't want you to ever regret them, because I don't."

She leaned close and kissed him on the cheek. "You're sweet. Goodbye, Bruce." She slid off the stool and left without looking back.

He watched her go with a lump in his throat, his eyes blurring. He wanted to rush after her, take her in his arms, tell her he knew everything and that he could help her if she would let him. But he knew he didn't have the right to do that. She disappeared through the front door, her head erect; and she was gone. For minutes afterward all he could see was that image of her, strong, independent, and alone.

He ordered another drink, the first of many more before the night was over.

Kathy reached her apartment shortly before twelve, having stopped off at one of her other haunts for a few drinks. She had had time to give the affair with Bruce some thought, and the booze had dulled the pain.

After everything was said and done, she rationalized, she was glad he had broken it off. Bruce had meant little more to her than diversion, a handsome face, a willing partner for stolen evenings. But there were other men to be found for that. She could not afford an affair with entanglements. Her involvement with the Russians was bound to come out sooner or later; she knew that. And when it did, if she were associated with the White House in any way, it would mean a scandal. That was something she did not want.

She turned the key in the lock and pushed open the door. The apartment was completely dark, all the curtains drawn. Before she had a chance to remember that she had left them open, someone pushed her into the room with tremendous force and slammed the door behind her. She hit the coffee table with her shins and toppled over it, landing on the couch with a shriek.

From out of nowhere, a man's hand clamped over her mouth and she could smell his sour breath hot against her face. She struggled, trying to scream, but he held her firmly and tightened his grip until she thought her neck would snap. She went limp.

"That's better, Miss Karpovich," the thick Russian voice said. She recognized it at once, and tried to speak, but he held her still. "Don't worry, I'm not going to hurt you. I'll release you if you promise not to scream."

She nodded her head eagerly and he loosened her grip, withdrawing into the blackness.

"What do you want?" she whispered in terror. "Why did

you come here?"

"Did you forget our appointment last night?"

She suddenly felt nauseous. She *had* forgotten all about it. *Now* she remembered what Sergei had said. They would contact her the following Thursday. *That was yesterday!* "I forgot!" she exclaimed. "I got it mixed up."

"That is very dangerous in your new line of work, Miss Karpovich," Aleksay said.

"I told you, I just forgot! I've had a lot on my mind."

"Nevertheless, we cannot afford to be too careful. I thought I would remind you of your vulnerability."

"Well, you succeeded," she said, starting to cry. The strain of everything she had gone through that day was finally too much.

"There's no need for tears, my dear." Aleksay said in mock sympathy. "I'm not going to hurt you. Have you any information for me?"

Kathy suddenly realized the implausibility of her story under the present circumstances. What could she tell him? How could she make him believe? Best to tell him the truth. There was no other way. "I've got some bad news," she gasped.

"Oh?" The chill in his voice horrified her.

"It's about Bruce. Bruce Wilson."

"What about him?"

"He broke up with me, tonight," She waited in the darkness for what seemed an eternity.

"I don't understand," he said at last, his voice icy calm.

"We broke up. We're through. We're not seeing each other anymore."

"How could that be?"

"It was his idea. I had drinks with him earlier. He said he'd met someone else, and he and I were through."

Suddenly he was in her face, his hands at her throat, rage trembling in his huge fingers. "You're lying!"

"No!" she screamed. "You've got to believe me! It wasn't my idea. He called it off. What could I do?"

His hands gripped so tightly around her throat that she could barely breathe. In the darkness she could just see his cruel flat face inches from hers. "I can check your story," he snarled.

"Check it," she choked. "I'm telling the truth!"

He released her and she collapsed coughing.

"You are a disappointment, Miss Karpovich. A woman of your talents. How could you lose such a relationship so easily? I think that you did not try to save it."

"What did you want me to tell him? That I was a spy? That I needed his help to get information for the Russians?"

She heard the sudden shattering of glass from the direction of the dining room, and saw his shape pass by the breakfront. The bastard had smashed her crystal in his rage. She cowered, afraid to move or make a sound.

"I should kill you now," he said with agonizing calm. "But I do not have the authority. You are Zeitsev's, not mine. If you were mine, I would kill you."

Suddenly she began to vomit. He paced to the windows and stood in silhouette, peering out through the parted curtain at the street.

"Control yourself, you disgusting slut!" he said tightly. "You are in no danger. You can be grateful that your position is of some value to us. But let me warn you. If you ever again miss a meeting, things will not go so easily for you. We are not playing a game. Lives are cheap. Do you understand?"

"Yes, she gasped, spitting the vile fluid from her mouth. The stench rose from the soaked carpet and her head reeled as another wave of sickness came over her. Desperately, she fought for control.

"We will contact you next Thursday in the appropriate manner," he said. "You will remember this time?"

"Yes!"

"Good. Sergei has worked very hard setting you up. I would hate to ruin his work."

He opened the door and closed it softly behind him, leaving her in the darkness. She was quivering, too weak to move. She began to sob.

. . . 2 October 1989 — 1 April 1990

The remaining days of 1989 passed swiftly, rolling down the year like marbles through a child's fingers into a fractured pile swept by the bitter winds of growing discontent.

October 2 brought a cautious proclamation from Enrique de Gonzales-Perez to the effect that the United States and Mexico had reached an impasse in diplomatic relations. He called upon the United Nations to castigate any attempt by the United States to intervene in Mexico's domestic affairs and warned that Mexico had entered a new era of sovereignty characterized by increasingly rapid economic growth and far-reaching political interrelations with foreign world powers. The latter was a euphemism for broadening ties with Russians, who continued to show increased interest in the Mexico's development as a third world ally.

Parker received the news with moderate annoyance and issued his own statement to the press, expressing distress that such a misunderstanding between the United States and Mexico should have come about and urging renewed negotiations toward a mutually beneficial settlement of all differences.

Privately, Parker met with Ralph Owens and Montie Montgomery on October 3. They reached a quick consensus. Should the United States be pushed to the brink of economic disaster, Parker would order a full-scale embargo on all Mexican imports, similar to the one issued against Cuba in the early sixties. In addition, all Mexican nationals would be deported, and the border would be fortified to prevent further illegal immigration. They were already aware of the build-up of Mexican troops along the border.

As a further contingency, it was agreed that should drastic

actions become necessary, the United States would invade Mexico, destroying Mexico City with saturation bombing, and secure the oil fields currently under the protection of the Mexican army. From there it would be possible to strike south into Central and South America, seizing the Canal Zone, and pushing on into Venezuela if necessary to ensure control of the Western Hemisphere.

These plans were for their eyes only, merely projections of last-resort alternatives, but they were feasible and would be implemented if conditions grew unbearable and the national security was threatened by the growing and crippling effects of the oil shortages.

In the period since 1979, crude oil prices had risen with only minor adjustment, creating a price at the gas pump in the range of $5.25 per gallon. The resulting impact on the American economy and the American way of life bordered on cataclysmic. The American people bore the heavy burden.

The strikes began in early November of 1989, wildcat walkouts, unpredictable and skillfully planned to thrust at the heart of the financial community. It seemed that Benest's demise had done little to soothe the ardor of the remaining conspirators to reduce the economy to cinders rather than see their power diluted by the government.

First the Carriers struck, protesting the gouging price of diesel fuel. Most of the nation's leading trucking firms were virtually shut down along with some of the airlines, causing havoc in businesses from Maine to California. Then, just at the onslaught of winter, the coal miners began sporadic walkouts in protest of runaway inflation and contract disputes arising from negotiations. Stockpiles were low, as more power companies had begun to reconvert to lignite with fuel oil growing more and more scarce no matter the price. It promised to be a long, cold winter.

From the beginning, Parker warned that he would invoke the Taft-Hartley Act at the earliest possible opportunity, but the unions had plenty of time to turn the screws.

But who were the strikes actually hurting? The big industries? The so-called fatcats who were alledgedly raking

269

in the obscene excess profits? Absolutely not! The word "profit" had become alien to most big companies, and the term "excess profits" would have been laughable were the realities not so grave.

No, the unions were not hurting the supposed villains of big business. They were hurting the little guys, their neighbors, their neighbors' children. Because of the decrease in available heating fuels, schools were being forced to reduce classes to three days a week in most northern regions. And the corner grocers who relied on southern produce and midwestern beef were also being hurt. After all, if the trucks weren't rolling, how could they stock their shelves? How could they stay in business? And what of the people of the neighborhoods who relied on those grocers? Who would feed those people when the food stocks no longer came? There would be nothing left to do but close the doors and turn them away. And what then? The truckers were not listening. They claimed they were losing money, just by rolling. And the Carriers were forcing more and more independents off the roads.

And what of the violence on the picket lines? Nonunion workers, eager for some income, no matter how little, desperate to feed their families, swarmed to fill the void left by the strikers. But they were beaten, stomped, driven away, their houses bombed and torched, some were even killed. And what were the police doing? Looking the other way. They were on strike too. They had the legal right. "To protect and to serve" meant nothing when the picket signs went up.

At hundreds of plants across the country, people were marching the sidewalks. Assembly lines were closed. There was no one to operate them, and why bother when the trucks weren't rolling and products weren't getting to the markets?

In mid-November, New York, Cleveland, Detroit, and Chicago defaulted on their loans. Millions of dollars of uncollectable debts, provided by individual savings accounts in thousands of banks across the country, were written off. At first there were no real shock waves. Everyone had expected it to happen; and everyone had carefully maneuvered to place the blame away from the real source of failure. Each of the mayors had his speech carefully worded, bitingly bitter about being abandoned by the federal government, claiming martyrdom and casting the brand of shame at the Parker Administration for ignoring their fervent pleas for help.

No one thought to condemn themselves or the unions which for years had so throttled the major cities that their collapse was inevitable. No one paused to consider the fact that at some point in time, the federal government had to stop printing money, had to put the brakes on inflation somewhere. It was clear that the citizens were not going to do it, so they had to be shown; they would have to witness the shutdown of entire cities in the wake of municipal defaults and empty treasuries.

Based on the current tax schedules, civil servants had to take a cut in pay to balance the municipal budgets. But that was abhorrent to their way of thinking — what about the new car, the new TV, the Friday night dancing and drinking?

There was not going to be a new car. The plants were closing. The dealerships couldn't sell the supply on hand because no one could afford the high prices of gasoline.

And the new TV? Japanese imports had dropped off sharply as their prices had risen due to the decline in the value of the dollar. No one was buying the imports; and even the domestic sets were sitting in boxes, gathering mildew. And the dancing and drinking? Who could dance when they were worrying about where their next paycheck was going to come from? Of course, people were drinking. There was plenty to worry about, and drinking helped assuage their fears. The bars and liquor stores did a booming business.

It didn't happen all at once. It grew like a cancer, for the same reason the gas lines grew, for the same reasons banks had begun to close as patrons withdrew their dwindling savings, until deposits no longer covered demands. Panic! People had lost faith. The system wasn't working. They wanted what was theirs, there and then. People began hoarding, stockpiling for the harsh winter months, afraid the supplies would run out.

Parker had warned them. He had begged them from the

271

beginning to listen, to sacrifice for the long run. But greed had become the American creed. *All I can get as long as it lasts, who cares about tomorrow?* Tomorrow will never come. It won't happen to New York. We're too great a city. The rest of the country owes us for the centuries of commerce and culture. It did happen there. Banks closed, brokerages went bust, the lights began to wink out on Broadway.

It can't happen here. Not in Detroit. We make the cars. There will always be a demand for new cars. They are the American status symbol. People will always buy cars as long as there are roads to travel and gasoline to fill their tanks. It did happen there. Millions of dollars of unsold automobiles sat rusting in the deepening snows of late November.

It can't happen here. Not in Chicago. We're the market center, the hub of American farming, the commodities exchange of the Western Hemisphere. Not when farmers don't have diesel fuel to fill their tractors and combines. Not when the crops can't get to market. It did happen there.

The riots began in December. Shops were looted, TV's stolen, stereos carried away by the armful, and truckload, and the child's wagonload, down brawling streets into dark freezing houses whose occupants were finding it hard to pay the utilities, where the booty was stacked high in containers never opened, strange modern relics, anachronistic before their time, memorials to overproduction and runaway consumption.

And where were the police? They weren't any police. They had been on strike. But now they were unemployed. What about the fires? There were no firemen to put them out. They too were unemployed. Who would help? Someone had to help. People—Americans—couldn't live like this! After all, this was the twentieth century, not the Middle Ages.

Parker immediately declared a state of emergency in the beleaguered cities and ordered the governors of the respective states to send in the National Guard to establish peace in the streets. The soldiers would help. They would put out the fires. They would stop the looting.

Armed patrols marched in the streets of New York. Armored cars and tanks roamed the waterfront in Chicago.

Roadblocks were established on once busy thoroughfares of Detroit and Cleveland. Honest citizens when forced to go out were stopped, I.D.s were checked. Curfews were the order of the day. And the few functioning engines of commerce ground miserably to a standstill

Even Wall Street was closed. It was closed because prices were falling like the heavy snows that wrapped the eastern seaboard. It was closed because the fighting in the streets had reached the front doors of the Stock Exchange. Windows were broken, fires were set in the lobby, the soldiers could not promise to protect the traders inside who were frantically trying to salvage some capital from the worst bear market since the Great Depression. At the depth of year-end trading, the market closed.

When it reopened four days later, it was announced that the exchange would be moved to Newport Beach, California, where the climate was more conducive to general business and the mood was better for continued efforts to restore the delicate balance of Wall Street's crumbling mentality.

By the first of the new year, the riots had ended for the time being, the panic selling had ceased, the plunging dollar had found a tenuous hemostasis on the foreign money markets, the armed forces were manning many of the mines and some of the trucking firms. America was becoming an occupied country, and everyone blamed the man in the White House, the insensitive monster in the Oval Office, the incompetent idiot who called himself President. A crisis of such proportions had never happened in the United States before!

They were correct. America had never before been so dependent on foreign production. America had never before been so bent on wanton consumption. America had never before been so profligate, so nearsighted, so self-centered, so lazy, so top heavy, so peaked for collapse!

And it was happening just as he had warned them it would, and they were all to blame; Parker, the garbage man, the truck driver, the student radical, the banker, the filling station attendant, the grocer, the cop, the fireman, the stewardess, the coal miner, the bus driver, the window washer, the foreign importer, the postman, the engineer, the developer, the damned fool who paid too much for too little too often. But people had not listened.

Now they heard.

They heard the rumble of tank treads on Park Avenue. They heard the wailing curfew sirens on Chicago streets that once had pulsed with commerce. They heard the erratic sniper fire in the cold dark Detroit nights, shattering down canyons of dark stone buildings. They heard the pounding of their own hearts at every creak on the stair, every shuffle in the hall.

They heard the news reports that the weather in California was warm and sunny. They heard that business was never better in Miami Beach, Atlantic City, Galveston, Nevada. People in their frenzy to escape the present horrors were desperately throwing away their life savings searching for that one big score, hoping for that one ride on Lady Luck's saddle that would vault them to financial security.

And they heard the bump-bumping of suitcases in stairwells, the slamming of car trunks, the grinding of old engines, sputtering on the last few precious drops of gasoline. People were moving out of the crippled cities. Where were they going? They wouldn't or couldn't say. Were they ever coming back? Probably not. What would they do when they got where they were going? They didn't know. Why were they going? There was nothing left to stay for.

The cities were dying. Four had begun, others would follow. For over two hundred years they had stood; grown higher and higher, wider and wider, dirtier and dirtier, new built upon the old, crumbling into stinking urban slag heaps. Once they had been great monuments, tributes to the American spirit; their museums had been marvels of the world, their universities had schooled the great minds of their youth, educated them to the growing ills of modern society, taught them to consider the greed and danger of capitalism without conscience, encouraged them to question, distrust, demand, resist, reject the successes of the past, tear gas politicians, stone their classmates, burn the lecture halls,

274

fight. What more was there for these great cities to do but die?

And were they really worth saving after all? They were too old, too battered, too clogged with the refuse of ten generations. They were like terminal patients on life support machines. Eventually, the plug had to be pulled, as soon as brain activity had stopped. And it had.

But there were other cities less battered by time and fate, ready to conquer and subjugate. There was open land to litter, green forests to defoliate, rolling hills to subdivide, sparkling rivers to pollute. Opportunities abounded for the brave, the adventurous, the ruthless. Why there were actually a few states that still had right-to-work laws, where open shops still existed and a person didn't have to join the union in order to work. That would have to be taken care of, of course; especially in Texas.

That state was wide open with grassy prairies, virgin mountains, oil beneath the ground, timbered forests, coal to be ripped from the Earth's belly, shining cities, thriving on growth and prosperity, glimmering meccas to the uprooted, the ambitious, waiting to be looted. It was almost too good to believe that such places still existed. But they did. And they thrived because a man was still paid what he was worth and not what a consortium of strongarm artists could extort from his employer.

Yes, that would all have to change. Shops would have to be unionized, workers brainwashed, dues extracted from them. After all, it took money to organize a union, and that money had to come from somewhere.

. . . 30 April 1990

In the great basin of Death Valley, far removed from the tremoring din of human turmoil, far removed from center stage of the drama that seemed like a horrifying prelude to the last act in the tragedy of the human race, the gaping caverns of the Oasis Project had taken shape.

Months of laser blasting had created all but the peripheral cavities necessary to house the massive underground complex. Already teams of carefully selected, highly trained construction crews, reams of technicians, scores of architects and engineers, scientists, and aerospace consultants were sculpting from the heat-seared silicon labyrinth the facility that quite probably was the last hope for the survival of the United States.

Hundreds of miles of conduits, tons of electronics, mountains of cement and steel, millions of man hours — all were pitted in a desperate race with time and circumstances against disaster.

The main cavern had evolved on schedule, and already the massive canopy was in place, shielding the frenetic activity from intruding eyes, while hundreds of feet below the surface, the labor continued. First the main chamber would be finished, but while that work proceeded, the auxiliary chambers for dormitories, recreation facilities, power plants, offices, tunnels, and the central computer complex were being fashioned. It would be months before the ASP assembly could be begun, and each person, no matter how menial his job, was aware of the time schedule, the intense pressure they all were under.

All twenty-one hundred miles above the apparently peaceful atmosphere of the precious blue planet, in a frail metal tin can called Skylab V, the top technical minds of SPEC and NASA were preparing the fission reactor thruster for its first test.

The new Skylab had been launched with scant notoriety, and was followed shortly by the first of the planned Shuttle missions, which relayed the SPEC-NASA team and the components of the nuclear reactors to the awaiting space laboratory. All had proceeded without a hitch, but the reactor had yet to be fired.

Early on there had been a delay, which had cost them over a month. The diamond bottle had failed in its first ground-based tests. It had been necessary to return to the drawing board, to rethink the theory, and to reframe the formation process. Painful extra weeks had been expended, tedious calculations had been forced on a schedule already stretched to the tearing point. But, at last, two prototypes existed which had survived preliminary testing.

If the reactor tests were successful, twenty more bottles would be ordered; but each took seventy hours to form, and there were only two molds from which to strike them. That process would require at least another two months. But if the prototypes were not successful, would there be time to rethink the formation process again? Would it be possible to redesign the entire reactor? Would the basic concept ever prove sound? There were a million variables, and precious little margin for error.

"Gentlemen, I don't want to sound like the voice of doom, but I have the unhappy duty of informing you that Libya, courtesy of the PLO, has the bomb." General Owens spoke to a somber gathering in the war room of the Pentagon. Among those present were Parker, Montie Montgomery, and the joint chiefs of staff.

Parker sat stoically at the head of the assembly, haloed from above by a solitary spotlight, softly drumming his fingers on a bulging dossier in front of him on the table. He had been in office hardly more than seventeen months, but already he appeared older. The suit that had once fit his broad, trim shoulders now hung slack ever so slightly. His once swarthy skin was sallow, his face was thin, his hair had greyed noticeably. Only his eyes remained unchanged. They were the same sparkling, intense emerald green, and shone with unbroken determination.

Parker asked, his voice low, "Do you mean they actually have in their possession a functioning nuclear weapon, Ralph?"

"Yes, Mr. President. We think two. Our sources reveal that the weapons were purchased from an intermediary source; without a doubt the organization responsible for the theft last January of the weapons lost in transit to Britain over the North Sea."

"Then we're lucky," Parker scowled.

"Lucky?" Montie asked in surprise.

"Yes. It's fortunate they only have the bomb and not the technology to make one. They will have to study them for at least a year to perfect the technique necessary to manufacture more. And then there is the problem of obtaining enriched uranium."

"Absolutely correct, Mr. President," Owens agreed.

"Unless they're crazy enough to detonate the ones they have!" Montie said.

"Highly unlikely, Mr. Secretary," Owens replied. "These are long-range warheads. Dirty little devices. The Libyans neither have the ability to deliver one nor the incentive, since their primary target would have to be Israel. That would mean dirtying up their own air with fallout. They're definitely not going to explode them. They are planning to copy the technology and adapt it to their needs."

"What about the source of enriched uranium?"

"Our guess is the heavy uranium plant in Kahuta, Pakistan. They'll most likely approach the Pakistans, if they haven't already."

"I assume you've taken steps to ensure that plant will never survive to provide them."

"I was going to suggest that, sir."

"I concur."

"Very well, Mr. President. I'll put the necessary arrangements together immediately. We'll train a special team to go in and knock out the plant and make it look like an accident."

Parker nodded his approval.

"Now, with that out of the way, let me apprise you of the latest developments as they affect national security. The situation in Saudi Arabia is shaky and in all probability will degenerate into civil war within the next twelve months. At best we could hope for only massive demonstrations. But even that is going to negatively affect the Saudis' petroleum output, which in turn will create havoc in most parts of the world, on a scale that will make the revolution in Iran look like a Sunday picnic. Presently, the world is running at a deficit of some two million barrels of oil a day, even with the Saudis' heavily increased output. Any cutback could prove disastrous."

"Any chance of us intervening to head off such a confrontation?" Montie asked.

"That's doubtful. The Russians are increasing their support of the Fedayeen, and we've got Satellite pictures of substantial troop activity along the Turkish and Iranian borders. We think it's a bluff, a warning for us to keep our noses out. But that bluff could turn into a threat if we try to intervene."

"You mean we just have to sit here and watch it happen?" Montie asked.

"Unless we want an open confrontation with the Kremlin. This is their first major test of your Administration Mr. President, but unless our sources are gravely mistaken, and I don't think they are, they intend to maintain their presence in that region and want us to know that they won't stand for any meddling in the Saudis' internal affairs.

"Also. We have reports of some major Soviet troop deployments along the Chinese border. We think we can expect some skirmishes there before the year is out. Nothing serious. A show of strength on both sides, on the Russians' part mainly to let the Chinese know they aren't happy with our growing relationship. But it could also mean that they are preparing for a counteroffensive should China mount an assault in response to any major confrontation with us in the Middle East. They're showing us they're prepared, in other words.

"Another serious note. The Israelis have promised swift retaliation for this morning's raid on Tel Aviv by the PLO. We've already got unconfirmed reports of heavy missile strikes in Lebanon northeast of Beirut, as well as some shelling in Beirut by Israeli warships. The prime minister has warned that he intends to push beyond the forty-mile DMZ boundary and establish fortifications if necessary to keep the PLO from returning. Naturally, Habash has labeled the assault as antagonistic and an example of Israel's fascist behavior. So far there has been no official reaction from Cairo, but there have been reports of troop movements on Egypt's Libyan border. Again, we think this is only a display of strength, but skirmishes could break out. It's very similar to the situation before Israel's last foray into Lebanon that touched off the ten-day war in '85."

"As long as the Russians don't get involved," Parker snapped, "I don't give a goddamn what the hell they do to each other, treaty or no treaty. Those assholes act like this is a fucking game of soccer, and I'll be damned if I'm going to support either side. Let them tear each other apart over that worthless desert!"

"In all fairness, Mr. President," Montie interrupted, "I don't see how we can turn our backs on the Camp David Accord. That would be exactly what the Russians are expecting. It would be a sign of weakness."

"Goddamnit, Montie! Do you want to start a shooting war with the Kremlin? I sure as hell don't! And if we make a move to intervene in any of this . . ."

"But . . ."

"But nothing! The goddamn Russians are no fools. They don't want to drop the first bomb, and they know we don't either. For the last two decades they've had two basic objectives. First to build up their military machine to exceed ours in brute strength. They've largely financed this by dumping huge quantities of crude oil on the market, regardless of the short term effect on price. Now that their military power is greater than ours, they are faced with their own oil shortage, which leads to the second phase of their strategy. For over twenty years, they have been establishing strategic footholds around the shipping lanes and in and around the major oil reserves, with the intent of isolating us from our sources of petroleum imports. They know that our need for foreign oil is greater than theirs and they intend to put as much pressure on us as they can without firing a shot.

Now that their plan is coming together, now that Iran is toppling again and Saudi Arabia is within reach in the next couple of months if they just wait, do you think they're going to sit by and let us march in? We lost all hope of that when the Iranians threw us out in '79. And do you know the reason Carter didn't respond then? The same reason we can't respond now. The threat of a direct confrontation with Moscow. The Russians can virtually do what they want in that part of the world and we can't do a damn thing about it. By the time we got enough troops over there to effect any sort of intervention, the Russians would be dug in along the Persian Gulf and the Red Sea; the Straits of Hormuz would be sealed, and by God they'd blow us out of the water if we tried to move in. The same thing we'd do to them if they tried for Mexico or Venezuela."

"So in the meantime we sit and wait while they gobble up territory all over the globe?" Montie asked incredulously.

"Exactly. It's a stalemate, and it buys us time until the Oasis Project is operative. When they know what we've accomplished, the Russians are going to back off, I'll guarantee it. They will know that with the amount of gold we can bring in, we can virtually bankrupt them. They'll have to negotiate with us. It's pure economic and communist governments have to respond to economics just like we do. When we've got the dollar back in line, gold prices are going to drop. Oil prices are going to stabilize and that means the Russians are going to have to be responsive to our demands or we'll threaten to flood the market with gold and destroy their lines of credit. When we can manipulate the international money markets, we'll have them in a corner."

"What if what we end up doing is driving them into

invading the Arabian peninsula? They're still running out of oil, remember," Montie challenged.

"There's nothing we can do about that if they want to do it, short of pressing the button. They know it, and we know it. World opinion is the only thing keeping them out. You saw how pissed they got when the world reacted to their invasion of Afghanistan."

"They're still occupying Afghanistan," Montie reminded him.

"But they haven't attempted to move any closer to the Gulf. The reason they moved in 1980 was because they perceived us as weak, and our allies abroad perceived us as weak, both economically and militarily. Reagan kept them at bay because they knew he wasn't going to take any aggression lightly, not like his predecessor. And now, if we can reestablish the gold standard and regain control of our domestic economic problems, our allies and our enemies are going to perceive us as stronger than ever and they will either respect us or fear us. Once they learn we have the technology to mine the moon, they are going to think twice about its military applications. That should give them second thoughts about challenging us outright."

"I hope the hell your right, Mr. President," Montie responded gruffly.

"Is there anything else, Ralph?" Parker asked, without looking at Montie, who was obviously dissatisfied.

"No, sir. I'll attend to the heavy uranium plant project. We'll have it inoperable within three months."

"Good. Then I'd like to wrap this up with a few comments. Whatever we do in the coming months, we avoid any confrontation with the Soviets. Our allies are going to scream like hell, but there's nothing we can do until the Oasis Project is operative. I don't even want as much as a border dispute with Mexico over a sandbar on the Rio Grande. In the meantime, I want every branch of the service put on standby red alert. Combat readiness is to be maintained at all times. If it does become necessary to move, I want an army trained to strike and strike without mercy. Gentlemen, to quote a very famous man, this is *our* darkest hour. But I'll be damned if we're going to take it lying down. In chess terms, we're castling, building our strength for when we really need it, and I have no doubt that some day soon we're going to need it."

Parker fell silent, his words echoing from the cold grey walls. Every man around the table felt the chill of dread run down his spine as he realized what course had been set for them and the role they were to play in the history of the human race.

The Florida sun beat down on the glistening white sands of Key Biscayne. The sky was clear, the day hot. A stout breeze blew from the northeast, driving a pounding surf onto the eastern shoreline of the island. It was one in the afternoon, and Roger Davis languished in the shade of the boat's canopy. His craft was anchored half a mile offshore, and he had several fishing poles secured to the bulwarks with lines in the water, but they were not baited. From time to time he turned his field glasses toward the rambling one-story Mediterranean-style villa sequestered in the midst of swaying palms and dense tropical vegetation.

The compound was Cubbi Bertone's southern retreat, his stronghold, from which he had ruled his Carriers empire for the past two months, having sought seclusion after the deaths of his associates in the unholy alliance once ruled by George Benest. Of the five who had met that day in The Madison, he was the last alive. Each of the others had met an untimely, and highly unpleasant death.

Alfredo Fontana had fallen within a month after Benest's death, another apparent victim of gangland violence. His body had been found by a servant, sprawled across his blood-stained billiard table, a piano wire garrot still embedded in his throat. The authorities had repeated their contention that Benest's murder and now Fontana's had been tied to gangland union power struggles, but no suspects had been arrested, no indictments handed down.

In December, Rudi Markowitz had met with a freak accident while skiing in Aspen, Colorado. His mangled body was found by the ski patrol at the bottom of a rocky gorge. He had apparently lost control while trying to negotiate an expert run and plunged over the edge of a precipice to his death. It had been impossible for even the coroner to distinguish the place where the steel ball bearing, shot from a powerful slingshot, had struck the dead man's left temple because of the multiple contusions all over his body. Davis had sat unobserved in the snowy timber until well after dark, when he had skied down by the light of a waxing moon.

Wallace Penchinski had gone down next, the victim of an apparent mugging. His body had been found on 53rd Street in Manhattan, one block from the East River, a single .22 caliber bullet in his heart. His wallet and jewelry had been stolen. The police had simply added his name to the list of unsolvable murders in a city of burgeoning violence.

Cubbi Bertone saw the pattern. He knew that his life was in danger, but little good that did him. The authorities would be unable to protect him, and judging from the stance taken by the FBI in their investigations, he knew that they considered the country better off without his type around. Thus his seclusion had begun.

Davis had watched him for almost three weeks and had discovered the one constant in the man's habits. Each day before lunch, Bertone would swim a mile or more in the ocean; and because of the security with which he surrounded himself, that was the only time he was vulnerable.

He was late that day, and Davis was beginning to wonder if his victim were going to show. Lunch was usually around two, and it was approaching one-fifteen. He was going to be damned angry if Bertone had picked that day to break his habit. The wind was high, the surf was up, the water along the shore was murky. The conditions were absolutely perfect.

Suddenly, there was a movement along the open rear veranda of the house, and then Bertone appeared in the sunshine, wearing a white terry cloth jacket, dark glasses, and swimming trunks. Davis raised his field glasses to make sure. It was Bertone, and he was heading for the beach surrounded by his four bodyguards, each of whom carried a pistol under his shirt in the waistband of his trousers.

Davis watched as Bertone crossed the lawn to the beach and dropped his towel on the sand. He took off his jacket and let his dark glasses fall on top of it. Then he walked purposefully to the water, waited for a larger swell to break, and dove in, appearing a few seconds later just beyond the shorebreak, swimming strongly out toward a buoy that marked the first run in his daily course.

Crouching, Davis slipped on the single scuba tank and fitted the mask over his face. Taking his fins in one hand, he put the regulator mouthpiece in his mouth and dropped over the side into the cool deep waters of the channel. He let himself sink slowly as he pulled on his fins, then clearing his mask, checked his wristwatch compass and headed along the prescribed coordinates. There was a strong current running, and he made allowance for it as he pumped vigorously with his fins, driving himself toward the shore.

He had to work to fight the current and felt the pressure in his chest as his lungs and heart responded to the exertion, his breath coming in regular popping hisses through the mouthpiece. The water was beautifully clear outside the reef; he could see for at least a hundred feet. So it was with little difficulty that he spotted the basket, buoyed at a depth of thirty feet. He rose to intercept it. He had positioned it there a week ago, and had checked it repeatedly in the interim to make sure it remained in working order.

The basket was metal; it contained a powerfully hinged trap with metal teeth filed to razor sharpness and a long length of nylon line fed through a ratchet that was bolted to the basket frame. The whole assembly was secured to the bottom by a heavy chain attached to a cement anchor.

Davis swiftly removed the trap from the basket and checked to see that it was properly set. Then he double-checked the line and the ratchet through which the line was fed so that it could be pulled in without slipping back. Everything was in order, and he played out two hundred feet of line as he swam away from the basket, the trap in one hand, the line secured around his wrist, toward the point where he anticipated Bertone would pass. He was thankful for the increasing cloudiness of the water as he approached the reef,

285

and soon was sitting on the sand bottom in forty feet of water, gazing up at the mirror-like surface, watching for the man's form to appear out of the haze.

The waiting seemed interminable. Maybe the swells had been too rough and Bertone had turned back. What if he had altered his course? No! There was a bright flash on the surface some fifty to seventy-five feet away. Davis withdrew against the base of the reef, limiting his breathing to reduce the stream of bubbles escaping to the surface. He wanted nothing to alert Bertone to his presence before it was too late.

Suddenly, the form of the swimmer took shape above him in the washing swells. He could see Bertone's face underwater, his eyes were closed. He swam with easy, powerful strokes. Davis waited. In another minute, Bertone was directly overhead.

Whipping his legs, Davis shot upward, holding the open steel jaws of the trap in front of him. As he closed on his target, he made sure that the line was taut—that was important. Ten feet, five feet, four feet, three, two; a leg flashed white in the sunshine from above. Davis thrust violently upward with the trap, slamming into Bertone's right leg just above the knee. He heard the hinge pop, felt the trap spring shut, saw it sink its razor sharp teeth into the man's flesh.

He dove immediately, pulling in the line, taking up slack through the ratchet as he went.

On the surface, Bertone screamed and rose from the water, his arms flailing as blood swirled around him. Something had seized his leg just above the knee, and he felt its teeth pressing against the bone, grinding sickeningly, tearing at his flesh. "Help!"

One of the guards on the beach heard something and turned to look at the swells. He saw Bertone waving his arms frantically and wondered what was wrong.

At a depth of thirty feet, Davis tugged violently on the line, drawing in almost fifteen feet.

Bertone screamed, then was dragged under, his cry swallowed.

The guards gathered at the edge of the shore, their eyes

trained on the bloodslicked swell where their boss had disappeared. One of them started to wade in. Suddenly, Bertone popped to the surface some twenty yards farther out to sea, screaming hysterically, a cloud of blood rising around him, coloring the foam which he churned with his arms.

Again Davis jerked in the line and Bertone was dragged beneath the surface

"Shark!" one of the guards gasped. "Get the launch!"

One of them ran off toward the boathouse, but he knew it was too late. The others stood frozen on the shore.

Again Bertone erupted from the water, his lungs exploding in an inhuman howl of pain and terror; but almost at once he was dragged screaming below the surface.

Davis pulled with all his might, backpedaling out to sea, drawing in yards of line. He could just see the man's writhing form in the expanding greenish cloud of blood. Suddenly, the line went slack and he tumbled backwards. When he looked again, he could see something thrashing toward the surface above the cloud. Then he saw an object floating toward the bottom, the lower part of Bertone's leg, trailing a stream of blood, still gripped in the powerful steel jaws.

Bertone broke surface and began to swim wildly toward the shore, aware that he no longer felt the pressure on his leg. He no longer felt his leg, but was afraid to think what that might mean. The guards spotted him, and yelling frantically to the man in the boat, ran into the surf and began swimming toward Bertone.

Davis swam swiftly forward, caught the leg and freed it from the trap; letting it sink to the bottom. Turning, he swam back out to sea, seizing the basket as he passed and dragging it with him toward the edge of the channel. Just over the drop off into deep water, he deflated the buoys and let the whole rig sink into the blue.

There was no time to lose. With that much blood in the water, the real predators of the deep were certain to appear at any minute. He churned back toward the boat, glad for the assist of the current which had buffeted him on the way in.

Bertone lost consciousness fifty yards from shore, but one

of the guards reached him just before he slipped under and dragged him frantically toward shore, cursing aloud in fear, followed by a stream of blood that stained his clothing and turned his skin red. He was certain in the last few moments before reaching the sand that he would also be attacked, but he struggled on and at last pulled Bertone's near-lifeless body out of the surf with the help of his companions.

The man in the boat watched helplessly as Bertone was laid on the sand, his blood spurting onto the beach, staining a patch deep red-brown.

Davis climbed aboard his boat on the windward side out of sight from the shore and slipped off his diving rig in the shelter of the day cabin. Then he returned to the deck and trained his binoculars on the shore. At first he could not see Bertone for the guards gathered around him, but when one of them ran for the house, he saw the fallen union boss lying motionless on his back, blood still squirting from the stump of his right leg. The men around him were trying to apply a tourniquet, but by the low pressure of the blood flow Davis knew it was already too late. Bertone would be dead within a matter of minutes.

The job was done. Davis weighed anchor and started the inboard engine. It was a thirty-minute cruise back to the harbor where he had rented the boat. He popped a bottle of beer and relaxed as he churned away through the rolling swells, enjoying the fresh salt air and the afternoon sun on his wet body. He thought suddenly of Mercedes. Why, he did not know. Perhaps it was the sun and the sea. She had never returned his call, and he had never called her back. Her silence had been her answer. Still, he felt a pang at the thought of her. She had been the only thing in his life that he had wanted and been unable to possess. The thought of her dampened the triumph of his afternoon.

Somewhere over the western coastline of Australia, twenty-one hundred miles up, an EVA was in progress. The space shuttle Cosmos had docked with Skylab bringing a support team of technicians from SPEC and NASA to conduct the first hot test of the Alpha nuclear reactor.

The payload bay doors of both craft yawned open, bright work lights casting hard shadows across the cold steel bodies of the vessels. Six silver-suited astronauts dangled like marionettes under the canopy of space, above the arc of the darkened Earth, rimmed by the gauzelike film of blue atmosphere.

From the command center in the basement of the Pentagon, Arnold Kemper and the mission control crew monitored every phase of the mission with multiple video transmissions, which were scrambled to prevent any possible interception from an outside source. What they saw on their bank of video screens was the transfer of the heavily shielded reactor, dubbed the "brick," from the Skylab bay where it had been assembled to the shuttle bay, where it would be transported into position for the test.

In silent pantomime, the astronauts guided the black monolith as easily as if it had been a balloon above the wing section of the Cosmos and gently into its cradle in the payload bay, where it was locked securely into position.

"Skylab, this is Mission Control. How do you read?"

"Loud and clear, Mission Control."

"How's it going?"

"A-OK, Mission Control. The brick is in its basket. We expect embarkation in about thirty minutes."

"Roger, Skylab. We're standing by."

Far below, in the blackness of night, the Great Barrier Reef drifted by, and beyond lay the unbroken Pacific. Within the half hour, the loading crew had returned to Skylab, and the shuttle crew was prepared for separation.

"T minus, ten, nine, eight, seven, six, five . . ."

"Ignition."

"Four, three, two, one, zero."

"We have burn."

"Roger, Skylab. We confirm that burn."

"We have separation."

"Roger, copy separation."

Like a gigantic toy model, the Cosmos drifted silently away from the seventy-five ton Skylab, its tiny reaction rockets spitting blue flames into the void. At a distance of half a mile, the pilot turned the nose toward deep space, and fired his rockets, driving the shuttle with terrific thrust toward a higher orbit. On the ground, and in Skylab, the crews nervously ran through the final checklists.

At an altitude of twenty-five hundred miles, the Cosmos went into a parabolic orbit in preparation for jettisoning its payload. The bay doors spread open like an enormous clam shell, emitting an aurora of blue light into the pitch black-ness of space.

"Mission Control. Cosmos ready to jettison the brick."

"Roger, Cosmos. Begin countdown sequences."

"Five, four, three, two, one, zero."

Four explosive bolts fired simultaneously in perfect balance, lifting the nuclear reactor from its cradle out of the bay doors and clear of the orbiting space shuttle, where it assumed a similar orbit a quarter of a mile higher.

"Mission Control, we have a perfect jettison. Returning to Skylab."

"Roger, Cosmos. Copy perfect jettison."

Nosing his craft earthward, the commander of the Cosmos fired a two-second blast, launching the vessel back toward Skylab. Inside of an hour they had docked and were awaiting further instructions.

In the interim, Mission Control had confirmed that the reactor was ready for testing and the ignition sequence was begun.

"Skylab. Heat the brick." Kemper said.

"Roger, Mission Control. Heating the brick." "Heating the brick" was the code for starting the reactor. Uranium rods were lowered into the core by radio instructions to the tiny computer on board the reactor vessel; everyone waited and watched.

Thousands of calculations began to feed into the Skylab computer terminal, all indicating that the heat-up was going according to program, and at last they received confirmation of full heat build-up. The reactor was ready.

"The brick is hot, Mission Control."

"Roger, we copy that. Commence burn."

"Roger, commencing burn."

The computer command was given. All eyes on board Skylab trained on the area of space where radio telemetry told them the brick lay. At first they saw nothing. Then a ball of light glowed out of the twinkling heavens, brighter than the shimmering sun which was only then striking the edge of the Earth, driving the darkness from the face of the waters. Suddenly, there was a jet of white orange light, which moved away at a sharp angle, accelerating rapidly until a tail of flame trailed behind the unseen obelisk.

Such a small payload and so much thrust produces enormous acceleration, and the manmade comet roared into the abyss in seconds, and was soon lost in the blanket of stars. But delicate on-board laser sensing devices plotted its course; for fifteen breathless minutes, the photographic equipment clicked incessantly and the computers registered every minute detail fed back to them. All indications were that the reactor was stable, the burn consistent, and the acceleration greater than had been expected.

Four minutes before the fuel was to be exhausted, Mission Control gave the order. "Skylab, this is Mission Control. We confirm a perfect burn. How do you read?"

"A Roger, Mission Control. We copy that."

"Commence destruct sequence, Skylab."

"Roger, Mission Control."

Skylab's computer operator programmed the command and a digital clock began the ten-second countdown. All eyes turned to the blackness of space. Then in one blinding second, a boiling fireball erupted in the void and quickly dissipated into the proscenium of space.

"Cosmos, this is Mission Control. Mission accomplished. Transfer test team to Shuttle and return to base. Good work fellows. Looks like the project is a go."

Kathy straddled the papers on the floor of her office; her desk lamp leaned against an armchair shining on the documents she was photographing. She worked swiftly and easily, although her heart was pounding in her throat. The file was one that had recently appeared in the library records. It had something to do with a new reconnaissance aircraft which was about to be deployed. She was sure that the Russians would be pleased, especially since it was the first really fresh material she had been able to secure in almost two months.

Security at SPEC had intensified ever since the transfer of the Top Secret section to the new facility. In fact, it was so tight that she did not even know where the new facility was. It had become harder and harder to get the kind of information the Russians were asking for. Nevertheless, necessity and the memory of the confrontation with the brutal Russian in her apartment had driven her to taking greater risks.

Their desire for information was insatiable, and they went about their business with a zeal she found surprising for men their age. They were like children playing hide and seek, deadly serious about the rules of the game yet relishing the thrill of challenging the opposition without being caught. This attitude made her very uncomfortable. She knew that each day she continued, her time was running out. She only prayed that she would see it coming, because it seemed very unlikely the Russians were going to allow her to retire.

Suddenly, Kathy froze at the sound of approaching footsteps in the tiled corridor. That would be Gus making his rounds. She doused the light and stood in the darkness, listening as he came step by patient step closer.

All at once she had the sickening feeling that she had forgotten to lock her office door. Gus knew that she was still in the building but thought she was in the library doing research. That was an area he did not have access to, so he had no way of knowing whether or not she was actually there. But would he think to check her door?

Breathlessly, she waited as his footsteps slowed and then stopped in front of her door. Through the thick opaque glass, she saw a flare of light and knew that he was pausing to rekindle his pipe. For what seemed an eternity he must have nurtured the embers, and she stood watching his silhouette on the door. Finally he moved on toward the rear of the building to check the outer doors.

She knew she had ten more minutes to complete her work

and get the material back to the library before he would return. Even so, she waited a full two minutes more before turning the light back on and resuming the job. When she reached the last item she fired two quick shots to finish the roll, but before closing the folder she glanced at the page with mild curiosity. It contained a list of cities, alphabetized by country. What could the list be? she puzzled momentarily.

Then she forgot it. She quickly folded the dossier, cut the light, and in the pitch blackness rolled the film back in the camera and opened the casing. Deftly she rolled the film into one of Sergei's special pens and resealed it. Her hands had grown sure from weeks of practice. Stowing the camera in the false bottom of her purse, she slipped the pen into the zippered pocket, replaced the furniture in its normal position, and stepped to the door. She listened, but heard nothing in the hollow emptiness of the corridor beyond. Cautiously, she opened the door and stepped out, pausing to look around. The hall was empty. She hurried toward the east wing staircase that would take her up to the third floor library.

Kathy's heart was still racing as she exited the specially coded, locked security door of the library five minutes later and started down the nearly blackened corridor which only moments before had been brightly lit. Her footsteps echoed eerily in the silent building and she was very uneasy as she approached the main stairwell, wondering why the lights were out. Suddenly from the darkness, Gus appeared before her.

She shrieked and staggered backwards.

Gus looked surprised, then chuckled softly as he took out his lighter and fired his pipe. "Sorry, Miss Karpovich. I didn't mean to startle you."

"Gus!" she gasped. "It's you. Why are all the lights out?"

"New company policy from Kemper himself. Conserve energy. I've been cutting most of the lights after working hours. I forgot you were up here or I would have left them on for you."

"Oh, I see," she said, still badly shaken.

"Are you OK?" he asked.

"Yes, sure. I've been up here so long, I sort of got spooked. I'm leaving now if you don't mind letting me out."

"Sure. Why don't you walk with me down to the other stairway so I can finish my rounds, and we'll go down that way?"

"OK," she said, not wanting to appear too anxious to get out. She followed him in silence as he checked every door that they passed, and she wondered why he had not checked hers. Probably because he had been fiddling with his pipe. She knew that to a pipe smoker, lighting the bowl is a ritual for which everything else is sacrificed.

The walk to the lobby was one of the longest she had ever made. Gus didn't say much. He wasn't a talker. What night watchman could be? Still, there was something else about him that bothered her, and she couldn't place her finger on it. Perhaps it was his calm manner, overly calm, confident, if not cocky. He was a veteran of nearly twenty years with SPEC and had grown to view the facility as his domain during the hours of darkness. Maybe that caused his almost imperceptible aloofness, although, he had always been polite to her and even kindly. Nevertheless, she sighed with relief as they turned into the lobby and reached the receptionist's desk.

She picked up the pen to sign out, but it ran dry in mid-signature. Gus looked surprised and fiddled with it, but the ink was gone. Shrugging, he dropped it in the trash can and checked his desk. "Gee, I don't have another one," he said.

Kathy was getting nervous, realizing she still had to make the drop, and before she knew it she had reached into her purse and pulled out Sergei's special pen. She held it frozen in horror. But there was nothing else she could do. She pressed the button and prayed to God it would write. To her joy it wrote beautifully, and this once she thanked heaven for the little Russian's ingenuity. "There," she said. "Goodnight, Gus."

"Goodnight, Miss Karpovich." He escorted her to the door and opened it. "Say, you wouldn't mind lending me that pen for the rest of the night, would you? I'll put it in your office in the morning."

Kathy almost fainted. She had to think quick. "Oh, Gus, I

would but it was a present. I know it sounds silly, but it's sort of sentimental, and I'd feel awful if for some reason it got lost."

Gus smiled at her queerly and shook his head. "Must be a pretty special fella, huh?"

She stared at him. "Yes," she stammered. "I guess he is. Goodnight, Gus."

"Goodnight, Miss Karpovich."

Kathy got in her car, locked the door, and drove past the guard at the gate, saluting him with a friendly wave. Only when she turned toward the river did she begin to tremble. It was times like these that made her think prison might have been a better choice.

She drove directly to the designated debok, a park near the river. She curbed her car in the shadow of some trees and reaching under the seat pulled out an empty coke can and a brown paper sack. She took the pen out of her purse, placed it in the coke can, put the can into the sack, and a minute later deposited the sack in the trash can that Zeitsev had specified. Then she returned to her car and drove away to mark the mailbox as she had been instructed. Since her encounter with Zeitsev's associate, she had been very careful to adhere meticulously to orders, and she had had no more trouble. That was the way she wanted to keep it. She would do her job, take the money, and wait for the day when she would be free.

Fifteen minutes after she had marked the mailbox, a small figure moved out of the darkness of the bushes across the street from the park, crossed the street, and plucked the sack from the receptacle, continuing on across the quadrangle toward the lights of the buildings on the adjacent street. As Zeitsev reached the curb, the dirty blue Dodge edged around the corner, the bulk of Aleksay Kurochkin behind the wheel. Zeitsev climbed in and they moved away in the sparse traffic.

From a white Ford van parked down the street, federal agents snapped their high-speed cameras at the receding vehicle, catching the license plate before it moved out of range. They had the whole scene on infrared film, frame for frame, from the moment their operations coordinator had signaled them of Karpovich's approach. One more night's work for the Russian apparat on the record. Secretly, the agents wondered how long it would be allowed to continue to operate unchecked, but they did not question their orders not to interfere no matter what happened. They knew the time to move would come soon enough.

Roger Davis stood on the balcony of his hotel suit overlooking the peaceful Atlantic. The wind had died and the sea had calmed. The sky was bright with stars and he wondered about the white dot, which he thought was probably a satellite, moving high overhead from West to East. He did not know he was looking at the Shuttle, and he probably would not have cared. He was bored.

There he stood, dressed in his white dinner jacket with nowhere to go. From the casino below came the sound of music and the incessant jingle and ringing of the one-armed bandits, the slots. He noticed a group of people by the pool, drinking and laughing. They were having a good time. He thought briefly about going down and doing a little gambling, but somehow he couldn't get into the spirit of gambling in Miami Beach. It was not like Monte Carlo where everyone wore formal evening clothes and spoke softly, moved gracefully, lost and retired with dignity, won with reserved modesty. Downstairs, he knew there was a surging throng of coarse, loud, drunken people who cared little for the oppulent casino that had been expensively prepared for them. They were too busy drinking the free booze and throwing away their year's savings and probably the next year's as well.

"Fuck it," he muttered. He thought about getting something to eat but wasn't hungry, so he decided to take a walk before turning in.

The boardwalk was lighted with torches, and music floated from numerous casinos as he passed them one by one. He walked aimlessly — for how long he did not know — his hands in his pockets, thinking about little else but Mercedes. He did not like it, but he could not put her out of his mind.

Finally, near some cabanas, the boardwalk played out and he stopped and turned back.

As he did, he noticed two dark-skinned men in casual clothes veer sharply up the steps of the last casino and disappear through the open doors. Nothing about them struck him as particularly curious, but his inner sense told him there was danger. He removed his hands from his pockets and pressed his left arm against his side, feeling the cold pressure of the Browning. He began to walk, casually glancing at the hotel to see if the men were lingering in the doorway or on the open veranda. He sensed that he was being watched but could not see them.

If they were going to make a move, however, it would probably not be there. They would wait until he was more vulnerable, or until they thought that he was. On impulse, he turned up the steps and entered the casino, his eyes sweeping the jostling crowd. He did not see them. The chances were that they had slipped out the front. He moved to the nearest twenty-five dollar limit blackjack table and threw five hundred dollars on the felt. The dealer fed him the proper amount of chips and stuffed the cash into the slot on the table top.

He played with apparent intensity, but his eyes roamed the crowd, looking for the two men. He was almost certain they were foreigners from the one brief look he had had at them. Were they Italian? Was the mob onto him? No one remotely resembled the two, and he continued to win at the game he considered boringly simple. His eyes came to rest on the face of a gorgeous young blond sitting at the other end of the table. She was obviously well into the booze already and still drinking heavily, throwing black hundred dollar chips around like they grew on the palm trees on the beach.

By consistently hitting breaking hands she was either lucking out or busting, most of the time the latter and at last the guy next to her could take no more and stood up cursing. "You stupid fucking broad! Anybody that keeps hitting breaking hands has gotta be working for the management."

A big guy behind the dealer stepped forward menacingly, but the pit boss stopped him from belting the poor loser, which was apparently his intention. The pit boss gave the loser a twenty-five dollar chip. "Here, pal. Why don't you cash this in and buy a couple of drinks on the house?"

The loser stared at him incredulously, took the chip without saying thanks, and wandered toward another table muttering. The pit boss smiled and the game continued. Davis picked up his chips and moved down next to the blond.

"That gentleman didn't seem to enjoy the way you play blackjack," he said, smiling.

The blond looked at him as if through a magnifying glass then smirked. "That was no gentleman." She laughed and drained her glass, which she then raised and almost shouted. "Cocktail!"

The dealer turned to the pit boss. "Cocktail here." The pit boss looked annoyed but waved the waitress over and gave her the order.

"Winning or losing?" Davis asked.

"Does it matter?" she drawled.

"Only if you have to work for a living."

"Say, you a comedian or something? Don't you work here in the hotel? Sure I saw your act the other night in the lounge."

"No, dear. You must be mistaken. I'm not a comedian. Just a tourist."

She looked at him with a queer expression, then leaned closer to peer into his cold blue eyes. It was clear she liked what she saw, even if there were two of everything. "You know? You're not half bad looking."

"Some girls have told me that," he said and doubled down on an eight and a three.

The blond flipped up a twenty-one, then moved closer to him until her lips were almost touching his. "I might like to fuck you," she whispered.

The dealer dropped a couple of cards and nervously glanced at the pit boss who was also keeping an eye on what was happening. Davis was aware of their interest.

"Your place or mine?" he said, half jesting.

She smiled a smile that showed her straight white teeth and a hint of pink tongue. "Yours. My old man is upstairs doing business with his buddies. He's always doing business."

"Won't he miss you?" Davis teased, watching the dealer flinch.

"Hell, no. He has his boys come find me about five when he's ready for a fuck. I'm usually passed out in the bingo parlor or the lounge. He's a bastard."

"I see," Davis said, studying the dealer's expression as he laid a ten on top of Davis' eleven and paid twenty-one. "Why don't we make this the last hand?" he whispered to the blond.

"Sure," she said. "Load up." She pushed her entire stack of black chips onto the felt square and stared directly into the dealer's eyes. "If I win, Fred, I'll suck you dry!"

Fred flushed and looked over his shoulder uncomfortably. The pit boss set his jaw but didn't make a sound. Davis put two hundred on the line and the cards came around. His first was a nine, the lady's was a four. The dealer turned up three on the second pass, and they were looking at a breaking hand. Davis had a seven, making sixteen and he stuck, wanting the dealer to draw the inevitable ten. Blondy, however, had drawn an eight on the second card and had a total of twelve.

"I'd pass if I were you," Davis said. "Let him bust."

"Hit me, sweet cheeks," she squealed with delight. Davis winced as the card came down and then stared in amazement. A nine, making twenty-one. Fred looked over his shoulder uneasily as he dealt his final card. A king. Bust! The pit boss glowered balefully as Fred paid the winners and was replaced an instant later by a new dealer.

"Come on," Davis said, taking her by the elbow. "Let's get some fresh air."

"Sure honey. Anything you say. Cash these in for me, fellas," she said, sliding her winnings across the table. Davis led her toward the front.

"Better go tell the old man," the pit boss told his young assistant. "She's at it again."

"You want me to take care of the dude?"

"No. Leave him to me."

Davis spotted the two dark-skinned men at a craps table on the way out, and they were so busy pretending not to be watching him they forgot all about the game in progress. They were definitely Latin, not Italian. One was smoking a short dark cigar and had a thick mustache. The other was thin. Both had wavy black hair. Somehow, they looked vaguely familiar. Davis searched his memory but couldn't place them.

Just as he and the blond reached the front door, she decided it was time to powder her nose. "Hold on, honey. I gotta pee. I won't be a minute. Why don't you get a cab?" She scuttled off and Davis turned to see the two Latins enter the foyer and try to melt into the woodwork when they saw that he was watching them. They continued past him and took the first cab in line without looking back. Davis noted the number, 2481, then glanced around to look for his new companion. There was no sign of her. Davis didn't want to lose the two men now that he had them on the run, so he hailed the next cab and jumped in. "Follow that cab."

A minute later, the blond appeared at the front door about the same time her husband's henchman did. She saw him and tried to duck out, but he caught her. "Come on, Connie. The old man's askin' for you."

"Fuck off, shithead!" she snarled. "Where is he? What'd you do to him?"

"Look's like he cut out on you, baby. Good thing for him." Grinning, he took her firmly by the arm and squeezed it much harder than he had to, pinching the skin between his finger tips. She squirmed.

"Ow! You son of a bitch!"

"Don't make a scene, honey. Old man's orders," he said and dragged her toward the elevators.

Five minutes later, Davis rolled up in front of the Hilton. They had lost the cab in the heavy traffic, and Davis had decided to return to his hotel. There was no sign of the cab. No doubt the two Latins had realized they had been burned and had beaten tracks for home, wherever that happened to be. He paid the driver and entered the hotel lobby, which was jammed with an Elk's club convention just checking in. While waiting for the elevator, he noticed that the pool was still crowded with drinkers and the casino was in full swing.

300

He exited the elevator on the floor beneath his own, and walked the last flight, carefully opening the fire door to survey the hall before moving into the open. The hall was empty and quiet. He walked briskly to his room but paused before putting the key in the lock. The fine strand of blond hair that he had left over the keyhole was gone. The hair on the back of his neck prickled and he slipped his hand into his coat and gripped the handle of the Browning.

Sliding the key noiselessly into the lock, he turned it, pushed the door open and flattened himself against the inner wall as a muted burst of gunfire erupted from near the sliding glass door, the silenced shots smashing into the door frame near his head. He slammed the door and dove toward the bed. The man near the window bolted into the open, firing wildly, each of his shots thumping harmlessly into the carpet.

Suddenly, Davis heard a noise behind him and whirled to see a form rushing out of the darkness. He drove his foot up sharply at the man's groin, lifting him off his feet with an agonized cry, sending him crashing back into the closet doors.

Again Davis wheeled around, this time to see the first man in silhouette against the open glass door, just about to reach the balcony. The Browning roared three times in rapid succession, each shot hitting the man in the upper back. A fine mist of blood sprayed from the man's chest as he toppled forward, struck the railing, and flipped over with a horrified scream.

Davis heard a distant splash and the sound of shrieks from the pool below but did not hesitate as he turned back to the second man, who was painfully rising from the floor. There was a glint of a knife blade in the darkened corner. Cursing in Spanish, the man lunged forward flailing with his weapon. Davis blocked with his forearm and smashed the butt of his pistol into the side of the man's face, dropping him to his knees at the foot of the bed.

Davis seized his wrist and wrenched the knife from his hand, then pressed it to the terrified Latin's face. "Who are you?" Davis hissed. He was conscious of the fact that he had

301

but a few minutes to effect an escape if he wanted to avoid an incident.

The man groaned. Davis put the knife to his throat. *"I said who are you?"*

The man whimpered as the blade cut into the flesh of his Adam's apple, and began to speak frantically in Spanish.

"Son of a bitch!" Davis croaked, recognizing the accent. Suddenly he placed them. "Did Perez send you?"

The man shook his head and Davis slid the knife a fraction of an inch to the right, and felt the blade sever the flesh and grate along the man's larynx.

"Aiyee!" the man cried. "Si, si, Perez!" The rest was choked off by a sharp flick of Davis' wrist. He let the man drop to the floor, gasping and sputtering as he drowned in his own blood. Davis rose to his feet. There wasn't much time.

He had to think quickly. Stepping to the balcony, he eased out for a look. The pool had emptied, and in the middle of it, half submerged, awash in his own blood, was the first assassin. A crowd had gathered at poolside and some were looking up at the hotel tower.

Davis turned and left the room as it was, locked the door and dropped the key down the mail chute after carefully wiping it clean. He paused in front of a mirror to straighten his clothing, ran a hand through his tousled blond hair, then stepped onto the elevator and pressed the lobby button.

When he reached the lobby, the place was buzzing like an angry beehive, but he walked casually out the front door, hailed a cab and smiled to himself as it pulled away past the arriving squad cars and ambulance.

"Miami International," he said.

Parker slumped in his desk chair in the Oval Office, watching a special satellite transmission of the Moscow May Day celebration currently in progress. It was a bright sunny morning in Moscow, and the military was on display, as were the party and government leaders. All of them were present, despite the President's failing health and the supposed rift

302

with the Premier, who was standing stiffly next to the Party Chief.

Red Square was teaming with civilians and military personnel, and caison after caison bearing ballistic missiles rolled to a tumultuous ovation and the bombastic pomp of the marching bands. As in so many years past, this was a heavy display of Russian might, a warning to the West of the Kremlin's preparedness and the support of its people. Tanks and missile launchers followed the caisons, and thousands of troops marched smartly in cadence past the head of state, their chests thrust forward, their hard-soled boots tramping resonantly on the square. It was hardly a joyous celebration of spring.

Parker raised his head slowly at the sound of the knock at the door. "Come in," he said softly. He had not realized until that moment how drained he was. The mere use of his voice had been an effort.

Shirley opened the door and allowed General Owens to enter. He was carrying a black case under one arm and wore a broad grin. "Thank you, Shirley. Mr. President, how are you?"

"Fine, Ralph. Pull up a chair."

The General sat down, pulled his chair around, and leaned forward intently at the sight of the huge military display. "Is this the live transmission?"

"Yes."

"They're really putting on the dog for us, aren't they? The whole fucking Kremlin's there. Actually, I just stopped by to show you this." Owens said, patting the small black case on his lap.

"What is it?"

"A surprise. May I?"

"In a minute. I want to get another look at the President. He looks tired. As tired as I feel."

They sat for a while in silence, watching the Russians parade across the square, listening to the pulse of the enemy's nationalistic heart, recognizing the implied challenge in the Kremlin's display of might. Finally, a close shot showed the group of dignitaries. They were somber, silent, intent.

"Well, I've seen enough. What's in the case, Ralph?"

Owens opened the case and removed a video cassette. "May I?"

"You know how to run that thing?" Parker asked, indicating the cassette deck just beneath the television set.

"I think so." Owens slipped the cassette into the deck and soon had the bars and tone running on the screen. Then it went to black with a ten-second countdown, after which a picture faded in. It was a view of the Cosmos over the edge of Skylab, with the black box of the reactor being settled into its cradle by the EVA crew. In the following moments, they watched an edited version of the Alpha test. As the fireball faded into the blackness, and the screen went blank, Parker sat forward, a narrow grin creasing his face.

"I wanted you to see it for yourself, Don."

"The test was successful?"

"Beyond all expectations. There'll be another one in a month, but Kemper has already given the go-ahead for production of the remaining diamond bottles and the reactor units. As far as he is concerned, the Oasis Project is a "go."

Parker sighed audibly and slumped back in his chair. It was a tremendous weight off his shoulders. Had the reactor failed, his alternatives would have been severely limited and altogether unpleasant. "And the construction?"

"Ahead of schedule by three days. The crews are working around the clock and we anticipate the hangar section will be finished out sometime late in September."

"And the ASP?"

"The mock-up has been wind tested and passed on every count. So far there are no problems."

"That's good news Ralph. I mean it. This display of Russian militarism is a clear indication of their intentions. Did you notice how the Premier was there, right next to the President, even though they've been at each other's throats for the past year?"

"I noticed. But I don't think they're going to make a move. Not yet at any rate." Owens placed the cassette back in its case and cleared his throat as if he had something more to say.

Parker looked at him questioningly. "Is there something else?"

"You remember the situation at SPEC with Kathy Karpovich?"

"Of course. What's happening with that?"

"Well, as it turned out, we let her stay longer than we had expected. It was necessary to keep the heat off the Project for as long as possible, and the amount of information we had let us feed the Russians a little at a time and really string them along. But during our surveillance of the embassy officials, we discovered that one of them was following one of our own diplomats when he wasn't working with Zeitsev, the Russian who first approached Karpovich. We had tentatively identified the second man as a Russian journalist on assignment here, but we have only recently discovered that the real journalist hasn't been in this country for some months now. And when we realized that the man he was following had been a visitor of yours over the past two years, we thought it might bear some closer scrutiny. The diplomat's name is Roger Davis. He was formerly assigned to the embassy in Moscow."

Parker paled but recovered quickly. "Davis? Of course. Davis. He's done some work in . . . Mexico for me, with Perez."

"Yes, well, apparently the Russians have got some interest in him, and when we finally found out who the Russian agent really was, I thought I'd better bring it to your attention."

"Who is he?"

"His real name is Aleksay Kurochkin. He's with the GRU, military intelligence, and apparently reports directly to the Center in Moscow. He's got a reputation on the continent as one of their more successful enforcers. In fact, the CIA thinks he's responsible for at least eight of our agent's disappearances over the last decade."

"What the hell is he doing following Davis?"

"We don't know. If, as you say, Davis has been on special assignments, it could be he is monitoring your foreign policies, perhaps with the intention of undermining them."

"How did you happen to discover he was following Davis?" Parker asked, trying to shield his discomfort.

Owens pulled a dossier out of his valise and produced several black and white photographs. He handed one to Parker. It featured Davis in the foreground in soft focus, with Aleksay in the background in sharp focus on a crowded sidewalk.

"That picture was taken here in Washington shortly after we began tailing Kurochkin." He handed Parker a second still.

This photo showed Kurochkin in three-quarter profile with Davis in the background in a ticket line in a busy airport terminal. "This was taken in Miami three weeks ago. One of our agents was struck by something in the picture, and when he realized he recognized the man in the ticket line, he went back through the files and found the first photo. A thorough check turned up three more such stills. Of course, we didn't know who Davis was at first, and we had to do some digging. We found his picture in the diplomatic corps files. That was earlier this week."

"Where is he now?"

"Davis?"

"No, the Russian."

"He came back from Miami this evening. We had a man on the plane, and we followed him all the way back to the embassy."

"And Davis?"

"We put several men on him, and as far as I know he's still in Miami. He's staying at the Hilton."

"Does he know you're watching him?"

"No. I thought it best to provide protection for him just in case and consult with you before doing anything else."

Parker's mind was racing, wondering how he could get Owens to call off his watchdogs before they discovered the connection with the mysterious occurrences that seemed to follow Davis' wake.

"Is he on assignment there for you, Don?"

"No." Parker said. "I haven't spoken to him for some time."

"I see. I wasn't prying, but if you want me to provide a special security team for him, I'll give the order right now."

"No. He's not involved with anything sensitive. I don't see any reason. I can't imagine why the Russians are interested in him."

"The only thing we can figure is that he was involved in something in Moscow, but we don't know what."

"What do you propose to do about Kurochkin?"

"Well, considering he's one of the GRU's top agents and on the CIA's hit list, we thought we ought to go ahead and pick him up. That might mean compromising their apparat at SPEC, but he's too big a fish to let go."

"How did he get into the country?"

"We don't know. He obviously came in under deep cover, then arranged to have the real journalist sent home and took his place. It's a pretty bold move, but this guy's renowned for that sort of thing."

"I suggest you get rid of him," Parker said.

Owens looked surprised. "Permanently, you mean?"

"Yes."

"Without questioning him?"

"What do you think you'll get out of him? If we arrest him, the Russians will claim diplomatic immunity and the best we could expect to do is deport him, unless we want to make a real issue out of it, which I don't. Killing him is the simplest way."

"You surprise me, Don."

"Why?"

"Well, I thought of suggesting the same thing, but I didn't know how you'd react."

"I may be cautious in foreign affairs, Ralph, but I'm also aware that sometimes we have to use other methods. I say get rid of him and see that the body doesn't turn up. Then the Russians can't say anything at all."

"There's a score of agents who would love to get him under the gun, Don. I'll pass the word along. As for Davis, I don't know what kind of a diplomat he is, but I suggest you consider getting him some protection if you think he's capable of being compromised."

"Leave Davis to me, Ralph."

"All right. Well, at any rate, let me be the first to

congratulate you on the tests, Don." Owens rose, extending his hand. Parker shook it, and glanced once more at the photos on his desk.

"Do you mind if I keep these to show to Davis, Ralph? He might be able to shed some light on this."

"No problem."

"And, Ralph. Keep this whole thing quiet will you? I mean within the service as well. I don't want this sort of thing getting around. It could be bad for morale."

"I'll take care of it."

. . . 5 May 1990

The Compound at Camp David was painted in the shades of spring. The day was warm, the sky filled with billowing thunderheads, and the air was still and sullen.

Parker and Davis walked by a sparkling brook, through towering pines with only the sound of the birds and squirrels in the trees to break the silence. Here and there, scattered around them in the woods, dark-suited Secret Service men moved like shadows, automatic weapons over their shoulders, their eyes sweeping the fringes of the forest.

"I'm very disturbed, Mr. Davis. The General was aware of your movements, even though he's obviously not made any connection with your activities. Were you never aware of a tail?"

"Frankly, sir, if someone wants to tail you, and if he's good enough, which I know Kurochkin is, he can do so for years until he decides to make a move. It's pure luck they picked him out. He's been in and out of this country a hundred times in the past twenty years, carrying out operations on various levels, and we were never able to get wind of him until months after he was gone."

"Do you think he was sent here for you?"

"Definitely. All they had to do was put a few pieces of the puzzle together and pull my name out of the hat. I spoke of this risk when you first suggested the operation to me."

"Then why didn't he do what he came for?"

Davis smiled at Parker's bluntness.

"I don't mean to sound calloused," Parker said.

"I understand. He certainly could have tried to take me any time he wanted to. But if my guess is correct, somehow he caught on to what I was doing. If what you say is true, that he was in Miami last week, then he's got a lot of circumstantial evidence linking me to the killings."

"What do you think this Kurochkin is going to do?"

"He's probably had orders from the Center to follow me and build up a case. They're trying to figure out what the hell I'm doing, and if there's any direct link to anyone higher up, namely you. So far, I think we've kept that clean, and unless they are able to penetrate White House security, I doubt if they'll be able to come up with anything conclusive."

"And if they can't."

"Then he'll be instructed to eliminate me and come home."

"I've instructed Ralph Owens to have him killed."

Davis looked slightly disappointed.

"I know you'd like to do the job yourself, but I think under the circumstances you should keep out of it. We've got to maintain your cover; so I'm afraid you'll have to sit on your hands for a while until this thing has blown over."

"Whatever you say, sir. At least we've accomplished something."

"Precious little, I'm afraid. The unions are still continuing with the old policies. All we've done is eliminate a few of the more criminal element."

"I'm willing to continue if you think it will help, Mr. President."

"No. I only have one thing in mind right now."

"Is it something I should prepare for?"

Parker looked at him gravely, then stared down into the water of the brook. "I'm not sure how you're going to react to this, Mr. Davis. So I'll try to put it delicately. I'm considering a move against Enrique Perez."

Davis showed no outward reaction, but his eyes suddenly glowed and his pupils widened slightly at the rush of adrenalin.

"You see, Davis, I'm aware of your relationship with his daughter."

Davis' mind reeled with twisted images: of Perez sprawled in a pool of his own blood, of Mercedes whispering "I love you." He relived the scene in his hotel room, saw the first assassin toppling over his balcony, heard the grisly death throes of the one whose throat he had cut. No doubt his expression revealed more than he had expected it would.

"I see," Parker said. "I had hoped that your affair would not color your judgment, but apparently it has."

For the first time since he had known Parker, Davis saw something he did not like. He wanted to strike out at him, but it was an emotion he could not explain. He felt nothing for Perez. Perhaps it was the thought of being personally violated by Parker; having his affairs scrutinized. But those things had never affected him before. He knew, even though he refused to admit, that it was because of Mercedes that he felt the sudden rage. He knew that he was still in love with her.

"I think I'd better tell you, Mr. Davis, that I had your phone tapped."

Davis glared at him, but made no effort to respond.

"It wasn't personal, and I assure you that I did not doubt your loyalty. It was merely a precaution. I happen to know that you are not seeing the young lady any longer. I took that as a good sign."

"It is, sir. I'm not seeing her. I haven't seen her since my trip to Cancun."

"I see."

"There's something else I think you should know, sir. Perez tried to have me killed."

"He what?"

"In Miami. He sent two hit men. I got them both. I forced one of them to admit that Perez had sent them. You probably saw the headlines about the double killing in the Hilton."

"That was you?"

"I had no other choice. There's no way it can be traced to me."

"Son of a bitch! Do you think . . ."

"I'm sure it was personal. I'm sure Mercedes' father found out about us and put out a contract on me."

"There *was* something between you?"

"Yes, sir. There was. But that's over now."

"How were they able to trace you?" Parker asked.

311

"Obviously Perez had his agents operating in this country. But I know for a fact there are no witnesses—living at any rate—who can link me to the operations."

"Nevertheless, your activities haven't gone unnoticed. You'll have to take greater precautions from now on. And that's going to be difficult because you'll be operating in Mexico. You realize it isn't a personal thing against Perez. He's forcing my hand. If he'd simply agree to cooperate . . . but then he hasn't, has he? So I have no other choice. Our embargoes are going to cause some problems down there, but I want Mexico brought to its knees. That means Perez must go."

"Has it gotten that bad, sir?"

"I'm afraid it's worse than that. Much worse. The Mexicans are gradually cutting down their oil exports to us. That's one of the reasons I've been forced to reduce domestic petroleum allocations. Our reserves are dropping too low. Perez knows this and thinks we'll have to come around to him. But it's going to be the other way around. His death will almost certainly cause a disruption in the country, and the disorganization that will follow will either prompt his successor to come to us on our terms or leave the country vulnerable. Either way, we'll be able to move in if we have to and take over the oil fields, which is my sole objective."

"Just what the Russians are doing in the Middle East."

"Exactly."

Davis nodded solemnly. "If you want Perez killed, I'll do it, sir."

"It isn't that I want it, Davis. It's necessary. He isn't a bad man. He's just shortsighted. I'll leave the details to you, but I'll plan the timing. It will have to be coordinated carefully."

"I understand."

"And you're sure you don't have any misgivings?"

"If there's no other way . . ."

Parker shook his head and continued to walk along the path, absentmindedly watching the rippling patterns of reflected light on the brook's rocky bottom. "What we've been trying to do is buy time."

"Yes, sir."

"That's why I have to act without compassion. But something keeps nagging at me, Davis. Something I guess you'd call a conscience, although by all rights I shouldn't have one. Are we right, Mr. Davis? Is what I've tried to do justifiable? Can we claim the same license allowed to soldiers in wartime?"

"Do you want an answer, sir?"

"If you've got one."

"I'm not saying what we've done is right or wrong, because I don't think we've acted like men with the luxury of choice. As far as I'm concerned, these were acts of war, against the enemy, and in some cases against men who were little better than traitors. We've tried to undo what it has taken two centuries to do, and the fact that our actions haven't had too much effect may mean that we started too late. If that's true, I don't see the future of life on this planet extending much past the end of the century. If this country goes down because of its unwillingness to fight for its survival, then the rest of the world is going with it."

Parker closed his eyes and raised his head, feeling the sun beat down on his face. "There's so little time, Mr. Davis. So little time. The final crisis is inevitable. It's just a question of where and when. It might start in Saudi Arabia with a religious rebellion or in Lebanon if the Israelis keep gobbling up territory. Already the Sudanese, Libyans, and Syrians are deploying troops along their frontiers. What would happen if they somehow decided to move en masse against Israel and Egypt? We know that Israel has between twenty and thirty nuclear devices, and our intelligence reports that in the 1973 war they were on the verge of using them if the tide had not turned in their favor. It was *that* close in 1973—even closer than with the Cuban missile crisis. And if something starts in the Middle East, how can the superpowers stay out of it?"

Parker lowered his head and rubbed his eyes wearily. "I haven't slept for more than five minutes at a time for the last six months, Davis. I keep seeing a blinding flash, hearing the roar and feeling the Earth tremble as a huge mushroom cloud boils out of the horizon. I see wasted landscapes that were once cities, skeletal remains of buildings reduced to charred rubble, the soil blowing in whirlwinds of lethal dust. I wake up in a cold sweat afraid to close my eyes again, but too tired to keep them open. and I keep asking myself *why?* Why does it have to be this way? What do they expect to gain? The Russians don't want to destroy the world, they want to rule it. The Chinese don't want war, and we certainly don't want it. Nobody wants it, but one false move and the whole thing could blow up in our faces. And for what? A couple of thousand square miles of sand and rock? A country once called Palestine? Crumbling ruins someone calls a holy city? Religious hatred five thousand years old? Is that any reason to decimate the planet and every living creature on it?"

He turned to Davis, who had remained silently by his side. Parker's eyes were welling with tears. His emotions were strained to their limit. "Don't you see, Mr. Davis? We have no other choice. We have to prepare for the inevitable. If we don't do something, it will be too late."

Aleksay stared thoughtfully at the latest developed photographs as Zeitsev took down the coded communique from Moscow. Miss Karpovich had done well indeed. She had managed to obtain almost all the current material on the new top secret reconnaissance plane the Americans were developing. The "Drone" they called it — capable of unmanned flight over a distance of six thousand miles, capable of pinpointing a target and photographing it from an altitude of ninety thousand feet, with a cruising speed of Mach 4, and the same radar jamming design characteristics as the Stealth bomber. It was a formidable tool, one that his country would be grateful to know more about.

While Zietsev decoded the message, Aleksay stared at the list — the projected targets. He was aware of the purpose of the pilot project: to survey population flows and activities, to try to anticipate and interpret psychological trends by these changing social patterns. He had heard that the Americans were prone to making outlandish studies, such as the cost of preserving an endangered species of fish, versus the building of a new hydroelectric dam facility. It was the rationale of children, and this project was no better. But the Drone was something else altogether. Its uses were multifold and could be damaging to Russia's national security by allowing the Americans to monitor any future arms agreement.

He dropped the list back into the dossier and stared out the window at the city lights, thinking of Davis. Since he had been following the American agent, he had witnessed several trips to the White House and one to Camp David. He knew that Davis had carried out acts of violence against persons in opposition to the Administration, although he had never actually witnessed one. He wondered what the Kremlin would recommend. How could that information best be used against the American President, since it could be reasoned that the directives for these operations had come down from his level? He was convinced that there was no coincidence, but would his superiors feel the same way? He was anxious to resolve the situation one way or the other, however, for he had wasted too much precious time on the operation.

At last, Zeitsev looked up from his ciphering, but did not speak. He was pale.

"Well?" Aleksay asked.

Zeitsev slowly read the message verbatim. "Concerning the American agent. Terminate him at once. He is of no use to us. Pertaining to the operation at SPEC, maintain the apparat. We are very interested to know more about this 'Drone' project. Send all materials through normal channels." Zeitsev looked up and saw the frown on Aleksay's face, and so continued before his companion had a chance to speak. "Finally, Brutus has revealed the existence of another more delicate program under development. Find out what you can about the Oasis Project."

Aleksay looked confused. "Who is Brutus?"

"He is another operative functioning in Washington. I do not know his true identity nor have I ever communicated with him directly. I only know that he is in deeper cover and has been in this country since the end of World War II. From time to time, the Center gives me leads based upon his information. He is too valuable to risk in an apparat. He merely points the way and others pursue."

"The Oasis Project? Have you ever heard of it?"

"No."

"The wording of the communique indicates that this project might be under development at SPEC, doesn't it?"

"It seems to."

"Interesting. Instruct Karpovich to pursue this."

"And the American?" Sergei asked timidly.

Aleksay's face darkened. "I have my orders. If they do not wish to use the information I have provided, who am I to judge?" Aleksay rose and dropped the Drone dossier on the desk. "He will be eliminated."

Aleksay left the embassy by the back way and walked along the darkened alley to a side street. He paused in the shadows to observe. The sidewalks were empty, the windows of most of the buildings dark. It was late, and in Washington, D.C., it was not wise to walk alone at night. Such a thought never entered his head. He had walked far more dangerous streets than those of Washington, D.C.

The night air smelled sweet with the fragrance of blossoming trees along the river and in the parks. The breeze was soft and gentle, the temperature mild. It reminded him of summer nights on the Black Sea. He turned north to the next corner, where he crossed and entered another alley between two apartment buildings. Approximately two hundred feet in, there was a T-shaped intersection, and in the almost complete darkness, he took the left hand artery and stepped softly past the blackened first floor windows to a door hidden in the recesses of a fire escape.

He turned the knob cautiously, eased the door open, and stepped into a dark hallway. He paused to listen, the hairs prickling on the back of his neck. Suddenly, a blast of fire spat from the end of the hall, the spray of bullets riddling the door and walls around him. Miraculously, in the instant before he dropped to his knees he was hit only three times, twice in the abdomen and once in the shoulder. Lurching back into the alley, he pulled the door behind him.

The CIA agent ran to the alley door and threw it open. The last thing he saw was the muzzle blast inches from his face. His body slammed backwards into the splintered wooden door and he dropped to the blood-spattered floor. Aleksay leaned for an instant against the building. People were shouting and lights were coming on. The police would be there any moment. He did not know how badly he was hurt, but he did not intend to stand still as long as he had the strength to move.

Staggering doubled over, clutching his pistol to his chest he ran with all his strength back along the way he had come, but instead of turning to the right up the intersecting alley, he continued on straight, out onto the street. Struggling to right himself, he managed to walk the three short blocks to the embassy.

He paused at the entrance to the alley behind the embassy and fed a fresh clip into his pistol. Then with his last reserves he managed to reach the back door and pounded on it. A peephole opened and an eye peered out.

"Open," he stammered, his tongue thick, his head filling with cobwebs. The door opened and he collapsed into the arms of the startled security guard. He was aware of his blood spotting the linoleum tile, then his eyes blurred, the pain in his chest seared up into his throat, and darkness closed around him.

. . . 13 June 1990

The announcement from OPEC that they were cutting production and curtailing exports to the United States came on the morning of June 13, a sultry steaming morning under a heavy grey sky. The night before had brought torrential rains and violent winds, and the streets were littered with leaves and broken tree limbs in the storm's wake. Washington lay beneath a canopy of gloom like a defaced relic, her mood as sullen as the tenacious heat that gripped her.

Already, the summer had been much hotter than normal, with temperatures in most parts of the country climbing consistently into the nineties for days on end, stretching into weeks since mid-May. Under the untimely surge in energy consumption sporadic brownouts had occurred along the eastern seaboard, and those unfortunates who had never been without the comforts of air conditioning soon received a crash course in what it was like in the good old days, as power companies imposed severe rationing. There simply wasn't enough fuel, whether coal or oil, to meet the demand, and companies had been instructed by the Administration as early as April to begin stockpiling for the winter months because of drastically reduced reserves from the previous winter strikes and the continuing labor problems in the mines. If conditions were to continue as they were, brownouts were anticipated from New York to Florida, and the announcement by OPEC had Capitol Hill in an uproar.

OPEC's action was based upon America's unwillingness to accept the idea of an independent Palestinian state. Though it was by no means a unanimous decision among its members, the Saudis were unable to counter the move with

318

increased production as they had so many times in the past, because their own domestic turmoil was draining the workers from the oil fields and filling the streets of Mecca, Jiddah, and Riyadh with angry demonstrations against the ruling family.

Where there had been a steady, albeit inadequate flow of crude oil from the Middle East, there was to be a mere trickle in terms of American demand. The situation called for drastic domestic action, and to this end Parker met with his chief advisors in the War Room of the Pentagon. The atmosphere was as bleak as the leaden sky over the city that morning.

"If this thing in Saudi Arabia erupts in violence, what the hell are the Russians going to do Ralph?" Parker asked.

"We don't know, Mr. President, and we have no way of knowing. So far, there have been no official reactions from the Kremlin. Personally, I'd say they're probably jumping up and down with excitement over OPEC's announcement. It's something they've been setting up for close to twenty years. We know they are supplying advisory personnel to the radical faction in Saudi Arabia, which we think is the Fedayeen or some equivalent thereof. They may also be supplying arms, although we have no confirmation of that so far."

"What could we do if we had confirmation?"

"Nothing, short of committing to a head-on confrontation with the Kremlin. As it is, I strongly suggest you issue a warning to the Soviets to maintain neutrality in any conflict that should arise and urge the United Nations to intervene before this thing gets out of hand."

"Have we got the votes in the UN, Montie?"

"It's marginal," Montie said.

"All right, we don't know what's going to happen, but we can predict an escalation, is that right?"

"It's probably inevitable," Owens said.

"What can the Russians do on a global level if they decide to play hardball?" Parker asked.

"A hell of a lot," Owens said, rising and approaching the world map that spread over the better part of one wall. "Let me direct your attention to the big board. As we've outlined

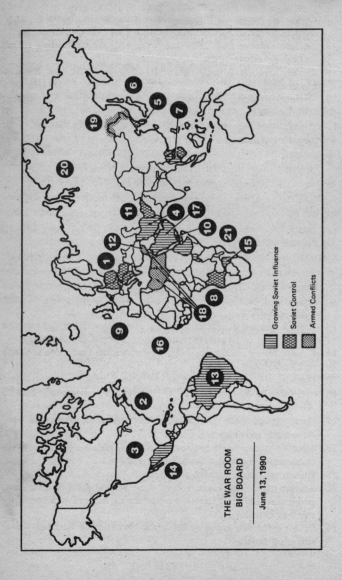

THE WAR ROOM
BIG BOARD

June 13, 1990

Growing Soviet Influence

Soviet Control

Armed Conflicts

LEGEND

1. Ongoing Soviet arms buildup greatest in history—jeopardizes peace in Europe and Middle East. 1979-present.
2. Serious defense cuts 1976-1980. Subsequent rebuilding effort behind schedule 1988.
3. Carter cancels Minute Man III Missiles, with no Russian concession.
4. Soviets exploit revolution in Iran, warn U.S. against interference.
5. Carter unilaterally withdraws troops from So. Korea, jeopardizing peace in North Asia.
6. Japan and Indonesia threatened by U.S. troop withdrawal from So. Korea, vital shipping lanes jeopardized.
7. Soviet-backed No. Vietnam conquers Cambodia—no Carter response.
8. Cuban/Soviets take over Angola, 1978.
9. Carter's neutron bomb decision shocks NATO allies.
10. Russian/Cuban advisors support attempted invasion of No. Yemen by So. Yemen.
11. Afghanistan falls to pro-Soviet takeover, no Carter protest. Russian invasion of Afghanistan draws weak U.S. response, jeopardizing Persian Gulf.
12. Israeli/PLO conflicts continually threaten stability of the Middle East.
13. Cuban backed rebels continuing guerilla warfare against the government of Brazil, threatening security of So. America.
14. Covert Mexican/Soviet/Cuban relationship threatens security of Central America.
15. Growing Cuban/Soviet influence in Rhodesia.
16. 105,000 Cuban troops and Soviet advisors now operating in 16 African states.
17. Growing domestic discord in Saudi Arabia, threatens pro-American government, 1990.
18. Massive troop deployments, Libya, Sudan, Jordan, Syria threatening Egyptian/Israeli peace accord.
19. Russian/Chinese border disputes.
20. Soviets undertake massive civil defense and factory relocation programs. 1976 to present, strengthening fears of an impending nuclear conflict.
21. Soviet influence grows in Ethiopia, threatening Red Sea—vital shipping lanes.

here, the Soviet strategy has been to gain influential positions in key locations around the world. In 1979 procommunist South Yemen invaded democratic North Yemen with Russian aid and Cuban advisors. Though that incursion was repelled, they're almost certain to try again. In 1980 Afghanistan fell to a pro-Soviet takeover and Russian invasion forces. I feel that OPEC's announcement might be related to these and subsequent events since we haven't been able to appreciably change our posture in ten years. OPEC may be hedging its bets, hoping they can appease the Kremlin by cutting us off. Maybe they think they can forestall an invasion of the Persian Gulf. We know they can't, but we're looking at it from the outside.

"Now, farther south, the government of Ethiopia is under strong pressure from communist-backed forces and the situation there is deteriorating daily. Our intelligence sources report the influx of Cuban advisors as recently as three weeks ago, and there are reports of Cuban troops being involved in some of the fighting in the outback. And the situation in Rhodesia is not much better. The black majority government is struggling with their own radical factions and the threat of tribal outbursts.

"The Cuban inspired revolutions in South and Central America since 1980 have had the same intent and that is to isolate the primary sources of petroleum production, namely Venezuela and Mexico. Thus the invasion of Honduras by Nicaragua, the guerilla attacks by Surinam on Guyana, and of course the rebellion in Brazil. All of it has been a master plan coordinated and financed by the Soviets. They're isolating the North American continent. Carter cut U.S. ship-building by fifty percent in the first two years of his administration and despite our attempts to catch up, the Soviets have been outspending us by nearly five percent per annum since 1982, spending an estimated twenty percent of their GNP on defense buildup, which makes the START negotiations a complete travesty. Their May Day display was designed to show off their latest technology, which if not quite as sophisticated as ours, certainly makes up for it in fire power.

"Add to this all the buildup in Eastern Europe and on the

Chinese border, and it spells potential disaster if it comes down to a shooting war. Using conventional methods, they might be able to cripple and isolate us, and that would leave us no alternative but to surrender or use nuclear weapons."

"And NATO forces?"

"Badly outnumbered, but situated in key defensive positions. Our conventional weaponry is far more sophisticated. Nevertheless, Russia's crack tank corps could sweep into Western Europe and we'd be hard pressed to hold them back without using a weapon like the neutron bomb. What's more, without immediate support from home, NATO forces would be swamped, and since the Soviets might be able to dominate the sea lanes in the Atlantic, there would be little we could do."

"Then we're back to the threat of nuclear weapons?"

"Any way you look at it, unless we're willing to concede Europe and the Middle East, it shapes up to nuclear confrontation."

"Is that deterrent enough?"

"That's questionable. As you know, starting in the mid-seventies, the Soviets began massive relocation programs of all civil defense and factory facilities. That's still going on, and we've got to assume it has been done for a purpose, which I frankly relate to military actions they've encouraged throughout the world. The Russians feel pretty confident they'd come out on top if it came down to what they've been referring to as limited nuclear confrontation."

"I see," Parker murmured. "All right, I want the selective service system completely refurbished and prepared for immediate implementation. In addition, I want all able-bodied individuals currently in the work camps to undergo induction physicals. If we need readily available manpower, the camps could provide at least a hundred thousand recruits. I also want an immediate build-up of defense oil reserves to maximum capacity. Notify the oil companies. We're going to have to cut domestic allocations to the bare bones for at least the next three months and absolutely no oil is to be exported, is that clear? Not to Israel or anyone else. In the meantime, intensify the combat readiness of all troops and notify me of any development in Saudi Arabia. Gentlemen, we're approaching a state of war, and I think it's time we faced it."

"My God, Don! Do you realize what you're doing?" Preston Holmes' face was bright red and the veins bulged in his neck. He stood beside the President, who was jumping rope in the White House gymnasium. It was almost midnight, but Parker had missed his morning workout, a ritual he had resumed recently to combat the psychological strain he was under.

"Preston, I know exactly what I'm doing."

"But the Congress is never going to stand for it. We can't cut back allocations any more or we're going to have riots!"

"We have no alternative. The coal companies have been trying to stockpile, the oil companies are refining at maximum output, the atomic plants that were shut down are back to full capacity, but we're still consuming more energy than we produce. With OPEC's cut back, we're going to drain our reserves if we don't make the people conserve, and the only way to do that is to give them no choice. I hate to have to ask you, but you're going to have to get me the authority from Congress to stockpile."

"How Goddamnit? Just tell me how! I've spent the last eighteen months beating my brains out, pushing through legislation that makes federal income tax look like a godsend. And nothing we've tried has worked. The people still think the oil companies are holding out, they're still picketing the nuclear plants, and you're asking me to take away still more? My credibility has hit bottom. Hell, I can't even get the House majority leader to return my phone calls! And your popularity in the polls is lower than any president since Jimmy Carter's at the end of his administration. So how in the goddamn hell am I going to sell another allocation cutback?"

"It's not a public issue, Preston. It's a matter of national security. What I want is the authority to stockpile military reserves. With the activity in the Middle East, we need to be ready to move on a global basis, and that means we need our reserves at peak capacity. If the Russians decide to make a move we're sitting ducks. That's what you've got to sell!"

"Isn't it possible that the Security Council might be exaggerating the danger?"

"As I recall, the initial reports before the Shah was toppled were considered exaggerations. Up until a few days before he was thrown out, the CIA still thought he could hold on. I don't intend to be caught with my pants down the way Carter was."

"You know you're asking Congress to give you the right to change the whole pattern of American life?"

"If that's what it takes to survive, then that's what I'm asking. You don't seem to understand, Preston, we're not talking about a hypothetical economic model. We're talking about a real economy, a real threat of collapse, and a real enemy waiting to move on us the minute we show signs of weakness. What do you want me to do? Wait until the Red Army marches down Park Avenue? The people of this country have got to be made to understand that there are no absolutes. Times and conditions change, and as self-centered as people are, they can't ignore reality. In this kind of situation, there are no rights or wrongs; there's only survival. That means we have to sacrifice. I don't care how loud the people scream or how low I sink in the popularity polls. My job is to provide leadership for the common good, and if that means forcing a bitter pill down people's throats, that's what I'm going to do, no ifs, ands, or buts!"

Parker dropped the jump rope which he had been swinging around wildly as he gesticulated. He picked up his towel and wiped his face, forcing himself to maintain his composure. "Preston. I know you've done a great job so far. No vice-president has ever done so much for an administration. The way you've handled the opposition on the Hill has allowed me the freedom to develop the Oasis Project the way I knew it had to be done, without interference or public scrutiny. You've kept labor off my back with the work camps and how you got that legislation through Congress I'll never know. But the tough part is still ahead of us. We need to buy time, and by keeping the Russians at bay we do that. But in order to keep the Russians at bay we need full military energy reserves. It's as simple as that."

The two men stared at each other in silence, both wondering about the future; if one really did exist for them, for the country, for humanity.

"You really believe that the Russians are going to make a move, don't you?" Holmes said at last.

"Everything that they've said and done since the end of World War II has indicated that they would one day move against us. Only, if we don't do something, they're not going to have to lift a finger. We're going to drive ourselves into oblivion by being too damned naive to see what's coming. I'm telling you, this country could completely collapse if we reach a level of economic turmoil much greater than we have right now. If the Saudi oil fields are shut down by a civil war, that could do it. Look at what's happened with the cutbacks they've already made. Businesses are going under, produce is rotting in the fields, banks are in danger of closing, loans are being defaulted, unemployment is growing. It's all interrelated and it all goes back to one thing—oil! Without oil, this country is dead!"

Holmes nodded solemnly and shoved his hands into his suit pants, staring at the hardwood floor. I'll do what I can, Don."

"I know you will, Preston. But make sure it's enough."

. . . 4 July 1990

People had begun to cultivate the ancient art of walking. Children rode their bicycles to school once more, and even fathers and mothers dusted off their old rusty two-wheelers to ride to work or to the market. The pace of American life had slowed, and somehow, in an unexpected way, people were happier, not to mention much healthier. It was a time of rekindling family ties, reshaping friendships, stopping to look around at all the things that had been forgotten. The rat race slowed to snail's pace, and a speeding society on wheels crept quietly to a halt.

In the small towns, July 4, 1990, was a day much like any other July Fourth. There were parades on Main Street, bottle rockets soaring above treetops, Black Cat firecrackers popping, watermelons dripping with icy sweetness, hotdogs, three-legged races around the town park, speeches from perspiring mayors, who mopped their brows with great white kerchiefs. There were concerts in the park, sailing contests on the town lakes, swimming meets and bright red, white, and blue ribbons for the winners.

There were the smells of charcoal fires, fresh cut grass, and home-baked pies and cakes. There was ice cream, and soft drinks, and rosy-red sunburned noses tipped with zinc oxide. Fathers gathered in the shade to pitch horseshoes and sip mint juleps on the sly. Mothers exchanged pickle recipes and hot pepper-eating contests brought cries of joy and admiration from one and all.

There were ice chests full of beer, potato salad by the gallon, hamburgers loaded with relish and catsup, mustard dripping ham sandwiches, and John Phillip Sousa marches floating on the wind. Birds sang in the trees, bees flitted from flower to hive, butterflies danced in graceful ballet across the parks and meadows, dogs yelped and whined in protest at the spattering of fireworks, and cats dozed on shaded porch swings, too wise to venture forth into the summer sun.

But what of the cities? People were not so gay about the Fourth of July. To most it meant another sweltering day of unbroken heat. Here and there, groups gathered on door stoops to sip tepid beer and grouse about the weather and the price of gas. The cities had grown grim and silent.

Every day, the freeways had grown less crowded. Not that there weren't cars or even gas to fill them. There was gas, enough to drive to work, enough if one cared to wait hours in line while listening to the radio or reading the newspaper accounts of strife in the Middle East, truckers' strikes, food shortages, murders and suicides.

People walked the streets afraid to speak, afraid to look anywhere but straight ahead. The subways still ran, and so did the elevated railways; both kept regular schedules, but they too were less crowded. The cities seemed to be emptying. Each day, more and more people failed to show up for work, and if they did not bother to call, the employers did not bother to inquire. They knew that someone else had fled the insanity of the metropolis. And all the while, others wondered, "Why don't *I* leave? What am *I* staying for?"

The once vital cities were becoming empty shells, and soon anyone who had the fare, anyone who could afford to fill his tank would leave. Maybe soon, those who didn't would pack a few bags and begin walking, over the bridges, across the polluted rivers, past rusting junk yards and stinking trash piles, never looking back, afraid to see what had become of their lives, their hopes and dreams, their futures.

There would be those who would remain. People who were too old or too sick or too alone to care where they were. People who were too poor, too disheartened, too battered by life to strive for more. People who were too lazy, too stupid, too stubborn to see the writing on the crumbling walls and cracking sidewalks.

The museums were closed and empty. Not just of people but of the priceless treasures they had once housed. They had been sold at auction to cover the municipal debts. The masterpieces of centuries that people had clung to in times of prosperity suddenly had become expendable. They had been immediately gobbled up by private sources, often at prices far below market values. But what value could a scrap of canvas with yellowing paint actually have, when children were in rags and bellies were empty?

The once great universities were closed too. Their windows were empty, broken out, the desks and chairs and books sold to whomever would buy them to cover the debts. The hallowed halls of learning were now rooming houses for rats and vagrants. The churches which had once supported these institutions could no longer afford the costs; their congregations — and their revenues — were dwindling rapidly.

And the young people who had once flocked from the farms to these great icons of wisdom now stayed home to help with the crops, to mend the fences, and milk the cows. Food on the table and a roof over one's head were the important things in life. Forget the excitement of the cities, the hustle bustle, the thriving pulse of the cosmopolites. That had all vanished into the choking fumes of the gas lines.

A section of downtown Detroit was ablaze as the President's plane circled overhead and received clearance for an immediate landing.

"The bastards," Montie snarled, chewing vigorously on his cigar.

"What did the mayor say, Montie?" Parker said.

"When I spoke to him last night, he said the city was peaceful; that the rioting was over. He thought your appearance would help prevent further violence, but it looks like he was wrong. I think we ought to turn around and go back."

"I promised him I'd be here to make a speech, and I intend to keep that promise."

"Under the circumstances, Don," Ralph Owens said, "I don't think there's going to be much of a Fourth of July celebration."

"I might be able to help. It's worth a try as long as we're here."

"I think you're a goddamned fool, Don," Montie snapped.

"We all are, Montie. Every last one of us." Parker closed his eyes and leaned back in his seat as Air Force One began its descent. It had taken so little time, he thought. Just over two hundred years. The rise was complete, the fall was imminent. The great American empire, the wonder of the modern world, the open arms and brimming treasury for the poor, the wanting, the suffering, the starving, the enslaved, the lazy; the mother lode of bounty was finally played out; the country was paying for its naive, misguided philanthropy.

The world that it had tried to shape, that it had fed and clothed and defended for so many years, had changed very little in all that time. But the country and the courageous people who had sacrificed so much to give to their brethren of so many races had changed dramatically. They now knew the meaning of the word "need," felt the gnawing of hunger in their stomachs, understood the pain of being jobless and helpless in the face of disaster.

And there was no one to extend a hand, no welcome mat at the doorstep of any country where they could retreat from their grief. America was alone, as she had begun, struggling for survival in a world that had forgotten her kindness and selflessness, a world torn by petty conflicts that could at any moment erupt into a conflagration the likes of which mankind would never see again.

In the city below, a crowd of blacks moved angrily up a deserted boulevard — a howling mob swinging baseball bats, brandishing firearms, smashing windows with bricks they ripped from the corners of buildings, overturning cars, setting them afire. They had had enough. They were out of work, hungry, and frightened. They were going to vent their frustrations on the establishment. They were going to burn the city to the ground.

Most people sat in their sweltering living rooms, listening to the sound of distant gunfire, wondering what was happening, staring at darkened TV screens. The TVs didn't work because the power companies had shut off the power from noon to four to conserve energy. Some men got out their old guns and loaded them, just in case.

But some went out to see what was happening. It was better than sitting inside listening to themselves sweat. On their way, they met a few friends or other curious people, and joined them to feel more comfortable. They did not use the word "safe." One of them picked up a stick from a garbage pile that was decomposing after three weeks on the sidewalks. Another person stole a chain off an open link fence. The owner would not miss it; he had moved away the previous week.

Those at home paced the living room floor, wondering what they should do. It was damned inconvenient not being able to turn on the TV and get the news. "Maybe we'd better go out and see?" "Take your gun, but put it under your shirt so you don't get arrested." "Make sure it's loaded." They went out in ones and twos, but soon became tens and twenties. They walked in the direction of the noise, which came from the now defunct central business district, and saw the columns of smoke rising over the roof tops.

From another direction, the sound of sirens wailed down the canyons of flying brick and shattering glass. The national guard and what remaining police there were, were racing to head off the confrontation.

Suddenly, a few people began to run, thinking it was better than walking with the crowd. Others became angry at being jostled, and they began to push. Their companions did not like being pushed and struck back with whatever they held in their hands. The violence spread from the rear of the crowd, and it turned into a charging mob, an unstoppable stampede of human hatred. They ran straight ahead, neither knowing nor caring where they were going, for the mob had a mind and body of its own now.

And in another crowd, on another street, the same hysteria broke loose. They ran in fear and anger and frustration, smashing windows, elbowing, kicking, biting, stomping anyone who fell into a grisly pulp.

The converging masses clashed in an intersection and melded into a bleeding mound of writhing, dying bodies, where people were pressed so tightly together they could not breathe and died of suffocation or were beaten, stabbed, and shot to death by the person next to them. They fought with a will to die, with anyone and with no one. They were all their own enemies, life was their enemy, their tormentor, and they had to kill and be killed.

The army and the police arrived too late to stop the melee and were forced to retreat as those on the edge of the mob turned on them, hurling themselves in frenzy on the uniformed enforcers of the peace. The street was theirs to do with as they wished, and no one had the right to stop them. The troops fired in self-defense, at first above their heads, but to no avail, then into the mass of bodies, killing indiscriminately by the dozens. But those who fell were trampled and replaced by a hundred more until the street was awash with their blood. And still they advanced.

The troops fell back, to the steps of the city hall, where the tanks were waiting and reinforcements were arriving. There was no place to retreat. The mob was upon them. At the Colonel's command the tanks opened fire.

The bodies lay twisted in mangled heaps and bloody mounds. The bewildered wounded and the miraculously unscathed looked up from the street where they had fallen. Carnage surrounded them, more horrible than they could have imagined. Reality returned and they rose one by one, dropping their weapons, staring at the rifles trained on them. It was over.

The President's motorcade arrived as the last prisoners were being removed to detention centers. The street was still littered with the dead and the dying. Medics attended them and emergency vehicles screamed away bearing casualties.

General Owens stepped from the President's limousine and stared in horror. The Colonel in command came forward and saluted, his face ashen.

"We had no choice, General," the man stammered. "We were outnumbered. There was no other way to stop them." His voice dropped off when he saw the President advancing past the line of silent guardsmen.

Parker surveyed the scene, his face like chiseled granite.

"Didn't you get my message at the airport, sir?" the Colonel asked Owens. "We tried to warn you not to come."

Parker turned and walked stiffly back toward the limousine. As he reached the car, another black limousine wheeled up and screeched to a stop. George Works, the mayor of Detroit, jumped out looking disheveled and frantic.

"Mr. President!" he gasped. "Are you all right? I thought they told you not to come!"

"You asked me to come, Mr. Works and I came. It's a blood bath."

"The situation was out of hand before we even knew it was happening. They damn near burned down the whole downtown district."

"It never should have happened," Parker said grimly.

"They were out of work. Their families were starving. But without the welfare programs there was nothing I could do . . . nothing any of us could do!"

"There are jobs out West, Works! We're building power plants, damming rivers, irrigating desert. We need labor, muscle, sweat, and hands, Mr. Works! Thousands of willing hands. The expense in human lives and energy wasted here today would have gone a long way."

"You can't blame me for this," Works squealed. "This is your fault! You're the one who cut off the funds. You're the one who let this city go bankrupt! We told you what would happen and it has!"

"Wrong, Mr. Works. I told *you* what would happen and it has. And I also told you what I would do if it did. As of now, you no longer have control of Detroit, Mr. Works. I'm placing this city under martial law. You'll continue to administrate what services remain, but you will report to a military advisory board."

"This is outrageous!" Works cried.

"You're goddamned right it is, Mr. Works! And it's your fault, and it's labor's fault, and it's the people's fault, and it's my fault. We're all to blame. We all looked the other way for too long. None of us are without blame."

"You're not going to get away with this! I've got friends in Washington, too. People who supported you. You can bet your ass they're not going to support you in 1992!"

"I'm not running in 1992, Mr. Works, so I don't give a good goddamn who they support. I don't even know if there'll be a 1992!"

Works's mouth dropped open, but he said nothing.

"Now the first thing I want you to do is organize a recruitment program for relocating the unemployed to the projects out West. I want this ghetto emptied and all able-bodied people shipped out or otherwise gainfully employed. The aged and sick are to be cared for according to the program guidelines. You are familiar with the program, aren't you Mr. Works?"

Works was ashen, and he stared at Parker speechlessly.

"I'm going to send in a high-ranking Army executive to make sure you do your job properly this time, Works. And if you don't, you will be removed from office and the military government will carry out my orders. Now I suggest you get busy. You've got a hell of a lot to do and not much time to do it in!"

Parker brushed past the man and climbed into the limousine. Montie followed close behind with General Owens, and the motorcade wheeled away up the deserted boulevard and was gone.

Circling over the city after take-off, Parker glanced out the window only once at the glowing fires that were only now being extinguished. "That city will be a ghost town inside a year," he muttered and opened one of his many dossiers. Montie and Ralph Owens stared at each other for a moment, then got up to make themselves a drink. It had been a long hot afternoon, even for the Fourth of July.

"How are you feeling today, Comrade?" Zeitsev asked, stepping onto the shielded rooftop garden of the Russian Embassy.

Aleksay Kurochkin lay on a chaise lounge, naked from the waist up, reading the morning paper. From the streets below came the sound of firecrackers and bottle rockets—and police sirens. It was a sweltering July Fourth afternoon. He looked up at Zeitsev and stretched stiffly, somewhat painfully. "A little better, Comrade. My shoulder is still sore, but the stiffness is going away. Have a beer," he said in an unusual gesture of friendliness. After his long weeks of convalescence, it felt good to be out in the sunshine again. His skin had darkened and the scars left by the bullet holes had become ugly red bubbles. He was thinner, but he remained solid.

"I have just received a communique from Moscow," Zeitsev said.

"Read it, will you?"

"Of course, Comrade. 'Regarding agent K. Maintain isolation until further notice. Make no more attempts on the American's life, as CIA is aware of K's activities. Must lead them to believe that K is either dead or has fled the country.' " He paused.

"Is that all?" Aleksay asked, sounding rather irritated. He had been cooped up too long and eagerly awaited the day when his doctor would give him a clean bill of health. He personally wanted to end the life of the man who had nearly cost him his own.

"No, there is more."

"Read it, then."

"It is on another matter. 'On April 30 last, our observatories reported the first of two sizable blasts at an altitude of nine thousand miles above the Earth. On May 31, the second such anomaly occurred of the same proportion and relative altitude. After careful examination and analysis, our scientists have determined that these detonations were atomic. No natural phenomenon we know of could have caused such occurrences, and we conclude that they were of man-made origin. Since only the U.S., besides ourselves, has sufficient technological capability to effect such explosions, we believe they are testing nuclear weapons in outer space. We fear that this might be a prelude to some form of aggression on the part of the Americans, in the event of serious complications in the Middle East. You are therefore ordered to attempt to discover the source and status of these operations. We suggest that they might coincide with the

Space Shuttle program, since Shuttle launches occurred in close proximity to the aforementioned dates. Press your contact at SPEC, and if necessary we will enlist the services of Brutus for this operation. Consider this top priority.' " Zeitsev paused and looked up at Aleksay who remained expressionless.

"It is curious that Karpovich had not provided us with more information than she has, especially concerning the Space Shuttle program," Aleksay mused.

"She apparently does not have access to the files."

"Perhaps. Or perhaps she is not willing to take the necessary risks to obtain that level of information. After all, she is cleared for high-level security, is she not?"

"That is our information."

"Then what is restricting her?"

"I don't know, Comrade."

"We must confront her directly and press her to take the necessary actions to penetrate the program security."

"And if she cannot?"

Aleksay's eyes turned toward the smaller man. "Then she is of no further use to us and should be eliminated."

Sergei looked down at the communique, but made no reply.

"Don't you agree, Comrade Zeitsev?"

"What? Oh! Yes, by all means, Comrade, I agree."

"Good. Send a communique to Moscow. Request them to arrange a meeting with this Brutus. I have a feeling that we may need his help. After we have spoken with him, we will deal with Karpovich, one way or the other."

In the hinterland of America, in small towns, on the farms, the night sky glistened with fireworks. Streamers of glimmering gold and blue, shimmering showers of silver and green, bursts of bright orange, cascades of crimson and purple bombarded the heavens.

Crickets harmonized rhythmically to their age old verse, small boys set off spattering strings of firecrackers on street corners and ran screaming with delight across the dewy grass of the town square. Bottle rockets and Roman candles, cherry bombs and sparklers, twisters and nigger chasers spewed their festive fires; and young lovers embraced in darkened tree-sheltered lanes.

For the moment America paused to reminisce on happier times and former glories, and the words "Oh say can you see, by the dawn's early light . . ." echoed faintly in hazy memories of the past. Better not to think about the present, the rumblings in the Middle East, the turmoil in the cities. They were like tales from other worlds, to be whispered about at coffees and bridge club luncheons, or at the Elks Club over the second bourbon and Seven-up.

"Have you seen the news?"

"Doesn't New York look just like one of those sci-fi movies?"

"Why don't those people just pack up and leave?"

"They are."

"I hope they don't come here. Lord knows we've got enough problems of our own what with the price of diesel fuel the way it is and the government rationing program. We'll be lucky to get the crops out of the ground, that is if they last through the summer without the proper care."

"Doesn't the government know that if we don't have fuel, our equipment won't run, and the crops will suffer? That'll mean a food shortage on top of it all."

"What good would a bumper crop do anyway? The trucks aren't rolling fast enough to get it to market. It would probably just rot in the fields."

"Of course, you've heard of the car graveyards?"

"No."

"People are just abandoning their cars, walking away, leaving them in gas lines when they run out of gas. It's happening every day."

"I've got an old surrey my grandfather kept from his child-hood days, if things ever get that bad around here."

"Have another beer, let's not think about that now."

They stood on front lawns, necks craned watching the fireworks, sharing misty feelings of patriotism, faint remembrances of piping fifes and popping snare drums, long-ago parades on Main Street, when apples were two for fifty cents and soda pop only cost a quarter. Why had it all changed? Where had the good times gone? It was a beautiful night to celebrate the Fourth of July, but few really remembered why they were celebrating.

. . . 10 September 1990

Death Valley appeared unchanged as the jets streaked down out of a clear blue sky toward the rippling white hot earth. Only a single line of fence, then a curious series of earth mounds spaced at regular intervals broke the salt flats. They followed a faint road in a north/south direction until the landing strip came into view and the jets fanned into formation and landed one after the other in a roar of flying sediment.

From ground level, the desert appeared as it had the first day Parker had visited the site thirteen months before. There was no trace of human habitation, and only a faint breeze moaned eerily out of the Black Mountains, raising swirling dust devils from the lifeless waste. A cluster of three white limousines materialized out of the shimmering heat and approached like spectres.

Arnold Kemper stepped from the first limo a few moments later, wearing a khaki bush jacket, a pair of rumpled slacks, tennis shoes, and a baseball cap with the Oasis Project insignia emblazoned on its brim. Grinning broadly, he greeted his guests warmly. "Welcome Mr. President, Mr. Vice President, General Owens, Mr. Secretary. You picked a perfect day. The temperature hasn't been under one-ten for the past five weeks," he laughed. "It's one-twelve in the shade right now!"

"It's hellish, Arnold," Montie groused.

"That's what I mean. You're seeing the facility in its best light. If you all would like to ride with me, the others can follow." They entered the first limo and pulled away across the salt flats, gliding noiselessly on a sea of shimmering silver heat that stretched to the horizon on all sides. No one spoke.

They drove for approximately a mile, then suddenly out of the earth, a massive opening yawned to swallow them, and they began to descend on a gentle grade in a tunnel lighted by heli-arc lamps, wide enough for three semitrucks to roll abreast and high enough for them to easily clear.

Deeper and deeper they wound in a gradual circle, feeling the pressure build around them the farther they sank beneath the surface. It was difficult, almost impossible in fact, for Parker to imagine that only thirteen months earlier none of it had existed. But the advanced capabilities of the Sevrensen laser had made conventional excavation obsolete and allowed for what could only be termed a miracle of modern technology.

Parker glanced once at Kemper, who was smiling with some private pleasure, then diverted his eyes ahead and saw a massive opening appear around the curve of the tunnel, and beyond, as bright as daylight, an immense cavern. They stopped at a heavily secured checkpoint where even Kemper had to personally be cleared before they were allowed to enter. On seeing the President, however, the guards snapped to attention and the motorcade passed.

What met their eyes was something that all the miles of blueprints or months of discussion and debate could not have prepared them for. The chamber walls rose two hundred feet in a gentle arc toward the massive hangar doors and enormous steel girders. The length of the cavern was perhaps one thousand yards, the length of ten football fields, and the width was two hundred and fifty yards, creating a floor space of some two hundred and fifty thousand square yards, or roughly five times the size of a modern domed football stadium. It was like being in an underground city.

The motorcade stopped some distance inside, and at once an honor guard approached and opened the doors. Parker and Kemper stepped out first, followed by the others, who stood gaping at their surroundings.

"Mr. President," Kemper smiled. "This way, please."

He indicated the raised dais and led the way. As Parker mounted the steps the public address system piped in "Hail to the Chief." Nearly five thousand workers raised a shattering din of applause. Parker stood, his chest swelled with pride, his head held high, flanked by Holmes and Montgomery, with Kemper close behind him.

A precision rifle team performed in their honor, their youthful eyes sparkling with pride. They were spit and polish, young Marines who looked tempered by training and the knowledge that they were sharing a unique moment in the history of mankind.

In the vacuum that followed his reception, not a soul broke the almost religious silence that settled over them. They were countrymen, joined by a common belief in freedom and a cause that was known only to them, confident that with the grace of the Almighty they would succeed and deliver the world from destruction.

At last, Parker stepped to the podium and spoke in what could only be described as a reverent whisper, as if he were standing in a cathedral, afraid to raise his voice and violate the holy silence. "Good afternoon, gentlemen . . . and ladies, if there are any present. It's hard to tell at this distance." His voice carried the length and breadth of the chamber, and was remarkably devoid of distortion or echo.

From somewhere, several women's voices whooped in response, and a surge of laughter swept the congregation. Parker laughed and waved his hand in acknowledgment. "Good. It pleases me to see that there are also women who are willing to devote themselves to the causes of patriotism and freedom. Ladies and gentlemen, if what I have just seen and what I am about to see this afternoon is anything as inspiring as your spirit and dedication to your country, then I will return to Washington a much more consoled and confident President, who believes that the future of our great land is not in jeopardy knowing that it is in the capable hands of people like yourselves." The throng broke into a thunderous ovation that took almost two minutes to subside, during which Parker smiled and waved. His eyes were suddenly misted, but no one noticed.

"Thirteen months ago, when I first came here, I stood two hundred feet above this spot, gazing at a barren wasteland. The Oasis Project was a concept on the drawing boards and in the imagination of a very few men who saw the impending collapse of our society and the hope of freedom for all of mankind. What you have wrought, with your skill and dedication, must be rated as one of the wonders of the modern world and I commend you for it one and all.

"But let us not forget that there are many hours, many days and weeks and months of diligence and sacrifice ahead of us; and if we are to achieve our goals, each and every one of you, from project supervisors to arc-welders, must respond to the call of duty. We are at war, ladies and gentlemen, and you have been chosen to fight this battle for independence. You out of all Americans have proven yourselves capable and responsible for the tasks that will be demanded of you. We have all been chosen to fulfill a destiny that was ours from the inception of this country, which our forefathers prepared for us and delivered into our hands for safekeeping. We have been entrusted with a solemn oath to preserve the freedom of mankind, by salvaging our dying democracy from the ravages of apathy, greed, waste, and jealousy. We stand united, but greatly outnumbered, against a world of conflict, the heart of a new movement on earth which will drive the armies of oppression from all lands and bestow the graces of freedom and equality on all men, women, and children for generations to come.

"We are the hope of the future, the promise of peaceful coexistence on a planet swollen with starving billions, a planet shriveled and wasted by wanton misuse and overconsumption. Our goal is the rejuvenation of our country, so that we may guarantee the survival of America and indeed the entire human race and all other forms of life on our precious planet. God willing, we will be successful.

"And now enough with ceremony. I will be moving among you during the course of the afternoon, as the esteemed Dr. Kemper allows me, that is, and I hope to be able to visit with some of you personally. But, please, continue your work. We cannot spare one irreplaceable minute for idle protocol, because I am not here as your President, but as one of you; your partner in this venture for peace and prosperity."

The caverns resounded with their cries and cheers, an

outpouring of affection and good will such as he had not heard since that cold winter morning in January of 1989, which now seemed several lifetimes ago. He turned to find Montie smiling, his mood changed. Kemper smiled and shook his hand. Holmes, who had not been adequately prepared for anything such as this, seemed still overwhelmed by the enormity of what had been accomplished.

"Come along, Mr. President," Kemper said eagerly. "I've got a little surprise for you."

"After this, Arnold, nothing could surprise me."

"Oh no? Well, we'll see."

They boarded electric carts and traversed the chamber, the President shaking hands with the workers who pressed around him, smiling, waving, cheering. They made their way toward the far end of the cavern, where rising out of the mist of arc-torch flares a huge metal structure loomed like a skeletal praying mantis, swarmed over by hundreds of white-suited engineers and technicians.

Parker's eyes widened as they approached the structure, and Kemper could scarcely control his enthusiasm as they rolled slowly to a stop beneath the gargantuan girders of the starboard wing supports of the first ASP.

All were presented with ceremonial hardhats bearing the project insignia, and Parker donned his reverently, but his eyes never left the colossus towering above him.

"You are impressed?" Kemper asked.

"I'm stunned, Arnold. Absolutely stunned. I didn't expect . . ."

"We were able to complete construction at this end several months ago, and I ordered work to begin immediately on the first ship. You're standing under the starboard wingtip. It's fifty feet to the bottom of the superstructure from the ground. Two hundred and eighty-eight feet from wingtip to wingtip and one hundred forty-four feet from nose cone to tail. Eventually, there will be twenty of them, side to side, nose to tail, being assembled simultaneously. But this baby is the prototype. We'll fly her before the others are ever completed."

"I'm speechless, Arnold. It's like something from another world."

343

Kemper turned to Parker and their eyes met for an instant of complete understanding. "It is Mr. President. It's from the world of tomorrow."

They met clandestinely at a modest steak house near Baltimore, Maryland, on the night of September 10, 1990. They came in separate cars, two of them in a blue Dodge with diplomatic plates, the other in a red and white Ford pickup truck with Virginia plates and a gun rack in the rear window. To anyone, they might have been three friends from the nearby factories, meeting for a few beers and a cheap steak dinner. But they were Soviet agents.

Sergei and Aleksay sat across the chipped Formica table top from the aging, bulky, cheery-faced man whose code name was Brutus. He did not look the part of a spy; rather he had the appearance of the average grandfather. His eyes were bright, still sparkling despite his advancing years, his English was unflawed without a hint of the accent which he had painstakingly suppressed many years ago, when he had come to America after World War II. He had the habit of repeatedly glancing at his wristwatch between spells of rekindling his pipe which was forever dying out. They spoke in guarded tones, their eyes sweeping the dark interior of the restaurant for errant glances, curious listeners.

"We are pleased that you could meet with us tonight," Aleksay said. "We know that it was difficult."

It had been eight weeks since they had requested the Center to make contact with the man they called Brutus, and since then they had waited in frustration as the precious days had slipped away. Both knew full well the sensitivity of the situation, the danger of making contact with an agent in deep cover, but it had been imperative to the success of their mission.

"It is good to meet you after so many years," Sergei said. "You have become quite a legend within the organization, an example for us all."

"I have only done my job, Comrade," Brutus said. He paused, aware of the unfamiliar taste of the word on his tongue. It had been forty years since he had spoken it.

"Your service record is commendable, Comrade," Aleksay said. "I admire your dedication, maintained so long under the American system, thinking only of your duty to the homeland."

"It has not been a bad life. You see, I have a wife and family; and you might say my life is really here, although my heart will always be in Russia."

"I did not know you were married," Sergei stammered. "Does she, she doesn't . . ."

"She knows nothing. To her I am a second-generation immigrant who has given her children and a happy home. And it is a happy home. She is a good woman. But enough of this. I don't have much time. The Center stated that you were in need of information concerning the Shuttle program. What is it you need to know?"

"As you are aware, we have another operative inside SPEC."

"Yes, Karpovich."

"Up until a few weeks ago, we did not know for certain that you were also employed there."

"I have been there since the early sixties."

"I see," Aleksay said. "What we are interested in concerns the real purpose of the Space Shuttle program. You have been briefed on the unexplained occurrences on April 30 and May 31?"

"I have."

"And you are aware that the Center suspects that the Americans are testing nuclear weapons in outer space?"

"I am."

"So far, the information we have received from Karpovich has mentioned nothing of this sort of testing. We have received in-depth information on an unmanned reconnaissance plane under development."

"The Drone?"

"Yes, the Drone."

"It was I who uncovered those documents. I managed to arrange for Karpovich to gain access to them. They were classified above her clearance."

"I see," Aleksay said. "But so far we have little information as to what the Shuttle program is doing, other than servicing the Skylab project, although we suspect it is involved in the nuclear tests, since we know that there were two Shuttle launches in the same time period during which the explosions occurred. Is it possible that these missions are carrying nuclear devices into space?"

"I don't know. Since its reinception, the Shuttle program has been impenetrable, even for me. You see, it was relocated almost a year ago."

"To where?"

"I don't know."

"Did you inform the Center of this?"

"Of course. I also informed them that several security personnel were replaced about the same time. I am positive their replacements are in reality American Secret Service agents."

"Why were we not informed of all this? Our entire apparat may have been compromised," Zeitsev gasped.

"I suspect that it already has," Aleksay said grimly. "That would explain why Karpovich has been unable to obtain more sensitive information. They know that she is working for us, and I suspect they have been purposefully feeding us declassified information, distracting us from the true nature of their development programs. I've been a fool not to see it sooner!"

"Do you think she knows?" Zeitsev asked.

"No," Aleksay snapped. "I would have seen it in her eyes. Have you revealed yourself to her?" he asked Brutus.

"Comrade, you forget that I was an operative when you were still a small boy."

Aleksay's eyes darkened, but he curbed his impulse to reply sharply and took the chastisement. "Then we must conclude that there is something of the gravest importance that we have been unable to breach. And we must also conclude that Karpovich is of no further use to us."

"She must be eliminated," Sergei said, his voice devoid of emotion.

"Not if the Americans are aware of her activities. It would

alert them that we knew about their surveillance and the doors would be sealed even tighter," Brutus said.

"Agreed," Aleksay said. "We will wait until we have gotten the information we need. In the meantime, she will be allowed to continue to perform her menial services as if nothing were amiss. However, it is imperative that we penetrate their top security. We must assume that this is a military operation and that it probably involves a highly sophisticated attack system. If this is true, it is a clear violation of all treaties and should be exposed at once. But we need proof."

"It will require great risk," Brutus said.

"I know. But the Americans' backs are to the wall. They are aware of the threat of our activities in the Middle East and Africa. They may feel that the only way to combat our superior strength is to move first with some secret new weapon. That is worth any risk we must take."

"So be it," Brutus said. "I will do what I can, and if possible, I will lead Karpovich into material I cannot myself provide. You may contact me in the same manner every other week on alternating Tuesdays and Thursdays. Goodnight, Comrades." He rose and left without looking back.

Sergei and Aleksay finished their steaks, although neither of them had sufficient appetite after their unsettling conversation with Brutus.

When they finally left the steak house, they crossed the lighted parking lot like two normal businessmen, got into their dirty blue Dodge and drove away. In the shadows of a plain white Buick sedan, Roger Davis sat motionless, his hands clenched on the steering wheel, his jaw set. He had not recognized the other man with Zeitsev on their way in, but he had seen him clearly when they climbed into their car. Aleksay Kurochkin, the Russian cat with nine lives, still lived. He had suspected as much when the service had been unable to confirm his death. It now seemed clear that he would have to do what all others had failed to do.

"He is still alive, Mr. President," Davis said calmly, facing the President across his drawing room table, which was

347

littered with open files and scratch pads.

"How do you know?"

"I saw him."

"Where?"

"At a steak house in Maryland. He was with Sergei Zeitsev, an embassy official."

"What were you doing there?"

"I've staked out the embassy on and off since Kurochkin was reported missing. I followed their car to the steak house and on their way out I got a good look at him."

"You suspected all along he was alive?"

"With a man like Kurochkin you don't believe it until you see the body. I thought I should consult you before doing what should have been done in May."

"You mean kill him?"

"Yes, sir."

"No. I don't want you involved in that. There's something more important now. I want you to move against Enrique Perez. I want him dead before the first of the year."

"Pardon me, sir, but . . ."

"No buts, Mr. Davis. You're too valuable to risk on a minor assignment. Let someone else go after him."

"I wouldn't call Kurochkin a minor assignment."

"Compared to Perez, I would."

"All right. Do you have any preferences as to the method?"

"I want it to be something public, something that will hit the world press like a bombshell. I want Mexico in turmoil inside of six months, and assassinating their President will do just that."

"Yes, sir."

"And don't worry about Kurochkin. I'll call Ralph Owens and make sure the Russian apparat is broken up immediately. I don't think we can afford to let them operate any longer."

Davis rose and nodded. "I'll take care of my end, sir. Goodnight."

"Goodnight, Mr. Davis. And good luck."

Davis left, and after he did, Parker picked up the phone and dialed Ralph Owens' home. The General himself answered.

"Ralph?"

"Yes, Mr. President—Don," Owens said, recognizing his voice at once.

"I hope I didn't wake you?"

"No, sir. I was watching the late movie. It's a classic war film, *Apolcalypse Now*."

"It's about this Karpovich affair, Ralph. I want it ended now."

"But . . ."

"The agent you were supposed to have killed is still alive, Ralph. I have an eyewitness report. I want him and the man called Zeitsev picked up, even if it means having them deported. And I want Karpovich picked up too."

"All right, Don. If you think . . ."

"Believe me Ralph. As long as they're operating at SPEC, there's a chance that they might get wind of the project. We can't take that chance any longer. One spy more or less isn't worth jeopardizing the nation's interests."

"I'll get on it immediately."

. . . 12 September 1990

Kathy pulled her car to a stop in the parking lot near the river and studied the darkened promenade. It was deserted. Down the river, the lights of the government buildings and monuments sparkled in the cool night air. A fair wind rustled the trees and she shivered, not from the cold but with a sudden feeling of foreboding. She wanted to be done with her assignment and home in bed, but there were those long empty steps to the trash barrel to cross.

She got out of her car and surveyed her surroundings. She was alone. She walked swiftly, carrying her purse in one hand, ready to strike out at anyone who might lunge from the darkness. In her other hand she gripped a brown paper sack with an empty pop can inside, containing one of Zeitsev's pens filled with more information on the Drone guidance system.

She reached the trash can and stopped to look around, unable to shake the feeling that she was being watched. Nervously, she dropped the sack in the can and hurried to her car. She had only to leave the signal at the mailbox and her night's work would be done.

Half an hour later, the blue Dodge pulled into the parking lot, and Sergei Zeitsev got out, wrapped in his crumpled overcoat, his hat pulled low on his forehead. He walked quickly to the trash can, plucked the sack off the top, opened it, withdrew the pop can and checked to see that the pen was inside.

As he turned, he caught a glimpse of movement out of the corner of his eye. A dark shape materialized from the trees—a man's form. He looked toward the car, and saw several more shapes moving toward it from the edge of the river. Whirling around, he raised his arm to fling the can into the river, but someone seized his wrist from behind and jerked him to the ground with enormous strength. He felt the tendons in his shoulder rip and he heard himself scream as he smashed to the cement and looked up at the black shapes above him. There were two men now, and one of them bent his wrist back until the pain was unbearable and he released his grip on the can.

At the sound of the scream, Aleksay threw the Dodge into reverse and gunned the engine. An unmarked vehicle with its lights off suddenly appeared behind him, blocking his path. Aleksay jammed his foot to the floor and crashed into it, slamming it into the curb, then threw the Dodge into forward and tried to spin out of the lot. But his way was barred by two men with drawn pistols. They fired point blank at the windshield, smashing it to smithereens, spraying him with glass; but none of the bullets hit their mark.

The two men dove for safety as he careened by, jumped the curb, and hit a tree. The hood sprung open and the radiator burst. He jerked the car into reverse and sped backwards, turned and lurched forward once more, heading for the street. Two more cars slid to a stop forming a barricade. He spun the wheel, jolted over the curb, and accelerated past them, sideswiping several lamp posts and two parked cars before he bounced back onto the street and pressed his foot to the floorboard.

Bullets thumped into the back window, glass flew around his head, and something struck him in the side of the neck. It burned, but he knew immediately he was not badly hurt. Three cars were in pursuit and he searched for a side street in which to lose them. An alley appeared and he cornered sharply, the other cars right behind him.

Out the other end of the alley and onto another nameless street, he sped, his eyes on the heat gauge which was now bright red. The car rattled and groaned and he was losing speed. He knew he had to do something and fast. Far ahead, he saw the glint of starlight on the water and realized he was headed for the river. Rolling down his window, he careened toward the guard rail at the end of the street and punched through it in an explosion of splintering wood. The Dodge floated through darkened space, hit the water with a violent concussion, and sank almost immediately. Aleksay's nostrils filled with water as he struggled out of the car window and swam toward the surface. He breached long enough for a gasp of air, then dived and swam with all his strength toward the far shore.

Searchlights swept the river, but there was no sign of the car or Aleksay. The agents cursed vehemently, and several of them stayed to supervise the retrieval of the embassy vehicle for evidence. The others returned to the park, where their associates had spread-eagled Sergei Zeitsev on the hood of their battered car. He was moaning in pain and looked like a frightened animal waiting for the *coup de grâce*.

The man who had broken his shoulder and wrist handed the coke can to the agent in charge, who removed the pen and studied it. "Well," he said caustically, "looks like we caught you red-handed, if you'll pardon the pun. Bring him in. I'll pick up Karpovich myself."

Kathy was having a glass of beer and a TV dinner when the knock came at her door. She felt a sudden rush of fear and for a moment thought she would not answer. Again the knock came, this time much louder.

"Who is it?" she said in hardly more than a whisper.

"Federal agents. Open the door!"

Numbly, she rose and walked to the door. She opened it and stared into the hard face of the veteran agent. He looked tired and angry, and she suddenly felt very small and alone.

"Get your coat and purse, Miss Karpovich. You're coming with us."

Hours later, Aleksay crouched behind a red and white pickup in the SPEC employee parking lot, while helicopters buzzed overhead, their spotlights searching the river banks and surrounding industrial complexes. The security guard on duty in the lot stepped out of his prefab shack to have a look, and in the moment that he was absorbed by the spectacle Aleksay deftly picked the truck's door lock, opened the door, and slipped in without being seen. He huddled on the floorboard and drew his knees up to his chest, hoping to retain his body heat as best he could.

Just before daylight, he heard voices in the lot, but kept his position with his pistol trained on the driver's door. Then he saw the faint silhouette of the bulky Brutus as he set the key in the lock and opened the door. Brutus covered his surprise like the professional that he was, and glanced around at the still hovering helicopters, summing up the situation almost at once.

Without hesitation, he climbed into the cab, started the engine and rolled out of the lot onto the empty street. Only then did he speak. "What happened?" he asked, his voice restrained.

"They were waiting for us at the *debok*. They have Zeitsev and the film, and if I am not mistaken they have Karpovich by now."

"What are you going to do?"

"You will take me somewhere where I can stay. Then you will bring me fresh clothes and food. I must have time to formulate a plan."

"Do you think that Zeitsev will talk?"

"No. He is not a big man, but I believe he is strong enough to resist their methods of persuasion."

"I know a motel. We'll get you a room and you can shower while I go for some clothes. Have a look at this." He slid a plain white envelope out of his coat pocket and handed it to Aleksay who was still crouched on the floorboard.

Aleksay opened it and withdrew several Xeroxed sheets.

"I found them in Dr. Kemper's desk and copied them on his office copier. They were in a file marked 'Guidance Systems: Oasis Project.' When I informed the Center of the Oasis Project the first time, I had only seen it written on a scrap of paper in the shredder, but here is concrete evidence."

Aleksay's eyes sparkled with sudden zeal, and he forgot the harrowing hours he had just spent dodging the American agents through storm drains and parking lots. He studied the sheets of paper, and with his trained eye recognized parts of the systems as being similar to those contained in the information that Karpovich had been providing. Then he turned to the last page and caught his breath. It was a list of cities, alphabetized by country, and if he were not mistaken, it was identical to the one they had found in the "Drone" files. "Take me to the embassy!"

"What?" The older man's voice cracked. "Are you out of your mind?"

"Take me to the embassy! I must get to the embassy!"

"But they'll be watching it!"

"Not for you. You can let me off near the alley and I'll slip in. It's still dark, I may have a chance. Believe me, this is urgent!"

Brutus shook his head. "Nyet! It is too dangerous, Comrade. I will take you somewhere . . ." He stopped at the metallic snap of the hammer clicking into place and his eyes widened as he stared down the barrel of Aleksay's automatic.

"I said, take me to the embassy, Comrade! This is an order!"

It was still dark enough not to be able to distinguish their respective faces, but each knew that the other's eyes burned with hatred and distrust. Nevertheless, the older agent turned his truck and headed for the Russian Embassy, muttering under his breath.

Fifteen minutes later, they pulled slowly onto the street bordering the embassy. Brutus noted several dark sedans parked at irregular intervals on either side of the road. "They are here, watching. It will be impossible for you to get inside unseen."

"Where are we?"

"We are approaching the alley."

"What side is it on?"

"My side."

"Go to the end of the street and turn around, then come back. Slow down as you reach the alley."

It was growing lighter, and the older man looked incredulously at his captor. "That will alert them."

"Do as I say, you bastard!" Aleksay snarled.

Brutus did as he was told and drove to the end of the block, turned around, and headed back toward the embassy. He slowed as they approached the alley.

"Tell me when we are within fifty feet of it and pull slowly to the curb."

The older man muttered but did not dare to disobey. "All right, we are within fifty feet." He turned the wheel and edged toward the curb.

Suddenly, Aleksay twisted on the floorboard, reached across, and slammed his foot on top of Brutus', driving the accelerator pedal to the floor. In the same instant, he pulled the door handle and hurled himself against the door, firing three rapid shots into the older man's chest as he toppled onto the sidewalk, rolled, and scrambled for the alley opening. The pickup roared forward simultaneously, struck a parked car, careened off it, and smashed into the embassy's outer wall, blocking the view of the alley from the street long enough for Aleksay to slip in and reach the rear door.

He pounded furiously, while on the street plainclothes agents materialized out of the shadows and surrounded the wrecked truck with pistols drawn. One of them approached and peered in at the man slumped over the wheel. He eased him back and looked at his lifeless staring eyes. Another agent heard the disturbance in the alley and bolted toward it, turning the corner just in time to see a dark form slip in the rear door and hear the sound of the bolts being thrown. The agent in charge joined them an instant later.

"What?"

"He went in the rear door."

"Did you see him?"

"Yes, well, I mean, yes and no. I saw someone that could have been him, but it's too dark to be sure. I heard them bolting the door."

"But you didn't see him?"

"I guess not."

"Son of a bitch!"

They walked back to the truck, where the other agents were rummaging through the dead man's wallet.

"Any idea who he is?" the agent in charge asked.

He was handed an I.D. card, and his face paled. "Holy shit! Gus Wallenski, the night watchman at SPEC labs! Wait till the boys in the back room hear this!"

. . . 13 September 1990

"Do nothing, Ralph. Absolutely nothing!" Eldon Parker looked pale but in control as he paced his office. He had just been informed of the incident at the Russian embassy, and he was in no mood for suggestions.

"But we have sufficient reason to believe that he has taken refuge in the embassy. We have the legal right to demand his release to us so that we can conduct a proper investigation."

"I've told you repeatedly that I don't want any confrontation with the Russians. This thing could blossom into a full-scale diplomatic embarrassment for both sides, especially if it comes out that this man Wallenski had penetrated SPEC as early as the sixties. How the hell is that going to look to the rest of the world, when we're trying to rebuild our image of leadership and solidarity? It'll make us look like the idiots we obviously are. And what if this Kurochkin spills everything, including the fact that we tried to assassinate him? No, Ralph. Definitely not! Let it die. The apparat has been broken, and we'll prosecute as best we can. That's going to cause enough flack."

Owens was livid. He took the entire matter personally, since his attempts had twice failed to eliminate the Russian agent from circulation. But he maintained his composure. "All right, Mr. President. If you're sure."

"I'm sure. And by the way, I want a full account of everything the Russians got from SPEC, from day one. And offer that girl immunity if she agrees to turn state's witness. As long as we have to come out in the open about this, we may as well try to make our side look as good as possible. Paint her up as being a double agent all along . . . what do you call it, build her a legend."

"OK. But with her background it isn't going to be easy, especially when the press starts digging."

"Fuck the press. Don't let them get past second base! I'm sure the combined talents of the FBI and the CIA can handle that, can't they?"

"Yes." Owens looked at Parker closely, wondering how far the man was willing to go in order to cover up the truth. Nevertheless he had his orders and he left without further debate.

Kathy Karpovich was placed in solitary confinement at the district jail, where her interrogation was slated to begin within a few days.

She had slept fitfully that first night, and awoke early to a tasteless breakfast of cereal and black coffee. She did not know what to expect of the coming days, but she knew that whatever happened her career in journalism was over and her future probably held a long term in prison. Those were not pretty prospects to consider. She wondered what had happened, what she had done to tip the FBI off. She had no idea what had transpired after her arrest.

She was shocked, therefore, to look up from the cold slab floor to see Bruce Wilson, entering with one of the agents who had been with her through her booking and preliminary questioning. Bruce looked drawn and thin, much worse than she did in fact, and she could not help feeling sorry for him despite her own somber circumstances.

"You've got a visitor, Miss Karpovich," the young agent said. "We'll allow you two to talk, but I've got to be present, and I've got to remind you that anything you might say can and will be used against you in a court of law."

Kathy nodded. Bruce stood awkwardly in the middle of the room staring at her. "Hi," she said.

"Hi," Bruce said. "How are you?"

"Oh, fine. Never better," she said and forced a laugh. She suddenly wanted to cry and rush into his arms. His was the only friendly face she had seen in hours. Her emotions began to come unglued. "I guess you're pretty disappointed in me?"

Bruce did not respond at first but sat down beside her on

the bed and took her hands. "I knew before."

She stared at him in disbelief. "You what?"

"They've been on to you for a long time." He glanced at the agent. "Is it all right to discuss this aspect of the case?"

The agent shrugged. "Talk about anything you want, as long as she realizes the implications. She has a right to have her attorney present."

"I've been instructed to represent her in an unofficial capacity for the time being. It's been cleared by General Owens."

The agent nodded.

"Kathy, I want you to listen very carefully. I've been instructed to make you an offer, in the interest of your own well being and the country's."

"What kind of offer, Bruce?"

"They want you to turn state's witness—fill in all the details of the Russian apparat."

"What do I get out of it?"

Bruce again glanced at the agent. The agent tried to look nonchalant.

"In return for your testimony, the government agrees not to prosecute; rather it will portray you as a double agent, working on its behalf to crack the Russian spy ring."

Kathy was silent wondering whether or not to believe him. "Do you have that in writing?" she asked at last. She had become suspicious of everyone since her involvement with the Russians.

"You have Eldon Parker's word on it. He's known about everything almost from the beginning. The FBI was following you and that led them to the Russians. They let you continue to operate on the premise that they would build up a case against the Russians so they could have them deported. Naturally, the President can't put any of this in writing because he would open himself up to some serious charges if it ever came out. But you can trust him, Kathy. I know. He personally instructed me to come here and present this deal to you. Apparently he's kept a personal interest in the whole affair."

"Why?"

"I don't know. He just said to me that it would be much better for the country, and you come out the winner in the long run."

"It sounds too good to be true."

"Quite frankly, Kathy, I don't see how you can refuse." He looked again at the agent, who stood with his hands in his pockets, his mouth twisted into a knot, as if trying to resist the urge to put in his two bits worth. Bruce smiled dryly. "I think you ought to take the deal, Kathy. Otherwise, it's going to get messy."

"All right," she said. "I haven't had a better offer since I got here. What do I have to do?"

"You'll be briefed. But let me warn you. It isn't going to end here. You may have to change your name, perhaps move somewhere and start a new life. That can all be arranged by the FBI. It's for your own protection."

"I understand," she said sadly.

"Chin up. You're getting off a lot easier than the Russian they caught."

"They caught them?"

"Only one of them."

"Which one?"

"The embassy official."

"Zeitsev! What about the other one?"

"I don't know anything about him. But I'm sure the FBI is going to want to know all you can tell them. That's part of the deal."

"It will be a pleasure. He's a lunatic." Kathy shuddered at the thought of Kurochkin and squeezed Bruce's hands tightly. "Thank you, Bruce. Thank you for coming . . ." Her voice trailed off.

"I wouldn't have had it any other way."

They smiled into each other's eyes, and Kathy began to weep softly. Bruce wanted to take her in his arms but didn't.

"There's one more thing, Kathy. I don't know if it's the right time to tell you, but I've got to get it off my chest." He turned to the agent. "Do you mind? This is personal, and the lady's already agreed to cooperate."

The agent looked reluctant but nodded. He left and closed

the cell door.

"I want you to know something, Kathy. It's about us. The reason I broke up with you . . ." He couldn't find the words, but it was clear to Kathy what he was going to say.

"You did it because of me and your position with the President," she said.

Bruce nodded. "I've never been so ashamed in my life. I knew you were in trouble, but there was nothing I could do to help. Not and keep my job at the same time. I placed my career over our relationship and it makes me sick to think I did it. To think why I did it."

"You didn't have much choice in the matter, did you?" she asked.

"Everyone's always got a choice. I made mine and for the reasons I told you. I'm not proud of it, but I couldn't let you go through with any of this without telling you. You have the right to know." He paused mustering his courage to find the proper words. "Kathy I haven't stopped thinking about you. I think I'm in love with you."

She couldn't have been more stunned if he had hit her in the face. "I think you're letting this whole thing get to you."

"I mean it," he said. "A day hasn't gone by that I didn't want to call you, warn you of what was eventually going to happen."

"But you didn't."

"I know. People do crazy things, myself included. I know I was a fling for you, maybe a way to get inside information. But I also thought there may have been something more than that."

"You were good in bed," she teased.

"Did anybody ever tell you were a female chauvinist?"

"All the time."

He clenched her hands tightly and drew closer, pressing his lips to hers in a brief kiss. He looked slightly embarrassed when they parted. "I'm sorry. I couldn't help myself."

"Don't apologize."

"I've got to go now. I'll tell the President that you've agreed. And I'll be back, you can count on that. I don't expect they'll hold you very long here, but they'll keep you under protection until after the trial. So keep the faith."

She smiled at his use of the anachronistic phrase. "You're a diehard phony, you know that?" she said. "But I love you for it."

He stared at her in silence, not quite believing what she had just said. He smiled and kissed her forehead gently. "Take care. I'll see you soon."

Aleksay Kurochkin paced his tiny third floor room in the Russian Embassy like a caged animal. Through the slatted blinds, he could occasionally glimpse an unmarked dark sedan cruising the street below, and on adjacent rooftops, he caught the glint of binoculars reflecting the sun's rays. He was hemmed in and confined within the embassy by order of the Foreign Secretary until further notice.

He paused by the desk where he had laid out the files obtained by their operation at SPEC. Something gnawed at him, something he had seen in the reams of material, but he could not decide exactly what. He sat down heavily and scoured the pages, searching for the key.

Was it the two lists? He had checked them against each other and found them to be identical. But one was from the file on the Drone, the other from the Oasis Project file. Was the Drone part of a larger plan contained within the Oasis Project? There was not enough evidence to make a reasonable deduction.

What of the guidance systems? He had gone over them both carefully and found them to be identical. That was understandable, considering that both projects would probably utilize the most advanced guidance systems in performing their prescribed functions. But *what were* the functions? The Drone was an unmanned reconnaissance plane. What then was the Oasis Project? Could it be linked to the Space Shuttle? And if so, did it have anything to do with the nuclear explosions in outer space?

He suddenly felt sick as he stared at the lists, one held in each hand. Nuclear explosions, detonations of warheads? What if those warheads were intended for the cities on the lists? Could the Americans possibly be considering such a move? It would mean the almost complete decimation of every capital and major city on Earth.

No, it was madness. They could never expect to deploy such an operation. And what of the American cities on the lists? Surely the Americans would not destroy their own cities, their own civilians. Or would they? Were the cities on the list not the same as the cities that were in severe difficulty? If such an attack were carried out, would not the civilian losses be minimal in light of the mass exoduses taking place? New York, Detroit, Cleveland, Chicago, Washington. Washington? No, surely he was wrong. It made no sense. Washington was a thriving metropolis. The Americans would never commit such an atrocity.

He did not have a chance to pursue his line of thought. The door opened without warning and the Assistant Secretary entered with several of his attachés, looking severe. Aleksay rose and waited for the man to speak.

"Comrade Kurochkin. You realize you have placed this embassy in a very difficult and embarrassing position? The Americans are considering filing a formal protest and we have information that they are going to prosecute Comrade Zeitsev for espionage. Now perhaps you can explain your actions outside the compound this morning."

Aleksay glanced at the two files. How could he convince his superiors of the threat that he instinctively felt? "My actions were necessary if I were to bring this file to your attention." He handed it to the Assistant Secretary, who passed it to his assistant. "The one called Brutus delivered it to me shortly before . . . his unfortunate death."

"Yes. Suppose you tell us exactly what happened."

Aleksay knew that he could never tell the truth and hope to make them see the necessity of his deed. "I do not know what happened, Comrade Secretary. I was on the floor of the vehicle. Suddenly shots rang out and I dove from the cab and ran for the alley."

"Are you saying the attack was unprovoked?"

"I can only say that we were fired upon and I escaped. I have already told you what happened at the river, so it is fair to assume that the American agents intended to dispense with us."

"Yet they have not dispensed with Comrade Zeitsev. How can you explain that?"

"I can't. They chased me and I eluded them, as I did the time before when they attacked me. Certainly they are aware of my identity and wish to do away with me so that there will be no necessity for a trial."

"Were you not instructed to confine yourself to the embassy?"

"I did not interpret my orders in that manner. I was told to keep a low profile and to desist in my pursuit of the American agent."

"I have been instructed by Moscow to see to your safe passage out of the country. You will leave tonight after dark."

"But Comrade Secretary. You do not understand . . ."

"I understand perfectly, Comrade. You must remember that this is America, and in America such methods as yours are undesirable."

"But the files . . ."

"I will see that they reach the proper level."

"But you must let me explain!"

"You will explain in Moscow!"

Aleksay stopped trying. He realized that nothing he could say would make a difference. The files would be sent to Moscow, they would be analyzed and catalogued, and nothing would be done past that point. But he was certain there was an answer to some larger question hidden in the classified documents. "As you wish, Comrade Secretary."

"Good day, then," the Assistant Secretary said and left with his entourage.

Idiots! If they would only take the time to consider the facts, to interpolate the missing elements, and think through the possible ramifications. But diplomacy stood in the way. The Americans were most assuredly testing some new military device and he had been ordered to obtain evidence to that effect. The evidence was in those files. But now it would be weeks, perhaps months, before the proper officials would be given a chance to evaluate them. Intuitively, he sensed that would be too long.

He knew what would await him in Moscow. He would be disgraced, dishonored for the actions he had taken in the interest of his country. This he could face. However, he could not bear the shame and the discredit it would bring to his mentor, Colonel Markelov. His only chance was to remain in the United States and discover the truth behind the enigmatic Oasis Project. He was sure that he could, but it would almost certainly mean contacting the American agent. It would be dangerous. He would be hunted by both sides, with death as his only reward if caught. But if he did not try, what would be the alternative? The Oasis Project would go unchecked. And then what?

There was really no alternative. The developments of the last few hours had ensured that. The cause of Brutus' death would be discovered, and there would be no way he could ever justify his actions to the Center; not with the threadbare evidence he had thus far delivered. He realized that he faced not simply dishonor but almost certain execution.

He turned to the mirror above the washbasin and daubed water on the laceration on his neck, and one caused by the shattering rear window. Another two inches and it would have severed his spine. Perhaps there was a reason he had been spared. He was a man without a country, abandoned by his government after years of faithful service. His future would depend upon his skill and instincts. But he sensed that his course of action was right, and that he alone could stop the Americans before their plans erupted in war.

At eleven they came for him, one of the military attachés and several security guards. They escorted him like a prisoner to the garage, where two cars were waiting. One was the embassy limousine. The other was a yellow late model Ford with New York plates, obviously stolen. They opened the trunk and the military attaché turned to him. "Get in, Comrade."

Against his better judgment he climbed in and allowed the trunk to be closed. Once inside he drew a stiletto from the sole of his shoe and lay back to reserve his strength.

Outside, on the street, several unmarked cars were parked at various locations, several agents inside of each, their eyes trained on the front and rear entrances of the embassy. At eleven-o-five, the embassy limousine rolled out of the rear alley and turned onto the avenue in the direction of the freeway.

The agent in charge of the surveillance tapped his driver, who started the car and pulled out after the limousine at a safe distance. The others followed, fanning onto parallel streets to effect the pursuit.

Five minutes later, the yellow Ford rolled out of the alley, turned the other way, and drove slowly toward the river, unnoticed by the back-up agents who were still moving into position.

In the trunk, Aleksay lay motionless, his mind a blank. He did not want to think of what he was being forced to do, but he was determined to survive.

The limousine pulled onto the freeway, heading for the airport, and the FBI agents followed, one car always in sight of their quarry. The agent in charge spoke briefly over the radio. "This looks like it could be it. They're heading for the airport."

The yellow Ford crossed the river and headed for the Virginia state line. It was not pursued.

As the limousine rolled into the terminal at National Airport, it was surrounded by federal agents. The agent in charge leaped from his car almost before it had stopped. Jerking the limousine's door open, he stared into the face of the Assistant Secretary. There was no sign of the Russian agent.

"Son of a bitch!" the agent gasped.

"What is the meaning of this?" the Assistant Secretary snapped.

The agent sighed and stepped away, allowing the diplomat to disembark. "I'm sorry, sir. There's been a mistake."

The yellow Ford reached a remote junk yard shortly after midnight just as the sound of a helicopter became distinguishable in the distance. The military attaché opened the trunk and Aleksay climbed out, looking sullen. His right hand was shoved into his coat pocket. He turned at the sound of the approaching helicopter and saw its running lights above the trees.

"You will be taken to Shippensburg, where a charter jet is waiting for you. From there you will be flown to Cuba and then to Moscow."

Aleksay glanced at the others around him. They were grim-looking men, younger than himself, all most assuredly armed. He would wait until the last moment.

The helicopter hovered overhead and one of the guards flashed the car lights on and off two times. With this the helicopter began its descent, showering them with dust. Now!

Aleksay turned on the nearest guard and slashed his throat. Blood spewed from the severed artery as the man went down screaming. Aleksay wheeled and caught the glint of a pistol out of the corner of his eyes. Two reports followed and he heard the bullets whistle past his head. He lunged for the man, rolling to avoid being hit and plunged the knife into his chest. The others rushed toward him. Sinking to one knee, he opened fire on them. The attaché was the last to die, his head exploding like a ripe melon. Aleksay bolted for the copter which was only then touching down. He snatched open the cockpit door and scrambled in, pressing the muzzle of his pistol against the pilot's temple.

"Take off! At once! Do you hear me!"

The horrified pilot made a sharp ascent into the cloudless sky and soon they were skimming over blackened fields and an occasional farm house. In the distance, he saw the lights of a small town. He pointed the way. "You will let me off there."

The pilot set the helicopter down in a deserted field on the edge of the sleeping community. Aleksay jumped out and waved the gun at him. "Go! Now!"

Gladly, the pilot set his machine in motion, and buzzed away into the night, leaving Aleksay to vanish into the darkness, thinking of the day when he would come face to face with the American agent.

. . . 31 December 1990

Like skeletal fingers, the blackened skyline of New York City rose above the East River under a leaden blanket of snow clouds. It was a cheerless December night, the last of the year 1990.

That night, like no other in history, held special meaning for the people of the United States. It was without the traditional broadcast from Radio City Music Hall, without the frantic jamming of Times Square and the raucous madness that had always infected such gatherings. It was the first New Year's Eve in many years when the strains of Auld Lang Syne did not issue forth from drunken street parties and penthouse gatherings.

The snowy shroud settled on the city of silent, empty skyscrapers, where once ten million people had clamoured with one voice at precisely midnight, an ovation heard round the world, heralding in the new year, banishing the old.

Now they were gone. Most of them at any rate. Commerce had died in the great metropolis. The Big Apple was reduced to its rotten core. Left were the sounds of tank treads crunching on the frozen streets, the marching cadence of armed patrols in Central Park. Broadway, Park Avenue, the Avenue of the Americans were barren tundras, wastelands of boarded shop windows and shattered dreams.

Elsewhere in the country, small groups of people gathered to sip champagne and cautiously wish each other better than the year before had granted them, but theirs were hollow hopes, riddled with doubt and fear, for they saw the message clearly, engraved on the worried faces of their companions. Could there be hope in a world fractured by hatred and distrust? How long would it be before the fate of the eastern cities would be theirs, when their businesses would feel the full impact of these troubled times?

The cycle had begun and for all intents seemed irreversible. Four of the country's major centers of commerce and industry had fallen, and others seemed poised to follow. Hunger, poverty, despair, crime, and violence spread over the land. Gone were the days of unlimited prosperity. Up and up, better and better, more and more; these were concepts of a tarnished age now trodden beneath the tramping boots of winter and deprivation.

In the cities, people did remain, and in great numbers. But they were the dregs; the thieves and looters, the ignorant and apathetic. They ruled the hellish world they had helped to forge. They were the defilers, the derelicts, the leeches, the bipedal remoras who had fed on the scraps of their providers as long as such had existed. Now they scavenged the disemboweled cities in packs, clashing in chance encounters, ravaging everything and everyone in their paths, destroying, consuming, discarding, desecrating. They were the malignancy, the cancerous pod that had seeded in the human spirit ages before, only to burst after generations of gluttony and squander. Time had sealed their fate, and the final hours would ring their death knell.

Two thousand miles away from the dreary squalor of New York City, Roger Davis sat at a sidewalk restaurant on the west side of the square of the Zocalo near the heart of Mexico City. His skin was tanned and his hair had been tinted brown, giving him the appearance of a Castilian Spaniard. He wore a loose fitting white shirt and a dark wool jacket, for the night was cool. His right arm was in a plaster cast and sling.

All around him, the plaza throbbed with life. In the shop arcades and on the square, a massive throng had assembled, dancing and singing to the gay strains of the wandering mariachi bands. Firecrackers spattered on the pavement, merrymakers swirled by in human eddies, heralding the New Year, the new prosperity, the bright future of their great country. And scattered throughout, grim uniformed soldiers patrolled in twos, machine guns slung over their shoulders, their eyes searching the mob for troublemakers.

On the rooftops of the Palacio National and the Palacio Municipal, dark figures stood silent sentry duty, watching the festivities below and the surrounding skyline. He could see their silhouettes above the lights.

It was eleven-forty-five when he checked his watch. Just enough time to make his way to the Cathedral on the north side of the Zocalo, where Enrique de Gonzales-Perez was to address the crowd at precisely the stroke of midnight. Leaving twenty pesos on the table, he rose and melted into the crowd, allowing himself to be drawn with the current flowing toward the Cathedral. He could see its spires rising into the night sky, its immensity dwarfing the thousands who danced in drunken zeal at its feet. It was the largest church in the New World, built upon the site of the ancient Aztec temple dedicated to their god of war. A fitting location for the events that would soon transpire.

The Zocalo itself lay on the original site of the ancient Aztec city which Cortés had razed in his ruthless overthrow of that glorious empire. Cortés had described it as the City of Palaces and the Venice of the New World, because of its elaborate canal system and splendid edifices. Nothing remained but the former glory of the artifacts in the National Museum and the shame of destruction that the conquerors had wrought.

As he walked, he flexed his fingers inside the cast around the stock of the pistol concealed within it. It was a twenty-two magnum, carrying a nine-shot clip loaded with explosive-tipped bullets. The cast was shaped to allow the slide action to function and a slot had been cut to enable the spent shell casings to eject to the outside. It had been necessary to shorten the barrel of the pistol so that it would fit in the palm of his hand and still be concealed within the plaster, and because of this he would have to work himself almost to the foot of the dais which had been erected on the Cathedral steps in order to ensure greater accuracy.

He knew that his one and only opportunity would come

during the fusilade of fireworks which was to precede the President's speech, during which he would empty the clip into the President's head, shed the cast from his arm and slip away into the confusion of the crowd before anyone knew what had happened. It was a bold plan, more dangerous than he would have liked, and had there been any other way, he would have chosen it. But not once in the five months that he had pursued Perez had the President made himself available as a target. Davis' repeated attempts to penetrate the executive's security had proven futile, as if Perez were aware of the danger stalking him.

The man had made himself inaccessible even to his own people, to the point of reclusiveness; and because of his actions, the people had grown increasingly discontented and uncertain. Finally, out of necessity, Perez had announced his intentions to make a major speech on the eve of the New Year. That had happened three days earlier, and Davis had had to prepare quickly.

Not once during his dauntless pursuit had Davis seen Mercedes. It was as if she had vanished from the Earth, and in a way, he was glad of it. He did not know how he would react, seeing her and being forced to face the reality of what he was planning; knowing what it would do to her, to her entire world. It was better if she were pushed out of his thoughts forever.

At four minutes to midnight, Davis found himself wedged in a wall of humanity, scarcely twenty feet from the Cathedral steps to the right of the raised dais. The people were packed so tightly that he suddenly doubted whether he would be able to take aim and fire, much less effect an escape; but he was committed and he resolved to wait for his opportunity and take it if it presented itself.

The people were singing now and chanting Perez's name. To many he had become a patron saint, the savior of their country. Under his regime, the Mexican oil reserves had begun to pump prosperity into an economy throttled by hundreds of years of poverty and ignorance. It did not matter to them that he and his cronies were growing enormously wealthy in the process. All they knew was that there were more jobs, and that spelled relief for the nearly twenty million people who now flooded the city.

Unknown to them, Perez had formed an un-Holy alliance with Castro, and in so doing had tapped the vast resources of the Soviet Union, its technology, its machinery. What would they do if they realized what lay in their future? Would they laud their revered hero when the iron fist of communism smashed their democracy? Or would it matter to them? After all, they were a people used to hardship, to deprivation. If communism meant food for all, clothing and education for the masses, could it be so very wrong?

At two minutes to twelve, the enormous Cathedral doors swung inward and a tumultuous din swelled up from the crowd. The Archbishop appeared first, bestowing his blessings on the faithful, followed closely by his coterie of clergymen and a swarm of dark-suited security agents who fanned out over the dais, taking up positions several feet apart around its perimeter, hands shoved into coat pockets, eyes sweeping the multitude.

Then Perez himself appeared, smiling and waving both hands above his balding head, his fat little brown face beaming. He was wearing a black tuxedo, a full length black overcoat with a sable collar, and white gloves. Davis glanced at the Cathedral clock high overhead. It was one minute before midnight.

Davis eased his cast out of the sling and worked his way into a position from which he could take aim if the pressure of the crowd subsided. For the moment, it seemed impossible. The people around him were jostling each other, whistling, clapping, shouting, and singing their adulation for the man they now saw as their messiah, the one who would lead them from the wilderness of poverty to the promised land of prosperity.

Perez stepped forward to the podium. Only his head was visible from where Davis stood, making the shot doubly difficult. Suddenly, however, the crowd grew quieter, anticipating the stroke of midnight. Perez looked to the clock behind him, and the crowd began the countdown as a death-like stillness came over the Zocalo. Ten, nine, eight . . .

Davis raised his arm slightly, aiming his pointed finger at the President's head . . . seven, six, five . . . the crowd began to vibrate with expectation . . . four, three . . . Perez turned and motioned to someone behind him . . . two, one.

He saw her as the Cathedral bells began to chime. She wore a flowing black dress and full-length mink wrap. Her skin was well tanned, her hair longer than he had remembered it. She was a vision of perfection, a goddess. She stepped to her father's side and he enfolded her in his right arm, waving to the cheering masses, his eyes sparkling.

He heard the roar of the crowd, felt the surge of humanity, saw the brilliant flashes above him and the shower of manmade starlight as the fireworks burst into the heavens. Suddenly, the crowd began to surge in their frenzied revelry, and his arm was nearly broken off. He jerked it back violently, cursing in pain and frustration the drunk who had cut in front of him.

The moment was gone, his opportunity wasted. He was a helpless victim of the crowd and he stared at Mercedes as memories raced through his head. He cursed himself for his weakness, for being distracted. Had she not been there, Perez would already be lying in a pool of his own blood.

He turned and fought his way through the pressing mob, away from the dais, away from the Cathedral, away from Mercedes and his memories. The crowd gripped him, tore at him in their excitement, jumping up and down, slapping his back, pushing and shoving. For the first time in a very long time he was afraid, not of what they might do, but what he might do in the next few minutes. His thoughts were flashing, his instincts were aroused. He had been heartbeats from snuffing a man's life and his emotions were boiling. He struggled for control.

Far behind, he heard the President's voice raised above the din. He did not turn to look back, but increased his efforts to retreat. He was reaching the edge of the mob. People were rushing past him, bleary-eyed from too much tequila, frantic to see their leader, to hear him, perhaps to touch him.

Suddenly, someone seized his left elbow with a viselike grip and whirled him around. Davis raised his plastered arm to chest level and looked into the cold brown eyes and flat white face of the Russian agent. He felt the nudge of cold steel against his ribs and his blood froze as he waited for the sound of the report and the crushing collapse of his lungs.

"I must speak with you!" the man shouted above the bedlam.

Davis stared in disbelief. Here was the man who had killed untold numbers of American agents. Here was his avowed nemesis, poised and capable of killing him in the wink of an eye. Had his ears deceived him? Was he already dead and falling, his mind hallucinating in the last few heartbeats before death?

"What?" Davis gasped.

"I must speak to you! Now!"

Aleksay fairly threw him in the direction of a darkened arcade and followed with his gun wedged against Davis' back, pushing him on. Davis had no choice but to obey, being unable to swing his plastered arm into position for a shot. In seconds they were alone in the darkness, their two faces glowing in the diffused light, the sound of the crowd seemingly miles away. High above, the fireworks boomed and showered the Zocalo with ribbons of sparks. The Russian looked around frantically. He seemed afraid, almost panicked. Was he aware of what Davis concealed under his cast? Would there be a chance for a shot? Davis swung the cast toward the man's midsection. If he were to die, he would not die alone. The Russian looked back at him, then down at the cast, an expression of realization crossing his face.

"I've got a gun aimed at your guts," Davis said. He had regained his composure and was now rock steady.

The Russian nodded and raised his own pistol again, pointing it at Davis' belly. "Stalemate," he said.

"What do you want?" Davis asked, his eyes never leaving the Russian's, watching for that glimmer of anticipation that would tell him the man was about to fire.

"I could have killed you at any time in the last five months."

"Then why didn't you?"

"I need your help!" Aleksay said, hating the sound of his own words.

Davis recoiled. "You what?"

"And you need me."

"What are you talking about?"

"Listen to me! There isn't much time. I know what you've done. The man at The Madison hotel, the one in Aspen, the one in Detroit, the one in Key Biscayne. And now this! I know what you're doing!"

"You're out of your mind!"

"You're working for the President, aren't you?"

"No!"

"Who then? The Senate? The Congress? I hardly think so. There's no need to admit it, I know! It doesn't make any difference now. I need your help!"

"I don't know what you're talking about," Davis said, trying to maintain his composure.

"Don't be a fool! Listen to me! I know he's planning something."

"You'd better pull that trigger, because I'm pulling this one!" Davis replied, knowing that his threat was idle. He saw something in the man's eyes, something that he had never expected to see—fear.

"You stupid son of a bitch!" Aleksay fumed. "Do you think that you are the only one? You are only a very small part of his scheme. I know he is planning something. I only have bits of the puzzle, but with your help we can stop him. It's your only chance!"

"You're insane! This is a set-up."

"No! I've defected. Nyet! I've deserted. I'm alone in this, don't you understand? Why else would I risk a confrontation? They were going to send me back. They were going to disgrace me. They wouldn't believe me. But I had the information. I had it in writing but they took it away from me! It was there. The two lists. They were the same. It all makes sense now. But they wouldn't let me explain!"

"What are you talking about? What lists?"

"The lists in the files. The lists of cities! Don't you see? Every major city on Earth. Without them, civilization as we know it, as we have known it, would cease to exist!"

"I don't know what the hell you're talking about!" Davis stammered, sensing that the man was close to the edge.

"I think you do! You've got to listen to me! I've thought it all through. Even the American cities! Don't you see what he's doing? His inaugural address, his speech about the oasis! It all ties in. They are testing atomic weapons in space! That is the Oasis Project! We've got to stop him. He's going to destroy . . ."

Four shots rang out from the pitch blackness of the alley. The Russian crashed into him, one of the bullets bursting out of his chest and striking Davis a glancing blow on the shoulder. Davis instinctively used the dying man's body as a shield and fired at the sound of retreating footsteps. There was no cry and the footsteps faded into the darkness.

"You've got to stop him!" Aleksay gasped. "It's our only hope. It's the world's only hope!" His knees buckled and he began to collapse.

Davis lowered him to the filthy street and stared down at him in confusion. "What are you saying? Who is going to destroy what?"

"Parker! Parker! The cities . . ."

"What cities?"

"The list . . ."

"What list?"

"My breast pocket . . . I copied it . . ."

Davis groped inside the man's jacket and removed a blood-drenched folded piece of paper.

"Get away!" Aleksay coughed. "Get away before it's too late. Stop him. Stop him before . . ." He caught his breath and began to strangle, the blood gurgling in his throat. "The Oasis Project! Stop the Oasis Project!"

He was dead. His massive body lay prostrate on the street. Davis rose and looked around quickly. The fireworks were soaring overhead. The President's speech was over. Soon there would be crowds of people. He had to get away.

Shedding the plaster cast, he left the arcade, entering the Zocalo and walking rapidly south away from the dancing masses. He fought the urge to run. His nerves were frayed, his mind reeling from the events of the last few minutes. Who had fired on them from the darkness? What was the Oasis Project? Why was it so important that the Russian had risked coming face to face with him, knowing that one or both of them would likely die in the encounter? At first he had thought the man mad, but now realized that he had been terrified. And a man like that did not frighten easily. What kind of fear could have pushed him to the point of hysteria? To the point where his own life became meaningless? To the point where countries and political philosophies were no longer a boundary?

Only when he reached the lobby of his hotel did he realize that he was spattered with blood. He slipped past the desk clerk and took the stairs, three at a time, until he had at last collapsed behind his own bolted door, gasping for air. Quickly, he stripped to his underwear and wadding his soiled clothing into a ball, stuffed it into his suitcase. He cleaned the flesh wound in his shoulder and put on clean clothes and his heavy wool overcoat.

At last he poured himself a glass of Scotch and drank half of it in one gulp. It burned like hell, but it calmed him and cleared his head for the moment. He needed time to think. Never in his entire service had something so bizarre happened to him. He had stared gunpoint to gunpoint with Russian agents before, but never had he been so shaken. The Russian's fanaticism, frenzied eyes, the absolute conviction in his voice made Davis wonder—could he have been telling the truth?

The list! The fucking list! He dug into the ball of clothing and withdrew the list, now completely soaked with blood. Gingerly, he spread it out under the desk lamp and studied it. It was a list of cities, alphabetized by country. What had the Russian said? "Every major city on Earth. Without them, civilization as we know it, as we have known it, would cease to exist." It was true. Remove the cities on the list, and man's systems of government, his central communications, his technologies, his religions, his works of art, his entire history would vanish. But why had Aleksay drawn that conclusion? Where was the evidence linking the list to the concept? Davis had only a crazed man's word for it. It was lunacy. Still, there was the list, stained with the man's blood.

He wondered again who might have fired the fatal shots. The Russians? If they had tracked their own man with the intention of killing him, would they not have killed anyone with him, especially if he were an American agent? But could it have been his own side? It was conceivable, in fact most probable. Someone sent to finish the job had failed so many times before. After all, no one else except Eldon Parker knew that he was working for the government. A CIA operative would have no reason to recognize him. Might not that agent have tried to kill him as well? That was general procedure.

Something else worried him. If Parker were capable of the covert measures he had taken, using Davis as his operative, was he not capable of conducting other activities that Davis had no knowledge of? He had made the assumption that he was in the President's confidence, but he remembered that the President had had his line tapped. Had he drawn the wrong conclusions about the man? Did he know as much as he thought about Parker? Or was there more? Much more! Might his intrigue not reach as high as the military brass? Was there a plan such as Kurochkin had suggested? No! It was out of the question! No man in his right mind could ever hope to perpetrate an act so horrible, so bold, without considering the possibility of retaliation. And he knew that Parker above all was a rational man. He would never do anything without evaluating the risks. The Russian was wrong! He had to be! One act of aggression would bring immediate retaliation on a world-wide scale, and life on the planet would be obliterated. And what was rational in that? It was insanity and Parker was not insane.

He glanced at his watch. He had just enough time to reach the airport and catch his flight. Once on the plane he would have time to think, time to formulate a plan. Then he would decide what to do, with the list, with Parker, with his future,

. . . 1 January 1991

A heavy snow shrouded the Northeast. Davis' plane was delayed nearly an hour in landing at Washington's National Airport. When he deplaned, he was rested and his mind was clear. He had had time to treat his flesh wound properly and rinse the coloring from his hair, returning it to its natural shade of straw yellow.

At customs, he saw several men in dark suits waiting, and recognized them at once as Secret Service agents by their manner of dress and deportment. He was not surprised, therefore, when one of them spoke to the customs agent and his bags were hustled through untouched. The agents greeted him in their typically formal manner.

"Mr. Davis?" one of them asked.

"I'm Davis."

"We've got a car waiting. Will you come with us?"

"What for?" he asked, suddenly on guard.

The agent who had addressed him leaned closer. "The President is expecting you."

Davis looked piercingly at the man, wondering whether or not to believe him. The man stared back without expression. Davis glanced at his two companions, and decided that if necessary he could take all three. "All right. Lead the way."

Forty-five minutes later, the black limousine rolled to a stop in front of the Executive Office Building, and the agents escorted Davis in through the President's private entrance to a seldom-used office created for President Nixon during his Administration. It was then—and now—used only for meetings of the utmost secrecy, when visitors were better unnoticed. The change in protocol did not escape Davis.

The agent who had spoken to him at the airport opened

the door and stepped inside.

"Come in, Mr. Davis. The President will be here shortly."

Davis entered and turned sharply as the door was closed behind him. He walked to the windows and stared out at the grey sky and the dreamlike white world. It was only a matter of minutes before the door once more opened and the President entered, waving to the agents to remain outside. He closed the door and stood motionless, staring at Davis, a look of veiled hostility on his face. His eyes were muddy green.

"What happened?" he asked, his voice cold.

"I wasn't able to pull it off," Davis said.

The President's face grew uncustomarily red. "I know that, Mr. Davis. I asked you what happened!"

"The crowd was pressed around me. I couldn't manage a shot."

"I gave you specific orders that Perez was to be eliminated by the first of the year. If you'll notice the calendar, Mr. Davis, it is the first of the new year."

"Yes, sir."

"Well?"

Davis grew suddenly angry, angry at himself for having failed, but also angry with the man he had served so faithfully, who had apparently turned on him in so short a time. "Well what?" he said harshly.

The President's face darkened in rage. "Do you realize what you've done?"

"Yes, sir. I've failed to carry out your orders successfully."

"No, Mr. Davis! It's much worse than that! You've placed this country in a very precarious position."

"I beg your pardon, Mr. President, but . . ."

"Keep your mouth shut!" Parker roared. "You'll speak when I order you to speak!" He paused and forced himself to regain control. "Don't you realize that this country is on the verge of collapse? We need that Mexican oil and we need it now! Our supplies are down to the critical level. We're having one of the worst winters in history. You blew it, Davis!"

"I wouldn't say it was entirely my fault."

"I would, Mr. Davis. I trusted you . . ."

"Did you?"

"What do you mean by that?"

"You use the word trust too freely, Mr. Parker," Davis said. His temper was beginning to boil. "I wouldn't call the way you've handled me an expression of trust."

"Oh, you wouldn't?"

"No. Not when you send your henchmen to meet me at the plane. How did you know I was going to be on that plane? I didn't fly under my own name. And I told no one that I had booked a reservation on that flight. You obviously had me followed."

"A necessary precaution in matters of this scope, Mr. Davis. You of all persons should realize that."

"I do, Mr. President. But I wouldn't call it an expression of trust."

"I don't think you quite understand . . ."

"I understand, Mr. President. I understand only too well. You put your bird dogs on me, just in case I needed silencing or in case I couldn't handle the assignment. Have they been there on all of them? Have I always been watched?"

"Watch your tone, Davis. I've got enough to hang you."

"And I don't have as much on you?"

"No. As far as the records go, you've been a discharged diplomat acting on your own volition, carrying out a private vendetta of terrorism. I've seen to that."

"Are you threatening me, Mr. President?"

"I don't think I have to threaten, Davis. Threats are for the insincere."

"I'm out," Davis said quietly, stepping toward the door.

"You're what?"

"I'm out of it. I quit. Find someone else!"

"It's not that easy, Davis. There is no getting out once you're in."

"I wondered about you, but now I know the truth. You're nuts."

"No. I'm as sane as the next man, if that means anything by today's standards. I put my faith in you because I thought you believed in what we were doing."

"I don't know what that is anymore, Mr. Parker. And I don't think you do either."

"That's where you're wrong. Davis. Dead wrong. I've known what I was doing since the beginning, since before the beginning. Long before you ever met me."

"Then what are we doing, Mr. President? Tell me that?"

"I've told you. We're fighting a war for independence."

"And am I an expendable pawn?"

"I hope not, Mr. Davis. Because despite what I've said, I need you." Parker's mood suddenly changed. "I've been up all night in meetings. I only heard this morning that your mission had failed." Parker's anger seemed to fade before Davis' eyes, and he paced to the window and stared out. "I'm sorry I said what I said. I was wrong. You're not a pawn, and I do trust you. I hope you believe that."

Davis made no reply.

"It's just that I have a timetable, and this delay has seriously jeopardized it . . ."

"What sort of timetable, if you don't mind my asking, as long as we're being honest with each other?"

"I'm afraid I can't tell you that, Mr. Davis. For reasons that . . . are of the utmost importance to national security."

"I see," Davis said.

Parker turned to him, his face suddenly open, his eyes pleading. "You've got to trust me, Davis. Believe in what we're doing! It's the only way!"

"What are we doing?"

"We're buying time! I've told you that before." Parker looked away. When he spoke again, his voice was cold and removed. "What did the Russian say to you?"

Davis jumped as if he had been shot. He looked at the back of Parker's head and wondered what was going on inside it. "Then it was one of our men in the alley?"

"Yes. He thought the Russian was about to kill you."

"So he sprayed the alley with gunfire on the chance that I wouldn't be killed in the process?"

"It wasn't that way. I've spoken with the man already. He could see you both clearly, but there wasn't time to warn you. His aim was true, wasn't it?"

"Aside from a flesh wound, I'm all right. What about him?"

"He was hit in the right buttock, but he's going to be fine. He's at Bethesda."

"Why did he run?" Davis asked.

"Because you were shooting at him. Now tell me what the Russian said. All of it. It's every important."

"To national security?" Davis goaded him.

Parker turned, his nostrils flaring. "Yes, to national security. You know he was involved in the apparat at SPEC and you also know that we've got some highly delicate operations going on over there."

"I'm sorry," Davis said. "I was striking back at you. The last twenty-four hours haven't been exactly pleasant."

"I know. Now what did he say?"

"He said he had information on a secret project. Something he called the Oasis Project."

Parker's face paled, and for a moment Davis thought that he might fall. "What kind of information?" he stammered. "How did he get it?"

"I don't know how he got it. I don't know much more than this." He pulled the bloodstained paper out of his pocket and handed it to Parker.

Parker took it and unfolded it. His eyes widened at what he saw. "Where did you get this?"

"Kurochkin. He said he copied it."

"That fits. This is a list of cities I gave Ralph Owens. It concerns a new reconnaissance plane called the Drone. It's an unmanned ship that we're putting into operation to monitor the Russian missile sites."

"What does that have to do with the cities on the list? If you don't mind my asking, sir."

"I suggested a new surveillance program for the Drone, dealing with population patterns. We were going to put it into operation until it proved unfeasible."

Davis looked at him sharply. "Kurochkin seemed to think there was more than that."

"Oh?"

"Yes. He thought it was a plan for a worldwide military operation."

"But I've just explained, the Drone is a reconnaissance

plane. How did he get that impression?"

"I don't know. He didn't have time to say. Maybe if we had taken him alive he would have told us."

"I doubt it. Did he say any more?"

"He said there were two lists. That they were the same."

Parker again flinched slightly. "I don't understand."

"Nor do I. He said he had more, but that his superiors had taken it away from him. They were going to send him home. Frankly, sir, he was terrified. He believed what he was telling me, about the worldwide operation."

"You mean he thought we were going to bomb every one of these cities on the list?" Parker scoffed.

"Yes, sir."

Parker began to laugh. "He was insane! Why would we bomb our own cities? How could he think that we would hope to get away with this type of destruction?"

"I don't know, sir. But I think he believed we were going to try."

Parker sighed with relief and sat down in one of the leather chairs. "That's a load off my mind, Davis, I don't mind telling you."

"What, sir?"

"He was so far off base, the Russians don't have any idea what we're really doing. For a minute there you had me worried."

Davis felt slightly sheepish, for the tension between them had completely melted and his anger had faded into confusion. "Don't you think they might draw the same conclusions?"

"What if they do? Let them think it if they want to. It might do them some good to sweat a little."

"What is the Oasis Project, Mr. President?"

Parker looked annoyed at Davis' persistence, but then smiled. "You're a strange cat, Davis. I never thought you would have spoken to me the way you have."

"Is it that sensitive, sir?"

"It's the most sensitive project in this nation's history, Mr. Davis. But it has absolutely nothing to do with warfare. Not conventional warfare at any rate." He studied Davis, considering how much to tell him. "I'll tell you only this, Davis. It has something to do with NASA and with the Space Shuttle program. More than that I cannot say."

For the first time in twenty-four hours Davis relaxed. It had all been a bad dream. His suspicion had been unfounded. He too sighed and sat down heavily in a chair. The President looked at him and smiled.

"I'm sorry I had to put you through this, Davis. I really am. I like you. I think we understand each other. Those things I said earlier . . ."

"Forget them, Mr. President. I was pretty out of line myself."

"You're still not off the hook for missing Perez."

"Believe me, sir. If . . ."

"Don't worry about explaining. You're going to get another chance at him, this time in this country."

"He's coming here? After what you two have said about each other?"

"He's coming to make an appeal to the United Nations."

"What for?"

"Since New York is practically a no-man's land, he's going to offer a new UN site in Mexico City. It's a power play against us, but we have to let him think he's getting away with it. The third world countries are really beginning to play hardball with us. They think we're on the verge of collapse."

"Aren't we?"

"Yes, if we're pushed the wrong way. But on the other hand, with the Mexican oil and our new technology, we're going to hand them a big surprise. I've been building up this collapse image larger than it really is, with the exception of those four cities. That's the real McCoy."

"And you're willing to take a crack at him here, that is in New York?" Davis asked.

"If you think you can make it seem like radicals, terrorists, are responsible. I had in mind a bombing. Everyone knows that his going into New York City in the face of the energy crisis, with the things he's been saying about Americans, is a tremendous risk. But he's getting pressure from the Soviets."

"I think it's a hell of a risk, sir. Couldn't I try again when he is back in Mexico?"

"Time is of the essence, Mr. Davis. We need to create chaos south of the border. It's part of my timetable."

"How do you want me to do it?"

"I've arranged for the word to spread around the city. We're almost guaranteed a mass demonstration. If not we'll stir one up."

"I've got to tell you, sir. I don't like it. I think it will look very bad for the country."

"I'm going to issue an official statement warning Perez of the dangers; that New York City is an occupied territory and that violence and civil disruptions are a daily occurrence. If he wants to come in the face of all warnings, the best we can do is try to protect him. Naturally, our efforts will fail."

Davis considered it as all his suspicions of Parker came rushing back. He said carefully, "I'll go on record against it, sir. But if those are your orders, I'll carry them out."

"Those are my orders, Mr. Davis."

That evening, Arnold Kemper met with Parker in his private study on the third floor of the White House. Both of them were grim, Kemper clearly worried by what he had discovered.

"It's confirmed, Eldon. Somehow, he got a look at the folder when it was locked in my desk."

"The night watchman? Gus, what's-his-name?"

"Yes. He was the inside man Ralph was looking for. I'll be damned if I know how he got away with it for all those years. He obviously was the one who slipped the Drone dossiers to Karpovich, then replaced them after she had done her job."

"Are you sure he got the information out?"

"Yes. I checked the counter on my copy machine in the office. There are five copies unaccounted for, the exact number of pages in the dossier."

"And what was in the dossier?"

"Some schematics for the guidance system we're using in the ASP."

"And the list?"

"Yes. I was beginning the program tapes."

"What can the Russians glean from what they've got?"

"I don't think very much, other than the name of the project and the fact that it has something to do with a guidance system and the same list of cities they got from the Drone project."

"And the two guidance systems. They're identical?"

"Yes."

"Then won't they possibly conclude that the Drone and the Oasis Project are one and the same?"

"From the information they have, I think that's the only conclusion they could make."

"Nevertheless, I think we have to step up the timetable. There can't be any slip-ups. The project must be operational by May 1."

"It will be, if we don't have any problems with the reactors."

"There can't be any delays, Arnold. It has to be May 1. Put on extra shifts, but get that thing ready."

"OK. Whatever it takes, I'll do it."

"When is the first test flight scheduled?"

"The prototype is finished except for the final electrical testing and the installation of the nuclear plant. I'd say we can target February 4 or 5."

"No sooner?"

"Don. What we've done is impossible by all manner of comparison. February 4 is pushing it as it is."

"Then February 4 it is. I'll be there."

Bethesda Naval Hospital was veiled in falling snow. Few lights burned in its upper floors, but the lower floor was brightly lit. It was past visiting hours. Roger Davis stepped from the cab, wrapping his overcoat around him.

"Wait for me. I'll be about half an hour at the most."

He entered the front foyer and approached the information desk. A plump nurse looked up from her Rolledex and squinted at him over half-moon glasses. The light was harsh, hospital blue.

"May I help you?" she asked, smiling impersonally.

"I'm here to see a friend of mine. I don't know what name he used; you see, he's on assignment." He flashed his diplomatic cards and the nurse raised her eyebrows.

"I don't see how I can help you . . ."

"He's in the Secret Service. And I know what his injury was."

"Oh?"

"Yes. He was shot in the buttock. The right buttock."

The nurse looked at him skeptically. "Is that all you know about him?"

"He was admitted last night or maybe early this morning."

She acted put out as she thumbed through a list of new admittances. She finished the deck of card and shook her head. "I'm sorry. There's no one here admitted for an injury in the right . . ."

"Are you sure?"

"If you could tell me his name . . ."

"I told you. He wouldn't use his real name. He's on assignment. I've got to speak to him. It's urgent."

"I'll check again," she sighed. She did, then shook her head resolutely. "I'm sorry. There's no one even listed in the Secret Service. Maybe you're mistaken."

Davis looked at her thoughtfully. He knew there was little chance of finding the agent he had shot by a front desk inquiry. That didn't mean the man wasn't there, however—just that there was no record of him.

"Well, thank you." Davis smiled. "I'll check the other hospitals."

"If you only knew the name," the nurse apologized.

"It's not your fault. Thanks anyway."

He left the lobby and climbed into the waiting cab.

"Where to, pal?"

"Drive."

"What?"

"Just drive."

"Where to?"

"Your choice. Some bar somewhere, I guess."

"It's your money, pal," the driver said and wheeled out of the front esplanade.

From a car parked near the front circle, a grim-faced agent spoke into his car radio. "He checked Bethesda, but he obviously couldn't get past the information desk."

"We'll have him moved to a private clinic tonight," the voice said on the other end of the transmission. "Follow Davis. Don't let him out of your sight."

"Will do."

The agents pulled onto the esplanade in pursuit of the cab. The snow fell in whispering flurries.

The word reached Parker just as he was turning in. It came from the agent who had met Davis at the airport that afternoon.

"Mr. President?"

"Yes?"

"I just thought you'd like to know, he checked Bethesda."

"And?"

"He didn't get past the information desk."

"Where is he now?"

"I'm having him followed."

"Eliminate him. Tonight, do you understand? He isn't to be trusted."

"Yes, sir."

Davis sat with his back to the wall in a booth draped in shadow. The place was hot and stuffy, smoke hung in ribbons in the air. The music was loud and jarring, and several drunk patrons undulated spasmodically to its neo-rhythms, emulating the latest dance craze. It was late, and he had had too much to drink. But he had needed it. There were things on his mind that he could not deal with in a sober state.

Suddenly, his world, which had always been printed in shades of grey, had taken on darker overtones. He was accustomed to doubt, uncertainty, even treachery, and he knew how to deal with them. But Parker's turnabout had caught him totally unprepared. The man was not the same person who had confided in him almost four years before at the ski lodge in Lake Tahoe.

He remembered the scene vividly. There had been a party, a diplomatic party of sorts, with many influential people in attendance; big contributors to Parker's campaign, regional party leaders, national caucus leaders, members of the foreign service. He had known at once that he did not fit in. But he had been invited.

He thought about the man Parker had been. He remembered the broad shoulders, the straight back, his powerful graceful manner, his smile exuding self-confidence, and a will power that made it hard to refuse his desires. And he remembered his stability. Something in the man had changed.

He also remembered who had given the party—Arnold Kemper—Dr. Arnold Kemper of SPEC Technologies. And there had been others there, now in the Administration; Montie Montgomery, Preston Holmes of course, and Bruce Wilson. It had been his first glimpse of the future Parker White House.

Their meeting had been brief. Parker had been characteristically blunt. He had laid out his cards, revealing his detailed knowledge of Davis' past activities and his political persuasions. The Said affair had been planned in Kemper's study, with just the two of them present, Parker and Davis. It seemed several lifetimes ago.

So much had happened. The days all ran together. The man he had met, the presidential candidate, had been so confident of his own election that he had given the go-ahead and pulled the necessary strings to have Davis assigned to the embassy in Moscow, despite his predecessor's presence in the White House. Even now, the realization of that kind of power gave Davis a sudden chill. How far did the man's influence reach? How far was he willing to stretch it?

There was little doubt in his mind that the relationship between them had been tarnished. And the plan Parker envisioned for Perez was lunacy. It would precipitate worldwide repercussions. So was it then a plan for Perez, or a plan for Davis? Wouldn't it be just as easy to eliminate *him* in the near riotous conditions surrounding the UN, as it would be to eliminate Perez? Somehow, he could still not see the logic in being rid of Perez. He knew that Mexico would fall quickly into line if the U.S. ever seriously threatened her.

His thoughts turned to Mercedes. He had managed to repress them up to now, but her face drifted back to haunt him. His mind, warped by booze and fatigue, painted grotesque images of her weeping over the bloodied carcass of her murdered father. He knew then he had had enough. He was no longer willing to be an actor — or victim — in Parker's drama. He felt more isolated than he ever had in his entire life, including the time he had spent in the tiger cages in Vietnam. Like Aleksay Kurochkin, he sensed he was a man without a country, or soon to be one; and he knew that to remain stationary was to become a target. He rose and weaved through the scattered tables toward the glass front door.

Suddenly, a hand landed on his shoulder from behind, and in the same instant, through the front windows, he saw several dark shapes approaching from across the street. Like lightning, he whirled, driving his elbow hard into the man's solar plexus as he turned. He heard his gasp, and saw his face turn blue as he staggered backward and crashed into a group of drinkers, who scattered screaming amidst shattering glass and flying chairs. He recognized the man at once as one of those who had met him at the airport that morning. Whipping his Browning from his shoulder holster, he fired pointblank, slamming two rounds into the man's chest before he could reach for his own weapon.

Hearing the shots within, the agents outside opened up with a volley fire through the front window, spraying the place indiscriminately. People were screaming, falling to the floor bleeding. The bartender was hit in the head and crashed into the racks of bottles in an explosion of glass.

Davis flattened himself on the floor and raised his pistol, firing wildly through the window, hoping to hit one of them or force them to take cover. It worked. The gunfire ceased for an instant, and he rolled toward the rear exit, feeding a fresh clip into his pistol as he did. Smoke hung heavy in the bar; bodies littered the floor; glass was everywhere.

Without hesitating, Davis threw open the rear door and stepped back as a blast of automatic fire riddled the bricks and doorjamb, spraying him with wood and mortar. He dived for cover in the darkness behind a trash bin and opened fire on the man standing in the middle of the alley. The man went down screaming and lay silent in the snow. Davis hesitated. No one moved outside, and he could hear the approaching sirens in the distance. His ass was cooked if he didn't get clear of the place right then. He knew that the men out front were either injured or gone by now.

Looking around, he saw two drainage pipes coming off the roof. He holstered his pistol and, grabbing them, shinnied up the wall, three stories above the alley to the slate roof. The sirens were very close now. He slid along out of the light behind a chimney and froze as the first squad car pulled into the alley, its lights flashing. Several officers jumped out with weapons drawn, expecting to have to shoot it out. He wasn't about to give them the satisfaction. Without the slightest noise, he stole across the roof, jumped down to the fire escape on the opposite side of the building and from there reached the street. He hurried toward another bar, anywhere he could melt into the crowd.

From the curb behind him, tires whined and an engine roared. He whirled to see headlights coming at him. Raising his pistol he fired, emptying his clip into the windshield and radiator. The horn blared, and the car careened and smashed into a storefront, showering the area with glass. One of the agents catapulted through the windshield and landed screaming in the wet snow, his legs severed from his body. The driver's head rested on the wheel, two bullet holes in his forehead. The last man, the man in the back seat, kicked at the window and managed to smash it out. He trained his pistol on Davis, who had by then fed another fresh clip into his automatic.

The agent was too late. Davis fired three quick shots slamming him back into the rear seat. By this time, a crowd had flowed from the thriving bars on the street and people stood gaping in confusion. Davis lowered his eyes, shoved his pistol into his coat pocket and walked swiftly through the stunned throng, letting no one look him in the face.

"Say, man, what's happening?" someone asked. "Is this a movie or something?"

Davis kept walking, as police cars skidded to a halt near the carnage and officers swarmed out, staring in dismay at the crowd and the bullet-riddled bodies. It was a hellish way to start the New Year.

. . . 13 January 1991

Men like Roger Davis need a place to go, to retreat from the world that they have chosen to inhabit. Such a place Davis had provided for himself years before, anticipating that one day he would need it for just such a reason as now drove him into the back country, far from civilization and the probing eyes of man.

The weather was bitter cold when he started out from Copper Mountain, Colorado, on a snowcat, bought that morning at the John Deere dealership, trailing a sled of supplies, enough food to last him several months when supplemented with the fresh game he would be able to secure. The mountains were full of deer, the back country, that is. And that was where he had built his compound, in the side of a mountain, high above people's normal haunts, on a remote parcel of land not recorded on any surveyor's map in the state. It was a region of endless mountain peaks and snow-filled valleys, flourishing timber, clean air, and isolation.

No one noticed him skimming up the back road into the wilderness. He was just one more winter hunter stocking his lodge for the weekend. Skiers were jamming the saloons and the mountainsides. Talk was of the World Cup races at Aspen and the rumbles in Libya, something about a border conflict with Egypt.

The road played out at last, and only virgin mountainside and soaring aspen and evergreen trees saw him pass along a faint trail, cut ages ago by deer and elk. It had become a hiking trail, then a cross-country ski trail, but no one followed it to the top of the pass in winter, some eight thousand feet above sea level and many miles into the interior, away from the glittering Christmas lights and fairy-tale setting of the thriving ski resort. To reach the pass was a day and a half on foot, but the snowcat took to the mountain like a flea to a dog's behind, and by late afternoon he stood on the summit, looking back into the valley.

A fresh wind whipped out of the north, harbinger of a new storm front. Though the sky was partially clear, he wasted little time. His retreat was still several hours away, down this valley, through a cleft in the mountains and into the next valley. He had spent ten summers building the trail, cutting timber, blasting out the mountainside, reinforcing it with steel and concrete brought in by rented helicopter in many harrowing trips over the pass. Each time he entered this wilderness, whether on foot or by snowcat, he felt the same way—free.

It was his wilderness, untouched by human degeneracy, where his life was in his own hands, where nature presented him challenges not found in his own world, and existence became the sole occupation of each day's labors. This was his haven, the place he had long intended to disappear to, for the old adage that old agents did not die, they just faded away, was untrue. Old agents did die, if they weren't smart enough to vanish from the face of the Earth under their own terms.

The shadows were lengthening when he reached the floor of the second valley, and bordering the river, skimmed over an unbroken carpet of snow northward toward the split towering spires, the Twin Spires, he called them. Below that rift in the mountaintops, nature had separated the bulk of the mountain range, a monumental achievement in tectonics. He called it simply the Divide.

The river flowed through its narrow bottom during the spring run-offs, leaving only a footpath high on the eastern wall by which to come and go to the next valley. But in winter and summer months, there was only a sparkling stream of fresh pure water, bordered by rocky till which was now covered by several yards of powder snow. Davis approached the Divide just as the light was failing and stood in the gathering shadows gazing up at the towering rock walls draped in shades of indigo and violet. The sky had dulled to a ruddy blue and over the high precipices grey clouds billowed. A stout breeze rustled the branches of the pines and aspen trees, shaking snow balls from their boughs.

The Divide was dark and still, sheltered from the elements, and at the other end, he could see a light shade of grey; the opening into his sanctuary. He shivered as the wind howled down from the icy slopes. There was little time to lose if he wanted to be inside and warm at the onslaught of the storm.

Gunning the snowcat's engine, he climbed the ragged Divide, the engine's roar resonating in the fragile silence off sheer rock cliffs a thousand feet high.

He emerged from the Divide in total darkness his head-lamp throwing a narrow tunnel of light for him to follow, and immediately started his descent into the valley below. His compound lay two miles in, on a bearing north by north-east, at the foot of a gargantuan granite outcropping that had been thrust from the Earth's crust.

He reached the entrance within the half hour. By this time the wind was fierce, blowing the powdery snow like piercing needles against his skin. Despite the cold, he felt warm inside; the feeling of coming home to a safe place after a long absence. He cut the cat's engine and waded through knee-deep drifts up the gentle slope to the granite face. From the outside, there was no trace of an entrance, no hint of human handiwork.

Removing a small electronic transmitter from his parka pocket, he pressed the red buttom and smiled as the wall of stone began to move, slipping into the earth, emitting a deep subsonic rumble. In less than a minute, the front of his retreat was revealed, the bay window, the four-inch thick lead-lined door. Inside, the lights came on illuminating the warm interior he had so carefully sculpted with his own hands; the stone walls, wooden rafters, hardwood floors, and strong masculine furnishings in colors of burnt orange and navy blue. A gas fire erupted in the hearth, and the front doors swung open with a pneumatic hiss.

This was his refuge, the only thing in his life he had ever created to last, the only trace he would leave on this world.

When found, archaeologists might wonder what manner of being had occupied such a dwelling, so remote, so intact, so utterly self-sufficient with its own air purification system, its own plumbing and waste filtration, tapped into a flowing brook of pure spring water. The power he drew from solar collectors positioned on the south and west faces of the surrounding peaks, connected to heavy-duty storage batteries by several thousand feet of cable. He had chosen natural gas as a backup and starter system, but was prepared to burn wood as an alternative to generate the heat he needed to operate the entire system. There were years of planning, scouting, designing, and physical labor dug into this mountain. He had built it as his last refuge.

He stepped through the front door and looked around, noting that everything was as he had left it. The heating system was working, indicated by the flowing plastic streamers on the vents. He began to unload his provisions. The thunder rumbled from the mountain tops, and he knew that soon the storm would break over the valley rim, dumping several feet of fresh powder to cover his tracks. He was alone, the way he wanted it for the present, with one exception; and in the coming weeks he intended to change that aspect of his life.

. . . 4 February 1991

The mountains were dark spectres in a moonless panorama, and the night air was cold and sweet. Hardly a breath of wind stirred the sagebrush, as if the desert itself had fallen silent in awe of its own tranquil beauty.

Old Jim Greely sat by his crackling campfire, sipping strong, black coffee, listening to the coyotes in the hills around him howling their age old song of loneliness to the vast empty wastes. He was a holdover from an age of dreamers, Old Jim was, and this was his country; remote, barren, hostile, but attuned to the natural order of things.

Emily, Old Jim's burro, brayed and tugged at her tether in response to the wailing calls of the four-legged hobos. Old Jim chuckled. "Easy, Em. They's only singing you good night." He looked up into the blue-black heavens over the great basin, which sparkled with a billion pinprick fires, and his eyes reflected their splendor. "Ain't it a beautiful night, Em? I don't think I've ever see'd the stars so clear. They seem like you could jest reach out an' touch 'em."

As if reminded by their luster, he rolled the gold nugget over in his palm and considered it thoughtfully by the light of the fire. He had caught sight of it just before pitching camp, coming up the slope from Jake's Spring, the ghost town on the flats below. There it had been, shining in the last of the sun's rays, beckoning him like a Holy Grail. He had stared at it long and hard before picking it up. For nearly thirty years he had been combing these mountains, sweltering by day and shivering by night, searching for that precious treasure so long forsaken — his dreams.

Had he ever really imagined he would find a motherlode, he might have given up. He had seen what wealth could do.

As a young man, he had struggled in the city, fought in the eight-to-five world, scrambled for his food and shelter with his sights always higher up, for something he did not have. In those days, he did not have time to reflect upon the night sky or the glowing sunrise. He had never felt the sweet dew on his lips at dawn or smelled the pungent aroma of the sage. Now he had more than he could have ever hoped to achieve through all his city-bound efforts; and he saw it in jeopardy as he stared at the gold nugget in his palm. All his years of searching had been ruined by that one moment in which his eyes had strayed from the path and fallen on that precious lump of mineral.

"What d'you think, Em? Have we got a motherlode here, or is this just a chunk somebody dropped a hundred years ago? Seems to me folks wouldn't have moved on if the gold had held out. So maybe it don't mean there's still veins in these hills. But what if there is? What would we ever do with all that gold? Give it to the government, I suppose. They's the ones own these hills, I reckon. Lord knows no one else would want 'em 'sides you and me." Emily brayed and nodded her head, shifting from foot to foot, and Old Jim laughed. "Well, no sense worryin' about it tonight, old girl. Tomorrow's another day, and we'll find out soon enough what's down there on that mountainside, 'sides the skins of rattlesnakes. And if it is a vein, we might jest keep it a secret, jest yours and mine. That would be one for the books wouldn't it? Let them suckers have their ivory towers. We'll have this here mountain; a mountain full of gold all to ourselves.

"Imagine if we told 'em they'd bring in bulldozers and dynamite; likely tear this here mountain range apart looking for the worthless stuff. I wouldn't like that, neither. This here desert is jest fine the way God made it. Who're we to change anything? We don't need no promoters settin' up hotdog stands and sellin' 'souveeneers.' Nope, I think it's going to be our secret. We'll be rich as Croesus and no one but us'll ever know." He laughed a crackly laugh and took a pull at his bottle of cheap whiskey; only one slug, his daily allotment. Then he rolled himself up in his tattered old Army surplus wool blanket and lay by the fire staring into the fathomless heavens. This was his country, the way he liked it. Silent, pure, clean, unblemished by the ways of man. He thought of the ghost town on the plain below and of how the desert had beaten them, driven them away. He felt at peace, knowing that here, at least, of all places on Earth, the Lord's handiwork had gone untouched. He watched a shooting star cross the arc of the sky and followed it into his dreams.

"T minus thirty minutes and counting," said the voice of Mission Control. "Ground crews commence final countdown checklist. Supervisory personnel clear the launch area. Maintenance personnel clear the launch area."

Eldon Parker stood on the observation deck of the central control tower, overlooking the voluminous main chamber of the Oasis Project compound through a wall of two-inch plate glass. The cavern was alive with activity, most of it centered around the distant shape of the first and only complete ASP, designated Alpha.

Nineteen more unfinished structures had grown seemingly overnight since the pandemonium of his last visit and were well on toward completion. But Alpha was ready, its giant delta wings arched like a huge manta ray's, seeming to hover on its massive landing pads, its nose dropping like a heron's beak, its gargantuan tail rising like a dorsal fin over a hefty fuselage.

Activity in and around the launch area was beginning to calm when Arnold Kemper and Ralph Owens entered from the computer room below.

"Well?" Parker asked expectantly.

"Smooth as silk, so far. If everything continues this way, we'll be airborne in about thirty minutes."

"I wish I could share your optimism, Arnold," Owens said, sounding tense.

"Relax, Ralph. Compared to the Space Shuttle this is a Sunday picnic. Remember, we're not using any rocket power tonight. Only jets."

"Are we on the computer?" Parker asked.

"Not yet. That comes at T minus fifteen minutes. We

decided to go ahead and test out the guidance system with the computer, but our mission control team will take over if there are any problems. We can fly her by remote control if it becomes necessary, the same way we used to control the early manned space capsules. But I don't think that's going to be necessary."

"You don't foresee any problems, then?" Ralph asked.

"Oh, anything might happen. But I don't think we've got much to worry about. This is going to take less than an hour. We've programmed some simple maneuvers to test the guidance system and the jets, and the laser. Our target is a ghost town, here." He pointed to a spot in the Black Mountain foothills about a hundred miles away. "It's on government land. Our people have set up TV cameras in the area so we can monitor the results. I think they might be just about to activate the system now." He flipped on a bank of TV monitors, revealing diverse images from the TV cameras near the ghost town and also around the perimeter of the hangar bay area, above ground level. "With these cameras, and the onboard units, we'll be able to watch every minute of the flight from right here."

Suddenly, an electronic alarm began to hum on and off, and red warning lights flashed in every room of the compound. "T minus fifteen minutes and counting. Secure all outer doors. Activate hangar bay doors. Ground crews clear the area. Ground crews clear the area. Switching to program operations."

Kemper turned to his two companions and smiled confidently. "We're on the computer now. Final countdown has commenced. If this were a real mission, only the three of us would have authority to countermand the program instructions from this point on. Only we three would know the recall code."

In the hangar section, one of the overhead doors had begun to move on monstrous rollers, rumbling ominously like distant thunder. The lights suddenly dipped to dull red, and the stars shone down through the widening aperture.

"T minus ten minutes and counting," said the voice of Mission Control. "All systems go. Air traffic control reports clear air space in the restricted zone. Edwards AFB standing by. Security checkpoints secure. At T minus nine minutes and counting, we have ignition sequence confirmation."

Like the droning of angry hornets, the turbo fanjets whirred to life, one after the other in rapid succession. All personnel had cleared the lift-off area, and all eyes were riveted on the giant black flying machine. From overhead, through the hangar door, the scene might have appeared like a vision from Dante's *Inferno;* the glowing red chamber, the ominous bulk of the ASP.

Parker, Owens, and Kemper sat in leather swivel chairs, eyes fixed on the ASP, waiting patiently as the countdown ebbed. "T minus one minute and counting. Engine functions ninety percent. All systems go. Final lift-off sequence engaged. Standing by with manual override."

Parker shifted anxiously now and glanced at Kemper who nodded to him confidently. Parker's doubts were not assuaged. There was too much riding on the test.

"T minus ten, nine, eight, seven, six, five, four, three, two, one . . . we have lift-off!"

The ASP began to rise gracefully despite its size, engines roaring, their force vibrating the thick plate glass of the observation window. Parker pressed closer to the glass, as the machine lifted on six columns of exhaust to their level and continued toward the opening in the ceiling. Toward the stars shimmering in the heavens, it rose like a prehistoric flying reptile, its strange elongated nose drooping as if to peer inquisitively back into its lair.

"Altitude, five hundred feet," said Mission Control. "All systems are go. Climbing to eight hundred."

"Let's watch it on the monitors," Kemper said excitedly turning around to face them. On the screens, they saw the black shape of the space ship floating into the night, blotting out portions of the vivid star canopy. It bore no running lights and was soon just a dim indistinct shape. "When it reaches eight hundred feet, the computer will convert from lift-off mode to forward thrust, channeling the exhaust through the nozzles on the aft of the wing section."

At eight hundred feet, the ASP slowed its ascent and

hovered momentarily. There came a change in the tonal quality of the engines' roar, which increased; and the craft edged forward, building speed rapidly, rising on a gentle slope.

"Thrust conversion sixty percent," said Mission Control. "Altitude fifteen hundred feet, airspeed two hundred knots. Thrust conversion eighty percent, altitude two thousand feet. Airspeed two hundred and seventy knots. Thrust conversion one hundred percent. Altitude three thousand feet and climbing. Airspeed three hundred and sixty knots. Four hundred knots. Four-fifty. Five hundred . . ."

Soon the ASP was lost to the ground-based monitors, but through the on-board cameras, they watched the Black Mountains loom closer out of the darkness as the ship's speed approached six hundred knots. Its first test was to simply fly on course at maximum programmed speed of six hundred and ten knots for a distance of seventy-five miles, which it did without difficulty. Then it described a programmed barrel roll and rose sharply toward thirty thousand feet. Kemper nodded as the data poured in.

Old Jim had been asleep for more than an hour when he heard Emily tugging at her thether and braying. He awoke with a start and looked around, placing his hand on the stock of his rifle, just in case a coyote or rattler had wandered into camp and was looking to stir something up. But the campsite was as it had been before he had turned in. Emily shifted and brayed again, her ears pricked straight up, jerking her head up and down.

"What is it girl?" Old Jim knew her well enough to sense that she was frightened, and little frightened Emily that didn't frighten Old Jim. She was a veteran burro, seasoned by many years in the desert, encounters with rattlers and Gila monsters, and days without water.

Old Jim glanced around once more, and as his head cleared and his eyes came into focus, he found himself staring off across the valley at the proscenium of the heavens. Something was moving out there in the sky, he thought. He couldn't really tell what it was. Perhaps it was a swarm of bats. No, it was too solid, its path was too steady. Bats swarmed erratically and almost always broke into a million different directions on clearing their cave.

Then what the hell was it? He definitely saw it now, a black shape against the star-spattered sky. And it was growing larger by the second, seemingly headed right toward him. Suddenly, he heard a distant humming, like the sound made by a swarm of locusts. That was it! Locusts! Son of a bitch! They'd eat him alive. The hair stood straight up on the back of his neck as he rose to his knees, preparing to flee or fight. But the humming increased in volume until it became too loud to be locusts. Then if it wasn't locusts, what the hell was it? He squinted into the darkness, straining to see, but it was useless. The object was merely a silhouette, with no other dimensions than height and width. But it was coming at him, and it was coming fast. Old Jim's jaw suddenly fell slack. "Goddamn Emily! That there's one of them UFOs! Holy shit, girl! Let's make tracks while the makin's good!"

He raced to her side and pulled frantically to free her tether from the sagebrush. Emily was braying and kicking, and what-ever-it-was-out-there was getting closer and closer, louder and louder. Now the noise sounded like the whining the big jets made on takeoffs, a roaring, metallic singing of the air whistling through their motors. Old Jim freed the tether and looked once more at the object in the sky. It was almost on top of him, kicking up a wind that raised the dust on the mountainside in swirling columns. If his eyes weren't lying to him, it was as big as any of those jumbo jets he had seen flying overhead near the air force base, but it was sitting stark still in the air, not moving an inch, and he knew no plane could do that, no way! It was just hovering there, right over the ghost town. What in the hell was it, and what was it doing?

He didn't have long to wait to find out. Near the front of the thing, or what he supposed was the front, a tiny red light appeared on the underside, the belly of the aircraft, for that's what it was. This little red light glowed brilliantly for several minutes, then all at once, a stream of blinding light streaked toward the ground, firing in repetitive bombardments at the town below for a period of not more than thirty seconds. So vivid was the light that he had to turn his head, and Emily took the opportunity to jerk free and run off kicking and braying into the sage, as fast and as far away from that thing in the sky as she could get. Old Jim covered his eyes, but curiosity kept him there. When the blasts of light ceased, he hazarded a glance, and saw the ship hovering motionless, above the glowing patch of earth where the ghost town had been only seconds before. He couldn't believe his eyes.

Then all at once, the droning increased in volume and the craft suddenly shot off across the desert, rising into the sky faster than any jet he had ever seen, or so he imagined. It climbed right out of sight into the stars and disappeared. Old Jim fell down on his knees and stared down the mountain at the fading glow of the heated soil. He could smell burnt wood and sage, strong and pungent odors on the light breeze left in the wake of the strange machine's passing. Out in the night, he heard Emily braying. He knew that she was scared out there all alone and was calling to him.

With his legs trembling, he rose and turned toward the blackened plateau. "Here, Em! Come on old girl. Here I am! It's all over, girl. Come back." He walked toward her forlorn calls, trying to forget what he had just seen. But it wasn't possible. He would never forget the noise the thing had made or the damage it had done in so little time. He knew he had to tell someone, and right away.

"That was one hell of a show, Arnold," Parker grinned. "How did it perform according to the data?"

"According to this, and this is only preliminary, it excavated to a depth of one foot, which was programmed, and only in the target coordinates, which we carefully chose as the perimeter of the town. That's why we used that site, to make sure detailed coordinates could be adhered to. We'll send out a crew in the morning to make on-site inspections and collect our equipment. Right now I'd call it a success."

"You're damn right, Arnold," Owens beamed. "If I could

use this laser in one of our experimental fighters, I'd have one hell of a fighting machine."

Kemper smiled grimly. "It's hardly designed for that, Ralph. But it's not out of the question in the future, with the proper development."

"What's next, Arnold," Parker asked.

"We've got a series of scheduled flights, gradually working into orbital missions, testing the rocket system in coordination with the jet system, and finally a deep space mission utilizing the reactor. We'll use Alpha for all of these, and concentrate on working the bugs out in her, then passing the information along to the crews so that the other ships will not have to go through the same trial-and-error routine. That way we should have a flying fleet in less than a year ready to mine the Moon or Northern Siberia if we want to."

"A year?" Parker sounded shocked.

Kemper winked at him clandestinely, and Parker understood.

"Yes, a year. But we'll be flying the others before that, I assure you. Now, how about some champagne? I think Mission Control has just about got our ship back by now."

The three entered the elevator and rode up one level to Mission Control. They entered, but not one head turned toward them. Everyone was concentrating on the returning ASP, which according to the monitors was closing at a fast clip over the desert, low down below the mountain tops. On one of the monitors, they could see the yawning red hole in the desert floor, that was the open hangar bay door.

"Touchdown in T minus one minute and fifty seconds. Looking good," the flight announcer said. "We have a confirmation of landing site coordinates, fixed and locked in. On-board computer control confirmed. Reducing power, airspeed three hundred knots and falling. Two-seventy-five, two-fifty, two hundred, range two miles, one-forty, one hundred, range one mile, airspeed ninety, eighty, seventy, sixty, fifty, range half a mile, altitude four hundred feet and dropping, airspeed fifty and holding, altitude three hundred feet, range one quarter mile, altitude two hundred feet, range two hundred yards, airspeed forty, thirty, twenty, ten, conversion to hover mode one hundred percent, airspeed zero, altitude one hundred feet, range zero from ground zero. Beginning descent."

The ASP drifted gracefully down through the open hangar door, into the glowing red chamber, and settled on its launching pad in the precise position it had occupied before take-off. The engines were cut and the compound erupted in celebration.

"Closing hangar door number one. Confirm engine shutdown. Alpha secured on launch pad." Almost no one heard these final words from Mission Control. Champagne corks popped, people were hugging each other, dancing and kissing, shouting at the tops of their lungs. Alpha was a success. The ASP flew. All their calculations and painstaking efforts had not been in vain. The vision that a few bold men had had was now a reality, and before them lay the goal they now felt sure they could achieve.

Kemper turned to Parker and Owens with brimming glasses of champagne brought up from the officer's club. "Gentlemen. To the Oasis Project . . . and the magnificent ASP."

"And to peace in our time," Parker concluded grimly, raising his glass in salute. But he did not taste the wine. He turned his eyes to gaze on the megalithic flying machine, resting tranquilly on its launch pad. He was trying to envision the future of the world, and what the Oasis Project would mean to it.

. . . 14 February 1991

The days had passed quickly since Davis' arrival in the valley. The storms had swept in, piling snow in drifts yards deep. By day and night he could hear the booming of avalanches crashing into unseen canyons, sweeping the mountainsides bare of tree and rock before them.

It had been a busy time for him, settling in, working the bugs out of some of the electronics, chopping firewood when the weather broke, and just that morning, in brilliant sunshine, trekking up the mountainside to repair his radio-television antenna which had been damaged during one of the storms. It had been an arduous climb, but the air was clean and cold and the valley white as a bowl of sugar. From the top of the slope where he had positioned the microwave antenna, he had looked out across the surrounding range, and for as far as he could see there was nothing but whitewashed mountain tops, glistening in the afternoon sunshine.

As he settled in for the evening news, picked up from one of many satellite superstations, he felt a sense of enjoyment in the soreness of his muscles. His body had been too long without strenuous exercise, and the day had been good for him, mentally and physically. He took the first appreciative swallow of a very dry manhattan.

He was amused to see the evening news begin with the story of a mysterious UFO sighting out of Nevada, and watched in fascination as they aired an interview with an eyewitness. He was an old-timer, and looked to be right out of the eighteen hundreds. It was Old Jim Greely.

"It was like a huge black bat," Old Jim began. "Only it weren't no bat. It was a space ship. One of them UFOs. I knowed it when it lit out with that stream o' far!"

"Fire?" the reporter questioned.

"Not really far. But farey light. Like in them science fiction comics in the papers. And when I looked, the whole dern town was gone!"

"What town was that, Mr. Greely?"

"Why, Jake's Spring! Only it ain't no spring no more. Not no town neither. One minute it was there, the next it weren't."

"And you say this flying saucer shot a bright light at the town and made it disappear?"

"I didn't say it was no flyin' saucer! It weren't no saucer at all. It told you it was shaped like a bat! And the town didn't jest disappear. It burned up!"

"And how do you know that?"

"I could smell it, you derned fool!"

The news anchorman came back on the screen wearing an amused grin, shaking his head. "That was Mr. Jim Greely, one of the last of a dying breed here in America. He's a prospector. And on the night of February fourth last, Mr. Greely claims to have witnessed an unidentified flying object destroy an abandoned mining town called Jake's Spring. According to our information, Greely headed for the nearest town to report the event, but ended up spending several days in the drunk tank at Beatty, Nevada, courtesy of the sheriff there who thought Old Jim was drunk. It took Old Jim several calls to the network affiliates in Las Vegas before anyone would listen to his fantastic story, but finally someone did, and other people started coming forward with similar stories of sightings since then. These stories have come from people in all walks of life, and most of them from California and Nevada.

"Our graphics department has drawn up two composite sketches of the types of craft described in this most recent string of UFO sightings and this is what they look like." An image appeared on the screen. It was the traditional flying saucer or cigar-shaped space ship. "This first sketch represents a minority of the sightings and bears a striking resemblance to traditional concepts about flying saucers," the anchorman continued. Then the image changed and this time a fairly good likeness of the ASP appeared on the screen. It was a black silhouette, the wings drooped at the end like a sweeping batray's, and the tail section rose sharply out of its thick fuselage. Davis leaned forward for a closer look, suddenly aware of a striking similarity of this shape to something else.

"Witnesses having seen this second type of craft—and most of the recent sightings have been of this type—have all reported the same metallic droning of engines associated with it, and they claim that at no time did these objects display running lights in the manner of conventional aircraft. We have spoken to the Air Force about these sightings, and here is their response."

They cut to another interview, this time with Ralph Owens of the Joint Chiefs. "There is absolutely no proof to date that what these people have been seeing have in fact been flying machines. We are looking into the matter and as of yet have found no reason to give credence to any of the reports; but as to the allegations from certain sources that these are in fact our aircraft, developed in secret by the Air Force, let me say that the notion is preposterous. I suggest a better explanation of these sightings, like so many in the past, is that people under stress, for whatever reason, see something or imagine that they see something in the night sky and convince themselves it is a ship from another world. As for the collaborative sightings, our experts can only conjecture that a form of mass self-hypnosis comes into play in people prone to see things that they wish to see when they don't actually exist at all. If this is the case, I'm sure we'll have a rash of similar sightings in the weeks to come before this hoax blows over like all the others."

The anchorman was featured again, looking amused. "And now, on a more serious note, in Rhodesia today, rebel troops . . ."

Davis switched off the set and sat staring at the blank screen, trying to picture the image that he had seen and link it to a shape that kept gnawing at his memory. Suddenly it struck him. Of course! The high tail section, the delta wing structure, the thick fuselage . . . the Space Shuttle! The designs were basically the same. Something else bothered him about the report. What was a man of Ralph Owens' rank doing on national television denying so minor an allegation, especially in the light of the military activity in almost every corner of the world?

What Parker had said to him suddenly came back, ringing in his memory. "It has somethng to do with NASA and with the Space Shuttle Program." Those were the words he had used to describe the Oasis Project. A new technology; The Shuttle Program? NASA? Who else but NASA and the Air Force could develop such an aircraft, if such an aircraft did in fact exist? On impulse, he rose and tore open his desk drawer, pulling out an atlas of the United States. He found the western states and located Beatty, Nevada, a tiny town situated in the foothills of the Black Mountains on the Nevada-California border. It was there that Davis would begin his search.

. . . 28 February 1991

War broke out on the Egyptian-Libyan border at four A.M.
the morning of the twenty-eighth. For months there had
been rumblings, charges, and countercharges accusations
and warnings. And finally the Libyans had made their move.
Urged on by the Soviets they crossed the border into Egypt
where they encountered the forces mustered to resist their
incursion. A pitched battle ensued, tanks and foot soldiers,
fighter bombers belching death; and when the forces parted
at midday, the Libyans had forged ten miles into Egypt and
secured positions to protect their supply convoys and reinforcements being transported to the front.

Parker was notified less than fifteen minutes after the
hostilities broke out, and he issued a statement denouncing
the Libyan aggression and calling for a United Nations
censure and an immediate cease fire. He did not mention
offering U.S. aid or troops, and within hours harsh criticism
came from both Cairo and Tel Aviv. Parker also sent an
angry message to the Libyan government, urging them to
withdraw their troops. But he received no response.

What the world had prayed was only a border dispute suddenly blossomed into full-scale war as the fighting resumed
shortly before dusk and continued into the night. Israel announced that it would honor its treaty with Egypt and
promised to mobilize her forces and put them at the disposal
of her ally. Air strikes began in the black of night, stretching
from the border to Bengazi. A PLO statement summed up
the situation as only the beginning of the end for Israel and
all who supported her.

Davis took a plane from Denver to Las Vegas the morning
of the twenty-eighth, and from Las Vegas drove a rented jeep

to Beatty, Nevada, where Old Jim Greely, had spent his time in jail. There was no doubt in Davis's mind that the old prospector was telling the truth. He only hoped he could reach him before it was too late.

Beatty is a picturesque mining town in the Amargosa River Valley, perched on the California-Nevada border. It is the Nevada approach to Death Valley National Monument, and like the country around it, it is remote and quiet.

There were the usual motels and diners, the bars and gas stations, and several tourist traps to greet Davis when he pulled in around sunset and found the sheriff's office.

"Can I help you?" the middle-aged overweight officer asked as Davis stepped into his office. The air was hot and smelled like sweat and stale coffee. A single ancient gas heater hissed in the corner.

"I'm looking for someone named Greely," Davis said cautiously.

The Sheriff smiled. "If you're a reporter you're about a week late. They done already picked Old Jim's brain and poured enough whiskey down him to kill a jackass, which is exactly what he is, if you ask me."

"Do you know where I can find him?"

"Sure. He's in the back. He won't be no good 'til morning though. If you care to stick around that long."

"Do you mind if I try to talk to him now?"

Now the Sheriff was suspicious. "Say, what's so important it can't wait 'til morning? Things moves kind o' slow in these parts, you know?"

"Do you mind?" Davis asked again.

"No. Don't reckon I do. Can't say how Old Jim'll take to bein' woke up, though."

"I'll take my chances."

"Help yourself to coffee, if you like. I think I'll mosey over to the diner for a spell. You watch out for the store since you're stickin' around."

Davis found Old Jim passed out on a cot in one of the cells out back. The cell door was unlocked, so he stepped in. Old Jim was snoring like an old grizzly bear, his breath smelling of sour whiskey and cigar smoke. Davis raised his head and managed to force enough of the thick black coffee onto his lips to get him sputtering and cussing. "What in tarnation?" Old Jim gasped.

"Take it easy, old timer. I just want to ask you some questions."

"That's poison, feller! Leave me be!"

"It's important. It's about what you saw."

"I didn't see nothin'. Tell that to them other fellers too. I ain't seen nothin', nohow. That's all I've heard fer the last two weeks. Flyin' saucers. Well, there ain't no such thing. I made it up."

"Who told you to say that?" Davis asked sternly, and Old Jim suddenly grew cautious.

"You one of them government fellers?"

"Have they been here?"

"You ain't one of them, is you?"

"No."

"How do I know you ain't?"

"Do I look like one?" He was dressed in a khaki-colored suit with a white shirt and no tie. The old man sized him up.

"No. I don't reckon you do. All those other fellers wore dark suits and ties. Ornery jackasses they was too."

"What did they want to know?"

"They wanted to know what I saw."

"And?"

"I told 'em."

"What did they say?"

"Nothin' much. Did some serious noddin' and throat clearin', then told me to forget what I seen if I knowed what was good fer me. An' that's what I been tryin' to do. But that whiskey ain't no good. I keep seein' it in my sleep, hearin' it roarin', like some dyneesore. It liked to froze the blood in my veins, I'll tell you truly. And it scared the livin' daylights out o' Emily. Made her charge right off into the brush."

"Emily?"

"She's my donkey. She's a good one, too. Right smart, as far as they go. She's the one woke me up when that thing come skimmin' in there over the mountains."

"Would you be willing to take me back there?"

"Where?" Old Jim sounded doubtful.

"To the place where you saw the UFO."

"No way. I been warned to keep out o' there. That's government land, you know. I reckon they got their reasons."

"Don't worry about the government. I'll take care of you."

"Ha!"

"All right, then tell me where you were."

The old man eyed him carefully. "You really goin' in there with or without me?"

"Yes."

Old Jim seemed to make up his mind. "In that case, I'll go. I left a lot of fear out there and a case o' beans to boot. I reckon I got a right to go an' get what's mine. Can you ride?"

"A horse?"

"A donkey."

"I'll do better than that, old timer. I've got a jeep. We'll do it the easy way."

The old man began to kaugh, and kept on laughing long after Davis had left.

. . . 1 March 1991

The dirt road played out twenty miles from the mountains, and the going was slow and dusty as Davis threaded the rented jeep up the gentle slope of the desert toward the foothills. Old Jim chortled every time they hit a bump, and Davis realized what he had been laughing at the night before. "You city fellers think you can jest hop in the car and go. But you don't do it out here. No sirreebob. Not in the desert. Donkeys may be slow, but they'll git you there. This pile of junk won't last to the foothills. Then we're on foot. I hope you don't need much water. It's two days to the top. That's where I seen it."

"Don't worry about that. You just make sure you've got the route right before we head up into those hills."

"Young feller, I been comin' this way for nigh on forty years. I guess I know my way by now. I could lead you there blindfolded."

The day passed miserably, and the heat grew stifling. It was fortunate that it was only early March, Davis thought. Summer weather would have prevented them from ever reaching the mountains, much less climbing their slopes.

By three o'clock, they had worked their way over the foothills and up a wide rift between the towering peaks all around them. "This is the way I come. It's a natural pass. The one the early prospectors followed when they first come west. The damn fools. Thinkin' Death Valley was a shortcut. That's how it got its name you know. Death Valley. A nice place to go if you want to die a slow, miserable death. I seen days so hot you could fry an egg on the salt flats. So hot the sand burned right through your boots, and you had to wear two pairs of socks to protect your feet."

"Are there any oases?" Davis asked.

"Any what?"

"Any *oases*. Watering holes. Springs. Anything like that?"

"Sure, there's some. But most of 'ems bad water."

By sunset, they had gone as far as the jeep would go. The pass narrowed and the trail was only a footpath. The old man climbed out, shaking his head and chuckling. "It's four miles on foot from here, young feller. I got to hand it to you. I didn't think you could get that critter up this far. But I wouldn't take odds on it makin' it back down."

"Lead the way, Jim," Davis said, grabbing a flashlight and a canteen out of the back. "I want to get a look at that place and get out of here before morning."

Two hours later, they stood on the slope looking down on the broad expanse of Death Valley, under the starry canopy, a cold wind buffeting them.

"There she be. Death Valley," Old Jim said.

"Is this where you saw it?"

"A little further down." He led the way to the edge of the bluff, and there were the scattered belongings he had left behind. "Here she be. An' down there is where the town used to be."

Davis started down the slope and the old man looked startled. "You goin' down there now?"

"Yes. I want to have a look. If what you say is true, there's bound to be something left of the town. Ash or cinders."

"Hold on there, then. Let me lead the way or you'll break your fool neck."

They started down the hill, Old Jim in front, Davis holding the flashlight to guide the way. Before long they approached the outskirts of where Jake's Spring had been. From their vantage they could see no trace of it, nor any charring of the desert. Davis grew more disturbed the closer they came to the site. At last he turned to the old man. "Are you sure this is the place?"

"You seen my camp up there, didn't you?"

"Yes, but are you sure this is where the town was?"

"Young feller. I slept in these hills long enough to know

where every town and prairie dog hole is . . ."

"All right, I believe you. But I thought you said the town burned up."

"It did."

"Then where are the ashes? Where are the charred timbers? Why isn't the sand scorched?"

Old Jim looked around and became puzzled. In front of them was a smooth expanse of snowy white sand showing no break in color suggesting that it might have been scorched. "I'm tellin' you the earth turned red the heat was so hot! I saw it with my own eyes. An' we're standing right at the edge of it." He stepped forward and suddenly froze.

"What is it?" Davis asked.

"There's something wrong here."

"What?"

"The ground. It don't feel right."

"What do you mean?"

"I mean it ain't right. It's too soft."

Davis rushed forward and pushed his hand into the earth at the old man's feet. Sure enough it was soft sand, completely unlike the hard-packed salt flat a few feet behind them. He dug his fingers as deep as he could, and it was still soft sand. then he began to dig with both hands, heaving the powdery sand out of the way. The old man stared at him in amazement, then began to help him. At the depth of one foot, their fingers raked the hard surface of glazed quartz, and the old man howled in surprise.

Davis smoothed away an area and looked carefully at the layer of quartz. The beam of his flashlight revealed that it was singed black, clearly altered by extreme heat. Nothing he knew of could change the composition of soil in that manner except the heat of a nuclear blast. But since the old man had witnessed the bombardment and survived, it could not have been nuclear. What then? What else could build such extreme heat? He thought of what the old man had said. A flash of bright light. He looked at the old man. "When the town caught on fire, what caused that to happen?"

"The light."

"What kind of light?"

"A light like in them comics."

"A beam of bright light? Like a laser beam?"

"Yeah! That's it!"

Davis stared at the charred earth as the pieces of evidence tumbled into their proper place. It was beginning to make sense.

"How long did the whole thing take?" Davis asked.

"Not more'n half a minute. Maybe less."

Davis heard the noise before the old man and turned to gaze out over the desert. It was the sound of a passing aircraft, moving at low altitude. He could hear the fanjets clearly; there were six of them, suggesting a B-52, but he could not make out any running lights. The old man began to tremble when he too heard the noise.

"That's it. It's back. It's coming back!"

"I don't think so. It's passing. Listen."

Sure enough, the jets faded to their right. Then suddenly, a thunderous roar shook the mountains, and they looked toward the sky to see a bright flame rising toward the stars, and in front of it, partially lit by its brilliance, they saw the delta shape of the ASP.

"That's it!" Old Jim screamed, covering his eyes. "It's from outer space!"

Davis stared coldly, watching the rockets burn, driving the ship higher at blinding speed. Suddenly, the rockets cut out and the noise ceased. There was no trace of the airship. He didn't know exactly what he had seen, but he was sure of one thing. It was not a flying saucer from another planet. It was a spacecraft, and he felt certain it was one of theirs.

Neither of them spoke as they climbed back up the mountain, gathered Old Jim's belongings, and returned to the jeep. The going was easier at night, in the cold, on the downgrade. But unfortunately, they were forced to use the headlights.

The aircraft came in over the mountains behind them, when they were nearing the dirt road to the highway just before dawn; three army helicopters, flying several hundred feet above the ground in tight formation, closing on the jeep at high speed. Davis saw them and immediately floored it, bouncing the jeep across the clumps of sage like a kangaroo. He was praying for a dry gulch that they could hide in, but prayed in vain. On their first pass over, the helicopters merely scouted them. Then they made a tight arcing turn and came back in, machine guns blazing, tearing the desert to pieces and riddling the jeep with lead.

"Jump!" Davis screamed to the old man.

Old Jim was just a little too slow. His body was drilled with holes before he hit the ground. Davis hit and rolled and scrambled out of the sweeping searchlights just as the jeep exploded, lighting the area with a fiery blaze. The helicopters whirred around for another pass, and this time spotted him by the light of the fire, dodging through the brush. He dived for cover as they swept overhead, somehow managing not to be hit. He came up with his pistol blazing and hit the gas tank of one. The craft exploded in a ball of flame and smashed to the ground half a mile away. He began to run again and ran into space, landing several feet down on the soft sand of an arroyo. He saw the remaining two helicopters circling and flattened himself against the bank as they roared overhead.

For almost an hour, he played cat and mouse with them; then suddenly, they gave up and zipped back toward the mountains, just as daylight was painting the eastern sky. Another hour and they would easily have been able to pick him off in the open. But their fuel had obviously run low, forcing them to return to wherever it was they had come from. That give him food for thought as he began to walk, hoping to reach the highway before noon, knowing that even the early spring sun would boil his brains if he didn't make it by then.

If the helicopters had come from some place close-by, their fuel would have lasted long enough to remain and finish him off. But since they had been forced to return, as he assumed, to refuel, they surely must have come from some distance. He guessed the range at between one hundred and one hundred and fifty miles at maximum. If he survived the next few hours, he would know where to search. What he was looking for, he did not know, but he was certain he would recognize it when he saw it. And if it were the Oasis Project, he knew that it had to be destroyed no matter what the cost, no matter the danger.

He thought of the old prospector he had left behind, and was truly regretful that the man had been killed. He had liked Old Jim, as much as any man he had met in the last twenty years. He had had a quality of purity about him, a simple innocence and wisdom.

Davis thought about going back and burying him, but to do so would endanger his own life, and if he did not survive, the lives of perhaps hundreds of thousands of other. He pointed his nose toward the east where the sun was just peeking over the horizon. In a few hours the desert would be an inferno.

Old Jim lay sprawled near the burned-out jeep, his hand out-stretched in the fine white sand, now stained with his red blood. In his palm he held the nugget of gold, and on his face was a peaceful expression. He had come to rest in the land that he loved, mercifully before it had lost its virtue to the spoiling hands of his species. Above him rose his mountain of gold; his secret was intact, for now, and probably for all eternity.

. . . 2 March 1991

The sun boiled the desert floor, shimmering in mirage seas. Davis staggered on, his body drained of fluid, his mouth swollen, his eyes blurred. How long he had walked he had no way of knowing. He had lost all sense of direction and time.

Out of the rippling heat waves, there appeared a vision; a white coach and a driver standing beside it, staring at him patiently. He wondered why the man did not help him. He tried to raise his hand to plead, but his strength was gone. His legs gave way, and he felt himself falling, but could do nothing to prevent it. He hit hard, with a loud thud, tasting the dust in his mouth.

The Sheriff picked up his radio mike and spoke calmly. "This is the Sheriff. Tell them I've got the fella they're lookin' for. I'm bringin' him in. There's no sign of Old Jim."

Davis awoke with a blinding headache, on a hard surface, looking up at a stained and cracked ceiling. He smelled a familiar scent, but could not place it. Looking slowly around, he saw the bars of the cell and his memory returned. He recognized the Beatty jail. He was too weak to move, and lay motionless, listening to a murmur of voices in the other room. As his head cleared, he began to distinguish what they were saying. He could make out the Sheriff's familiar twang, but the other voices were new to him.

"I found him near the highway, damn near dead. He must've walked for ten or fifteen miles in the heat," the Sheriff was saying.

"Can he be moved?"

"I don't see why not. I fed him some tap water and put

compresses on his head to bring down his body temperature. I got him locked up in the back."

"We'd like to move him now, if you will sign him over."

"I reckon it'll be all right. I don't much cotton to having no Russian spy in my jail any longer than necessary."

Davis, quickly filling in the gaps, realized that the Sheriff was speaking to federal agents. He had one chance, and that was to pretend to be unconcious when they came in. Maybe by doing so he could get the drop on them. He moved his legs to see if he had any strength. He did, but precious little. He lay still and waited.

There was the sound of the outer door opening on a rusty hinge, then he heard several pairs of feet on the stone floor. The key was inserted in the lock, and the door swung open. He heard the men approach his cot. They stopped short to look at him.

"Go get the car," one of the agents said, and a pair of footsteps retreated. "Give me a hand, will you, Sheriff?"

"Sure thing."

Davis waited until he felt both men's hands on him, then lashed out, kicking high with one foot, flailing his right hand in a side hammer punch. He opened his eyes in time to see the blow land against the Sheriff's temple and his eyes roll up into his skull as he collapsed. The agent had caught his foot and now drove it down toward him. Davis tucked his free leg and planted his foot in the man's chest, smashing him back into the adobe wall and springing up in the same motion. The agent gasped for breath and reached for his pistol. Davis flew at him with a whip kick, striking him in the jaw. He heard it shatter and the man went down screaming in agony. There was little time. He picked up the Sheriff's pistol and headed for the front door. By this time, his head was swimming and he could barely keep his feet. The other agent came through the front door, and seeing Davis, went for his weapon. Davis raised his and pointed it at the man's head.

"Don't!" he snarled.

The agent froze, then slid his hand from his coat.

"Drop it on the floor. Carefully!"

The agent reluctantly obeyed, and the weapon clattered to

the floor. Davis had to use the desk for support. He was much weaker than he had thought.

"Out the door!" he gasped. The room was spinning around him. The agent didn't move. "You're a dead man!" Davis roared.

"What do you want?" the agent asked.

"You're going to drive me out of here. Now move!"

"You'll never make it."

"Let me worry about that. Get outside."

The agent led the way outside and Davis nearly fainted in the intense heat of the day. He managed to stagger halfway to the car before he saw the soft drink machine by the garage next door. "Wait there!" he ordered, and the agent froze in his tracks.

Davis stumbled over to the machine, but found his pockets empty. Then he spotted a case of warm drinks next to the machine and opened one, drinking most of it in one draught. He at once felt better and opened another just as the garage attendant came around the corner. Davis leveled his gun on the man. "Put the case in the car."

Sipping his second drink carefully, Davis accompanied the attendant to the car and waited for him to put the case in the back seat. He had to use the car to support himself as the attendant backed away. "Beat it," Davis mumbled, and he did. Davis then turned the pistol toward the agent. "Get in." He watched as the man walked slowly around to the driver's side and opened the door. "In." The agent obeyed. Davis climbed in next to him. At once Davis noticed that the radio was on. He fired a single shot through the unit and that was that. "Now drive, asshole, and no tricks. I'm in a bad mood."

The agent started the car and wheeled out onto the highway.

"Where to?" he asked.

"Las Vegas."

The agent turned south and gunned it. Davis cut on the air conditioning and rested his head against the window, his gun trained on the man's guts.

By sundown, the shimmering Las Vegas strip was in sight. The highway was a golden ribbon leading to the city of lights, and the traffic was sparse. Davis had almost completely recovered, and aside from a headache and a case of nerves from all the caffeine he had consumed in the Cokes, he was feeling pretty well. He motioned with his pistol. "Put off on the shoulder."

"What for?" the agent asked, sounding frightened.

"Just do it and you won't get hurt."

The agent pulled over and put the car in park.

"Get out," Davis said.

The agent looked hesitant, and Davis pointed the pistol at his head.

"You'll never get away, you know. The whole country's looking for you."

"Thanks for the warning. Now get out."

The agent opened the door and stepped out onto the highway. Davis motioned him over to the soft shoulder. "It's a nice night for a walk," he said, and sliding over behind the wheel, put the car in gear and spun onto the pavement, flooring it. The agent kicked the ground in futile anger and stared at the receding tail lights. He looked around and tried to flag down an oncoming car, but was nearly flattened. The driver had no intention of stopping. Cursing, the agent began to walk toward the city.

In the air over western Arizona, Davis settled back in his first class seat and loosened his belt a little. He had just finished a steak dinner along with several beers. The cabin temperature was pleasantly cool, and he was feeling much better. The stewardess offered him coffee, which he refused, asking for another beer, and opened the newspaper that had been resting on the adjacent seat.

The headlines jumped out at him. "Special Mexican Envóy Scheduled to Address the UN." He read the first few lines, and his pulse began to race. "In an unprecedented breach of protocol, Mercedes de Gonzales-Perez, the daughter of President Enrique de Gonzales-Perez, will speak to the full assembly of the United Nations tomorrow morning calling for the relocation of the United Nations to Mexico

City, away from the chaos and degenerating conditions of New York City, which in recent months has suffered crippling collapse . . ."

He lowered the paper to his lap and stared out the window at the darkened country below. On impulse, he rang for the stewardess.

"What can I do for you?" she asked, eyeing him with more than a passing interest.

"Is it possible to make a reservation to New York before we reach Denver? I need to get there as soon as possible." He flashed her his diplomatic I.D.

"I'll have to ask the Captain, sir. There are only a few regular flights connecting from Denver each day now."

"Will you try? It's very important."

"I'll see what I can do."

"Thank you."

He leaned back in his seat and tried to clear his head. Somehow he had to reach her, and the only way was to go to New York. Perhaps if he could speak to her in person, see her face to face, he could make her understand. He had to warn her, and until he did, the Oasis Project would have to wait.

. . . 3 March 1991

Mercedes entered the hotel's presidential suite in the company of her entourage of advisors and bodyguards. It was nine A.M., and she was scheduled to address the General Assembly of the UN at one.

She walked stiffly to the window and stared out at the empty streets below a sullen grey sky. How strange it seemed to see the city that way. She remembered how it had looked to her as a little girl, the avenues pulsing with life and snarled with traffic. Now there were tanks on almost every street corner and armed patrols combed the parks. They had come from the airport in a heavily guarded motorcade, through vacant chasms of silent skyscrapers, past shops that were boarded up, sidewalks that were strewn with refuse. Although it was broad daylight, they had scarcely seen a soul besides the soldiers in their drab green uniforms. She wondered what kind of government could let such a majestic city fall into such decay and she thought briefly of the armed patrols on the boulevards of Mexico City.

She was weary from her long overnight flight and ordered her aides to leave her so that she could rest before her speech, requesting that they wake her at noon. Left alone in the massive suite, she entered the bathroom and turned on the water. She then returned to the bedroom and disrobed. Standing in front of the full length mirror she stared at her naked body, still perfectly tanned, untouched since her fiery encounter with the man whom her father had forbidden her ever to see again. She was as he had left her, alone and unhappy in her sheltered world.

"Hello, Mercedes." His voice came from behind her.

She whirled and tried to scream, but her voice would not

respond. He stood near the open closet door, looking tired and unkempt. She rushed into his arms, unsure until their lips met whether he was real or a fantasy that her troubled mind had conjured up. But he was real. He held her tightly in his arms, crushing her in his passion, and she exploded with sudden desire as all her frustrations and emotions came to a peak in that one moment.

Without speaking, he drew her into the bathroom and closed the door. He left the bath running but pulled the plug to let it drain. Mercedes looked confused, then frightened as he searched for and found an electronic "bug" under the sink. He removed it and dropped it in the toilet.

"What?" she asked, her voice desperate.

"Don't be afraid. No one knows I'm here."

"How did you get here?"

He handed her a towel and she wrapped it about her as he washed his hands and face in the sink. "That's not important," he said, turning to her. "What's important is that I'm here. I read about your speech in the paper. There isn't much time," he continued, "So let me speak first. I tried to call you, but I could never get through."

"I know."

"Your father?"

She nodded remorsefully.

He struggled for the words which did not come easily. "Mercedes. I came here because I knew I had to try one last time. Because I want you to come with me. But before I ask you to make that decision, I have to tell you some things that you aren't going to want to hear."

"What things? I don't understand."

"Hear me out. First, I love you. I've loved you from the first time I saw you that day on the beach. I've never felt this way about anyone. I want you to share my life. But there's no future for us in the world that he's shaping. Nothing is as it seems."

"Roger, make sense! You're talking in circles."

"I'm trying to make sense out of it, but it isn't clear to me."

"What isn't?"

"What he's doing?"

"Who?"

"Parker."

"The President?"

"Yes. He's going to do something . . . more horrible than Hitler or the Vietnamese or the PLO have ever done."

"What are you talking about?" she cried in total frustration.

"He's going to start a war."

"Roger, that's insane!"

"Yes."

"A President of the United States declaring war on the rest of the world?"

"He isn't going to declare war. He's going to create it. He's going to strike the first blow."

"Roger, are you out of your mind? You're talking . . ."

"Mercedes, I've seen a list. The list the Russians had."

"What Russians? What list?"

"Mercedes, I've got to tell you something. It's the only way to make you believe me. I told you that I was on special assignments for the White House."

"Yes."

"What I didn't tell you was what those assignments were."

"I understand that."

"No, you don't. Those special assignments were political assassinations."

She stared at him in shock.

"Ali Said was my first target!"

"Why are you telling me this? It isn't true."

"Yes it is. After that, George Benest, a powerful labor leader. And there were others."

"Stop it!"

"You've got to hear it."

"I don't want to hear it!"

"You must! It's the only way you will believe me!"

"No!"

"Mercedes, listen."

"No!"

"Listen!" he screamed, shaking her.

"Why are you saying these things?" she sobbed, her face

429

streaked with tears.

"Because it's the truth! And I want you to know what kind of man Parker is. What he's capable of. Only then will you believe what I'm going to tell you."

"I don't care about Parker. I care about you and I know you couldn't possibly do anything like that!" She was groping for hope in a world that was crumbling around her.

"Yes, I could," he said quietly, releasing her. "I'm a soldier. I work for the CIA. Or did until Parker turned on me. Mercedes, the men I killed, they were scum. They were filth. They were a threat to freedom and prosperity and peace. I was doing a soldier's job for his country. But then I became expendable."

"What do you mean?" She had quieted, exhausted from her outburst.

"I found out more than Parker wanted me to know. He tried to have me killed. In fact, I'm being hunted as a Soviet spy."

"Why?"

"Because of what a Russian agent gave me in Mexico City."

"Mexico City? When were . . ."

"New Years Eve. I was in the Zocalo."

"No."

"Yes," he said softly and lowered his eyes. "I was there on his orders."

Mercedes fumbled for the words, afraid to form them. "Who's . . . who's orders?"

"Parker's," he said.

"No!" she shrieked, her eyes burning. "You're lying! You're lying to me! You were never there! You wouldn't . . ."

"Stop it! Stop it, Mercedes! Listen to me!" He gripped her shoulders and shook her hard, his own frustrations boiling over. "Stop it and listen to me, goddamnit! There isn't time for hysterics!"

She fell silent and stared at him in horror, her face red, her hair mussed.

"I was there," he said. "On Parker's orders. To kill your father for refusing to cooperate with the United States in the

430

energy crisis. I was not more than twenty feet from him . . . or you."

"It's not true."

"He was wearing a tuxedo, white gloves, a full-length overcoat with a sable collar. You were wearing a black dress and a full-length mink."

"What kind of man are you?" she wailed.

"Not the kind to murder someone who doesn't deserve it. I couldn't pull the trigger. I saw you and I couldn't do it. Maybe if you hadn't been there I could have, but you were and I didn't. No matter what your father might have tried to do, I don't think I could have done it."

"What do you mean tried to do?"

"Nothing."

"No, it is something. You said no matter what he tried to do. Roger, tell me what you're talking about."

"No."

"Yes! He's my father. I have a right to know!"

He wanted to lie but somehow couldn't. "He tried to have me killed."

"You're lying!" she hissed.

"Why in the fuck do you keep saying that? Why the hell would I come here, risk my fucking life to come here and tell you goddamn fucking lies? Everything I've told you is the truth. I haven't got a goddamn thing to gain by lying. It's true. Your father tried to have me killed. The two men who followed us to Isla Mujeres. He sent them after me in Miami Beach. I don't know why, but he had ordered them to kill me."

He turned away. "This is getting us nowhere. I came here to try to convince you to go away with me. I must have been out of my mind. I should be after him right now. But I'm not. I'm here and I'm saying come with me now before it's too late."

"Why did Parker want my father dead?"

"To create a disruption in your government. He's planning to make a move on Mexico in less than six months. That much I know."

"What do you mean 'make a move?' "

"Make a move. Conquer! Do I have to spell it out? Mercedes, the world is at war, or will be in less than a year. And oil is the cause. Do you think a country like the United States is going to let a chicken-shit little country like Mexico keep its oil when the Russians are threatening at every turn? These are cold hard facts. If war comes, the U.S. is going to take the oil one way or the other. But I doubt your father will survive to see it. I don't mean to hurt you, but you've got to know the truth. Parker wanted me to kill your father here, today. But then he changed his mind and tried to have me killed. Your coming here probably threw that plan off, but I have no assurance that you're any safer than your father would have been."

"You mean he would have me killed?"

"I don't know! But I'm here to take you with me so he won't have the chance. I want you safe before I go after him."

"You are going after him? Alone?"

"It's the only way."

"What can you do?"

"Stop him from carrying out his plan. I've seen a list. On it is almost every major city on Earth including five U.S. cities. Four of the five have gone bankrupt and are virtually ghost towns; New York, Chicago, Detroit, and Cleveland. The other is Washington, D.C."

"But why? How?"

"I don't know why. And I'm only guessing at how. He . . . rather the military has developed a new airplane . . . or space craft . . . I don't know what it is. But I've seen it once. Over the desert in California. And I've seen what it can do. It carries a laser weapon that can vaporize its targets. The UFO sightings that have been cropping up. Those are real sightings. Only they aren't space ships from outer space. They're our own ships, and they're capable of destruction the likes of which we've never seen, *without* nuclear warheads."

"But would he destroy his own people?"

"Don't you understand that of those American cities, only Washington is still inhabited by more than just the dregs? If I'm not mistaken, he's planning to strike them first. To throw off the enemy. To buy time, introduce the element of doubt, the element of surprise. The Russian saw it and he tried to explain. But they killed him."

"And you believed him?"

"He approached me in the Zocalo that night. He knew who I was and what I was doing. And what I had done. And I think he had figured out what was going on, or at least most of it. But he never got a chance to tell me. He risked his life to get close to me after being assigned to kill me. I take that as an act of courage, spawned by a fear greater than the loss of his own life. He came to me for help, not for Russia, but for the entire world."

"How can you stop Parker?"

"I don't know. But I have to try."

"Then why are you here?"

"I told you. I want to take you somewhere where it's safe."

"But you must have known that I wouldn't go."

He lowered his eyes in exhaustion and surrender. "I guess I did. But I had to try, for my own sake if not yours."

"Don't you see that I have to warn my father? Maybe it isn't too late. Maybe he can still make a deal with Parker. Then it won't . . ."

"It won't make any difference, don't you see that?" Davis' face flushed bright red as his anger overflowed. "Your father is just one small pawn on the chessboard. Mexico is targeted, and so is almost every other OPEC producer as well as Russia, China, and the West—all the centers of culture and civilization. He's planning to strip the world of every shred of government and organization . . . and God only knows what he's going to do after that, if anything still exists of this miserable fucking planet! I'm sorry, Mercedes. I was wrong in coming here. I should have known how you'd react. It won't do you any good to tell anyone. No one would believe you. I could drag you out of here, but I don't want you that way. I want you to come with me freely. And it doesn't look like you're going to, so I'm wasting my time standing here."

"Isn't there any other way?" she pleaded, suddenly realizing that she was about to lose him again, this time forever.

"Don't you understand? He's holding all the cards. This is his game and there are no winners. There are only survivors. Who those lucky or unlucky people will be is anyone's guess. But if you go back to Mexico City and I fail, you're going to die, with your father and the other twenty million people there. Goodbye, Mercedes." He started to brush past her. She grabbed his arm.

"Roger!"

He looked at her coldly.

"Please try to understand. I can't go with you. Not because of what you told me about yourself. But because of my obligations . . . to my father and to my people. Try to understand that."

"I have, and I can't. You've got to do what you've got to do. I've got to do what I've got to do."

"Roger, what can I say to you? I'm all mixed up. Part of me wants to go with you now and never look back. Part of me is saying that I have to stay. I don't know what it means. Maybe I still love you. I must. I can't hate you. It isn't in me to hate you. But I can't go with you."

His face softened. "I can't understand what you're telling me, because I don't have anything besides you. If I did maybe things would be different. Listen. If for any reason you change your mind . . . I'll meet you at the Denver airport the morning of April fifteenth. What I have to do should be over by then, one way or the other. If I'm alive, I'll be there before noon in the main terminal. If you're not there, I'll leave and we'll never see each other again."

He opened the door and walked out without looking back. She sagged to the floor in total collapse, mentally and physically. Everything that she had thought was real was suddenly unreal. Everything that she had relied on had suddenly crumbled into dust. The game she had been playing had no rules. The game, such as it was, was up to the man in the White House. The future of the entire world hinged on that one man, if Roger were right. And if Roger couldn't stop him, he would die trying, and the last scrap of hope that she had would be gone. Then there would be no point in going on. She knew that she had allowed him to walk out of her life, perhaps for the last time, but nothing would make her get up off the tile floor to pursue him. She had made her choice for better or for worse.

. . . 13 April 1991

Parker and Ralph Owens had coffee in the Oval Office at nine P.M. Parker was grim, his eyes tired, the circles under them large and dark. Owens on the other hand was the picture of health and effervescent with the news he had to relate.

"I spoke to Arnold less than an hour ago. All twenty ships are being readied for the final tests. The reactors are going in, and all other systems are operational."

"That's the best news I've had all day, Ralph. When is he going to start flying them?"

"In the next day or so. Only . . ."

"Yes?"

"Honestly, Don. What is the point of testing them so openly? It doesn't make any sense. After all the attention Alpha has gotten, isn't it asking for trouble? Can't we run them over the valley and let it go at that?"

"Arnold explained that to me. He needs to check their range and accuracy, especially under rocket power. That means high altitude and supersonic. We're going to have to fly them over the ocean to do that, and unfortunately, we run the risk of having them seen in transit. You'll have to keep the lid on the UFO investigation."

But the press is really putting on the pressure. In the last month there have been forty-two sightings, some by persons in - respected places. We can't keep calling these people cranks."

"Stonewall it, Ralph. That's all we can do. We're almost ready, and when we are, it will be too late for anyone to do anything about it."

"The Russians, you mean?"

"Yes."

"They're bound to be getting pretty edgy, with what they know about the files. Don't you think they're going to put the pieces together?"

"Not in time, believe me."

"How much time do we have?"

"May 1 is our first launch. It will be a test run, and no landings. But it will tell us if everything is operating properly."

"Then we go public?"

"Yes. Then we go public."

Owens was silent for a moment as he gathered his energy for the next topic of discussion.

"I've just gotten word on the Middle East."

"And?"

"It isn't good. Israel is throwing in everything they've got, but Libya's moved deeper into Egypt in spite of them. And Syria has stepped up its attacks on Israeli troops in Lebanon, threatening to make it a two front war."

"Do you think they're stupid enough to use the bomb?"

"Libya?"

"Israel."

"Our sources say not. I've had our Ambassador working on the Prime Minister day and night, discouraging any escalation, and so far he's managed to temper their judgment. But I don't mind telling you, the Israelis are getting more and more hostile. I don't think we can go on withholding aid for very much longer, especially if Jordan—or God forbid, Iraq—makes a direct assault on Israel. So far Israel's only pushed past the DMZ in southern Lebanon to get at the PLO strongholds. But the Russians and Arabs are really raising hell about it."

"Any luck with the UN Security Council?"

"Montie's been working day and night, but we just don't have the votes. We're looked upon in a pretty poor light. Our allies are getting nervous, the more we delay in taking a strong stand. We're going to have to do something if the Russians make any kind of show of strength in the Persian Gulf. If we don't, the whole Middle East is going to go pro-

Moscow in self-defense."

"There's nothing we can do for now but wait."

"How long can we afford to wait? I've already told you, I think we're making a mistake."

"We wait until I say to move. You've sent the Fifth Fleet into the Indian Ocean?"

"Yes. They're under way now."

"Let's hope it keeps the Russians at bay a little longer."

"Did you hear the results of the trial?"

"Yes. I saw it on the news. You handled it very well. Too bad we couldn't hang that little bastard Zeitsev. He could have really been a problem, you know."

"I know. But at least we got Kurochkin."

"Any word on Davis?" Parker asked.

"No. He's disappeared. After he left Las Vegas, no one's seen him, and the whole service is looking."

"Keep at it. If he's in fact in league with the Russians, he's a threat to the Project."

"What can one man do?"

Parker looked at him, wanting to tell him the truth but knowing it was impossible. "Davis is a professional, Ralph. I'm afraid to think what he's capable of. I want him stopped. Do you understand? He's got to be stopped." There was just a tinge of fear in his voice.

"I give you my word. Davis is a dead man the minute he shows his face."

Bruce Wilson came home at the end of a long and bitter day battling the press. Since the hostilities had begun in the Middle East, he had fought a nonstop war of public relations. The press wanted to know why the President wasn't doing anything. It was hard to tell them that he was, when all indications were that he wasn't, even from the inside. He himself wanted to know why Parker had done little more than issue warnings to the Russians to maintain neutrality and urge the UN to step in with a peace-keeping force. The country was beleaguered by poor morale, a slumping economy, a failing currency, soaring inflation, and a

President who had taken to sequestering himself in the White House or Camp David or the Western White House, a private home in Lake Tahoe, Nevada, which in recent months had become a frequent retreat.

At least the ordeal of Kathy's trial was over. Sergei Zeitsev had been found guilty on ten counts of espionage and sentenced to deportation. It had given the Russians a black eye, but the affair had severely damaged America's faith in her own security—one more blow to crumbling confidence.

Bruce himself was caught up in the general malaise and had spent many sleepless nights fretting over the very real possibility of a hot war with the Russians. Parker's visitors in recent weeks had been mostly military or CIA or FBI, and the manhunt for the man that he remembered so well, the one with the ice blue eyes, had taken up more and more of Parker's attention. Preston Holmes was almost single-handedly running the country, not that he hadn't run domestic affairs from the very beginning. If it hadn't been for his efforts, none of the public works projects in the West, the work camps, the relocation programs for people in the failing eastern cities would have come about. The man was a tireless worker, and Bruce respected him immensely. But he wasn't the President; he wasn't the leader of the people.

Parker had started out strong, confident, bold. And the people had listened to him, believed in him. But his programs had had only limited success. Like his predecessor, the bureaucracy was working against him, and he had lost the trust of the people. There was of course the indelible stain on Parker's reputation of his refusal to help the eastern cities. And there was the blemish of the diplomatic rift between the U.S. and Mexico. The deportation of thousands of illegal Hispanic aliens had raised the war cry in the border states, causing Parker's popularity to slide severely. But Parker had said time and again that he wasn't interested in popularity and that he wasn't running for reelection. He was running the country, the way he saw fit, so that future generations would be free of the burden of economic dependence on foreign products, free of the spectre of economic blackmail from OPEC, Japan, and West Germany. Parker had not made many friends, there was no doubt of that, and it had made Bruce's job a nightmare.

He opened the door of his flat and stepped inside, grateful for some small relief from the clinging humidity of the unseasonably warm spring day. Even the tepid 78 degrees in his apartment felt good. He headed for the kitchen in the semidarkness of the hall light.

Suddenly, there was a sound in the shadows; then he saw the intruder's shape materialize in front of him, and felt the viselike grip on his throat. He choked for air, but there was none. The intruder stood a foot away, his grip tightening, staring dispassionately at Bruce as he struggled for breath. Just when he thought he was going to die, the intruder released him and he fell to the carpet, gasping and whimpering.

The intruder walked casually to the kitchen, opened the refrigerator, pulled out a can of beer, and threw it toward Bruce. It hit the carpet and rolled against his leg. Bruce didn't move. The intruder left the refrigerator door open, and its dim light stole across the living room. "Drink it," he said.

Bruce raised himself slowly and stared at the dark figure. Even in the faint light, there was something familiar about him.

"Drink it," he said again.

Bruce picked up the can and opened it, spraying himself with the foam. He took a tentative sip, and the cold liquid felt good going down his throat. He did not let his eyes stray from the intruder as he approached, looking casually around the room.

"Now you know how easy it is to kill someone," he said.

Bruce's teeth chattered on the rim of the can and he choked on the foam.

"I wanted you to know, just in case you have any second thoughts about cooperating."

"What . . . what do you mean?" Bruce stammered.

"Exactly what I said. I want your cooperation. In return for which you keep your life."

Bruce suddenly felt nauseous. "Who . . . who are you?"

The intruder stepped forward, the light from the hall spilling onto his face, his frigid blue eyes, and the thin scar under his right eye. Bruce sucked in a breath and withdrew instinctively.

"You!"

"You remember me, then?" Davis said.

Bruce was too petrified to answer.

"I'm not surprised. Half the country probably knows who I am by now. What they don't know is what I'm doing or where I am." He looked at Bruce with a hint of derision in his voice. "You can relax, Bruce. This is between me and Parker."

"What is?"

"I'll ask the questions. You provide the answers."

"I don't know what I could possibly . . ."

"What do you know about the Oasis Project?"

"The what?"

"The Oasis Project."

"I don't know what you're talking about."

"You don't know anything about the Oasis Project?"

"No."

"You've never heard of it?"

"No."

"You're either really stupid or you're lying. The Russians know all about it."

"Then you *are* working with them."

"That's what Parker would like the rest of the country to believe, but I'm not. I'm working for me."

"What is that supposed to mean?"

"I said I'd ask the questions. How much has Parker been seeing of Ralph Owens lately?"

"I don't know."

"How much?"

"A lot. Almost every day."

"Have you ever sat in on their meetings?"

"No."

"How about Arnold Kemper?"

"What about him?"

"How much has Parker been seeing of him?"

"Not much."

"No?"

"No."

"I'd think they would have been seeing quite a bit of each other. What with the Space Shuttle being Parker's pet project."

"I wouldn't know anything about that. I just know Kemper hasn't been around for some time."

"I see. Has Parker seen him at all?"

"I'm not sure. Maybe."

"Don't lie to me, Bruce," Davis said stepping forward menacingly flexing his fingers.

"Yes, he's seen him."

"Where?"

"The Western White House, Lake Tahoe."

"What is the military's involvement in the Space Shuttle Program?"

"I don't know."

"You don't know one hell of a lot, do you?"

"My job is to write press releases, not run the country or the military."

"Which is Parker doing?"

"What do you mean?"

"Is he running the country?"

"He's the President."

"That's not an answer."

"What do you want me to say?"

"Isn't it true that Preston Holmes is running the country?"

"No!"

"And Parker is running the military and the Oasis Project?"

"No! It isn't like that. Parker's in control. Of everything . . ."

"I never doubted that."

"Listen, what do you want with me? I can't tell you anything. I don't know anything."

"Maybe not. But you're going to find out some things for me and you're going to do it in the next two days."

"Like what?"

"Like what Parker's schedule is for the rest of the year."

"No way."

"You obviously don't put a very high value on your life, Bruce."

"Neither do you, coming here. I'm watched, you know. I've got security protection."

"I've noticed. They're very effective, as you can see." He moved closer, and Bruce shrunk back in fear. "Listen to me, boy. There's something going on and I want to know what. Parker's planning something with Ralph Owens, and I think it smells like World War Three."

"You're crazy!"

"Am I? A Russian agent gave me a list of cities and told me that it had something to do with a top-secret project called Oasis. He also told me that it had something to do with the destruction of all the cities on that list, and those were most of the major cities on Earth."

"That's insane!"

"I know. But I believe him. I've seen a spacecraft that the Air Force is denying any knowledge of. I'm positive it's one of ours. And I've seen a lot of people killed to keep me from finding out any more about it."

"You're nuts. Parker would never pull something like that."

"No? Well you're wrong. He fingered Said. How do I know? I'm the one who pulled the trigger. And the same with George Benest, and Cubbi Berone, and so on. Are you getting the picture?"

"You're lying," Bruce panted. "You're just saying that to frighten me!"

Suddenly, Davis jerked Bruce to his feet by the collar and pressed his face inches from the terrified press secretary's. "Fear me, boy! Fear me because it's the only way you're going to stay alive. I don't care who you tell, or how much cover they give you. I can get you any time I want you. You're not safe from me! Now I want Parker's schedule and you're going to get it for me. Do you understand?" He was shaking Bruce. "Do you understand?" His voice rose.

"Yes!" Bruce cried and began to sob in terror.

Davis threw him to the floor. "Good. That's all you have to

do. Get me his schedule and you're through. I give you my word you can call it quits."

"Your word?"

"It's either that or your life!"

"You don't give me much choice."

"I don't intend to."

"How will I contact you?"

"I'll contact you in the next two days. Have the information I want ready." Davis walked to the back door and unlocked it. "I won't indentify myself on the phone," he said. "So remember my voice. And remember, Bruce. This is no game."

. . . 14 April 1991

The President was sequestered in the Oval Office, gazing out over the blossoming Rose Garden and budding trees. The weather was warm, the sky filled with billowing thunderheads. But Parker's mind was far away from the beauty of an early spring.

Libyan troops were within four hundred miles of Cairo and advancing despite heavy air assaults from Israel. The Egyptian army was demoralized and in retreat. In response, the U.S. Seventh Fleet was steaming in the Persian Gulf, the Fifth Fleet would reach the Arabian Sea in forty-eight hours, and the Second Fleet was performing patrol maneuvers near Crete, ready to move in response to any actions taken by the Soviets near or in the Red Sea and Suez Canal. It was an uneasy silence that surrounded the Oval Office that morning.

There came a knock at the door and Bruce Wilson entered looking pale. "Excuse me, Mr. President," he said.

"What is it Bruce?" Parker sounded tired.

"I have this statement you asked for."

"Leave it with Shirley. She'll retype it."

"Yes, sir. She isn't at her desk . . ."

"She's in the cafeteria. Just leave it on her desk. And close the door, will you?"

"Yes, sir," Bruce said weakly and withdrew. He set the papers on Shirley's desk and his eyes came to rest on Parker's appointment calendar, near the phone. He realized this was the opportunity he was looking for, but for a moment he was unable to move. He was plainly visible from the corridor. The book was only inches from his fingertips, and he did not dare to extend them. Yet he remembered Davis' warning and knew that he had no choice.

He thought about walking into the Oval Office and telling the President all he knew. But what would Davis do in retaliation? And what if Davis had been telling the truth? What might the President do? What might Davis do to the President? Suddenly, he found himself pouring over the appointment calendar pages, beginning at April 14 and 15 and continuing all the way up to April 25. There was not a single entry until the twenty-fifth, and then there was only a simple note: "Western White House." Bruce thumbed through the pages for the rest of the year, but there was nothing more. Suddenly, he heard footsteps in the hall outside and frantically returned the pages to the right place before Shirley entered and stopped in the doorway, looking surprised to see him hovering over her desk.

"He asked me to leave this on your desk," Bruce said, straightening the single sheet of typing paper next to the calendar. "He wants it retyped."

She smiled. "All right. Is that for tonight?"

"Yes," Bruce stammered, trying to figure out the reason for the absence of appointments on the President's schedule.

"I'll take care of it," Shirley said, sitting down with a cup of hot coffee.

Bruce left, his heart pounding in his temples, his head feeling so full he thought it would burst. Somehow he managed to reach his office before he came unglued and collapsed at his desk, sweating as if in a fever. His hands were trembling; and he broke a long-standing oath he had made to himself and poured a strong drink. It was just after nine-thirty. Suddenly, he lost his stomach. His head reeled and he bolted for his private washroom, emptying his breakfast into the toilet. He huddled on the tile floor, heaving out his guts. He had never known such fear.

Davis sat on his bed in the Holiday Inn near the Denver airport, pouring over the map spread before him. He had plotted a circle roughly one hundred miles in radius from the place where he and Old Jim Greely had been the night they

446

had seen the spacecraft. It was an enormous area of desolate terrain, mostly desert and mountains, encompassing almost the entirety of Death Valley; stretching from Goldfield, Nevada, on the north, to Searles Dry Lake on the south; Indian Springs, Nevada, on the east, to Lone Pine, California, on the west. Somewhere in that arid, largely unpopulated area, he felt sure he would find the Oasis Project compound, if such a thing did in fact exist, and considering the alternatives, Death Valley seemed the most likely place to start looking. Nowhere else in the continental United States offered a more inhospitable, perfectly tempered climate and environment to ensure isolation and adequate space for a project the size of which Oasis had to be.

On impulse, he called the local Air Traffic Control and waited for a long time before someone finally answered the information number.

"Hello," he said in his most cheerful voice. "My name is Aaron Weston. I'm a writer doing a story about scenic national monuments, and I'd like some information about the air routes over Death Valley. It's part of my story to tell people what to look for when traveling cross country by air. You know, the natural splendor of the American wilderness and that sort of thing."

"I see," the woman on the other end of the line said with apparent understanding. "Can you hold the line?"

"Sure," he replied. He waited almost five minutes for her to return.

"Sir? I have that information for you."

"Wonderful," he said, readying his pencil and the map.

"As of today, most flights through that region pass south of a line drawn through Lone Pine, California, to Lathrop Wells, Nevada. East of a line through Goldfield, Nevada, to Lathrop Wells, Nevada. West of a line through Lone Pine, California, to Oasis, California. And north of a line through Oasis to Goldfield, Nevada."

Davis stared at the lines he had drawn on the map, and to his astonishment realized that they completely blocked out the northern portion of Death Valley, fully a quarter of the circle he had traced on the map. His pulse quickened. "And did you say there were other routes in that area?"

"Not according to my records, sir."

"I thought you said most of the flights."

"I meant, sir, all of the flights."

"I see. Can you tell me how long this has been in effect? You see, I remember taking a flight from Dallas to San Francisco that took us over the northern portion of Death Valley, but these routes don't do that."

"I wouldn't know, sir. I only have the most recent routes."

"All right, thank you." He hung up and scrutinized the trapezium shaped area described by the lines on the map, through which no civilian air traffic was permitted. Under ordinary circumstances, it would have been a coincidence. But he knew otherwise now. Only a few roads cut through the region, ones most assuredly seldom traveled. Coupled with the fact that the sightings in the past two months had all centered around the California-Nevada state line, the conclusion seemed obvious.

Folding the map into his coat pocket, he put on his overcoat, slipped his Browning into his shoulder holster, and packed the small leather bag he had brought with him. His eyes swept the room for anything he might have forgotten and he started toward the door. Something made him hesitate. He had heard the sound of footsteps on the stairs outside. That was not unusual, but still he faltered.

Drawing his Browning, he edged toward the bathroom. There was a small window above the toilet, just large enough to crawl through. Instinct drove him, the animal urge to survive. He closed and locked the door, then opened the frosted glass. It was about a fifteen-foot drop to the alley below, which ran the entire length of the back of the complex. Beyond was a shopping center. The sky was overcast and the light poor. He would have to time his landing perfectly to avoid injury.

Suddenly, the front door crashed in, and he heard the muffled sound of silenced pistol shots thumping into the walls of the bedroom. Throwing his bag out first, he scrambled through the window, teetered on the sill, and dropped, striking the pavement in a crouch, absorbing his weight evenly on both feet. His legs ached from the concussion, but he leaped forward, picked up his bag at a full run, and slipped through the fence into the parking lot.

The agents poured into his motel room, firing indiscriminately, only to find it deserted. Two of them charged the bathroom door, riddled it with gunfire, and smashed it in. Shattered tiles and splintered wood littered the floor, but the room was empty. One of them saw the open window and jumped for it. "He's gone out the window! Circle the block!" he shouted. Then he spotted the figure of a tall man in an overcoat running zigzag for the mall.

Raising his pistol, he fired, spraying shots wildly. People in the parking lot threw themselves to the ground, screaming as windshields shattered around them, showereing them with glass. Davis hit the mall doors at a run and burst inside, hoping to be swallowed up by the mob of shoppers. But the mall was strangely empty, and he walked quickly along the promenade looking for a clothing store.

The agents pured out of the motel room into their cars, calling for backup as they screeched out of the parking lot and roared around the block toward the mall. Startled motel patrons stood in their doorways, toothpaste and shaving cream on their faces, ties undone, curlers in their hair.

Davis stepped into a dressing room with a new dark blue overcoat and a pair of lightweight grey slacks. Changing quickly, he slipped his old clothes into his grip and hurried out again, paying the clerk too much. He was gone when she turned around with his change.

Back in the mall, he put on a pair of tinted glasses and a tweed driving cap he had had in his bag, then walked casually through the sparse crowd toward the east entrance, where he dropped his bag in the trash before exiting.

Outside, people were lined up for a shuttle bus to the airport, a few blocks away; and in the parking lot, Davis saw the unmistakable unmarked cars patrolling, looking for him. He saw several plainclothes agents approaching on foot along the sidewalk, walking quickly, hands in their coat pockets. He boarded the bus with several other shoppers and took a seat near the side door, his own pistol in his fist, shoved into his overcoat pocket.

The bus was only half full but filling, and he sat motionless, his eyes following the sedans outside and the men on the sidewalk. They were surveying the bus, and several of them were conferring. He knew they would search the bus before it pulled out.

At last the bus was full. In fact it was overfull. People were standing in the aisle and the frustrated bus driver was trying to convince them to wait for the next shuttle. But they shoved on board past him. "Please, folks. There'll be another bus in ten minutes. This is against regulations." His protests fell on deaf ears as a woman near the front snapped back. "I've got a plane to catch. You're going to make me miss my plane!"

Shrugging helplessly, the driver started to close the door, when one of the agents stepped on board and looked toward the rear.

"Sorry, mister. This bus is full. You'll have to wait for the next one."

The agent looked angry and tried to move down the aisle past the driver. The driver protested. "I said this is a full bus, sir! You'll have to wait." The driver placed a hand on the agent's arm. "Sir!" he insisted.

The agent turned to him snarling. "Can it, buddy. Unload this bus! Now!" He flashed his badge but the driver was not impressed.

"You got a warrant? If you got a warrant, I'll unload this bus. If not get your ass off it. I got a schedule to make!" Davis sank a little deeper in his seat, behind a man wearing a cowboy hat, and waited for the fur to fly.

"Driver, I'll miss my plane!" the woman up front railed, glowering at both men.

Just then another of the agents came on board and took the first aside, whispering in his ear. The first agent was fuming, but backed off and the driver at last closed the door and pulled away. Davis didn't raise his head until they were on the boulevard nearing the airport. When he did, he glanced behind and saw one of the unmarked sedans following.

The airport traffic was snarled, and it took twenty minutes

from the time they entered the esplanade until they reached the first terminal. During that time, the sedan slipped a couple of car lengths behind as the bus made several forced lane changes, cutting in front of hotel courtesy vans in the process. Davis knew that he had only one chance, and that was to get out before the bus reached the terminal building.

He waited until they were stalled in front of one of the baggage claim areas, then forced the side door open and ran around to a nearby Ramada Inn van. He pounded on the passenger door and the driver leaned over and opened it. "I got a full load!" he said.

"That's all right. I don't have any luggage. I'll just sit up here with you." Davis climbed in before the man could protest and hunched down in the seat.

The driver snorted in irritation and mashed his hand down on the horn. Davis watched with satisfaction as the sedan followed the shuttle bus up to the terminal. His driver slipped into the stream of moving traffic and headed for the airport exit.

A half hour later they reached the Ramada Inn, and Davis entered the lobby and found the pay phones. He dialed quickly, keeping his back to the door, and waited as the connection was made. "Calling collect, operator. For Mr. Bruce Wilson. He'll know who it is. Yes, I know what number I dialed. He's expecting my call. That's right."

Bruce sat at his desk, still shaky from his experience that morning. There was a pile of papers waiting for his attention, but he could think of nothing but the horrible dilemma that had been thrust upon him. He jumped when the phone rang and began to perspire, his heart pounding wildly as he listened to his secretary take the call.

"Mr. Wilson's office. Who? May I ask who's calling? I'm sorry I'll have to ask your name, Mr. . . . Just a moment please." She buzzed Bruce on the intercom. "A collect call, Mr. Wilson, but he won't give me his name. Shall I refuse the call?" Bruce was frozen, unable to respond. "Mr. Wilson?" she asked again.

"No! No, I'll take it," Bruce said, picking up the phone. "Will you get me some coffee please, Rita?" He waited as Rita left the office. "Wilson," he said softly.

"Listen to me and don't speak yet. Give me dates, then last names, then places."

Bruce's mind whirled, because the information he had suddenly seemed inadequate. What if the man thought that he was lying?

"Did you hear me?" Davis asked.

"Yes," Bruce gasped. "April twenty-fifth. No names. Western White House."

There was a long silence.

"Go on," Davis said.

"That's it!"

"The only entry for the rest of the year?" Davis asked coldly.

"Yes," Bruce stammered.

There was a click at the other end of the line and the phone went dead. Bruce hung up quickly, his hands wet and trembling, wondering if security had been tapping the call.

Davis left the phone booth and surveyed the motel lobby. There were a few business types milling in the checkout line. Otherwise, the place was fairly deserted. He crossed to the front desk.

"I'd like a room, please," he said.

The desk clerk looked up and forced a grimace. "A single or double?"

"A double."

The clerk looked around for the other person.

"I'm expecting my wife," Davis explained. "She's coming in on a later flight."

"I see. Sign in, please."

Davis signed in as Mr. and Mrs. Pendergast from Akron, Ohio. "We'll be leaving in the morning early, so I'll settle with you now."

"As you wish, sir." The man slipped him his key.

He paid the bill and walked through the inner courtyard,

up the stairs to the second floor, his eyes searching every stranger's face. He reached his room, entered, and bolted the door behind him. Immediately he checked the bathroom and found that the window opened onto a flat rooftop. His shins ached from his jump and he turned on the bath to soak them, then called room service for a bottle of bourbon, confident that he had lost Parker's agents at least for the present and could afford to relax.

He sat on the bed and studied his map again thoughtfully. There was no doubt now that Death Valley was the site. The only problem was how to scout it. He was looking at close to three thousand square miles of barren wilderness to explore in the next ten days, if the date that Wilson had given him was correct.

April twenty-fifth. The only entry in Parker's appointment book. A peculiar lack of contact for a man running a country in economic trouble, with a simmering international crisis in the Middle East. Why was he not swamped with appointments? Instead, he was planning to vacate the premises for the Western White House, a heavily fortified, remote chalet on the wooded slopes of the Sierra Nevada, overlooking Lake Tahoe. Considering the circumstances, what could possible draw him away from Washington?

Suddenly, he remembered the list. The cities on the list! *Washington!* He was not being drawn away. He was retreating! But April twenty-fifth. What was the significance of the date? Nothing. Yet something gnawed at him. There was a connection. There had to be. Nothing that Parker ever did was arbitrary. Why a day in the last week in April?

"Son of a bitch! May first!" he exclaimed. May first. The Soviet May Day parade in Red Square. Christ Almighty, that was the day! The entire Russian hierarchy would be assembled to review the massive display of troops and weaponry. Russia would be bristling her spines, showing the rest of the world her might, a special warning in light of the crisis in Egypt. The entire government leadership and thousands of people would be sitting targets for Parker's flying machines. It had to be the answer. Parker had planned it with his unnerving, meticulous precision. The attack would commence on April 30, at night, for it would be May 1 in Moscow. He had little more than two weeks to stop the man from committing an act that would surely lead to the total annihilation of the human race.

He jumped at the knock on the door. Slipping his pistol into his coat pocket, he stepped to the window and looked out. It was the bellboy with his bottle of bourbon. He opened the door and paid the boy, tipping him generously. The boy smiled. "Thanks a lot, man." He walked away whistling to himself, and Davis reflected ruefully how blithe the fellow was, blissfully ignorant of his destiny that was scarcely two weeks away.

Davis remembered the bath and found it overflowing. He cut it off and undressed, then poured himself a glass of whisky and flipped on the TV on the way back to the bathroom. As he was settling in, his attention was caught by an item on the evening news program, and he leaned forward so that he could see the screen around the doorjamb.

"In a rare show of candor, the Air Force today announced that one of its squadrons of interceptors out of Edwards Air Force Base, California pursued an Unidentified Flying Object north of Death Valley National Monument yesterday afternoon. Six F-15 fighters tracked the object at an altitude of fifty thousand feet, at speeds over Mach 2, that's two times the speed of sound, before the mysterious craft, which was reported to resemble a giant manta ray, accelerated to unbelievable speed and disappeared. Here is Jim Petersen at Edwards Air Force Base for the latest update."

They cut to a command room setup similar to NASA's mission control headquarters in Houston. The young reporter was standing in front of several large TV monitors displaying frozen images of the aircraft in question. They were of poor quality, but left little doubt that they were nothing anyone on Earth had ever seen before the recent rash of sightings. "This is Jim Petersen at Edwards Air Force Base in Southern California. What you see behind me on these screens is a video image of what Air Force officials are now calling the first documented sighting of a UFO. This object, which is reportedly entirely black and about the size of a modern jetliner, was intercepted by ground-based fighters out of this facility at just after ten yesterday morning. In a space-age version of the classic getaway chase, six Air Force F-15's capable of speeds up to Mach 3 or somewhere around twenty-one hundred miles per hour, gave pursuit for close to fifteen minutes before what the pilots and ground-based observers and tracking stations can only describe as the phenomenal occurred. Over the Nevada-Utah border, this mysterious aircraft ignited rockets and soared away at speeds in excess of twenty-five thousand miles per hour, or well over orbital escape velocity, leaving the fighters behind in its fiery wake.

"When questioned why the Air Force was so quick to acknowledge this sighting as opposed to the countless others in this country's aviation history, and in recent weeks as well, a spokesman said that the Air Force and NASA have no reasonable explanation for the vessel, that is not one of their ships, and that they feel it might present a very real threat to national security. In the meantime, NASA and Air Force officials are conferring and analyzing the meager data collected during this alleged Close Encounter, and will issue a statement tomorrow morning as to their findings. From Edwards Air Force Base, this is Jim Petersen . . ."

Davis sat mesmerized, staring at the screen, but not hearing the rest of the news. He was stunned. Parker's plan was a stroke of genius. By purposely revealing his secret weapon to the public, knowing that the reaction would be at once hysterical and fanatical, counting on the human instinct to accept the most bizarre explanation without question, he was diverting suspicion from the truth and setting the stage for the ruse he was soon to perpetrate.

This was his most brilliant gambit. If it worked, he would convince a frenzied world that it was being attacked from outer space by aliens of superior strength and intelligence, thus making retaliation impossible. Before anyone could act, the centers of government and culture all over the world would be destroyed, leaving him alone to pick up the pieces. How brilliantly conceived. How completely depraved! Yet it had a horrifyingly good chance for success.

Davis poured himself another shot of bourbon and tried to concentrate on formulating a plan of attack. But his thoughts kept coming back to what he had seen in the desert that night with Old Jim, and the potential destruction Parker's flying machines could unleash on the densely populated areas that were its targets. At last he concluded that there was no sense in seeking out the Oasis Project compound. He knew that if Parker were in fact going to make his move on the thirtieth, the only way to stop him was to go to him where he would be in eleven days—the Western White House. Until then Davis could do little else but prepare himself for the ordeal he would face. He knew that it would quite probably mean his life, but he was willing to sacrifice it for what he felt was mankind's only chance for survival.

He thought suddenly of Mercedes and realized that the next day was the fifteenth, the day he had promised to meet her at the airport if she were to change her mind. He knew that Parker's agents would be watching the terminal for him. It was a senseless risk, one that could jeopardize his mission. But he was determined to keep his promise. He cut off the television and closed his eyes, his body and mind drained. He was unaware that Eldon Parker was about to address the nation.

"Good evening, ladies and gentlemen, my fellow Americans. Tonight I want to address you on what I feel is the growing peril in the Middle East. As you know, hostilities between Egypt and Israel, and Libya have continued since February 28 last. Despite my attempts to initiate an enforced peace, the United Nations has taken no positive steps to effect any such resolution. The reasons for this seem clear enough. Our allies and friends throughout the world have grown skeptical of our intentions and our capabilities of backing up our commitments to them. Many are now leaning toward normalized relations with the Kremlin, as we in their eyes slip farther down the ladder as a world power.

"Indeed our history over the past two decades has given

456

them little other choice. We have consistently turned our backs on treaties and friendships. Past administrations have forsaken their duties, and in one sense, my administration has been accused of doing the same by refusing to provide military assistance to Egypt and Israel in this current struggle. But I must state emphatically that I feel it is imperative for the superpowers to remain completely neutral in this conflict, in the interest of world peace.

"Should the United States and the Soviet Union allow themselves to be drawn into these armed hostilities, we run the risk of inviting a war that no one could win. If we were to intervene in Egypt, we would open the door for the Russians to intervene in North Yemen or Saudi Arabia. I am therefore convinced that the only rational way to proceed is through the United Nations, by persuading them to condemn and bring an end to this unconscionable act of aggression by Libya.

"In that vein, I hereby give notice that the United States is immediately embargoing any and all goods from countries involved in this conflict and countries trading with the embroiled parties as well as shipments to these nations. I am also nationalizing all holdings of these diverse foreign powers in this country until such time as hostilities end and peace in the Middle East has been restored. These include bank accounts by major Middle Eastern depositors, and the major lending institutions are hereby given notice not to release any funds to these foreign entities or face the severest of consequences.

"I have reached this decision because it has become impossible to reason with the overemotional and overzealous leadership of the countries in that part of the world who have chosen to challenge world peace time and again without regard for the ultimate outcome of their actions. This administration goes on record from this moment on as demanding peace in the Middle East, full and complete compliance with the Peace Accord between Egypt and Israel, and the immediate initiation of similar negotiations for peace with all countries in the region. Furthermore, I urge Israel to reevaluate its position concerning the Palestinians and the proposed independent Palestinian state. Their refusal to do so can only impede the goal of peace and brotherhood that we all pray for.

"I feel it is necessary to also include a warning to the Kremlin that the United States will in no way tolerate intervention in any country in the Middle East, and that any such action will be regarded as an act of defiance which may precipitate consequences of the direst nature. In the coming weeks, I will be meeting with my advisors to formulate an overall plan for complete bilateral peace in that part of the world, and I will be extending open invitations for foreign heads of state to meet with me to discuss possible solutions. I hope that they will respond favorably in the interest of peace and understanding, and I hope that as a free and brave people, Americans will rally together in this troubled time, putting aside our petty differences in the realization that we are threatened as a nation by the seditious forces of those countries that wish to take from us everything we have struggled to achieve. I am counting on your support and I am asking for your prayers and understanding in the coming weeks so that together we can forge a new world, a world of promise, prosperity, productivity, equality, and compatability. Thank you, and goodnight."

. . . 15 April 1991

The morning headlines carried the story, the radios and televisions heralded the news, and speculations ran rampant. Had the Earth in fact been invaded from outer space? It was the hottest story in months. Overnight, thousands of sightings came in from all over the world; Mexico, China, Peru, Brazil, Japan, Australia, Israel, Libya, Saudi Arabia, India, Russia.

Soothsayers were predicting the end of the world, as usual, warning that these were super beings from worlds thousands of years more advanced than our own, come to destroy us for our petty savage tendencies. Others claimed that they were ancient astronauts, returning to evaluate the progeny that they were the creators, the gods from the stars, the overlords, the returning messiahs. The optimists looked to the heavens and the strange sightings for salvation.

Religious scholars, nuclear scientists, agnostics, NASA officials, politicians, evangelists, pop recording stars, movie stars, sports heroes, people on the street—everyone had an opinion, and the news syndicates devoted hours of special coverage to their innocuous drivelings. Sky watches and space patrols sprouted overnight, and some vestiges of American ingenuity and free enterprise again appeared with T-shirts and bumper stickers proclaiming, "Welcome to Earth!"

As for the President's speech, it took second billing. His warning had been too grave, his tone too severe, his message too real. His critics called it just one more display of his pessimistic attitude toward American society and social reformation. Various power groups, however, were up in arms about his decrees. Foreign businesses trading with Israel were raising hell. Egypt was raising hell. And countless Arab nationals in the U.S. were demonstrating in front of every college campus and government building they could find. They were also promptly arrested and immediately processed for deportation, as Parker had instructed local officials with a special communique only hours before his address.

Mexico was again in the headlines with Enrique de Gonzales-Perez threatening that any act of aggression by the United States against Mexico would be answered swiftly and harshly. Perez apparently intended to continue his trade relationship with Libya and OPEC despite Parker's warnings, and he encouraged other world leaders to do the same.

In the UN, the vote was again lopsided against the U.S. It seemed that there were too many special interests involved to even reach a consensus as to what the best format for negotiations would be in order to proceed to discuss a forced settlement and eventual peace. So while the diplomats played their games, the war machine ground up towns, littered the earth with the dead and dying, left thousands homeless, all in the name of nationalism.

The UFO mania that gripped the world was the one release, the buffer they needed, the escape they had prayed for, the distraction that the troubled minds of a crumbling civilization had needed to deny reality and the ugly spectre of war which hung over the planet like the sword of Damocles.

Davis sat reading the newspaper in the observation section overlooking the main terminal of the Denver airport. His back was to the windows, so that he was silhouetted against the glare, his face indistinguishable. He wore a cheap black wig and a huge pair of sunglasses. The day was warm and he wore only his slacks and shirt, which was open almost to the navel.

Though he had read almost every article in the morning edition about the speech by Parker which he had managed to miss, his attention never left the lobby, where Parker's agents were swarming around every incoming and outgoing flight, scrutinizing the crowds for anyone even vaguely matching his description. He had seen several people hustled off under duress, only to be released minutes later in confusion and anger.

He had no way of knowing if Mercedes would show, or even where she would be coming from. But from his vantage he could see every surge of arriving passengers as they came through. He knew that it was a long shot, but he had had to try for his own peace of mind, so that he would never have any doubt one way or the other about her, about them.

At eleven-forty-one he saw her moving through a heavy crowd toward the paging phones. He studied everyone near her, to see if she had been followed, but there was really no way of knowing. He folded his paper and walked down the stairs, hoping that his affected walk would shield him for the suspicious eyes of the agents who were everywhere, checking I.D.s, watching the baggage claim area.

He overtook her just as she was speaking into the red paging phone and disconnected her call. She looked at him in surprise, then disgust, clearly not recognizing him.

"It's me, darling," he said, his voice straining for a lisp.

She recoiled in shock. "Roger! What on Earth?"

"Don't say another word," he whispered. "Act like we're just old friends. Come on . . ."

"But . . ."

"Don't argue. There isn't time to explain."

"But my luggage."

"Forget it!"

"But . . ."

"I said leave it!" He squeezed her hand hard enough to hurt and winced at the pain in her eyes. "It isn't worth your life!"

They emerged on the street and moved toward the parking lot. He felt that people were staring at him, but remained calm long enough to get Mercedes into the late model Cadillac that he had rented. He slid in after her and soon they were on the interstate heading west into the mountains. Only then did he take off his disguise. Mercedes wouldn't look at him. She was hurt and frightened.

"I'm sorry," he said. "I had to get you out of there. I didn't mean to hurt you."

She turned to him with tears in her eyes. "Roger! What is going on?"

"The Secret Service was all over the airport looking for me. I've been dodging them all morning."

"If you knew they were there, why did you stay?" she asked.

He looked at her and smiled dryly. "For the same reason you came to meet me after all."

She embraced him, her emotions releasing. "Oh, Roger! I thought I'd never see you again. You don't know what torture I've been through these last few days, waiting, hoping I could get away. Never sure. Just last night father was talking about going to Cancun. That would have been the end of it. But when he heard Parker's speech he went into a rage and called a Cabinet meeting."

"You realize your father is committing suicide?" Davis asked frankly, but as kindly as he could.

"Yes," she said sadly. "If what you told me is true."

"It is."

"I also realized last night that he is wrong. My country should be sharing its resources with the United States. Father knows that we could never survive without your protection. But he is a stubborn man. He has refused to face the truth or admit defeat. I know he hopes to make a deal with Parker at the last minute."

"There won't be any deal."

"Is it happening?" she asked, not really wanting to hear the truth.

"It's going to."

"When?"

"I think May first."

"You aren't sure?"

"No. But everything so far points to it."

She sat back and stared at the mountains rising up to meet them. "Where are we going?"

"Somewhere where no one can find us."

She looked puzzled. The road rose up the mammoth slope of the Rockies toward distant towering peaks still snow-bleached despite the advancing spring. He would tell her later that she would have to remain behind when he went after Parker, that there was a probability he would not be coming back. But for the present he wanted her to be happy. There was still a momentary peace to be found in a world waiting for Armageddon.

"Ralph?" Montie spoke softly into the phone, seated across from Parker in the Oval Office. "This is Montie."

"Yes, Mr. Secretary," Ralph Owens said. He was buried under paperwork in his Pentagon office.

"I'm returning your call to the President. He's tied up in conference right now and asked me to get back to you."

"Oh. I see." Owens sounded slightly deflated.

"Is there something I can do for you?"

"Well, I don't know Mr. Secretary. It's about the news stories on the UFO sightings."

"What about them, Ralph?"

"Well, I wanted the President to know that I was tracking down their source right now. I wanted him to know that heads are going to roll."

"That won't be necessary, Ralph."

"It what?" Owens nearly fell out of his chair.

"It's all been taken care of."

"I don't understand."

"Don gave the OK on the release yesterday."

"He what?"

"It came through Arnold and NASA. They got the report and their people monitored the whole story. Everything is under control."

"Jesus Christ!" Owens gasped. "I get the feeling I'm the only one who doesn't know what's going on around here. Just who in the hell is running the military intelligence anyway? Those are my people . . ."

"Ralph, let me explain," Montie said calmly, more distant and reserved than Owens had ever heard him. "We felt it was in the interest of everyone to release the UFO story as it was, since six Air Force pilots as well as every civilian airplane in the area witnessed the chase, not to mention the radio chatter that went on. There was no way to cover it up. Since we're going public in a few weeks, we thought it would be easier to let the story run and blow over, rather than arouse any undue suspicions from the press or the Russians with a cover-up. Can you understand that?"

"But why in the hell wasn't I at least consulted?" Owens stammered.

"There wasn't time, Ralph. We had to make the decision in a hurry and we channeled it through SPEC."

"I see," Owens said. His nose was clearly out of joint.

"Is there anything else, Ralph? Anything new on Egypt?"

"No. I'm meeting with the Joint Chiefs in half an hour."

"You've arranged for them to be at the Western White House on the twenty-fifth?"

"Yes, sir."

"And the Security Council?"

"Yes, sir."

"Good. I'll expect you to keep us informed."

"I will, sir."

"Thank you, Ralph. I'll relay our conversation to Don." He hung up and Parker nodded.

"Do you think he's going to be difficult?" Parker asked.

"He sounds a little pissed off. I think Arnold should have consulted him."

"There wasn't time. He would have stalled for at least a day, trying to rewrite the statement. We needed the publicity."

"If you'd only told me everything at the very beginning, Don, this would have been a hell of a lot easier."

"I couldn't, Montie. I hope you understand; I wasn't sure how you'd react. Kemper and I have thought the same since the first time we met, but you were always independent enough to shoot back at me. That's good in it's own place and time, but with the Oasis Project I had to have complete autonomy and control. Now that you've expressed your willingness to go along, there's no problem."

"What would you have done if I'd refused?"

"That's not fair. You didn't."

"But if I had."

"I'm a good judge of character, Montie. I chose you because I knew you wouldn't."

"You're becoming a politician, Don. You still haven't answered my question."

"And I don't intend to. What did Ralph say about the war?"

"Nothing new. Is that the reason you and Arnold played

464

that little charade in your office the day of your inauguration?"

"What charade?"

"His pretending not to know about your plans."

Parker chuckled. "Yes. I'd forgotten about that. Now, is there any progress in the UN?"

"No. The Soviets are still blocking the vote."

"Good. That makes it that much easier."

"Can Arnold really pull this thing off, Don? I mean, isn't there any way anyone can stop us once we start it?"

"Not unless I issue the recall code."

"And the results?"

"Within twelve hours after launch, we expect total destruction of the targeted areas."

Montie stared at him, awed, perhaps frightened by the prospect of what he was now a willing party to. It was the boldest step in the history of modern politics, it's goal the most far reaching, the most ruthless, but the only rational choice in his mind in light of the world situation. Its means were less noble. In a period of less than twelve hours, the strongholds of nationalism and religious intolerance would vanish forever.

Bruce met Kathy at the train station at six-forty-five. She looked thinner than the last time he had seen her. The ordeal of the trial and the long weeks of FBI protection added to her months of covert operation had taken their toll. Nevertheless, she was free, if living under an assumed identity provided by the FBI with a future of guaranteed anonymity could be considered freedom. It was the price she had paid for remaining outside the walls of prison.

"How are you?" Bruce asked, forcing a smile.

"All right," she said, lighting a cigarette as they walked toward the boarding platform.

"Have you got your ticket?"

"Yes."

"It's going to be beautiful in upstate New York. I envy you."

"I'll send you a postcard."

Bruce stopped, stung by her cynicism. "I had hoped you'd

send me an invitation to visit."

She blinked her eyes but her expression remained unchanged. She was hardened by her ordeal, her emotions deadened. She began to walk again. Bruce hung back, trying to control his temper, searching for understanding. Yet he wanted to throttle her. He ran after her and grabbed her arm, whirling her around violently.

"Kathy! I'm trying to reach out to you, but you won't let me."

"Why, Bruce?"

"Why what?"

"Why bother?"

"That's a stupid question!"

"Is it?"

"Of course it is!"

"I don't think so. There are all sorts of reasons why you should want to avoid me."

"Name one."

"Pity. Guilt. Remorse. Embarrassment."

He now knew the full depth of her bitterness. "You forgot hatred and disgust, as long as you're into self-flagellation. What the hell is wrong with you, Kathy? You got off damned lucky, but you're acting like you were crucified. Remember, you're the one that got yourself into this."

"I know. You keep reminding me."

"Well, you can also remember that you had a lot of help getting out of it. So don't go pulling the martyr routine. It doesn't play."

"Fuck off, Bruce. Just fuck off!"

He slapped her, hard enough to turn her half-way around. Her glasses flew across the landing, and the tears sprang into her eyes. "You bastard!" she cried.

"Don't ever try this again, Kathy. The games are over. I don't know why, but I still care for you. Everything you've gone through I've suffered with you. I don't think I'm very smart, but I can't help the way I feel. I love you, and I won't let you destroy yourself with self-pity. Be grateful you're not in the slammer. Now, do I get to see you again, or don't I?"

She was sobbing silently into her hand, but suddenly she

threw back her head defiantly. "What do you want me to say? Yes? Come see me any time. We'll have a great time. I can take off from my job at the dime store, so we can go on a picnic. Everything will just be dandy." She began to cry and laugh all at the same time.

"You're acting like a shit, Kathy."

"I know," she sobbed. "I know I am. You're crazy to have anything more to do with me."

"I love you," he said simply, taking her hands.

"I don't know why. You deserve better. God, this is insane, but I think I love you too."

"I'll come see you as soon as things quiet down a little."

"I'll murder you if you don't."

"Anyway, you need a little time to get settled in. And I've got to go out West with the President at the end of the month. After we get back I'll take some time off. You've got a fresh start. Use it."

"I will," she said, trying to smile.

"Promise?"

"Promise."

The train whistle sounded.

"I'd better get aboard."

"Take care of yourself," he said, and kissed her.

Bruce watched the train roll out of the station and wondered if he would ever see her again. With heavy legs he headed back to his car. He wanted to disappear with her, but something called a sense of duty held him to his job.

. . . 18 April 1991

The setting sun was blazing on the snow-capped eastern mountain tops as Roger and Mercedes climbed toward the Divide. It was growing cool but the day had been beautiful — warm bright sunshine, clean fresh air — and they had shared the exhilaration of being isolated from the rest of humanity, sheltered in nature's own cradle of creation.

Mercedes had surprised him. Her stamina was far beyond what he had expected, and what he had anticipated would be a two-day trek up the mountain had taken only one. The spring runoffs were in full flow, and the normally placid stream was a foaming torrent. A rainbow rose above the Divide, struck by the refracting rays of the sun. Birds sang in the budding aspen trees, squirrels were busily rebuilding their nests ravaged by winter storms, and high on the mountain slopes deer could be seen from time to time slipping in and out of the sheltering stands of pine. The wind whispered crisply in still barren branches, and high overhead a Bald Eagle cried its hunting cry, then dived out of sight behind a rocky crag into the next valley, plunging on its prey.

They stopped near the foot of the Divide and stood for a peaceful moment pondering the regal beauty of the mountains, refreshed by a fine spray off the river flowing from its mouth. Sheer rock walls rose above them into a pastel sky. The smell of spring mingled with the bite of lingering winter in the damp air.

Mercedes turned to him, a look of enchantment in her eyes. "You told me but I still don't believe it, even now. It's beautiful."

He nodded reverently. Each time he returned, he too was overwhelmed with the simplicity of nature's design, the grandeur of the tableau she had painted, the defiant strength of the landscape she had sculpted. Nothing that man had ever created, nor ever would create, could ever hope to match the scope and power of this virgin country.

"Is it far now?" she asked, having to raise her voice above the rapids.

"No. But we'd better push on if we want to get there before dark. Follow me, and watch your footing. We have to take the high trail along the canyon wall. When I left, this was all covered in snow." He breathed in deeply, filling his lungs with the sweet cold air and started up the Divide.

They followed the narrow trail above the cascading aquamarine waters, and emerged in the next valley to find the mountain tops glowing fiery red in the sun's last rays. Without stopping, he moved on, down toward the lake which had been a sheet of ice when he left. Now patches of black, crystal clear water shown through the thinning icy crust. In the shadows of the ridges, drifts clung tenaciously to their footholds, hiding from the sun, fragile reminders of the winter's frigid hand.

The air grew colder and their breath came in glowing plumes of vapor. He took her by the hand and guided her through the gathering darkness to the foot of the mountain where he had chiseled his home. Smiling with a private amusement, he pressed the electronic transmitter in his pocket, and the rock wall began to move. Mercedes jumped back, looking startled, then her fear turned to amazement as the imitation rock facade slid into its recess and the front of his sanctuary was revealed.

"Roger!" she gasped.

He smiled, seeing her excitement. This moment was something he had imagined many times, but had secretly doubted would ever take place. Now that it had, he knew that he had everything a man could ask for, and for the first time he seriously questioned his decision to stray back into the troubled world.

They entered the subterranean compound and stood in the middle of the living room with its wooden beams, rock walls, and dark stained floors. He dropped his pack on the overstuffed leather sofa in front of the fireplace and helped her out of her harness. She was tired, but her enthusiasm far outweighed the effects of the climb.

"Roger, it's beautiful."

"For as long as I can remember I've wanted a place like this," he said, adding wood to the fire. Soon it would be blazing, bringing warmth and a cheerful glow. "A place where no one could find me."

"I still can't believe it's real."

"Would you like a drink?" he asked.

"Champagne?" she teased.

"Moet Chandon '61?" he responded to her total amazement and withdrew a bottle from the refrigerator behind the bar.

Mercedes' eyes grew wider by the minute. "How impressive," she marveled.

"I'm a compulsive," he said. "That's something else you don't know about me. What you see here is the grand total of everything I have ever saved or invested. The electronics, the furnishings, the cost of building this place; this has been my entire life aside from my work for the past fifteen years."

"You planned it that long ago?"

"Longer. For the past twenty years. I knew that one day, if I had a place like this, I might be able to survive . . ." he let his voice trail off.

She understood his meaning. "Could we survive?"

"We'd have a better chance than most. We're in a remote area, protected overhead by the mountain. The compound is lined with lead. The air filtration system is basically the same they use in the modern nuclear submarines, and our power is generated by several sources, the primary being solar. Even on a cloudy day we've got enough reserve power to operate our systems at full capacity. This is the legacy of modern technology, the only things that man has created that are of use to any of us. It's too bad they should have to be used to survive the outcome of our greatest failure."

Smiling dryly he poured her glass full and handed it to her. Their eyes met and he kissed her gently, realizing it was their first kiss since their reunion. "Thank you for sharing this with me," he whispered.

They ate a late supper of deer steaks he had stored in the fall, and supped a Bordeaux, '67 vintage. Before a crackling fire, nestled in each others arms, they shared the solitude of the mountain. In other parts of the world, men were

470

slaughtering, towns were burning, children were crying, blood was washing the dusty streets of tiny nameless villages. Young soldiers were screaming in pain and terror as generals hurled their troops into battle regardless of the human cost, fighter bombers were streaking out of the sky blasting the enemy with napalm and rockets. Heads of state were issuing threats, countries were flexing their military muscles, limbering their death-dealing fingers, sharpening their saberlike teeth for the taste of battle, and death, and conquest.

But in their valley, there were no countries, there were no enemies, there were no governments or generals, and the sounds of war dared not penetrate the holy solitude guarded by the mountain sentinels. There was only peace and time; time to enjoy life, what little there was left.

"I'll be leaving in a couple of days," he said softly, holding her close, afraid to look into her eyes.

She tried to face him, but he would not let her. "What do you mean?" she asked, already knowing the answer.

"I've got to try to stop him."

"Why?"

"Because it's the only chance we have."

"I thought you said we were safe."

"We are. But the rest of the world isn't."

"What chance will you have?"

He made no response.

"Then why?" she asked.

"Because of what I believe in. And because he betrayed me."

"I thought you were a man without a conscience," she said.

"Everyone has a conscience."

"But . . ."

"Just because I've done some things that you don't understand doesn't mean I'm wrong, or that I didn't operate under the guidance of my own conscience. There are no absolutes, Mercedes. Every situation presents a multitude of alternatives. The things that I have done were in the name of the country I believed in and in the name of the people I love—the Americans. Many of my ideals have changed, I'll grant you that; but I still believe in freedom of choice and the basic principles that this country was built upon."

"But you said yourself that you are an outcast."

"To Parker, but not the country. And Parker has to be stopped."

"What about me?"

"You're safe here."

"But without you . . ."

"Darling, I brought you here to show you an alternative. I won't force you to stay if you don't want to, but I wanted you to make your choice knowing what you now know and have seen. If you're here, I know you'll be safe. And if I succeed, I'll be back. It won't be safe for me out there. If I fail and somehow survive, we'll need this place because the world will be in ashes. If I fail and don't survive, then the decision will be up to you. If you choose to remain, this and everything I have created will be yours. If you don't there will be no one to stop you from returning . . . to whatever is left out there."

"Oh, Roger!" she sobbed clinging to him. "Has it come to this? Have we come this far to be torn apart by something neither of us has any control over?"

He made no response.

She gazed into his blue eyes, now strangely soft and shining into the glow of the fire. She had never seen such vulnerability in his face, nor felt such a tide of emotion rising within him. She knew it was no use to argue. His mind was made up. If he were to be taken from her so soon, then she would not think about the days ahead. She would think only of the present and being with him.

Slowly she unbuttoned her blouse. He watched her, entranced by her beauty. She offered herself to him, her eyes asking, demanding him to have her. He embraced her as he would have an artist's masterpiece, delicately, lovingly, with all the reverence and desire of a man enraptured by a rare creation.

Their bodies melded, their souls entwined for eternity, no matter what the days ahead held for them. This was their moment, their time and place in the universe. Their union was the sanctification of two lives, two loves, two dreams. From that moment, they would be bound together forever.

. . . 30 April 1991

Bruce paced the cavernous living room of the Western White House, high on the southern slope of the jagged mountain rim surrounding Lake Tahoe. The day was gloriously clear, the lake unbelievably blue reflecting the towering thunderheads building over the Donner Summit. He thought of Kathy alone in upstate New York, hiding from a world that was hostile and dangerous. He wanted to be with her but knew that he couldn't. And there was no way of contacting her. He had tried. All outgoing calls were being screened by General Owens' staff.

Since before dawn, Parker had met with his advisors and members of the Joint Chiefs of Staff. Shortly after daybreak, the Vice-President had arrived to join Parker, Kemper, Montgomery, and Owens in the President's library. Owens had come and gone several times looking grim and perhaps a little bewildered, but so far Bruce knew nothing but the fact that they were scheduled to depart for the airport at eleven sharp. Their destination was a closely held secret.

April twenty-fifth had come and gone without incident, and Bruce had a growing concern that Davis had compromised him for some purpose other than he had indicated. Why? Was the man planning to assassinate the President? Had Bruce made a horrible mistake? Would it be better to confess his crime and let the proper authorities handle Davis? Something in him held back. He did not trust Davis, but he was not sure that he trusted the men who were running the country either. There was something wrong, something very wrong. He could sense it in the absense of answers to his many questions. He was confused, his thoughts scrambled. And he was frightened.

Arnold Kemper appeared from the library at just after ten and handed Bruce a piece of legal paper with a handwritten message on it. "Retype this and release it to the news agencies at once, Bruce. As is."

"Yes, sir," Bruce said, taking the piece of paper, his hand trembling slightly. Only when he was in his private office did he pause to read the release, and what he read startled him. "NASA announced today that the reported sightings in recent weeks of certain Unidentified Flying Objects have thus far been impossible to evaluate. While not discounting the possibility of extraterresstrial spacecraft as an explanation of the sightings, NASA and Air Force officials concur that the craft in question are far superior to anything currently in use by either NASA or the Air Force. Barring the possibility that some new reconnaissance plane has been developed by a foreign power, authorities are at a loss to explain or even speculate on the origins of these mysterious ships."

His blood turned cold. Was this what it was all about? The sightings from all over the world of UFO's, which filled the world press; were they really alien in origin or were they manmade? Something told him the latter. He did not readily accept what the public frenzy had so quickly embraced as the truth. And if they were manmade, what nation of men? American or Soviet? He suddenly felt very small in a world grown too large and complex to comprehend. He sat down to transcribe the release, trying to blot out the future, which held only uncertainty.

Davis entered the operations room at the South Lake Tahoe airport at about the same time Bruce was retyping the press release. He was dressed in the uniform of the man he had just left bound and gagged in the closet of his hotel room, drugged so that he would not awake for hours.

He glanced around the small room and quickly spotted the pilot of Montie Montgomery's corporate jet checking over the weather charts and sipping a cup of steaming hot coffee. Davis walked over and stopped by the table. The pilot looked up and Davis flashed his CIA identification card. "Jim

474

Prichard. I've been ordered to replace your second officer."

The pilot looked baffled. "You what?"

Davis drew out a chair and sat down. "You're going to be carrying some special cargo this morning. The company wants someone in the cockpit."

"Has this been cleared with Mr. Montgomery?" the pilot asked, totally confused.

"He ordered it," Davis replied.

"But I spoke to Ron this morning and he didn't mention anything about this."

"He didn't know until a little while ago. I just left him at the hotel. He's going to take a few days off on company time. Don't worry, I'm checked out for jets, multiprops, and helicopters. I've got 2,500 hours, most of it combat, with some commercial time for the company."

"I'm not questioning your ability," the pilot said apologetically. "This is just kind of sudden."

"Don't worry about it," Davis said. "You can call in if you want to check it out." He held his breath, hoping the man wouldn't take him up on it.

"No. No, I believe you. What did you say your name was?"

"Jim Prichard."

The pilot extended his hand smiling. "Barry Keller."

"Have you checked out the weather?"

"Yeah. Clear as crystal."

"You want me to file a flight plan?"

"We're flying VFR," Keller said under his breath.

Davis nodded. "Good." VFR meant visual flight reference. They would file no plan and therefore no one would notice when they dropped off the radar screens with the President on board. "I assume that we're to maintain radio silence until we begin our final approach?"

Keller nodded. "That's right. Funny they didn't mention anything about you . . ."

"This only happened last night. Mr. Montgomery called me in L.A. and I flew in. I understand the locals are up in arms about you landing here last night."

"Yeah. This must be something pretty special to set a jet down here on a landing strip that has banned them. It's all over the morning papers."

"I saw. What time are we taking off?"

"Eleven-forty sharp," Keller said looking at him queerly.

"You want to take me out a little early and check me out? I've never flown a Jetstar."

"Sure. Be glad to. Were you in Nam?"

"Yeah. I spent most of my last tour in a tiger cage."

"Jesus," the pilot whistled. "Were you with the CIA then?"

Davis suddenly grew solemn. "We like to call it the company, just in case anyone is listening."

"Oh, sure. Sorry," Keller said, clearly impressed with Davis by this time. "I was in Nam sixty-seven to seventy-one. Got shot down twice but never was captured, thank God. How did you get out?"

"I broke out. Me and another fellow."

"Just the two of you?" Keller was now in awe.

"I wanted to go alone, but I couldn't bring myself to leave him behind. You want to show me the ropes now?"

"Sure. Why not?"

The Lockheed Jetstar was parked near the private hangars at the west end of the airstrip, under heavy guard. Keller and Davis passed through security without any problem and were soon in the cabin of the eight passenger Montgomery Mining jet going through the prescribed procedures. Davis caught on quickly although he was fairly rusty, but he was most attentive to the fact that the cabin had a door, which was strapped open.

"Do we close this in flight?" he asked.

"It's not necessary."

"I think we should. There're some pretty sensitive negotiations going on."

"Fine by me," Keller shrugged.

They were already warming up the engines when the Presidential motorcade approached, two black Cadillac limousines, sparklingly clean and polished. They pulled to a stop near the front of the plane and Kemper appeared first, then Montgomery and Parker. Ralph Owens was in the next car with Bruce Wilson and Preston Holmes and several of Owens' aides. They boarded the plane quickly and the limousines pulled away.

There was a knock at the cabin door, and Davis looked at Keller. "You want me to get it?" he asked. By this time, Keller was so impressed with Davis that he had almost forgotten who was the captain.

"No," he smiled. "They probably want to see me back there. Mr. Montgomery likes me to show myself sometimes." He crawled back and opened the door.

Bruce Wilson peered in. "Captain Keller?"

"Yes."

"Bruce Wilson, Mr. Parker's Secretary. All set?"

"Any time," Keller beamed.

"Good. Then let's get underway." Bruce glanced past Keller at the other pilot, whose back was turned to him, engrossed in his checklist. He was blond and wearing dark glasses. For a moment Bruce paused. The man reminded him of someone. But who?

"Does Mr. Montgomery want to see me?" Keller asked hopefully.

"He didn't mention anything to me about it," Bruce said. "I think they're ready to get underway."

"Sure. Well, buckle up. We'll be off in about five minutes." Closing the door, Keller returned with his ego somewhat deflated and strapped himself in. He was all business now, and taxied the jet to the end of the runway in preparation for takeoff.

"South Lake tower, this is Mining One requesting clearance for VFR takeoff."

"Roger, Mining One. You're cleared for takeoff."

The jet lurched forward, engines whining, building speed quickly on the short runway, the mountains rushing up to meet it. Keller pulled back on the stick and the Jetstar rose sharply, banked hard to the north gaining altitude out over the lake and in no time was soaring over the peaks of the Sierra Nevada, leaving the peaceful mountain valley in its wake. They climbed steeply to thirty thousand feet and leveled off in smooth air, heading southeast almost directly along the California-Nevada border at five hundred and forty knots. Suddenly out of nowhere, four F15s appeared on their wingtips, dipping their wings in salute. Keller smiled and returned the gesture gently so as not to jostle his passengers.

"Just like the old days," he grinned, feeling better now.

The flight was uneventful as they passed over Yosemite first, then Mono Lake. In forty-five minutes, the Panamint Mountains fell away below them and the lifeless void of Death Valley appeared like a sheet of white linen, spreading out to the horizon rimmed by the rugged Black Mountains.

"Descending to ten thousand feet," Keller said, and began a steady descent toward the salt flats. The air was choppy with thermals, but Keller was good and handled the aircraft like a brain surgeon would his scalpel.

At ten thousand feet, he leveled off and broke radio silence. "Oasis, this is Mining One. Ten thousand feet, fifty miles northwest for an approach."

Davis felt a rush of adrenalin and the hairs prickled on the back of his neck even as Keller spoke the words. There was only radio static in response.

"Oasis, this is Mining One. Ten thousand, fifty miles northwest for an approach," Keller repeated.

"Mining One, this is Oasis. Squawk 0115."

Davis tuned the transponder to 0115, the designated code, trying to keep his hands from trembling with excitement.

"Roger, Oasis. 0115."

"Mining One, Oasis. Turn to a heading of 180 radar vector to final approach course."

"Roger, Oasis. Turning to heading 180 radar vector to final approach."

Keller made the prescribed alterations in their course and both men strained into the distance for some sign of a field. There was only glaring heat.

"Mining One, Oasis. Descend to and maintain five thousand feet."

"Roger, Oasis. Descend to and maintain five thousand feet." Keller brought the Jetstar down and held it. The fighters had never left his wingtips.

"Mining One, Oasis. Descend to and maintain three thousand feet."

"Roger, Oasis. Descending to three thousand."

Breathless moments passed.

"Mining One, Oasis. Do you have the runway in sight?"

Davis and Keller squinted hard, but they could see only the shimmering white salt flats.

"Oasis, this is Mining One. Negative runway."

"Mining One, Oasis. Runway ten o'clock your position. Fifteen miles."

Again they looked and this time spotted the faint swatch of runway etched on the valley floor.

"Oasis, Mining One. Have runway in sight."

"Mining One, Oasis. You are cleared for visual approach, runway one-five."

"Roger, Oasis. Cleared for visual approach runway one-five," Keller turned to Davis. "Checklist?"

Davis began the checklist as Keller brought the jet into the proper approach altitude to the runway. "Airspeed reference set 140. Altimeter set 29.98. Flaps thirty. Gear down."

"Mining One, Oasis. Contact the tower 135.8."

Davis switched to the designated frequency.

"Roger, Oasis Tower. 135.8."

They stared hard into the white glare, but there was no sight of a tower. Only empty desert and the rippling mountains beyond.

"I don't see a tower, do you?" Keller asked.

"I guess we trust them," Davis murmured, his mind racing far ahead.

"Oasis tower, Mining One. We have you in sight. Cleared for landing, runway one-five."

"Roger, cleared for landing runway one-five."

Keller brought them down smoothly, settling on the salt flat runway in a shower of flying white powder, reversed engines, full flaps, and glided to a halt on the desolate tundra. Overhead, the fighters streaked by once, dipped their wingtips and were gone in the dancing heat. Davis was almost as confused as Keller looked. They sat on the runway, looking at what to all outward appearances was an empty tract of desert.

"What now?" Keller asked.

"I'd say we wait for instructions."

They didn't have to wait long. Out of the mirage of liquid mercury came two glistening white limousines. Keller punched Davis in the elbow and pointed. "Look at that."

Davis nodded grimly and pressed his arm against the pistol under his coat. The cold steel felt reassuring.

"Where in the hell did they come from?" Keller asked.

Davis did not respond. He was trying to think of his next move. For all he knew it was about to end there on the runway.

There was a knock on the cabin door, and Keller rose. "Sit tight," he said to Davis and opened the door.

Arnold Kemper peered in. "You two will come later with the plane. They're sending a truck up now."

Only then did the scope of the operation hit Davis, and the explanation was at once obvious and mind-boggling. The whole compound was underground. It sent a chill up his spine.

"Yes, sir," Keller said and turned back into the cockpit. "A truck?" he gasped, grasping Kemper's statement.

The hatch was opened and the heat rushed in like molten lava, suffocating in its intensity. Kemper led the way down the steps, followed by Parker, then Montgomery, Preston Holmes and Bruce Wilson, Ralph Owens and his aides. Davis watched out of the corner of his eye as the Presidential party climbed into the limousines and pulled away.

Keller shook his head in amazement. "What truck?"

"That one," Davis said, pointing across the flats.

A flatbed tractor trailer had materialized out of nowhere and was heading their way. On the trailer there was a large crane. Keller shook his head in disbelief. "I'll be goddamned! What the hell kind of operation are they running here?"

"God only knows," Davis whispered. "God only knows."

The jet was hooked up to the trailer, and inside of thirty minutes they approached the gaping hole that was the entrance to the underground. It was almost too much for Keller to take in all at once. He kept shaking his head, muttering. "I'll be goddamned. I'll be goddamned."

Then they were in the massive tunnel, descending into the bowels of the Earth, the slow spiral downward, the building

480

pressure, the mammoth opening at the end of the tunnel, and the final blow, the cavern itself. Davis caught his breath at the sight.

Lighted as if by the sun, the megalithic chamber stretched the length of ten football fields, and rising from the floor on huge steel support girders with landing pads the size of backyard swimming pools, were twenty of the enormous black aircraft that he had seen in the desert that night and in his nightmares ever since. Like huge bat rays, they perched, ready to take flight.

"Son of a bitch!" Keller gasped. "Will you look at this? What the fuck is going on here?"

The truck stopped and Davis and Keller were invited to disembark by a platoon of tight-lipped Marines, who politely ushered them into awaiting electric carts. Davis made sure that he kept his glasses on and his face tilted down so that no one could get a good look at him as they traversed the chamber past the towering spacecraft. He took the time to make a note of where the limos had been parked, at the foot of a cement bunker, rising from the center of the far wall and stretching all the way to the roof. From the looks of it, with the various levels of windows, he took it to be the mission control center, and just before they entered a small tunnel, he saw people moving high up in one of the rooms.

Without explanation, he and Keller were taken down a long corridor into the dormitories where they were given their own spacious suite, and informed of the facilities at their disposal; the gymnasium, the entertainment section, and the dining hall. They were also given strict instructions not to enter the black zones, so designated by wide bands of black paint on the walls at regular intervals.

Two solemn young Marines, who looked prepared to enforce these restrictions, were posted outside the door. So there they were, inside the Oasis Compound; and Davis had no idea what his next move was going to be.

He washed his face and hands and took off his tie. Keller wandered around the suite, looking at the books in the bookcases and discovered a closed circuit television. He turned it on and found a western in progress. "How 'bout

481

that! *True Grit!* Go get 'em Duke!" he whooped in mock enthusiasm. "Can you believe this place?" he said to Davis.

Davis shook his head but made no reply. His mind was racing. His one chance was to lose Keller, which he sensed was going to be something of a problem, if he wanted to avoid unpleasantness, which in Keller's case he did. He had seen enough innocent people killed and didn't want to add Keller's name to the list. Keller was a nice enough fellow, if somewhat ineffectual. He was a damned good pilot, of that there was no doubt, and had probably flown many successful missions, but he was the kind of pilot who went about his duty mechanically, even though his targets had likely been native villages and perhaps civilians. He had dealt from a distance. Davis on the other hand was used to delivering the kill at close range. Keller would be useless to him.

Assuming that Keller was out of the way, there would still be the two Marines outside. He doubted if he could take both of them without raising an alarm. They had the advantage of youth and training, but he had experience.

He glanced at his watch and mentally calculated the hours he had left. It was three o'clock. That would make it two A.M. in Moscow. Therefore he had less than twelve hours in which to stop the President, and if that meant killing him and everyone around him, he was prepared to do so.

The sun set over the Last Chance mountains, draping the valley in shades of deep purple and blue. The sky was a vivid lavender and stars began to twinkle in the heavens. A gentle breeze whispered from the foothills as the temperature fell. The valley seemed to be waiting in anticipation of the events to come.

At seven P.M., in the observation room just below Mission Control, the President was engaged in a critical strategy session. Ralph Owens was looking particularly severe, Preston Holmes' young face was ashen, Bruce was lurking in the background feeling sick. The others were placid as chiseled stone. Arnold Kemper had the floor.

"Gentlemen, it is now T minus two hours and counting.

482

All systems are go, including the reactors. At precisely four A.M. Eastern Standard Time, the cities of New York, Cleveland, Chicago, Detroit, and Washington, D.C., will be attacked. The Western White House will issue a worldwide alert that the United States has been attacked by an unknown aggressor. Eldon will personally call the Soviet Premier, urge him to take all possible precautions against attack, and assure him of our conviction that the Soviets did not initiate the destruction of our cities. At that time, he will reveal to the Premier that the UFOs reported in the recent sightings were responsible for the assault, and that the Air Force has advised him that they are definitely alien in origin."

"Isn't that going to give the Kremlin too much warning? We're losing the element of surprise," Owens complained.

"To the contrary. It will be too late for them to do anything about it. The city will be packed for the May Day celebration. It will be after one their time, and every government official of any importance as well as most of their military leaders will be in Red Square. At precisely one-fifteen, the two ASPs will dive out of orbit over Finland, knocking out the Soviet ground-based radar systems as they go."

"What about their satellites?" Owens asked.

"Two additional ASPs will simultaneously knock out the satellites monitoring that air space and then begin a systematic destruction of all low-altitude Soviet satellites around the world, thus crippling their communications and retaliatory systems."

"That still leaves the possibility of a limited ballistic missile attack from their submarines," Owens grumbled.

"Not so," Kemper replied. "A total of four ASPs will remain in orbit to monitor and knock down any missles that are launched from any source, including submarines, from a distance of up to 2200 miles. Any conventional aircraft the Soviets might launch will meet a similar fate. With the Soviet radar systems neutralized, the ASPs will descend on their targets—eight ships in all—and begin their programmed destruction of some 20 military installations. Interception of any kind is all but impossible since the ASPs will be traveling at Mach 10 and are programmed to knock down any unidentified aircraft or missiles at a range of 200 miles."

"This is incredible," Preston Holmes muttered.

"The remaining eight ASPs will begin attacking key military installations and major government complexes throughout the rest of the world."

"At that time," Parker interrupted, "I will take immediate action to form the first global government. I want to stress that these attacks are not targeted for population centers, but rather military and government installations."

"But what about New York and D.C., and the others?" Holmes gasped.

"These attacks will be limited. The White House and Capitol building will go, but we've arranged for a last minute evacuation of all personnel on the premises. The other cities will suffer destruction only in their central business districts which, as of today, are virtually deserted."

"What if the Soviets are able to penetrate our air space, Mr. President?" Owens asked solemnly. ". . . with conventional aircraft, I mean."

"It's highly unlikely, but SAC will be scrambled just prior to the attack on D.C., and the entire armed services will be on Red Alert. We'll be waiting for them. You, of course, will coordinate that aspect of the operation."

"The Joint Chiefs are in the war room downstairs," Owens acknowledged.

"Any local outbreaks of violence will be ignored unless they pose the possibility of nuclear confrontation. If that is the case, we will move swiftly with the ASPs and conventional weaponry to eliminate the problem areas. By this time tomorrow, gentlemen, I will have established the first Democratic World Republic. There will be no countries, no nationalities, no religious differences, no conflicting political systems. We will for the first time be one race of man, one civilization, sharing our resources equally for the betterment of all mankind and world peace. Hunger, deprivation, ignorance, persecution, will be nonexistent within the next decade. If all goes well, this will be the war to end all wars."

"What is the estimate in the loss of human lives?" Preston

Holmes asked dazedly.

"In the low millions," Parker said gravely. "It is estimated that in an all-out nuclear confrontation, only forty percent of our population would survive, whereas 90 percent of all the Soviet population would escape the initial conflict. This still equates into hundreds of millions of lives in our two countries alone. I ask you to compare this with the mere ten million or so that will be sacrificed in our initial assault."

"Goddamnit, Eldon!" Holmes shrieked, jumping to his feet. "This is insanity. You're committing mass murder!"

"This is war, Preston. And the alternative is complete annihilation of the human race in a nuclear confrontation that is almost certain to arise over the Middle East. There's no way it can be avoided. We must choose the lesser of the two evils. If we don't strike while we still have the advantage of technology, the Russians will eventually manage to cut us off and starve us. Believe me, if they could do what we are planning to do, they would."

"I won't stand for it!" Holmes shouted. "Eldon, you're mad! I've listened all morning to this like it was a bad dream, hoping I would wake up and it would end. I've had it. You're not going through with it!"

"I'm afraid you have no choice in the matter, Preston. The countdown is running. Be thankful that you are one of the chosen survivors."

"Thankful? Jesus Christ, man! Think of what you're saying! Those are real people you're talking about annihilating, not statistics. For God's sake listen to reason!"

Parker stared at him grimly, but made no direct response. He looked at Kemper, who nodded and pressed an intercom buzzer. Two guards came in from the outer foyer, heavily armed.

"Confine the Vice-President to his quarters for the next twenty-four hours," Parker said coldly.

The staff sergeant saluted and approached Holmes. "If you'll come with us, sir."

"Don, in the name of all that's holy! Stop this before it's too late!"

Parker glared at him in icy silence.

Bruce Wilson stepped forward, his voice quavering. "Mr. Parker. I cannot condone your actions. I hereby tender my resignation. I don't want any part of this." He was pale and trembling.

Parker nodded and the guards took Bruce in tow as well. They were escorted from the room and the door hissed shut behind them. Those who remained were silent. They knew the horror of what they were about to do, but they were committed.

Davis and Keller were returning with their escorts from the mess hall. Davis had not been hungry, but he had eaten to keep up his strength and to avoid suspicion. In the corridor, they saw a detail approaching with two men under guard. As they drew closer, Davis saw the Vice-President and then Bruce Wilson. They passed and at the moment Bruce spotted him. In one horrified instant, the look in his eyes went from shock to despair. Davis understood at once. They knew about Parker's plan at last and had refused to cooperate. In them he saw the way to Parker.

He and Keller were ushered into their own suite and Keller turned to him the moment they were alone. "Did you see that? That was the Vice-President. He was under arrest. And the Press Secretary, too! What the hell is going on?"

Davis stared at him sternly. "Listen to me, Keller. For your own good, no matter what happens in the next couple of hours, stay in this room. I don't have time to explain, but there's nothing you can do, and I don't want you in my way."

"What the hell are you talking about?"

"It's better that you don't know. Just keep out of my way and you won't get hurt. Try to interfere and I'll kill you."

Keller stood frozen in astonishment near the bar. "Who are you?" he gasped.

"I said no questions! Make yourself a drink and keep your mouth shut." Davis turned away and paced the room. He had to have time to think.

Keller poured a glassful of gin with trembling hands, then slumped on the couch downing it in huge swallows. He glared at Davis but was afraid to move. After several moments, Davis turned to him.

"I'm going to get those guards in here. I need one of their uniforms. You go into the bedroom and stay there until I'm gone."

Keller rose, confused and suddenly angry. "Listen, if you'd just tell me what's going on, maybe I could help. I know something . . ."

"I told you I don't need your help! You'll only get in the way."

"If you think you can take those two by yourself, you're crazy. They'll cut you apart. This isn't Vietnam and those aren't V.C. They're crack Marines!"

Davis thought it over carefully and realized that the man was right. He didn't like putting his trust in someone he didn't know, but he had to take the chance. "All right, Keller. I'll let you help me take the guards. But that's it. And if you turn on me, you're the first to get it." He pulled his Browning from under his shirt and snapped the safety off. Keller's eyes widened at the sight of it.

"Smash that bottle over the bar," Davis said.

"What?"

"You heard me. And be ready to take down the second one in."

"Whatever you say," Keller said, picking up the bottle.

"Go!" Davis said.

Keller dashed the bottle on the countertop and almost instantly the door burst open and the two guards appeared, weapons ready. Davis was by the door and seized the first one whirling him around and smashing the pistol across his face. A stream of blood gushed from the man's broken nose but he fought back. Davis struck him in the throat and the Marine collapsed, sucking for air.

Keller in the meantime had tackled the second one in the doorway, knocking the rifle from his hand, and immobilizing him with several well-placed karate punches to the side of the head. A final kick in the stomach silenced him, and Keller dragged him inside.

Davis looked at Keller's work appreciatively and nodded.

"Nicely done." He was thinking fast. "You still want in?"

"If you tell me what the hell is going on."

"I'm going after the President. If necessary I'm going to kill him."

"Son of a bitch!"

"If I don't he's going to start World War Three. Now I haven't got time to explain any more. Are you in or out?"

"Is that why the Vice-President is under arrest?"

"Yes."

"Then I'm in. What do I do?"

"Get into one of those uniforms, then find something to tie those two up with."

Moments later, Davis and Keller appeared in the corridor wearing the guards' uniforms and approached the Vice-President's suite, walking in formation. The Marines posted outside the suite were caught off guard. Davis pointed his weapon at their heads while Keller disarmed them before they knew what had hit them.

"Open it," he ordered.

The Marines remained rigid. Davis slammed the muzzle of his rifle into the nearest soldier's ribs with a resounding smack. The man yelped and doubled over in pain. Davis turned on the second one.

"I said open it."

The man obeyed and they pushed their prisoners in first and followed. They found Preston Holmes in his shirtsleeves, well into a bottle of brandy. Bruce Wilson was sitting on the edge of the couch playing solitaire, also into the sauce. Both looked up in surprise, and Bruce paled at the sight of Davis.

"Keep quiet, Wilson," Davis ordered. "Mr. Vice-President, are you all right?"

"Who the hell are you?" Holmes snapped.

"My name is Roger Davis. I work for the CIA. Or did until Parker sold me out as a double agent."

"You're the one they're looking for?" Holmes gasped. "What are you doing here?"

"Trying to stop him before it's too late."

"Then you know about his plan?"

"I have a general idea."

488

"But how?"

"There isn't time to explain. You had a falling out with him, right?"

"Yes."

"Well, I need your help to get to him."

Holmes looked questioningly at Wilson, who nodded his agreement. "What can we do?"

"Call upstairs and speak to Parker. Tell him you've changed your mind and want a meeting with him. We'll make up the guard detail. It's our only chance."

"Then what?" Holmes asked, afraid to hear the answer.

"That's up to him."

"What do you mean?"

"I mean if he listens to reason and calls off the attack, he may get out of here alive. If not . . ."

"You'll kill him . . ." Holmes said, his voice hollow.

"If I have to."

Holmes looked at the captive Marines. "Do you men know what's going on up there?"

"We're allowed to give our name, rank, and serial number, sir!" one of them responded.

"Goddamnit man! I'm the fucking Vice-President of the United States! And I want some answers now! Do you know what's going on up there?"

"It's my understanding, sir, that this is a NASA project. It's objective is to mine the moon of its natural resources and transport them back to the United States for processing and consumption!"

"Wrong." Davis interrupted. "Those ships are going to destroy every major center of government on Earth."

"He's telling the truth," Holmes said. "By tomorrow afternoon, millions of people will be dead and Eldon Parker will be responsible. We need you help to stop him!"

The young Marines looked baffled, then anguished as they realized the implications of the decision they had to make. They were not trained to do so.

"Your alternative is to enter the combat zone unarmed. You're going up there with us, like it or not," Davis said. "And you're dead men if you try to resist."

The guards made no response.

"Have it your way," Davis said. "Keller, unload their weapons. Mr. Holmes. Call up there and convince the President you've changed our mind."

Bruce rose shakily from the couch as Preston picked up the telephone. "Connect me with the observation deck in the command center. This is Preston Holmes. I want to speak to the President." He nodded as the connection was made. "This is Holmes. I want to speak to Eldon." He paused and his face reddened in anger. "Tell him I've changed my mind. I want to talk to him." Again he paused and fumbled with the phone cord searching for control. "Eldon? I want to speak to you. Wait, listen to me. I've . . . changed my mind. I want to come up. Uh, I don't think Bruce is in any condition to. He's drunk. Yes. We've both had a few and I've had time to think things over. I'd like to discuss it with you. I'd like to be there. Will you send the order down? All right. Yes, I'll be waiting for them." He hung up, visibly shaken. "I don't know if he bought it, but he said he would send the order down."

"All right, let's move," Davis said.

"What about the guard detail?" Keller asked.

"We'd better be gone before they get here. Give them back their weapons."

Keller gave the Marines their empty weapons.

"You men lead the way; any tricks and you're dead. Got that?" Davis said.

The Marines moved down the hall toward the restricted zone. Holmes and Wilson were next, then came Davis and Keller, their rifles trained on the two Marines. Past checkpoint after checkpoint, they made their way toward the command center elevator lobby.

Suddenly the voice of Mission Control came over the P.A. system. "T minus ten minutes and counting. Secure all outer doors. All systems are go. Open launch bay doors." A dull metallic horn began to sound at regular intervals, and security details ran past them intent upon their duties. At last they reached the elevator lobby below the command center. "T minus nine minutes and counting," Mission Control announced. "We have ignition sequence confirmation. All systems are go."

Through the ten-foot-thick concrete wall they could feel the vibration of the powerful fanjets revving up. Precious seconds ticked off as they waited for the elevator.

Suddenly, behind them, they heard the pounding of hard-soled boots and turning, they saw an armed platoon rushing after them. "Halt!" their commander ordered. "Drop your weapons!"

Davis stepped clear of the others and sprayed a blast at the oncoming soldiers, scattering them and dropping several. They returned fire and Keller joined in, helping to keep the platoon pinned down. The elevator was one floor above them.

"Come on! Come on!" Davis urged. He fired another volley into the corridor. Warning sirens began to sound and the lights went dull red.

"T minus eight minutes and counting. Security details to command center lobby. Secure all posts. Launch bay doors open. All systems go."

The elevator arrived. "In!" Davis shouted, pushing Holmes and Wilson first. Keller followed. Davis shoved the two prisoners out of the way and started in. One of them grabbed for him, but Keller riddled the man with bullets. The other bolted for cover and Davis stepped inside.

"What floor?" he shouted.

"Four!" Holmes screamed.

Bullets were hitting the walls, spraying them with plaster. Davis punched the button and the doors closed. The elevator started to rise.

They waited breathlessly, gathering their wits. Davis and Keller fed fresh clips into their weapons, watching the numbers click off. Two, three . . .

"Be ready!" Davis warned. Four! The doors opened. "Flatten!" Davis shouted.

The cabin was showered with bullets. Davis whipped his weapon around the corner and opened up. Marines went down screaming in the foyer outside.

"Now!" Davis yelled, and bolted into the open firing short

blasts in a wide arc, cutting down the soldiers that were waiting for them. The others followed. Holmes was the first hit, his chest exploding as the bullets struck; and he dropped like a stone to the concrete floor. Bruce dove for cover in an adjacent corridor and was hit in the legs. He collapsed screaming in pain. Keller and Davis rushed the remaining troops, their weapons glowing red hot, spitting death into the corridor. Keller was hit in the stomach and spun around, firing his weapon spasmodically into the air before he too crashed to the floor and lay motionless.

Davis, miraculously untouched, rushed past the carnage stepping over the bodies, his shoes slipping in the growing tide of blood awash on the floor. He slammed through the door of the observation room prepared to open fire, but found it empty. He saw an open doorway, with stairs leading up. Outside in the foyer he heard more troops approaching, and turning he bolted the door, then jumped for the stairwell, taking the steps three at a time, his weapon poised. Several Marines appeared above him on the landing, but he opened fire, dropping them before they could respond. He reached the top an instant later, exploding into Mission Control to find Parker's entourage clustered together with the horrified technicians.

Ralph Owens raised his .45 automatic and fired, his shot slamming into the cement inches from Davis' head. Davis returned his fire and the general reeled back into one of the computer consoles spouting geysers of blood in a shower of electric sparks. He hit the floor and no one made a move for his weapon. They were all unarmed.

"Parker!" Davis screamed, his blood boiling.

Parker stared at him with hatred in his eyes.

"T minus four minutes and counting," said the voice of Mission Control.

"Call it off, Parker!" Davis yelled.

"Give up, Davis. You're beaten. It's too late." Parker was as cold as ice.

"Parker, I'm warning you!"

The sound of boots on the metal stairs turned him back around. He slammed the door and bolted it.

"T minus three minutes and counting," said Mission Control. "All systems are go."

Davis sprayed the computers with rifle fire, showering the room with sparks. Red warning lights began to flash.

"It's too late!" Kemper shouted.

"You programmed it. You can stop it!"

"I can't!" Kemper returned. "It's on the computer!"

"Stop the computer!" Davis again blasted the consoles, but to no avail.

"T minus two minutes," Mission Control droned.

"It's no use, Davis," Parker said calmly. "This console isn't running the program. You're beaten!"

The guards began to lunge against the stairwell door and Davis opened fire, forcing them to beat a quick retreat.

"Parker. You know the recall code. There's bound to be a recall code. Use it you son of a bitch or you're a dead man!"

"Listen to me, Davis," Parker said. "It's the only way. In a few hours there will be no enemy, there will be no more wars."

"You're out of your mind! It's suicide!"

"T minus one minute and counting. Engine functions ninety percent. All systems are go."

"Kemper, what's the recall code?" Davis roared, out of control.

"Tell him nothing!" Parker shouted.

"Either you tell me the code or you die, Kemper."

"Why are you fighting us, Davis?" Parker asked, drawing out the seconds. "Isn't this what we've planned for? Everything we've worked for is riding on this moment."

"Not we, Parker. You! You sold me out, remember?"

"I had to. I had to do it, don't you see? I didn't know what the Russian had told you. I couldn't take that chance! But now it's all over. Join us! Be one of us!"

"Kemper, I'm warning you!" Davis snarled.

"T minus ten, nine, eight, seven, six . . . engines one hundred percent. We have liftoff power . . . two . . . one . . . we have liftoff!"

In horror, Davis looked past Parker out the window and saw the hugs ships begin to rise from their pads, engines shaking the two-inch-thick glass. They rose to the level of the window, past it toward the gaping hanger doors. He saw the stars shimmering in the night sky. Everything was moving in slow motion, like in a horrible nightmare. Frantically he whirled on Kemper and leveled his rifle. "For the last time Kemper. Recall them!"

"No!" Parker shouted.

Davis fired, driving Kemper against the computers in a twisting fountain of blood. His lifeless body struck the floor with a dull thud and Davis turned on Parker, who stood rigid in front of the glass, watching the ASPs which were just reaching the open doors. Montie Montgomery slumped into a chair unable to stand the strain. Alarms were blaring.

"Parker. I know there's a recall code. Use it! You can stop this!"

Parker turned to him, completely composed. "Listen to me, Davis. The survival of the human race depends on this action. Every country on Earth is in turmoil. Our economy is collapsing, and we are the only ones who stand between freedom and the Russians. But we're in a corner. The Russians are pinning us down, the Arabs are bleeding us. There's no alternative to this but nuclear war!"

"This will start it!"

"No, it won't. There won't be a chance. In a few hours every other major government except my own will be wiped out. There will be no one left to launch a nuclear attack."

"You're insane!"

"No. The world's insane. Everything we've stood for, everything we've fought for is being destroyed by insanity. We're battling for oil because one cartel uses it to blackmail the rest of the world. We're battling for peace because people all over the world are clinging to narrow-minded traditions and religious bigotry. No one is willing to give, no one will share for the common good. There is plenty of everything if only people were willing to share on a worldwide basis. Don't you see that after tomorrow there will be no countries, there will be no religious hatred, there will be no political differences? We will provide the leadership; create a new democratic government, a free world. All countries will

494

share equally in all the Earth's resources. What we've been battling — greed, hatred, prejudice, distrust — will no longer have any reason to exist. The Earth will be an oasis of peace and prosperity. There will be no starvation, no deprivation, no fear, no hatred, no blackmail, no oppression. In one fell swoop we can accomplish what the United Nations could never do. We can bring the people of the world together under one Democratic World Republic, under one economy. It's the only way to survive! If we don't do it now it will be too late!"

"Goddamnit, Parker, don't you realize what you're doing? You're killing millions of people in the name of peace. You can't justify that! How can you hope to build trust and harmony out of the ashes of worldwide genocide? Don't you see that there will always be nations? There will always be hatred, and greed, and distrust, and deprivation? That's the nature of man! He's a base animal. You can't change that! No one can!"

"I just have," Parker said calmly and turned back to the window.

The ASPs rose over the desert, twenty black ships, their engines roaring in the holy silence of the night. They rose and fanned out in the directions the computer told them, blindly obedient.

"Parker," Davis shouted, his voice cracking, his legs wobbling in fear as nausea swept over him. "Issue the recall code!"

"No," Parker said. "It's begun."

DYNAMIC NEW LEADERS IN MEN'S ADVENTURE!

THE MAGIC MAN #2:
THE GAMOV FACTOR   (1252, $2.50)
by David Bannerman
With Brezhnev terminally ill, the West needs an agent in place to control the outcome of the race to replace him. And there's no one better suited for the job than THE MAGIC MAN!

THE WARLORD   (1189, $3.50)
by Jason Frost
The world's gone mad with disruption. Isolated from help, the survivors face a state in which law is a memory and violence is the rule. Only one man is fit to lead the people, a man raised among the Indians and trained by the Marines. He is Erik Ravensmith, THE WARLORD—a deadly adversary and a hero of our times.

THE WARLORD #2: THE CUTTHROAT   (1308, $2.50)
by Jason Frost
Though death sails the Sea of Los Angeles, there is only one man who will fight to save what is left of California's ravaged paradise. His name is THE WARLORD—and he won't stop until the job is done!

THE WARLORD #3: BADLAND   (1437, $2.50)
by Jason Frost
His son has been kidnapped by his worst enemy and THE WARLORD must fight a pack of killers to free him. Getting close enough to grab the boy will be nearly impossible—but then so is living in this tortured world!

Available wherever paperbacks are sold, or order direct from the Publisher. Send cover price plus 50¢ per copy for mailing and handling to Zebra Books, Dept. 1296, 475 Park Avenue South, New York, N.Y. 10016. DO NOT SEND CASH.